DADDY, DEAREST. . . .

The woman's voice was changing, becoming more and more like Lylunda's; it had happened so gradually, she hadn't thought about what it meant, but understanding came like a slap in the face, She swung round to confront her father. "She's supposed to take my place, isn't she. To fool Grinder into thinking I'm tucked in and waiting for him. Well?"

"It pleases me that you're intelligent, Lylunda, though you do talk too much. I brought you here because I wanted to see you, that's the truth. And because it became clear to me that you'll probably get ground up and thrown away if you stay here, And because I don't wish to face the choices you're forcing on me. Ekateri-mun, do you have sufficient material?"

"I think so, Anaitar-jaz."

"Excellent. Janik bless you, daughter. May you fare well."

Lylunda saw the stunrod, started to protest. Before she got any words out, her father shot her.

JO CLAYTON'S
DAW Science Fiction and
Fantasy Novels:

THE DANCER TRILOGY
DANCER'S RISE
SERPENT WALTZ
DANCE DOWN THE STARS

THE WILD MAGIC SERIES
WILD MAGIC
WILDFIRE
THE MAGIC WARS

THE DUEL OF SORCERY
MOONGATHER
MOONSCATTER
CHANGER'S MOON

THE SOUL DRINKER TRILOGY
DRINKER OF SOULS
BLUE MAGIC
A GATHERING OF STONES

THE SHADOWSONG TRILOGY
FIRE IN THE SKY
THE BURNING GROUND
CRYSTAL HEAT

JO CLAYTON
CRYSTAL HEAT

The Shadowsong Trilogy #3

DAW BOOKS, INC.
DONALD A. WOLLHEIM, FOUNDER

375 Hudson Street, New York, NY 10014

ELIZABETH R. WOLLHEIM
SHEILA E. GILBERT
PUBLISHERS

CRYSTAL HEAT

Prologue:
Rumblings Before the Game Begins

A conversation by letter, or how to keep your thoughts away from a ubiquitous and apparently omniscient employer.

... so that's over. I really didn't want to send the disruptor back to Sunflower Labs, but it was Digby's call, so back it went. I believe he managed to duplicate it first and his techs are market cream, so could be he'll have a defense out before that thing becomes too much of a problem.

I've been called in tomorrow. It seems that there's another investigation that can use my talents. I'm beginning to have second thoughts about this job, Lee. And just maybe about Digby himself. Which is why I'm writing this, not just giving you a call.

Anyway, I'll see how this one goes.

Any Hunts on the horizon? Lilai should be old enough by now for you to leave her without worrying too much. Selfishly, I rather hope you'll be home when this new business is finished. I need somebody to talk things over with without prying little electronic ears straining to hear what I'm saying.

Aleytys dropped the letter on the table beside the drone capsule where it coiled up into the tight cylinder it'd been when she took it out of the capsule. She poked it with her finger, watched it rock back and forth till it settled to stability again.

"Was it worth the expense?"

Aleytys lifted her head. Grey stood in the doorway looking tired and cranky. She suppressed a sigh; she didn't want to deal with his crotchets, but she'd asked him to come. "Just a note from Shadow. She's got a new investigation. I want a Hunt, Grey. I don't care what it is."

"So that's what this is about. Every time that woman shoves her nose in here, you get all stirred up."

"No. This is me talking. It's been two years, Grey. It's time I was out again."

"There's nothing suitable. I told you. When something comes in that's right for you, I'll call you. Is there anything else?"

"No."

Without trying to protest further, she watched him turn and leave; it was only after she heard the whine of the lifting flier that she dropped her head in her hands.

1

Shadow on the Job

I refuse to be intimidated by a spook. Shadith folded her hands in her lap and smiled politely at Digby's simulacrum.

He'd been fiddling with it again. It was solid now, with the weighty feel of real flesh though it was nothing more than colored light she could walk through if the thought didn't revolt her. He sat at a real desk (a broad battered stretch of dark wood), in a real chair—an antique leather thing that swiveled and had micromotors installed to make it creak and tilt as if it moved to the shifting of his body. The instrumentation, though, was simulation. He had no need for exterior connections to the kephalos buried deep beneath the building, the kephalos which created the simulacrum and controlled all functions in here. In a sense, he was the kephalos.

Today he was being the academic in conference with the wayward student. He wasn't wearing the fez with the gilded tassel that he affected sometimes, but had gifted himself with silver-gray hair flowing in thick waves from a noble brow and a severe expression that went well with that beak of a nose.

Odd how recognizable he was in all his incarnations ... hm, incarnation was not precisely the right word

since whatever flesh he'd once worn must have long
ago rotted back to the earth it was born from.

The simulacrum looked up ... no. Digby looked up,
laughter in his eyes, a sly self-mocking twinkle. *He always puts a twist on things,* she thought. *He knows just
how much this isn't impressing me.*

"Hm." The voice he was using was a rough tenor.
"Your little Ghost Yseyl is profoundly insane in terms
of her culture. Quite at home in ours, though, perhaps
more than you are." With a twitch of non-lips into an
ironic smile, he lifted a simulated sheet off a nonexis-
tent pile, pretended to read it, then looked up. "The
disruptor is on its way back to Sunflower. The rep was
delighted with the swiftness of the retrieval. And most
impressed." He turned another page. "I begin to think
Ginny Seyirshi was right when he called you a cata-
lyst. By the time you were through with them, the Ptak
world was thoroughly chewed up, their commerce dis-
rupted, one war winding itself down through attrition
and a new one fruiting. The place is probably going to
be chaotic for years."

He dropped that last sheet, fitted his hands palm
against palm, and contemplated her. "You managed
with admirable discretion to keep any mention of Excavations Ltd. from notice. However, in other areas,
discretion was ... hmmm ... noticeably lacking. The
peripheral effects of your activities are ... hm ... disconcerting. Added to your tumultuous romp through
the assorted worlds during the Dyslaera affair, there's a
pattern that ... hm ... shall we say, limits your usefulness."

"So I'm fired?" Shadith slid forward in the chair,
prepared to get to her feet. She was getting irritated
and saw no need to listen to a bunch of painted light
scolding her.

"Jump jump, ha! Stop acting like a startled flea,

Shadow. No. Of course you're not fired. It just means I have to be careful to use you in places that I wouldn't mind seeing trashed in your inimitable fashion. As long, of course, as we are not visibly engaged in that trashing. The areas in which I can use you are limited but they do continue to exist." He leaned back, laced his non-fingers across his non-belly.

She watched his careful mimicry of the gestures of the flesh and wondered about it a little. *Is he trying to be sure that he doesn't lose that self which comes so pungently through his poses?* Odd how that chimed with what she'd written to Aleytys. *Maybe it's because he is like me, like Swardheld and Harskari, that I don't trust him.* Immortal and immaterial in that his essence lived in a matrix of forces with even less to hold his self intact than she'd had. At least she and the others from the Diadem had the body of the wearer to remind them what they were and the limits of the field that preserved them. Digby was, in a sense, scattered across half a hundred worlds—maybe more—with no limits, nothing but his will to avoid dissolution. *What's he up to? I see this manifestation of him, but how much of that is construct? How much is meant to reassure me and his clients?*

She pulled her attention back and saw Digby waiting with exaggerated patience. "So," she said. "Why am I here?"

"The Kliu Berej have hired Excavations Ltd. They've lost a Taalav Gestalt array from Pillory. The prison planet they run. Hm. Not a prisoner, a life-form native to the world. One of the weirdest I've ever come across. An assemblage. The various parts reproduce and grow to adulthood as separate forms, then in the last Change grow into each other to create the Gestalt. Which means to breed and grow a Taalav you need an assortment of smaller parts. Which is why they call it an array. I've put the information the Kliu provided in your packet, you can read the details later. Always remembering that clients have been known to lie their brains out. So don't trust it too much."

"They want the array returned? Sounds complicated."

"No. They want to know where it is so they can destroy it. The Taalav extrude a crystalline substance and shape it into complex forms. The Kliu have a monopoly on those crystals and mean to keep it. They wanted the thief, too, but weren't willing to pay double to include him in the deal, so all I contracted to do was locate the array. And to keep the search quiet. You can see why. Once something like that happens, every jack and smuggler with delusions of grandeur will be out trying to find it himself."

"Do they know who the thief is, or are we supposed to discover that also?"

"They know. He was one of the xenobiologists studying the Taalav. Making sure they stay healthy and producing crystal. Not a Kliu, a prisoner. A Cousin working in an exoskeleton because of Pillory's gravity. Don't know why he was sent there; they won't release his files or tell me anything about him, not even his name and description. I suppose they might have to refund some of their fee if his planet of conviction discovers he's gone missing."

"Just how much cooperation are we going to get?"

"As little as they feel they can get away with. We can't trust the Kliu, Shadow. I've had clients like them before. Letter of the contract and that's it. Keep that in mind. And there's this—the theft was almost a year ago. They've been using available resources to search for the array. But they're a cautious species and have decided on backup just in case their hands slip. That's us. You. If they spot you as my agent, they'll put a trace on you and as soon as you look to be getting somewhere, they'll zip round you and scoop the pot under our noses. Then they come round saying sorry, we found the smuggler ourselves. You get your one-percent kill-fee, no more. That's extrapolation, but you can be sure the conclusion is solid. If you need cover and can't arrange it, call me. I expect you to use your ingenuity, though. That is one thing you have plenty of."

"I think I'd better see an array in place. Flakes don't do it. And I want to question the people who knew the thief. Spla! If I don't know his history, how am I supposed to find the smuggler who took him offworld? I presume that was how it was done?"

Digby nodded, a lock of shining gray hair dropping into his eyes. He brushed it back with a flick of his hand. "Thought you might, so I've arranged for you to go to Pillory. There's a light exo ready for you in the equipment room. It's been tarted up with a few extras including a visor which you are to keep in place as much as possible. If anyone tries to take a template, what they'll get is hash. How much they know about my prime agents I couldn't tell you. There might be descriptions circulating already. How much good these precautions will do is not something I'd like to guess about. Nevertheless, get that fitting done as soon as you leave here. And pick up your Trick Kit, have the techs run through it with you, there've been additions since the last time you went out. Just one thing, Pillory's security is fierce, Shadow. Don't try anything with their kephalos. They have redundancies on that system that would frustrate a ghost."

"Speaking of ghosts . . ."

"No. Yseyl isn't ready yet. And this is too complicated. After the fitting, go to Briefing Room Three. I've set up a feed that will give you all we know about

Pillory. Eyes only, no duping, hm? Doesn't go beyond these walls except in your head."

"Discretion is us. To hear is to obey."

"Hmp. Watch your back, Shadow."

"You're a careful soul, Digby."

"You better believe it. I always get full measure. Keep that in mind."

2

Danger. Run for Home

Lylunda Elang rode the shuttle along the linktube that led to Marrat's Agency node, contriving to look bored and mildly stupid, as if she were a low-level worker in an office like the one she was planning to visit. She was short and broad across the shoulders and to her sorrow across the hips as well, with a round guileless face that had proved its worth more than once. The neat small waist she was proud of, she'd concealed under a loose tunic that hung in soft gray folds from the elaborate tucks of the smocking, the looseness concealing the Taalav crystal taped beneath her left breast. She'd brushed in temporary coloring to hide the white streaks at her temples, pulled her coarse, springy hair into a tight bun that tugged up her eyebrows and gave her a look of continual astonishment.

So far she hadn't seen any faces she knew. And she was happy about that. She didn't want anyone recognizing her before she reached the broker's office and shed the crystal.

She stared out the window by her seat, past the ghost images of the other riders reflected in the glass, watching the pewter glitter of the translucent tube walls slip quickly by. Though you could see nothing worth looking at, she was glad of the windows, being uncomfortable hurtling along in a capsule she didn't control without access to the outside, however illusory such access might be.

After a short while, though, she used the mirroring effect to study the other riders. Innocuous as they looked, this was Marrat's Market and any of them could be predators or scam artists.

The shuttle had twenty rows of seats, four seats in each row with a narrow central aisle passing between the middle pair. She was sitting on the left side in the first row, and there was no one in the seat beside her. The rest of the capsule was about half full. The others riding with her seemed to be shift workers heading for their jobs, some sleepy, dozing in their seats, some staring at nothing, a few busy with notepads; they were mostly an assortment from the Cousin worlds, though there was also a pair of Tocher femmes chattering in Tochri gutturals and a lanky Lommertoerkan male immersed in whatever it was he was reading off his sheet screen.

A small wiry man sputtered awake, met her eyes in the window mirror before she had time to blank her gaze. He took this for an invitation, grinned at her, and moved up to the seat beside her. "Haven't seen you before. Me, I'm Exi Exinta, I work at the Nut Tree, it's a food place over on the Barter Strip. Lots of people who work the AgentNode eat there. Be seeing you?"

She gave him a bovine look, blinking slowly as if she had to take time to process the words. "All right," she said finally. Then she turned away to stare out the window again.

Exi Exinta shifted nervously in his seat; after another stretch of silence, he got up and went back to where he'd been sitting before. Lylunda kept the apathetic look, but she wondered about him. His had been a very nice performance, but alarms were going off inside her. It wasn't the first time she'd trotted out this persona, and she knew well enough what reactions it got. Moving in on her showed a kind of blindness on his part, as if he thought that she'd be so flattered by the attention she wouldn't question the reasons behind it.

She was annoyed because it meant she had to drop deep into the role she was playing; if you were supposed to be dull and self-absorbed, you couldn't let an experienced op catch you peeking. There was something else to worry about. This could be a double up. Mr. Ex—the gall of the man, playing that kind of names game—Mr. Exi Exinta might be the throwaway, the one she was supposed to watch while his partner got inside her boundaries and dropped the sack over her head.

Which brought up another problem. She must have tripped an alarm that her ship's sensors missed because the Kliu tagged *Dragoi* just before she 'splitted with Prangarris and his catch. Probably got enough for an ID. Were these two or maybe three working a standard scam, or were they setting her up for a snatch? Marrat's OverSec ran a tight Pit, stomping hard on industrial spying and any physical violence beyond the drunk fight and the one-on-one duel, but they weren't set up to guard against the one-off, the quick snatch and scamper.

When the shuttle sighed to a stop and the exit slid open, she walked out, moving with a heavy stolidity meant to underline her lack of curiosity about the world around her. She climbed aboard a chainchair, tapped in her destination, and went clanking off, tensely aware that Exinta was behind her and that she still hadn't identified his partner. If he had a partner.

The chair's back curved up round her shoulders and head, a not so subtle reminder of the possibilities of backshooting. The composite wouldn't stop a cutter beam, but cutters would bring peacer 'bots swarming and trigger a shut-off of the Node gates. Didn't do much good if the shooter was a berserker intent on suicide, but it tended to discourage the less committed.

It'd been a while since she'd been along here. There were some changes, new signs on the restaurants and the other small shops on the lower floors of the buildings, but the broad squat structures with their complex of offices were much the same as always; there wasn't a lot you could do with prefab office stock except stack it and paint it and maybe squirt a few curlicues about if that was your taste. *I'm dithering,* she thought. *Jaink! Get your mind back on the job, Lylunda my girl. Almost there. Moving between the Chain and the door, that's going to be the tricky time. Let's see . . . how do we handle this. . . ?*

The Chair string clicked to a halt outside Jingko iKan's building. She stepped down, moved at a heavy jog across the walkway, and reached the deeply inset door without any trouble, something that bothered her rather a lot. She wasn't mistaken about Exinta, she was sure of that. But . . .

"Lylunda Elang," she told the small Blurdslang when he opened the shutter and blinked at her. "By appointment with Desp' Jingko iKan."

One of the Blurdslang's large watery eyes slid to the left, then he thrust a hair-thin fingertip into a receptacle and the door slid open.

Lylunda glanced over her shoulder as she moved inside, but what she could see of the street was empty. She shrugged, walked at a brisk clip toward the lift tube, glad to shuck that bovine cover.

* * *

"I'm carrying," she said. "Block."

Jingko iKan sat mantis still, his eyes expressionless as obsidian marbles, but the two short feathery antennae that served as eyebrows twitched into a nervous dance. He tapped a sensor with the tip of a polished claw, and a shimmercone sprang into being over the desk area. "You said it's good."

"Taalav crystal." She reached up under the smock and jerked the packet loose, brought it out and laid it on the desk, a grubby wad of tape and blancafilm the size of her fist. She took a pin from the hem of her sleeve, pricked her finger, and dripped some blood on the seal. It shriveled and the packet began opening itself until it lay flat on the desk, exposing the thing it had contained.

The crystal was an intricate lacery of the clear resin secreted and shaped by a Taalav Gestalt. As it woke from its shielded sleep, it began a series of faint but exquisite chimes in response to the whispers of air that passed through its interstices; pulses of pale light flowed through the twists and turns of the shimmering threads.

Jingko iKan leaned closer, blew gently at it. As the crystal changed its song to something that was his alone, his dust lids slid over his eyes and his monkey face went momentarily slack. After a moment, though, he leaned back in his chair, sat rubbing the callus patches on his wrists together, using the skrikking sound to counter the spell of the crystal.

"Wrap it again," he said. "I can do without that enchantment dulling my sense of what thing is worth. How hot is it?"

She refolded the film around the crystal, tucking the ends under without sealing them. "Cold as winter on Wolff. It's unregistered."

"You got through Kliu security?"

"Let's just say I had help. And it's not something I can repeat. This is part of my share of the deal. I've got another stowed away, a bigger weave. I thought one at a time would get a better price."

He rubbed the calluses together once again, the skrikking this time filled with satisfaction. "That is truth. For sure, for sure. You do bring me such interesting items, Lylunda Elang. Hm. To get the most out of this little item will take some time. Are you pressed for coin?"

"I'm well enough, desp' Jingko. Take what time you need." She reached under the smock again, brought out a much smaller packet, unfolded it, and pushed the one-time flake it held across the desk. "The blind drop on Helvetia. Transfer the credit when you get it, less your commission and five perc over for expenses."

"The expenses might be rather large. Security costs."

"You and I both know what the total take is likely to be. With five perc of that you could buy your own army."

"We'll see. Yes, we will." He lifted the packet with finicky care, rose from his chair, and moved two steps back. A curtain of darkness cut suddenly across the room, hiding him and the crystal.

Lylunda rubbed at the underside of her breast where the film and the tape had irritated the skin. She hadn't told Jingko the exact truth. She had two more crystals, not one; they were tucked away in a lock box on Helvetia, the safest place she could think to leave them. It was a problem, when to get rid of them. She didn't want to overload the market, but there could be a limit to the time in which she could get the best price. Prangarris expected to have his Taalav array established and producing within five years. If he succeeded, the rarity factor would be lost; people would still pay a good price for them, given their beauty and their charm, but not the world's ransom they paid now.

The black curtain vanished and Jingko iKan settled into his chair again. "One other um . . . difficulty. I had an intrusion that tells me the Kliu know about this. About you."

"Ah?"

His antennae twitched through a slow dance as he stared past her at the door. "Yes," he said finally. "I was approached. Asked if you were one of my clients. Most annoying. They have no tact at all. And no common sense. If you're worried about me, to turn a client would destroy my reputation and my earnings would stop. No mention was made of your having the Taalav crystals."

"If I were worried, I wouldn't be here, desp' Jingko."

"They will have approached others. I have informed OverSec that attempts on a client of the Market might be made. They also are annoyed, but it would be better not to have to call on them."

"Hm. I'm going to be at the Marratorium for a few days. Better to find out here what's coming at me. Easier to watch my back." She got to her feet. "Take care, desp'."

2

Hair flying, feet kicking through the intricate patterns of the voor tikeri, Lylunda sucked on the pelar pipe and danced to and away from Qatifa, the Caan she'd run across watching the knife cotillion at the Pertam Darah arena. She'd shucked the neck-to-ankle cover of her disguise and wore her play clothes, a black-washed-to-gray T-shirt sliced to ragged fringe for the bottom six inches, some ancient cutoffs that she hadn't bothered to hem, plus a pair of supple foot-gloves with roughened soles to give traction for the dancing. The pelar bowl was tucked into the T-shirt's pocket and bounced with her breasts so she had to keep her teeth clamped on the stem or she'd lose it. Now and then she grinned at Qatifa and blew a cloud of dreamsmoke in her face.

Qatifa's plush fur was a dark chocolate brown with russet and occasionally gold glimmers when the light hit it in just the right way. It smelled faintly like cinnamon, was impossibly soft, and was matchless as a teaser against bare skin, at least in Lylunda's view of such things. The Caan's eyes were narrowed to slits against a puff of smoke, the light catching glimmers of gold in the darkness of her round blunt face.

When the music stopped, they elbowed back to the chip of a table they'd claimed, settled into the instruments of pain the Tangul Café had attached to the tables, mislabeling them as chairs. Qatifa rolled her tongue and cut through the noise with a whistle that brought the tiny jaje waiter scrambling over to them.

"Double shot of Nibern for me, mineral water for that dancing fool across from me." She waved away Lylunda's motion to pay and dropped a credit chip in the jaje's palm.

"How you can drink that syrup?" Lylunda shuddered.

"How you can smoke that crap?" Qatifa chuckled, a rumble deep in her chest. "I like sweets. You should know, gula-mi. One splendid thing about skin people, you can smear them with all sorts of lovely goo and lick it off without getting fur in your teeth." An ear twitched. "The sale came through just before you called, Luna. I'm out of here before the next pay cycle at the tie-down. Which means a couple hours and see-ya."

Lylunda grimaced. Before she could respond, the

waiter was back with their order. She took the flask of bubbling water and gloomed at it. "It's been fun," she said finally. "Maybe we could do it again sometime."

"That's what you said the last time. You should work on your valedictions a bit, gula-mi." Qatifa's grin faded. She gulped down a mouthful of the Nibern, sat chewing on the fruit. "Luna, my friend, I've heard a rumor or two. Why don't you tandem your ship on mine and come fool around a while with me on Acaanal?"

Lylunda smiled. However much she liked Qatifa, she'd be jumping out of her skin by her second week of undiluted Caan company. "Thanks, Qat. I've got commitments elsewhere, but I appreciate the thought."

Qatifa looked at the glass, wrinkled her blunt nose. "I'd better go pee 'f I don't want to disgrace myself next time we hit the floor. Besides, the hornman promised me a slow dance and it's about time he came through on that."

Alternating sips of the water with draws on the pipe, Lylunda watched the tall femme undulate through the closely packed tables, using the tips of her claws on hopeful hands trying to cop a feel of Caan fur. For a moment she was tempted to change her mind and go with Qatifa, but common sense returned when the sleekly graceful form vanished behind a bead curtain.

She felt something brush against her neck and turned to see the back of a man moving away from her, a stranger as far as she could tell. When nothing else happened, she forgot about him and let the pelar float her off to a place where she wasn't worried about anything.

The man calling himself Exi Exinta came out of the drifts of smoke and stood beside her. "Come with me," he said.

Larr off, Ziz, she thought, then was startled as her

body rose and walked after him. *What the . . . Zombi! That snake shot me up with Zombi juice.* She drew in a breath to yell, but Exinta heard and turned. "Be quiet," he said.

Her throat closed and the words died there as she shuffled after him, the pelar countering the Z-juice enough to let her drag her feet. She contrived to bump heavily into tables, to slam into people, to swing her arms so she knocked over drinks, creating a commotion that set Exinta cursing under his breath as he grabbed her arm and tried to hustle her along faster.

Lylunda fixed her eyes on the door, sweat coiling down her face, fear and rage knotting her insides. It drew closer and closer. She tried to pull loose, but the hold of the drug was too strong even with all the pelar in her system. Her tongue was locked, she couldn't even form words, let alone say them.

"Oy! Luna. Where you going? Huh?" Qatifa's voice, filled with anger and alarm.

Exinta yanked on her arm. They were almost to the door. She managed to turn her head, to open her mouth. She couldn't speak . . . not a word . . . not a word. . . .

Golden eyes widened as Qatifa understood what was happening. "Zombi," she roared, her voice cutting through the noise of instruments tuning and the undertone of conversation, shocking the place to silence. She came plunging through the tables, claws out, mouth stretched in a threat snarl, teeth glistening in the light from the pseudo torches.

Exinta ran for his life, diving under the arm of a peacer 'bot that came clanking into the café.

Most of the crowd in the Tangul faded as the 'bot hummed over to Lylunda and clamped his cuff claw around her wrist. Qatifa patted her cheek. "Gula-mi, don't take this wrong, but I can't afford to get hung up." Then she faded with the rest.

3

Lylunda Elang sat on a couch in the armored peaceplex, cursing Exinta and trying not to think about the headache that was sitting behind her eyes ready to sink its claws. She rubbed absently at the itchy place on her wrist where they took blood to make sure what she'd been given. *Jaink! I'll be glad when I'm finally flushed clean of that stuff. I want a full spectrum clear, who knows what that ziz blew into me. Not from this lot either, I wouldn't trust them with a cotton swab. What's holding things up? I want to get out of here.*

The door slid open and a nutrient dish with an immature Blurdslang hummed in. "Des' Ela'?"

Lylunda got carefully to her feet, trying not to jar the lurking headache awake. "I can go?"

"I' you 'ollow me?"

She sighed and moved after him.

The elder Blurdslang contemplated her for several moments, then played his fingerlings over the speaker cube. "The Directors are considerably disturbed by the use of a will suppressant; I am sure you can understand the reasoning behind that, smuggler, so I will not elaborate. The user has been located and probed. There was a confederate, a brother, but he left before we could lay hands on him. By the end of the diurn, the user will be wiped and sold to a contract labor firm. The Kliu will be informed that they are not welcome here. We have discussed what to do about you, Lylunda Elang. There was a suggestion that since you drew those men here, you should share their fate. The Broker Jingko iKan spoke for you and convinced the majority that you are a valued client and will continue to be one."

Too angry and alarmed to speak, Lylunda pressed her lips together and tried to ignore the throbbing in her left temple.

"The will suppressant was a bootleg version of c5 Z juice as it is called in the vernacular, overage, with a number of impurities that could cause you some difficulty. The medtechs suggest you prepare yourself for several days bed rest and a bland diet, eschewing all caffeine and other drugs. The Directors suggest you do it on board your ship, bound elsewhere."

"All right. Can I go now?"

"In a moment. The Directors of Marrat's Market are not banning you; they simply suggest that you clear up this difficulty before you attempt to return. Have you any questions?"

"No."

"Your gear has been collected from your room in the ottotel and will be waiting in a transfer pod. A peacer 'bot will escort you to the pod. I am told to inform you this is a courtesy not a constraint."

4

Migraine auras invading her eyes like flags of crumpled cellophane shivering in a high wind, Lylunda brought her ship to what counted as a stop at the Limit, drifting into a slow orbit about Marrat's sun while the ottodoc grumbled at her blood and she ran a disinfect over the outer surface of the ship. The crawler dislodged three tags, one obvious and meant to be found, one subtle and one she didn't understand at all that she found only by chance, a shift in the solar wind that jogged the crawler in just the right way.

By the time the doc's notifier pinged, she was blind

in large areas of her vision field and her head hurt so much that she couldn't bear to move. She turned and almost drowned in the vomit that caught her by surprise as she groped for the slot; she slid her arm in and waited for the shot she hoped would give her some relief.

She felt the sting against her wrist, a moment later the burn of stomach acid in her throat, a shiver in her knees. She just had time to withdraw her arm before she collapsed in a heap on the floor.

When she woke, she knew there was only once place where she could feel safe for the next year. She had to go home.

3

Worm's View

"Your jodidda juice din't work. They got Xman, stinking slinkies. Almost got me, but I slid."

The ears on the Kliu image curled tight and the eating mouth opened to show the tearing teeth. The speaking mouth rippled as if the old male wanted to chew the words, but when the sounds came through the twit cones, they were mild enough. "The woman remains at the Market?"

"The smuggler? When slinkies let her go, she took off. I got an idea where, but I don't say no jodidda thing, and I don't go nowhere till you pry Xman loose."

"That requires consultation. I will get back to you."

For several minutes Worm stared at the glassy blankness of the screen, fingers of one hand plucking at the plas cover on the chair arm. He moved his shoulders finally, straightened his back, and reached for the flake case.

"Da, Xman got snicked by the slinkies."

The old man glared at him from the snakes' tangle of wires and tubes of the Sustainer. "How come you clean?"

"Way we planned it, I zombi the femme and get out,

he fetches her, I hit for the ship and get ready to go. When that don't come off, he hits out for me anyway, but he don't make it. I see peacer 'bots globe him and they got one jodiddan huge shaker with 'em, wouldda dusted me good if I'd tried snatching 'im. I cut out but stay in system, get through to Sniff Herk and he tells me that the slinkies, they read Xman's head, blew it clean and laid a contract on him. And they got a pickup for me, so I can't go back. I get on to the scivs, tell ol' jodface he gonna buy Xman out or I don't go nowhere. They don't come through, you better send Dogboy and Trish to see if they can lever him out."

"You shoot y' mouth too fast, boy. You gonna have some backin' down to do if scivs set their claws and won't move. They still got Mort, so they got us by the cojos. You gotta get that femme, so we hold value for the trade. When they lookin' at her meat 'n all, they know they gotta do a deal."

"Sorry, Da. I was so burned they give Xman junk juice, I din't think. Da, call light's on, I gotta go."

"Since our investigations indicated that it was indeed a failure of the drug that led to the capture, we will extract your brother from his current situation. We will place him with your other brother to wait a successful outcome of this business."

The screen blanked.

Worm swore and reestablished the link with his father to let him know about this turn in their collective fate.

4

Pillory is Not
a Nice Place

1

When the Pillory shuttle landed, Shadith stood, the servomotors of the exo doing most of the work and the muscle braces shifting to optimize their restraints. She sagged everywhere—which was disconcerting because she had thought she was in fairly good shape. And Digby was right about the Kliu trying to template her; she could feel the exo's defenses powering up as probes licked at them. The interference waves gave her a low-level headache that was like an itch inside her skull.

The shuttle was the one the Kliu used to transport prisoners. The seats were fitted with massive restraints, there were ominous apertures with metal snouts in them, the unpainted walls were scratched and dull, marked with stains she didn't want to think about.

She tapped alive the robot mule, clicked along behind it to the exit and stood waiting for the lock to cycle open, wondering as she waited if transporting her in this thing was a deliberate insult. It seemed likely. *Well, Shadow, take it as a warning and let Autumn Rose be your model. Cool is it. Losing your temper isn't an option.*

She wrinkled her nose as the slide chunked back, exposing a battered wooden ramp shoved up against the shuttle. The air smelled like the backside of all the Star Streets she'd ever walked through.

She let the mule haul her gear outside, then followed it down the ramp, happier with the exo as it settled into the performance mode it was made for. A juvenile Kliu was waiting at the foot of the ramp, a crocodilian centaur, his six stubby legs stirring up the noisome dust of the enclosure, the lips of his eating mouth clicking together with disgust and disgruntlement. His ears were rolled tight—which was another sign of discourtesy if the diplo guide Digby had secured for her was accurate. He was signaling that nothing she said had enough worth for him to bother giving her more than the most marginal attention.

He swung his body around and marched away as soon as she reached the end of the ramp, his clawed feet going stomp stomp crunch crunch creak creak, the thick arms swinging, hands closed into fists. *Digby said they squealed as if he were chewing on their soft parts when he insisted his agent look over the scene herself. He had to threaten to give back the advance three times before they capitulated. It was obvious they grudged every second of her presence on planet. Their suspicions weren't all that unjustified either, considering Digby's instructions about remembering and reporting everything she saw.*

With the mule humming beside her and the exo doing its job, cradling and supporting her and powering her walk, she followed her escort through a series of dingy, badly lit corridors. Empty corridors. *Servant stairs. So I won't offend their delicate eyes with my alien verminhood.*

Muttering in his guttural Kliubre, the guide plunged ahead, turning corners until Shadith was dizzy with the circles she was being led in; finally, though, he slowed, slapped at something on the broad belt where his horny torso joined the horizontal portion of his body. The thing let out a blat like a hungry tantser calf and repeated the blat at fifteen-second intervals as he went stumping down a broader corridor.

Shadith followed, her annoyance increasing. She didn't think much of being treated like the carrier of multiple plagues.

Her guide waved at a door, shut off the blatter, and settled into the Kliu equivalent of parade rest. She exoed past him, the metal sponge pads of her soles clinking and scraping against the metacrete floor, the 'bot mule humming beside her.

The Kliu subadministrator inspected her in heavy silence. His speaking mouth made a few preliminary twitches; the sound that came out was a musical tenor that made her want to giggle at the absurd contrast with that mass of muscle and armored skin. "We have few facilities for srin in the Island Chains."

Srin, she thought. *Small itchy pests that infest the anal glands. That's not what the book says, but it's what you mean. I can see you sniggering with your peers at how you've got over on those stinking aliens.*

"The prisoners we get here are a dangerous, desperate lot," he said. "Lifers, all of them. Many of them are political with very little concern for the lives of those who do not share their particular beliefs or belong to their genetic group."

Takes one to know one.

"You must understand, we do not guard the prisoners. We guard the world. Those who refuse the work we offer are provided with materials and tools so they can build their own shelters, and with adapted seedstock so they can raise their own food. We have a series of satellites watching them to stop any activities we consider dangerous to us and we do occasional ground checks for various reasons. Otherwise we leave them alone. It will be difficult, if not impossible to protect you in these circumstances."

Bite your tongue, Shadow. You don't want to tell ol' crocface he lies in his fangs. That's not tactful. "Come now, Exalted Cheba, I'm sure you don't mean that the island where you harvest the crystals is unguarded."

His ears crumpled, the edges rolling inward, and a film dulled his large black eyes, nocturnal eyes, unused to strong sunlight. "That is another difficulty, Desp' Searcher. The exact location of the island and the Taalav beasts is a security matter. You're a pilot, a view of the night sky, even a strange sky, would yield sufficient data for you to work out the island's location."

Shadith blinked at him; she found that degree of idiocy in a subadministrator rather hard to swallow. "It may have been a secret before now," she said as mildly as she could, "but it has certainly lost that status with the departure of the thief. Right? In any case, I need to study everything the thief left behind, and of course, the physical requirements of a Taalav array. That last will set important parameters to the search for the world where they were taken. I'm sure you understand that."

"You'll need living quarters. That will take time to arrange."

"I assume you have a new xenobiologist in place by now. Is that person Kliu?"

"The Kliu do not concern themselves with such matters."

Why was I so sure what your answer would be? Hah! "Another prisoner? Or have you gone outside this time?"

"It is not necessary for you to know that."

"In any case, you will have set up accommodations for this person and his aides. It should not be difficult to find a spare room for me in that facility. Especially since you've known I was coming for over a month standard. And that I was female—if that is to be your next objection."

She read his burst of anger with no difficulty, the overtones of petulance and distaste. Her exoed hands clasped in her lap, she waited with stiff patience for him to realize that stalling to the point of forcing her to walk out on him would win him nothing but a reprimand from his superiors.

He ignored her last response as if she hadn't spoken, tapped a sensor with the longest of his eight fingers. When her erstwhile guide shuffled in, he flung a spate of Kliubre at him in the expectation that Shadith wouldn't understand what he was saying. She listened carefully. A lot of cursing and nasty epithets, but basically he was doing what should have already been done, ordering a flier and pilot to take her to Glin Paran which was apparently the name of the island in question.

2

The dot in a semicolon of islands trailing across one of Pillory's southern seas, Glin Paran was a wheel with a lake at the hub and a high jagged rim around the periphery. It was a big island, almost a subcontinent.

Shadith suppressed a sigh as the flier dipped from the scatter of clouds and fought the choppy winds; the trip had been as rough as the Kliu pilot could make it and Pillory cooperated with his malice by throwing storm after storm at them. Despite the support of the exo, she was battered and exhausted; some of her bruises felt as if they went to the bone.

The Kliu slammed the flier down, waited only long enough for Shadith, the 'bot mule, and her sullen guard to disembark, then he shot away, vanishing into those clouds they'd left such a short time before.

Shadith glanced at the guard, but he had his eyes nearly shut against what was for him the glare of the sun, though the reddish light was more like a cloudy twilight to her. He was radiating stubbornness and revulsion and his speaking mouth was pressed shut with such determination that she didn't bother saying anything to him. She looked around.

They were standing on a gritty landing pad, wind whipping debris against their legs and into their faces. On every side there were tangles of squat trees. Several stands of reeds taller than the trees grew out of the water, a cross between tules and bamboo with short stubby leaves like knife blades, tough enough to stab with. Each reed was different from its neighbor in color and configuration, a red like dried blood, a green so dark it was almost black, fire orange, a deep sapphire blue, plus blends and shades of all these colors, mottling and stripes; a few had feathery sprays of seed pods bursting from their tops.

In the open spaces between the tree clumps there were patches of low brush with brown, dead-looking leaves clinging to branches that were as crooked and knotty as arthritic fingers.

The xeno settlement was sited a short distance into the lake with only a spidery catwalk joining it to the bank. The buildings were constructed from those reeds and took some getting used to because whoever supervised the construction seemed to have been colorblind. Apart from that, though, they were simple boxes with peaked roofs made from the leaves of the reed, over-

lapping like shingles. The area where the catwalk
reached the bank had been cleared though she could
see new sprouts just breaking the surface of the water;
apparently the reeds had to be cut back again and
again. She wondered about the catwalk and why the
Kliu had gone to so much inconvenience with their
building. It seemed to suggest that the Taalav arrays
were hostile and dangerous. If not them, then some
other predator flourished here. Which made the guard
rather more useful than she'd supposed. Or maybe it
was simply because they didn't want to harm the juvenile body parts of the Taalav.

Reasoning without data was a singularly futile process, so she gave it up and followed the guard toward
the settlement.

A man in an exo stood on the platform at the end of
the catwalk. He had a shaggy black beard and heavy
eyebrows, so his face seemed mostly hair. Despite that
there was something familiar about that face. She
didn't know him, but she'd seen his phot recently.
Ambela? University?

She tapped the mule with her toe, sent it humming
onto the narrow walk, followed it. Halfway across, she
remembered when and where she'd seen him and
nearly misstepped off the edge.

It was a big scandal around the middle of her first
year at University. His picture was everywhere. Saklavaya. That was his name. He'd been skimming and
selling exotics from expedition stocks—which would
have been bad enough, but he had the misfortune to be
caught pinching off genetic material from the rarer of
the alien sentients he had access to and selling these
interesting bits to one of the Gray Market meatfarms.
The uproar when this was discovered nearly destroyed
the Xeno School. The Regents Board fined him all his
voting stock and convinced Helvetia to freeze his ac-

counts; then they barred him from ever returning to University or using University services. If he was here as a result of some further predations and not just hired, she suspected the Kliu had better keep a close eye on their crystals.

She'd gotten to watch his hearing. Her friend Aslan was a member of the Xeno Department and went every day to glare her fury at this man who'd polluted everything she believed in. Shadith wasn't afraid he'd recognize her. She was in the Music School and the various Departments of University were self contained units.

She stopped in front of him. "You are?"

"Vannar. I run this place. What'n pyag you think you're going to learn here? The last xenobi is long gone and I've got his rooms. There's nothing there."

"Desp' Vannar. If you'll show me where I'll stay while I'm making my investigation, I can get on with it and out of your hair."

3

"That's all?" She looked at the small stack of printed readouts. "I asked for every offworld contact for the past three years. I was very careful to specify that proprietary data could be privacy blanked, but I wanted the contacts and context."

Vannar shrugged. "Don't ask me. None of my doing, I passed on the request as you framed it. You should have taken care of that while you were still at Base. If you don't mind, I have work I need to do." He sauntered out of the room.

Shadith wrinkled her nose. One of the drawbacks at having a touch of empathic intake, you had to endure silent snickers like that one. She had to concede, though, that Saklavaya/Vannar was right. There wasn't much here. It was as if they fumigated the place once the

former xenobi took off with the array. As she leafed
through the skimpy pile of printouts, she grinned at the
thought of a gigantic vacuum hose chasing down fugitive glyphs and sucking them up.

She noted the business entities addressed, but didn't
expect them to lead anywhere. *Digby's right,* she
thought, *we're strictly backup and will only get left-
overs and things the Kliu consider last hopers.*

She leaned back when she was finished and stared at
the wall. All the aides had been changed, there was not
a single individual left who'd worked with the old
xenobi. He must have had some rep outside Pillory, if
they were that reluctant even to name the man. She'd
requested interviews with the prisoners involved, but
was told they were not available. *Dead or gaga,* she
thought. *Probed to their backteeth, and not daintily.
Hmp. Smells like this is a lost cause gambit. I'm on my
own, Digby said. I thought it was a compliment then.
Right now I suspect what that mainly means is you
don't get no support no way, Shadow. Ah spla! I hate
letting these fugheads win. Well, there's no point in
putting this off. One more step, then I pack it in. We go
out and take a look at an array on site tomorrow. No
more stalling out of ol' Saklavaya. If I have to call the
boss and put a rocket under his tail . . .* She giggled at
the thought of the subadministrator's double gape at
fireworks popping in his anal orifice. *Give him a new
appreciation of srin.*

4

The creepler was an odd vehicle with six articulated
legs on each side, each leg moving independently, lifting and setting a broad foot down with slow care,
guided by a thick array of visual sensors so it wouldn't
step on any of the juvenile forms. It followed a pre-

programmed path with all the alacrity of an arthritic land tortoise.

The Kliu guard propped himself into the arrangement that Kliu used as chairs, a complicated mix of bellybands and stout rods. Shadith rode in the reed chair that had belonged to the former xenobi, an unpadded contraption that ground against her exo straps.

The area near the lakeshore was fairly deserted, but after the creepler picked its way through a stand of low, broad trees, climbed up a hill covered with grass tall enough to brush its frame, grass that looked capable of stabbing through solid wood, she saw a grove of taller trees, widely scattered, with clumps of vines growing about dryland reeds. Under those trees a score of odd creatures moved in a loose herd.

"Red Riding Hood," she said aloud, remembering a child's tale from a world she visited in her first incarnation.

The bodies of adult Gestalts looked approximately like mottled green and black grasshoppers the size of a large dog, long insectile legs bending through a sharp angle, six knees raised above the carapace. A flexible nose tube brushed along the ground, sucking up bits and pieces of plant stuff. There were two eyepits on the subsidiary head at the base of the nose tube, but these had either grown over or like a viper's pits collected heat rather than light. Above the first set of shoulders the chitinous material that covered the body turned a bright cherry red and rose into a sort of hood with the main head of the Gestalt tucked into the hollow of the open front. This head was round and soft, with huge dark green eyes, a doughy greenish tint to the skin; it had a button nose and a handsome, mobile mouth. There was a fringe of tentacles around the body head, their skin sharing its consistency and color.

These tentacles were in constant movement like a nest
of snakes; she watched their movements for a short
while, decided that they might be sense organs as well
as graspers.

Under the feet of the adults in this array dozens of
tiny body replicas were skittering around, whistling
and making small chuckling sounds, chasing each
other, playing with a cheerful intensity that brought a
smile to Shadith's face. Tiny blobs pulled themselves
along by nests of tentacles growing beneath their rudi-
mentary chins; these were the infant heads. There were
fugitive movements in the litter of grass and old
leaves, but she never got a good look at any of these
bits of the array.

The adults were hosing up seeds and insects from
the ground, nuzzling at the trees, and poking among
the leaves of the vines. She watched one of them fooling about a bush for several minutes, the neck tentacles
busy about something. It was only when the Taalav
moved on that she saw it had been tying stray canes to
smaller reeds it had thrust into the ground.

All this while the adults were silent, going about
their activities as if they were alone, though they
sneaked glances at the creepler as they moved about.

The largest Taalav moved closer, scuttling sideways
on those long, bent, tippy-toe legs. It stopped a body
length away and stared at her, ignoring the Kliu almost
as if it considered the guard a part of the machine.

It started making noises. Excited noises. Exchanging
noises with the other Taalavs as they gathered around.
Noises that blending into song, complex and lovely
music.

Sudden pain jagged behind her eyes, intensified by
the itch from the distorters in the exo.

Shadith clutched at the chair as she sought to make
sense of what was happening. The translator didn't

work on animal sounds, only on organized speech. And that meant the Taalav were not animals, they were sentient beings.

The more they chattered, the worse her head felt. This langue had to be a mass of peculiarities because she'd never felt the translator labor so hard. *I've got to get out of here. Now.*

She slapped at the controller, got the creepler moving once more on its programmed path, this time turning round to head back to the lake.

As soon as the machine began moving, the Taalavs backed cautiously away, then stood watching as the creepler picked its careful way up the slope and into the trees.

5

She lay in semidarkness, a damp compress spread across her eyes and dripping into her pillow. Despite the exo's support, the days she'd spent on this world kept layering exhaustion on exhaustion so even in the best of circumstances, thinking would have been difficult. Now she had a moral dilemma to complicate matters.

If the Kliu didn't know the Taalav Gestalts were intelligent beings rather than beasts, they had to suspect it. So if she piped up like a good little phenom with her discovery, the least she could expect was a sudden accident that would leave her a grease spot on some mountain between here and Base. No wonder they wanted to erase all instances of the Taalav outside their control. Discovery of the Gestalt's intelligence would complicate their lives enormously. And it wouldn't help the Taalav all that much either. Instinct said this is slavery and it has to stop. Instinct was an ass.

Even if she managed to get them taken from the

Kliu, how long would they last without an equally powerful protector? *Protector? Call it what it was. Exploiter. Once they're discovered, they're going to be exploited. The only big weapon that small people have is Helvetia's adamant stance against slavery. Getting that evoked would take a whole lot of proof, not just her word.*

There were a few comforting things she'd noticed. They seemed healthy enough, and the abundance of the tiny body forms meant that reproduction was continuing. She'd felt no rage or fear or frustration from that lot. And loathsome exploiters as the Kliu were, they were also protection as long as the Taalav kept producing their crystals.

Well, Digby, I think I've just quit. I can't do this, but I can't not do it either. Can't take your pay and work against you. Can't let the Taalav array be murdered. Because that's what it would be. How do I ... hmmm ... I'm going to keep working to find that smuggler and hope I get to him before the Kliu. I wouldn't put it past them to use a planet cracker on the place just to make sure they eradicated the array. Can't leave them with that thief either. He's no better than the Kliu ... get them away ... take them somewhere ... they'll need looking after for a while ... Sar! What do I do with them? I have to think ... hunh! Maybe I'd just better ask them what they want. If my head ever settles down....

The decision made, tension drained from her; her breathing slowed and she slept.

6

She sat in the chair on the creepler, listening to the Taalav chatter their symphonies and growing fonder of the odd, ugly creatures as the hours slipped past. They were as playful as otters, and they punned relentlessly in a langue that was a gift to wit-snappers and persifleurs. She nearly fell out of the chair in her efforts to stifle laughter when they threw quips back and forth describing the Kliu guard, especially when they were speculating about his sexual involvement with the creepler.

She sobered rapidly as the implications of that came clear. This new xenobi might be studying the Taalav, but the Gestalts were studying them back with an equal intensity and making some amazingly accurate deductions despite their isolation here.

They were more serious about her.

It took a while, gathering hints from the flow of their speech, to understand why. Their eyes were very good; they saw finer detail in the reddish twilight that was Pillory's high noon than a hawk hunting in the brilliant light of a yellower sun. And they were clever at patterns, not just with words. They noted the basic similarities between her and someone else. They wondered if Shadith and this other woman were a separate species from the men in the lake place. They didn't say men and women, of course, but talked about the diamond-shaped ones with the double-lumped high front and the wedge-shaped ones with the single smaller lump at the crotch.

They grumbled at her, wanting her to stand up so they could get a further comparison of heights. They speculated on the reason for the different skin colors of these two-bump people.

She glanced at the guard. He wasn't technically sleeping on the job, but he'd let his body slump down on his support limbs and his secondary lids had slid across his eyes. She *felt* at him and came up with a sense of relaxation so deep he couldn't be aware of much going on around him.

Still *listening* to him, she got carefully to her feet and walked to the lowering platform of the creepler.

They were excited about that, a little wary, but still not afraid even when the descent of the platform was finished and she stepped off of it.

She walked toward them, stopping when their nervousness increased sharply, then stood where she was and used the motors to help her stretch her arms out straight from her shoulders.

When she didn't move, they edged closer, the biggest one taking the lead. It lifted its nose tube, hesitated, then brought it closer and closer to her, until it was finally nuzzling at her clothing and the metal skeleton of the exo.

Gentle touches. Tickling her. Getting very personal at times.

She twitched away, giggled—which they found fascinating so they repeated the touches. She lowered her arms slowly so she wouldn't frighten them, moved the nose tubes away, then licked her lips and attempted a crude version of their langue, a kind of pidgin whistle talk.

===

Greet you **tied to the land**
    I, Singer   No-harm **offered wanted**
This one **who stands here**

===

They were enormously excited by this. It was the first time anyone had ever attempted to talk to them. They hurled a whole symphony of questions at her, not giving her a second's opening to respond until the biggest one swung its armored tail about and made some peremptory clicking sounds.

When there was silence, it eased its head from under

the hood, raised it on a thin muscular neck until the round naked head was almost level with hers; it stared at her for several moments. Then it spoke slowly, but did not try to mitigate the complexity of what it said, weaving the tones and undertones into a song. Though what Shadith heard the Taalav saying was simple enough when stripped of the qualifications and multiple meanings, it was also a great beauty that pierced her through and through.

The Taalav said:

where do	**stilter**	creep	(our)
how do (the being that you are)		walk clumsily	the
what are	**stranger**	invade	**this**

space	and **hear us**	?
topological landscape	and bespeak us	?
stone/plant/we life	and **know what others do not**	?

Included in the question were asides that mentioned her coloring, her size and shape, the features that were like the Taalav and those that were radically different, the features (fewer) that she shared with the Kliu, her smell, her strange attempts at truespeak and other things that were too subtle even for that most subtle of instruments, the translator she'd inherited from Aleytys.

As she contemplated her answer, knowing it would be so crude that she'd better not try anything but the simplest response, she glanced at the guard and was startled to see two of the smaller Taalav standing close to him, making soft steady humming sounds; then one of them flipped its long tail forward and inserted the thorny tip between two folds of the Kliu's skin. Amazing. They'd somehow understood that she didn't want the Kliu aware of what was happening.

She sang/whistled:

===

This person I am that you are touching **need
curiosity**
Maker of songs called Shadow am I being here
liking you

===

The Gestalts chattered among themselves, sorting out to their satisfaction exactly what she meant by each nuance of sound, some of their conclusions making her grin, though she didn't try to correct them.

There was a tickling around her ankles. She looked down. Several of the tiny body forms were starting to climb up her legs.

She didn't try form a request, just whistled and pointed.

A few slaps of the nose tube by the largest Taalav and the curious infants scuttled away to hover under the legs of other adults and stared at her with tiny pinpoint eyes until she wanted to giggle again.

The Taalav fixed its eyes on her. When it spoke, it had carefully stripped away the harmonics and all it asked was, **why**?

She drew in a breath, sang/whistled to them:

===

A part of you   **adult forms**   **taken away**
        family   juvenile forms   the one-bump stilter
plants/land/bugs   eggs   **the two-bump stilter**

===

Her face twisted in a fury of concentration, she told them of her need to find the missing array, stressing that she wished no harm either to them or to the others. She tried to impress on them that the others would be in great danger if she did not find them before those like him—she pointed at the dreaming Kliu—came across the absent and destroyed them. . . .

=====================================

this one before you	**politely**
with no call on you	**asks** to save the absent
but a desire to help you	**urgently**

=====================================

. . . so I ask you to tell me as much as you can about the two-bump person . . . *female smuggler,* she thought, *just knowing that is a step up* . . . what its colors are, how high it is . . . *do they know about names?* she asked the translator, *ah! yes, I see they do. Names as descriptions, so intricately nuanced they can only belong to one Gestalt among the many* . . . did you hear the name she gave herself, the sound of it?

Listening with such concentration her head started hurting again, she picked out of the weave of sound they gave back to her an astonishing amount of data:

There were too many sounds exchanged between the two-bump and the one-bump who studied them and whom they studied in their turn. Too many to remember. And they had no way of deciding what was name and what was just talk.

The two-bump was wider than Shadith, the bumps were rounder and bigger and it showed brighter colors than Shadith though it had a carapace very like hers.

The growth on its head was longer and thicker than

Shadith's and a different color, it was a shiny
black and hung all the way to the bending part of
its body; there were two white streaks in the
black, very shiny, too.

It came on a flying thing, broad and flat like the
creepler, but far more silent and more subtle.

It argued with the one-bump stilter; the argument
made lots of noise, but the other stilters didn't
come out to see what was happening.

The speaker Taalav thinks the one-bump fed (un-
translatable and untranscribable noise) to the others; this (noise) was the poison the Taalav collect
in their stingsacs. The one-bump had taken sacs
from Taalav in earlier days.

It took the one-bump most of four days to collect
two full arrays and shift them on the transport. In
all this time, none of the six legs or the other stilters appeared.

By the time this was done, Shadith was shaking with
fatigue, sodden with sweat rolling down inside the exo,
soaking the spongy cushions supposed to protect her
body from the abrasion of the metal supports. She took
a step toward the creepler, then turned again. She
thought a moment, shaped a question, sang/whistled it
to the Taalav: When I find your others, shall I bring
them home to you?

She expected another cascading consultation, but the
large one answered immediately.

==

| Maker of Songs | **if they thrive, let them be** |
| **Shadow** | plant the spirit/essence in another place |

Two-bump friend   **let them shape another
                           home**

==

After she rode the platform up and settled herself in
the reed chair, Shadith watched the Taalav arrays go
spreading out beneath the trees, taking up the lives
they'd put down to talk to her. She heard the Kliu
guard's breathing start to change and knew he was
about to come awake.

She touched the sensor and set the creepler going on
the trek back to the lake. *A little tact and some patience and I'm off this stinking world.* She smiled at
the burp from the Kliu's eating mouth. *Sounds like
crocface there OD'd on (noise); may his gut rebel and
his head feel worse than mine.*

7

A drone from Digby was waiting for her when she
reached the ship, but she didn't access the data inside
until she was well away from Pillory and 'splitting for
Spotchalls.

Digby was sitting behind the desk again, wearing
the face she'd seen when he set her to work. "A
bit of information has come into my hands,
Shadow, which you might find interesting and
perhaps even useful. Word has come from
Marrat's Market that the Broker Jingko iKan has
on offer a Taalav crystal. Guaranteed genuine and
not stolen. Seems clear to me this is the smuggler's payoff and he's getting his money out of it
as fast as possible. I want to remind you of the
strictures of this search. You're to be invisible to
the Kliu. I leave it to you to figure out how."

Shadith watched the image dissolve as the message erased itself from the ship's memory. "Complications. So I'm supposed to get past OverSec without letting anyone know I'm looking for that smuggler. Cover? Spla! Can't sneak in and disguise won't do it. OverSec took that template of me when I went into Sunflower Labs. Said it would be erased. Not likely.

Cover . . . cover . . . a job that'll be plausible and get me in without airing the Kliu connection. Lee? No. If she were hunting something, she'd do it herself. Swarda would do, but he and his crew are on a run out to the Hevardee. Aslan's Mama. Yes. She owes me. Doesn't like me all that much, but she likes feeling obligated even less. I need to talk to her first, though. Droom. That's another month of traveling while the trail freezes on me, but with Digby's strictures . . . Shayss!"

Sighing, she called up the destination code of the Hegger Combine and fed them into the router, then dealt with the disorientation as the ship phased into the new course and 'splitted for Droom.

5

I Forgot What Home Was Like

1

Lylunda crawled from the sludge of the ocean called the Haundi Zeön, wriggled through the tangle of baifruit vines and into the clump of tall, thin rynzues with their woody braided stems and the dusky black heat-collector nodules on the spray of branches at the top. Half an hour ago she'd brought her ship down through a foaming red light, Ekiloré's sullen fire filtered through an abundance of cloud fleece as the sun rose above the horizon; they were dry clouds because the rainy season was still two months off. She'd settled it in the tangled mass of vines and trees on the largest island in a spray of islands that ran parallel to the coast, covered it with camou cloth and left it with a low-level shield in place, a smuggler's special.

On her feet again, she looked back at Nameless Island, only one end of it visible past the tangle of vines and the droop of the rynzu branches.

They were all nameless islands. Behilarr notion—why bother identifying something so useless? The Zeön was a soup of poisons infested with eels that were mostly mouth and vast schools of small, black swimmers that could strip flesh from bone in seconds.

All of these died when they ate Behilarr flesh, but the Behilarr died as well, ending as vomited chunks on the ocean floor. She was only half Behilarr. She grinned at the thought; maybe she'd only half-poison the fish.

No one went boating for pleasure in the waters round here and swimming was a skill only the very rich with their pools of filtered water could afford to learn. Her ship would be safe out there until she came back for it, though she didn't look forward to the long dangerous swim to reach it.

In the strengthening light of the steamy dawn, she slipped off the impeller harness and laid it on the ground, unclipped her dita sac, took out the can of cleanser and the packet of blancafilm, and began the long process of cleaning and stowing her aegis suit and all the appurtenances that let her come safely through the hazards of the Zeön.

2

By the time she reached the coast road, most of the morning was gone and she wasn't quite so pleased with herself for finding a perfect place to stow her ship. The burlap sack she'd used to conceal her offworld gear was a hot wet spot on her back, the rough weave rubbing a rash through her blouse and T-shirt. *Smuggler on the brain,* she thought. *I probably could have parked the ship in the tie-down at the transfer station and come in legit. And saved myself a lot of trouble. . . .*

She started walking along the edge of the unpaved road, a line of dirt beaten hard by the hooves of cattle driven from the nearby arranxes, the estates of the Highborn Behilarr, to the feed lots and slaughtering houses outside Haundi Zurgile. Zurg. Where she was born. Hutsarté had only been colonized a little more than a hundred years ago, and Behilarr were slow to spend money on things like roads even though floats did need fairly level ground to operate efficiently.

Dream on, Luna, if you came in legit, your name would be on the list. How long would it take a hired snoop to find you then?

Her ankle turned as her foot slipped into a rut. Arms waving, she found her balance again but winced as she took the next step. "Jaink! I think I sprained the thing."

She settled herself on a clump of irratzy, the curly leaves and rubbery stems of the fern grass poking at her through the cloth of the long skirt she'd pulled over the underpants she'd worn beneath the aegis suit. The road curved here and a stand of prickle pipes with their twining side growths and spongy foliage blocked the wind and the fine white dust that wind blew like heat clouds along the ruts.

For several moments she just sat, pulling her knees up, folding her arms on them, resting her head on her arms while she wondered if this homecoming business was worth the pain it was going to bring her. Then she sighed, turned back the hem of her skirt, and prodded at the ankle. She was wearing low-heeled boots she didn't want to take off because she'd never get them back on again. With stingworms, pincer mites, and the other small biters that Hutsarté grew in the millions, walking barefoot wasn't a good idea.

Barefoot. Every summer when she was a subteen she'd spent a lot of time in a local clinic, waiting for a purge to expel one parasite or another from her system. Jaink only knew what passengers she was picking up right now, just by sitting on this patch of fern grass.

She pulled the skirt down and tucked her feet under her when she heard the hum of a float, the first in several hours. It was a hiccuping hum, as if the lifters were ready to scatter their parts to the four winds. When it came round the stand of prickle pipes, she saw a small battered vehicle that looked old enough to be one of the firstdowns. The driver matched it, his face a mask of wrinkles, his clan sign so faded she couldn't read it. He was one of those rambling peddlers who moved from arranx to arranx, selling items and occasionally buying handwork to resell in Zurg.

He saw her and brought the juddering float to a gentle stop, twisted his body around, and called back, "Shouldna sit there, neska. Some mean biters wud soon be chewing your sweet little poto. What's wrong? You not feeling good?"

"Give my ankle a turn, jun."

"You aiming for Zurg? Hoy! twanghead question that. Where else would you be going? Want a ride?" He grinned at her, showing a good set of yellow fangs. "Got all my teeth still, but I don't bite."

She pushed onto her feet, winced at the twinge in her ankle, bent, and picked up the gunny sack. "'Preciate it, jun," she said and limped around to the rider's side.

"You make it all right?"

"Give me a minute." She tossed the sack into the cargo bin, pulled herself up, and settled onto the grubby seat. "Drop me at the Izar Gate if you don't mind."

The old man tapped and pushed and jiggled the controls, and after a while the float coughed and lifted onto its airpad; he started it wheezing forward, then leaned back, one hand on the joystick. "You a working girl? Izar, I mean, that's why I ask."

"Nah, just visiting kin." She drew her sleeve across her face, grimacing at the smear of mud on the cloth. "Been gone a while. Anything I should look out for?"

"Thought I hadn't seen you round. You wanna keep your head down. The Ezkop is on a purification rage, he's got Mazkum and Jazkum in High Zurg wearing out their knees and burning their silks. He's threatening to harrow the Izar next in the name of Jaink and Virtue. Ever been through one of those?"

The float whined and labored as it began climbing the long slope to the top of the gorge where the River Jostun ran down to join the sea.

Lylunda shivered. "When I was little. My mother was scourged. How likely are Duk and Dukerri to allow that?"

"The Ezkop Garap has the ear of the Dukina and the Mazkum ladies. They don't like it when the Jazkum go slipping round to Izar to sample the housewares, but they can't say it. Now they got a chance to use their claws. If I had kin in the Izar, I'd slip them away somewhere till the rain sends the Maz and Jaz out to the hills."

"I'll think about it. Thanks." She wiped her face again, then sat forward tensely as he took the last bend around the huge clump of ancient rynzues that marked the end of the bridge over the Jostun. After fifteen years away, this would be her first sight of Haundi Zurgile.

The city was on the far side of the gorge where the Jostun ran, rising up the slopes of a dead volcano whose dark gray summit she could see beyond the rynzues; the higher you lived in Zurg, the classier you were, the more money and power you controlled. The Izar was on the flat land around the base of the mountain, the folk there breathing in the air of the feedlots

and slaughterhouses as well as the factories and the hot
air wafted over from the landing field a few kilometers
off. As the float hummed and choked up the approach
to the wide bridge, she could see the red tile roofs of
the tenements poking over the whitewashed walls that
shut the Izar away from the rest of the city, beyond
them the painted 'crete of the Low City like the colored filling between the layers of a torte, and above all
these the black and gold citadels of the Jazkum who
ruled the place.

Her father lived up there still, a Jaz of the Jazkum
with a Maz wife and a High Family, all of whom refused to know about her and her mother the whore.
Her mother died before she reached her fortieth year,
brought down by a fever that a gray-market antibiotic
couldn't cope with. The old anger came back as the
float hummed and coughed across the bridge, a fury
not diminished by the fifteen years that had passed
since the day she found her mother cold and still, her
bed stained by her body fluids. To get access to good
medicine and good care you had to be sealed to one of
the Seven Clans; brought in by birth, adoption, or pur-
chase; your name writ in the Temple register; your
body marked as Jaink's own by the clan sign tattooed
in the center of your brow. Most of the people in the
Izar hadn't a hope of any of these things.

Lekat—that was what the Behilarr called them.
Mongrels. A collective name for a heterogeneous
swarm of entertainers, exiles, and half-breeds, a mix of
Cousins from a hundred worlds: thieves; fugitives from
contract labor gangs; smugglers and arms dealers
who'd made elsewhere too hot for them; crewmen and
women so drunk or drugged their ships went on without them; embezzlers; dethroned dictators fleeing war
crime tribunals; lost souls yearning for something they

couldn't name who ran out of money before they found whatever it was and others who had reason to cut loose from their former lives; misfits of every kind there was. They were free to come and squat in the Izar, they were free to do those jobs the Behilarr considered beneath them, they were also free to starve, to harbor such diseases as they brought with them, free to pass them around as far as they would go among the others in the Izar, free to steal from each other, rape, plunder and kill each other. Free as long as they didn't discommode the Marked Pure among the Behilarr.

Except when the Ezkop, the High Priest of the Temple, or the Sorginz, the Priestess of Groves and Peaks, except when that holy pair fell into one of their frenzies of purification, except for those harrowing times, the Behilarr tolerated the Lekat and by their very contempt protected them. As they'd protect her now, once she was lost in the Izar.

The old man stopped before an open arch in the high white wall; black Behilarr glyphs painted above it spelled out IZAR. "I'm not asking questions," he said. "But don't forget what I told you."

She summoned a grin, leaned over, and kissed his leathery cheek. "And best you disremember me, my friend. Jaink smile on your and yours."

3

As she limped along a narrow cobbled street, the weight of the sack disturbing her balance, making it difficult to keep weight off her ankle, she looked around with a sense that she'd stepped back in time. She'd been gone fifteen years, but the graffiti on the walls looked much the same; the names might be different, but she couldn't remember the old ones anyway.

There was a new cook shop on the second corner—new to her at least—used to be a dressmaker there. Eskoziaka, that was her name. She made costumes for dancers and working lingerie for the housegirls.

She hobbled on, noting other changes. Halak the Spice Man was gone; the windows were whitewashed so she couldn't see in and some stars and crescent moons were painted on them. Lester the Knife Man was still there, with Halfman Ike in his wheelbox by the door, looking older than time and stony as the Mountain, his sharp black eyes missing nothing that went on in the street.

He was the first to recognize her. "Ba da, if isn't Meerya's girl. What you doing back, 'ska? Should we expect a plague of space marines any day now?"

"And a good morning to you, Ike. Auntee Zaintze still with the living?"

He blinked at her a moment, considering the bulging gunny sack and the shabby skirt and blouse. If she hadn't been who she was he'd have lied flat out. "In the flesh? Yawp. You wanting something outta her?"

"I owe her a greeting. Old times, you know. And I want to catch up on what's what." She tapped her nose, offering a snippet of her own news. "Met a peddler outside the city, give me a ride, he said the Ezkop and the Sorginz, they're working up to a harrowing."

"Peddler, eh? Just yammer or did he look like he knew what he was talking about?"

"Old git. You know what it takes to last that long fiddling the arranxes. Mid city. Canto clan."

"You know Zitz Alley? Back end by wall, go up stairs to first landing, bang loud, she don't hear so good sometimes."

"Owe you one, Ike." With a flip of her hand she moved on. After a few paces, she looked back, saw him talking earnestly to a skinny dirtyface boy. *What a hoot! Me bringing news to Halfman Ike. After all these years, me!*

4

Zitz Alley was the noisome dead-end offshoot she remembered all too well, rats feeding on garbage, not bothering to run when they saw her, stench of urine strong enough to rival poison gas, scraps of this and that rotting into slime after sitting there through four, five, six rainy seasons. A narrow path swept relatively clean led back to a framework of rusting metal that was only a sketch of a stairway.

Lylunda climbed the ladder, trying not to touch the worn oily rail. Going up wasn't that bad, but she did her best not to think of coming down again.

The door had a coat of shiny black enamel that had been washed or repainted recently. An iron knocker was bolted beneath a shuttered slit too narrow for even a child's hand to pass through. When she banged the knocker hard against the door, the resulting boom sent her brows up toward her hairline. Steel? Looks like dear auntee has prospered since I left. She knocked again.

The shutter slid open. "Who's that?"

"Lylunda Elang. Auntee Zaintze, want to talk to you."

"Luna?" Quick glitter of an eye at the slit. "Ahh, it is you. Just a minute. This takes some doing, you know."

The slide snapped shut. Lylunda heard scribble-scrabble noises muffled through the steel and stepped back when the heavy slab began swinging open.

"Hurry, child. Jaink knows who's watching out there."

* * *

The hallway inside the door was short, narrow, and lined with metal plates. There were a pair of dim presslamps stuck up on the plates, casting just enough light to let her see the tiny bent figure scuttling along ahead of her.

She turned a corner, went through another door into a small, bright jewel of a room, clean and filled with light from a line of small windows up near the ceiling and mirrors everywhere that caught the light and passed it about.

"I was just about to make some tea. You used to like Auntee Zizi's tea. I've got some of those macaroons baked fresh today, from Okin the Baker, you remember him? He's been doing well enough, he's thinking of sponsoring his youngest daughter, the pretty one, into Canto clan, she's classic Behilarr, even more than you, luv. Got white wings in her hair and a profile pure as a coin. He's got some families interested and there're those in the Izar who'd be willing to add to the dower. Just put that ... um ... sack down anywhere, I've got a tiny little fresher if you'd like to wash off the dust."

Lylunda bit into the crispy macaroon and sighed with pleasure. When her mouth was clear, she said, "No one in twenty star systems bakes like Okin."

Zaintze smiled and refilled the two delicate china cups. "Which brings up a point, Luna. You got out. Why'd you come back? You in trouble?"

"Let's just say I annoyed some folk and I need some time to cool off."

"Law trouble?"

"No warrants out, Auntee Zi. Hired noses doing the looking. Private thing."

"Going to follow you here?"

"Depends. I don't do a lot of talking about where I

come from, but there are sniffers who might figure it out."

"Was what you did worth it?"

"Oh, yes. I'm not hurting for the coin, Auntee Zi. I just needed a place where I could watch my back."

"Good. I'd hate to see Meerya's daughter hopping from fire to fire for nothing. Talking about watch your back. . . ." She broke off, frowned at Lylunda.

"Yah, I figured ways haven't changed all that much since I left. Who do I see for protection and how much will it cost?"

"You remember Grinder Jiraba?"

"Big kid, a year older than me. Had girls for every day of the month and two for JainkEve." She didn't say that she'd been one of those girls, using sex with Grinder to keep the others off her, though she suspected Zaintze knew it well enough. "And he was a lot smarter than most rip-and-runners."

"That's him. Hasn't changed his ways either when it comes to women, so if you don't want to play, let him know up front. What it is, about five years ago, he went head-to-head with Pouska, I know you remember him. They say Pouska's poisoning Haundi Zeön's fish these days. No one knows anything for sure except he's not around any more and Grinder's running the Izar." She slipped a slice of ranja fruit onto Lylunda's plate and set another macaroon beside it. "Protection won't be cheap, but it's good. And it'll cover Star Street. Fifty zilars a week." She made a deprecating gesture with one thin, bony hand. "You count as an outsider, Luna, can't do anything about that. "Hundred zilars bonus pay if he has to off a nose that gets too pushy and won't take no. Fifty zilars bonus for a discourager."

"You're right it's expensive. Could be worse, I suppose. He have a credit comm?"

"What do you think?"

"I think he does."

"Good to see you haven't lost your edge. Account on Helvetia, eh? Not just brag, then."

"Trapped account with a dead drop, Auntee Zi. You and Mum taught me to keep my cash away from sticky fingers."

"Gratifying to see something we said finally sank in." Zaintze grinned and tapped the back of Lylunda's hand. "Another lesson. We'd best find you some work. Don't want the blood lice thinking you're a lady of leisure."

"I don't know how long I'm going to be here."

"More than a month?"

"Yah. Maybe as much as a year. Depends on if things start hotting up."

"A year? Oo-ee, child. That is some mad you conjured."

Lylunda shrugged.

"Hm. You went for to be a pilot. Make it?"

"Yah. Why?"

"Was thinking. Grinder might eat the protection fee for a favor or two."

"I won't work on my back, not now, not ever."

"Not that kind of favor. Grinder's been bringing in stuff, tapping into the Star Street kephalos to slide the goods past Behilarr eyes, but the keyboarder was a graghead and ODed last month."

"Weapons?"

"We're not that stupid, Luna. 'Tronics and medicas."

We, Lylunda thought. *I begin to see the back-behind of all these pretties.* "I've done this before and no brag, just truth, I'm rather good at it. Set up the meet and we'll see how it goes. But he'd better find someone for me to train. Make it real clear, Auntee Zi, this isn't a permanent thing. I'm outta here soon as I think it's safe."

"Grinder's second son, his name's Herred, they call him Bug, he's near as much a whiz as you were, Luna. But he won't be going anywhere. Some sickness that come off a tradeship when he was just four killed his Mam and a lot of others and gave him brittle bones. Has to wear an exo all the time which is why he got the name Bug. But bright, yah, he's bright. Plays with numbers like some boys play with knives. He's holding shop, working the lines Lerdo the Graghead set up, but he's not ready to make new, though he thinks he is. Better if you handle the tap a while and teach him enough to make sure he doesn't slip and blow the whole operation."

Fun, Lylunda thought. *Bug, huh! Like me? If I'd had to deal with me that age, I'd have strangled me. Ba da, what I have to, I can do. It'll save a lot of potheration, having Grinder's shadow on me.* "I need a room. Somewhere I won't be hassled."

"I know just the place."

5

The room was small, but solid—grills on the windows, a door with a bar-lock and a sheet of plasteel laminated to the inside, up on the third floor of a five-key building. It had a tiny alcove with a hotplate and a miniature oven set into the wall, and the bed was a narrow cot, hard enough to pound yams on. There was a coinbath down the hall and a small greengrocers on the ground floor where vegetables and eggs were expensive but available without having to face the dangers of the street, especially after dark.

On her first day in the new place, Lylunda soaked the ankle and wrapped it in a pneumabrace, shot it with

pain suppressant, and gave herself a full spectrum
kataph to flush out the parasites she'd picked up on her
way into the city.

She dozed for a long time to let the drugs work, then
spent the evening planning and revising plans until she
was tired of tramping along the same ruts. It was full
dark out when she woke to a chime that left her confused until she remembered what the concierge had
said about the mail warn.

It was a note from Zaintze giving the details of
her appointment tomorrow with Grinder Jiraba—and
along with the note, a parcel with clothing the old
woman had bought for her. Plus a hefty bill for that
clothing.

She looked it over and grinned. "Cunning old lukie.
Wonder how much she padded this."

There were two plain black skirts with narrow bands
of embroidery about hems that would hit her around
the ankles, two plain white blouses with high necks
and long sleeves and two hemmed lengths of black silk
for folding about her head. She wrinkled her nose at
the thought of wearing long sleeves and a demi-turban
in the steamy heat that belonged with this time of the
year, but Auntee Zi was right. This was righteous garb,
announcing *don't mess with me*. There were also half a
dozen pairs of silk underpants and three sleeveless un-
dershirts. And Zaintze'd got the size right. Cunning old
lukie indeed.

She fixed an omelet and sat on the bed to eat it, her
injured ankle propped on one of the straightback
chairs. When she finished, she set the plate on the bed
beside her, propped the second foot beside the first,
and watched the sky turn improbable colors through
the bars of the window.

How very strange . . . she hadn't thought about it until now . . . until she saw the calendar in the greengrocers. . . .

You don't think about planetary dates much when you're 'splitting here and 'splitting there. It doesn't seem worth the bother, all those different ways of reckoning. Ship's kephalos stayed on universal time, that's all you needed.

She'd looked at the calendar because of the picture, a phot of Hutsarté from the transfer station with the interesting pale fan of the River Jostun's outflow. Then she read the month. Begiberru, the Month of Buds. The days were numbered in their forty small squares and twenty-five had been crossed off with a red crayon. Twenty-sixth of Begiberru.

Fifteen years ago to the day, her mother died.

Three months later she had her place as trainee and she'd left, so filled with anger it was not possible to grieve.

The layered colors of the sunset blurred as she finally wept for Meerya and her useless death.

6

On her second day in the Izar, Lylunda dressed in the new clothing, tucked Zaintze's note with its instructions into a wristpouch next to a small stunrod, and left the rooming house with her keys on a chain round her waist, dropped inside her skirt where they'd be less vulnerable to a snatch-and-grab.

Grinder's Place was on the far side of the Izar, a huge old warehouse tucked between a slaughterhouse and a flash freeze plant, its back butted against the Wall. From its flat roof you could look down into Star Street or watch the shuttles from the transfer station and the Freeships landing most hours of the day and night.

The sour stench from Star Street mixed with the sweetish aroma of old blood to thicken the air until you almost had to chew it before you could breathe it. She'd forgotten that stench and had trouble keeping her lunch down as she turned a corner and the full glory of it hit her in the face. She thought about it and decided that she appreciated Grinder's subtlety. Those who lived here got used to the smell; intruders tended to betray themselves as they leaned against the nearest wall and vomited.

The warehouse was a busy place, sleds moving in and out, crates and barrels crowded into every inch of space. Drunks and other sentient debris of various shapes and species sprawled beside the walls in the meager shade provided by shallow niches. In the alley between the warehouse and the flash freeze plant, a standup whore with dead eyes endured the grunting efforts of one of the derelicts who'd panhandled some coin and spent it on her instead of his usual brand of self-destruction.

Lylunda stepped over a sprawled drunk, ignoring his mumbled comments that she couldn't understand anyway, waited for a sled to whine out, then moved quickly through the opening into the vast dim interior.

Several men moved to meet her, the leader a tall thin man with a face she almost remembered.

"I think you're lost, woman. This isn't Star Street."

As soon as he spoke, she knew who he was. He had a high whiny voice that hadn't changed at all. "You forgot me already, Krink? I've an appointment with Grinder. Tell him Luna's here."

"Walking with your head up, huh? Amu, go see if the Jun Jiraba wants to see this urd."

Grinder Jiraba leaned back in his chair and rubbed a broad hand across his chin. He'd lived hard since last she'd last seen him and had lost bits of himself in the process. Two of the fingers were nubs; a scar just missed the tip of his right eye and slashed a ravine across his check. His coarse black hair was still thick, but peppered with white and gray. He wore it clipped almost to his skull, barely a centimeter long all over. His shoulders were meaty and his once slim body had acquired a thin padding of fat that did little to conceal the hard muscles beneath, while the weight gave him a force he hadn't had when he was thin and beautiful.

"Sorry to see you back here," he said.

"When you have to go to ground, best do it where you know the traps."

"You think you know them?"

"Better than some. It's been a while and things change, but not that much from what I've seen."

"You aren't on any passenger lists."

"Sure of that? What about a Freeship or a false name?"

"I know everyone who goes in and out of Star Street. It's my business to know. And my business to know who's chasing you. Don't play the fool. I remember you too well for that."

"I've been smuggling this and that since I got my ticket. Smuggled myself down. Didn't want my name on lists Jaink knows who gets a look at."

"You didn't answer the question, Lylunda Elang. Who's chasing you?"

She hesitated, but she'd been over this before, over and over it till she was sick of it; it was a danger to tell him, but if he picked up someone coming after her, he'd squeeze it out of him anyway. Besides, he was right; it was his business to know what was going on in his patch. "The Kliu Berej. They've set a bringalive price on my head. It'll probably take them a while to

track me here, but there are noses around able to follow a grain of salt the length of a star arm."

"Hm. You snatched some Taalav crystals?"

"I'm a smuggler, not a thief. Say someone did and
they want him and they think I can tell them where he
is. Easy money for you, Grinder. All you have to do is
go over the Wall and walk down Star Street." She
waited for his response, more tense than she'd expected to be, watching his eyes, seeing the heat of
crystal fever wake in them. She thought she'd judged
Grinder and the circumstances that bound him well
enough, but you never really knew how people would
jump when pressure was on them.

She knew the moment he made up his mind. He
wouldn't sell her. Not yet, anyway. Not till he lost
hope of squeezing crystals out of her. . . .

"I wouldn't hand those borts on Star Street a used
turd," he said and pushed his chair back. "We'll go to
my house. Want to show you what you've got to deal
with." He stood, came round the desk. "Zaintze said
she told you about my Second. Herred, he's not an
easy boy. Other kids called him Bug because of the
exo. He picked it up and that's all he lets anyone call
him now. Kids, you can't beat that sort of kak out of
them. Bug's mad all the time at me because I didn't try
it. He's too young yet to understand that it'd just get
worse if I did. Be a favor if you got him to see that, but
I won't be holding my breath."

She put a hand on his arm, stopped him before he
opened the door. "Speaking about holding your breath,
what about Krink? You trust him?"

"The length of a micron if he's wearing handcuffs
and leg irons. He does work I don't want to do myself.
Efficiency, Luna. Remember ol' Efficiency Gidur?"

She chuckled, chanted, "The right tool for the right
job." Sobering, she tapped her fingers on the hard mus-

cles. "Watch out this one doesn't turn in your hand. He's ambitious. I could smell it on him."

"Ba da, he's already tried it and got kicked in the butt for being an idiot. Better the flaws you know. He's a little worm, thinks little, and couldn't plan his way out of a paper bag. He doesn't know it, though, and that's one of the things that makes him dangerous." He opened the door, stood aside to let her pass. "Luna, arguing life with you is one of the things I missed most after you took off."

As they walked down the stairs together, she murmured, "I never understood why you stayed. You were smart enough to get out."

He didn't answer till they reached the main floor. "This is my place. I wouldn't feel right anywhere else. I'm not like you. You cut your ties so easy. You were gone even before you left."

"I never had ties, Grinder. Not then. Not now."

7

Lylunda stood on the balcony outside Grinder's company parlor. His house was on the high side of the Izar, tall enough to catch breezes over the Wall, breezes not tainted by ship exhaust and slaughterhouses. It was a big place, built in a square about a large central court with a fountain and trees and flower beds. And children everywhere.

"Kak! Grinder. They all yours?"

He grinned. "That's what their mothers tell me. Actually, no. Couple of the youngest are my grandkids. Would you believe it, Luna? Me, a grandpa."

She watched him beaming down on the busy scene and felt a coldness start to gather under her ribs. There was something so . . . proprietorial and . . . oh . . . lethal about him. *This is my place, he said. My place. My house. My children. My women. If he starts thinking about me like that. . . .* "You'd best let me have a look at Lerdo's documentation. I have to know what I'm talking about when I meet your son."

6

Worming into Haundi Zurgile

1

Worm slipped the *Kinu Kanti* into Hutsarté's atmosphere above the major continent of the Wild Half, the hemisphere the Behilarr hadn't bothered to settle yet. He went warily at first, then relaxed as the readouts told him that what he'd picked up about the place was true, not enough security to keep out a tesh fly.

When he was at a level to go on visual screens, he looked at the tangle of unsavory vegetation sliding beneath him and decided the Behilarr didn't have to worry about anyone coveting this place. He shifted direction, went circumpolar, and began a metal scan of the coastline that belonged to the settled continent, keeping the visuals on to give him a look at what was being probed. Low and slow ate power, but he was operating on the Kliu's credit chip, so he'd topped up at the transfer station and was feeling comfortably prodigal at the moment.

He slowed further when he began picking up a signal as a string of islands came into the screen. Metallic smear, size uncertain, shape uncertain—he was nearly on top of it before he could nail which island it was on.

There was a hollow in the vegetation with withered

edges, enough to suggest a ship had put down here and the very faint traces he was picking up had to mean it was a smuggler's ship, equipped to escape most detection.

He chortled as he changed direction again and started back across the ocean. "Lylunda Elang. Gotcha."

He set the *Kinu Kanti* down in a small stony canyon in the coast range of a continent in the Wild Half and started cycling through the shutdown/conceal procedures, brooding all the while over the last thing his father had told him. *Keep those scivs sweet, Worm. They've got your brothers. Two of them now because you din't bother using that useless lump a gristle atop your neck. You shouldda known we couldda fetched Xman out of contract easy enough. I tell you to your face, we gotta get Mort loose, he's the only one of the lot of you who's got the guts to run this place. Snake over 't next Rift, he been shooting eyes this way. So you keep 'em happy till we get that girl and make the trade.*

Worm shivered when he thought of his older brother and some of the things that Mort had done to give him the rep that kept Snake and Herbie and the other Riftmen backed off. If Mort hadn't been his brother and blood was sacred after all, he'd have been just as happy to leave him scrabbling about Pillory scurfing off other gits as murderous as him.

Time to do the sweetening, to let the Kliu know he was on the job and making time. He worked over the message for several minutes, then played it back. *Am down on Hutsarté, Behilarr Colony. Have got suggestive though inconclusive evidence the smuggler is here. Will be going undercover for close-up observation. Will keep under advisement the listed possible agents of Excavations Ltd. and report if any such are spotted. Clandestine conditions of investigation require limiting exposure to detection, so contact will be sporadic for the next few weeks.*

It seemed adequate, saying as little as possible while giving the impression he was being forthcoming. *As good as anything Xman could write.* Xman was the talker of the family, the tongue that was quicker even than Mort's knifes. Worm sighed, missing his brother a lot as he coded and compressed the message, squirted it on its way. "Choke on that, stinking scivs."

He waited a while longer, watching the readouts to be sure the squirt hadn't pinned him, then he extracted the ship's flikit and once again started across the ocean.

2

After he hid the flikit, Worm spent the rest of the night trudging across prickly wasteland. He detested walking, he hated all this ugly nothing full of dust and stinks and malevolent thorns doing their best to rip his flesh; but he wanted to be sure the flikit would be where he put it when he needed it again, so it had to be in a place no sane man would bother looking at.

He reached the Landing Field in the gray dawn light, brushed himself off, and caught a jit heading for Haundi Zurgile's Star Street.

He found what he was looking for at the end of a narrow side alley, a hole-in-the-wall called The Rainy Season. The name didn't matter, it was the smell he recognized. Xman said it was cheap drink, cheaper brainrot, mixed with the stink of maybes never gonna happen and the lowgrade fever of hate/fear. Sure enough, whenever he smelled it, Worm knew he was in a place he understood and with people he knew even if he'd never seen them before.

He dumped his gearsac on the floor between the stool and the bar, then slid onto the stool so the sac lay between his feet.

The barscort was an old, sad Lommertoerkan, his facial folds so deep and packed so tightly together, he looked like someone had shoved his skin through a pleater. "Ya?"

"Any cohanq?"

"Five minims a shot." The Lommertoerkan's voice was high and sweet; if Worm closed his eyes, it could have been a woman talking. "See the coin before I pour."

Worm set a brass gelder on the wood. "Local exchange will do me, gonna be here a while."

He sipped at the cohanq, expecting the hard bite of barrel squeeze and was surprised to find it sliding down without ripping the lining off his throat. "Good stuff," he said and could've kicked himself when he heard the surprise in the words.

The pleats on the Lommertoerkan's face spread slightly around what could have been a smile, then he said in his soft, sweet voice, "Trade's brisk. Should you pick up something good, I can find it a home."

"Luck up and bit me in the ass or I'd do a deal." He drained the last drops of the cohanq and inspected the pile of local gelt, turning each plaque over, scowling at the holoed face and the enigmatic inscriptions. They were all alike. Fifteen of them. Twenty to a brass unless the Toerk was cheating him. He pushed five of them back. "Again."

When the barscort slid his glass back to him, Worm took another swallow and felt a warm buzz forming in his head. He enjoyed it for a moment, then blinked at the Toerk. "Be here a while."

"So you said."

Worm moved the plaques with his finger. "All outgo 'n no in don't play."

"Labor exchange over by the Tinkerman's lot. Ask anyone, they'll point you right."

"Could do, uh-huh. Could drop by here again, maybe you'd know someone could use a good lock man."

"Drop a name. References as it were."

"Texugarra. Gran Jalla Pit."

"Ah. Sweet lady that she is."

Worm snorted. "Texugarra would drop his beard should he hear that."

"And what a beard it is, heh?"

"Every hair white as Menaviddan monofil and twice as tough."

"Let us say you come along here round midafternoon tomorrow. You've found a place to stay?"

"Just got off the jit."

The Lommertoerkan found a stylo and a bit of paper, scrawled a few words on it. "Empling has a room or two, I put down where to find him. If you don't take to that place, look round there. Plenty of others." He dropped the paper in front of Worm, swept the rest of the plaques into a side pocket of his tunic, and went to serve another patron.

Worm finished the drink, sipping slowly, savoring the sweet fire of the cohanq. In a little while he'd have to go to work again, but for the moment he was just Worm and nothing more, no worries to twist his gut and give him nightmares where he relived things he hated having seen the first time.

3

The night was hot and sticky, a cloud layer blocking moon and starlight and pressing on the air until it was so thick it was more like breathing water. Worm ignored the sweat rolling down his back and inside his barrier gloves and huddled in the deepest shadow he could find while Keyket went through the ID dance with the guard inside. The man had taken the bribe all right, but he was making sure he opened to the right thieves. Worm didn't blame him, knowing how pissed a type like Grinder got when someone swooped in and snatched his prize; he just wished the git would hurry and make up his mind.

And he wished it would rain and wash the crud from the air. He was working up a real hate for this stinking world. The sooner he got off it, the better he'd like it, but it was going to be tougher than he thought glomming that femme. She was here all right; he'd seen her ambulating around with Grinder's crippled kid. Hadn't figured she'd have that kind of connections. Meant he had to be jodaddin sure he had it right, 'cause he wouldn't get a second chance.

A siss from Keyket brought him out of shadow. The door opened, and they hurried inside.

"Bug has the sec sys tamed." The guard was whispering, the sweat on his face from more than the heat. "Says you got a clear hour before the bypass starts to strain."

Keyket nodded. "Gotcha. Where?"

"I better show you. This setup's so messed only the keph can keep straight what's where. Bug's got dollies already there."

* * *

The first lock took the longest time, almost twenty minutes of their hour. It was a tricky bit of 'tronics with layered freeze triggers and a mutating key, but he'd done tougher and he knew better than to lose hold on his patience.

He'd just got the lock to signal open when a brief waggle on the readout warned him there was another trick in the shipper's bag. He swore under his breath and ran the palmscanner around the crack where the lid fitted onto the base. Just a pressure spot. Simple but wicked if you missed it. He pressed his thumb onto the spot, the lock hummed, and the lid to the container cracked open.

He left the loading to Keyket and the guard, and moved on to the next container. The pattern was the same, so he went through that one fast as kobber beer through a gut. By the time he finished the third, they'd lifted the packets they wanted from the first and transferred them to Grinder's box. He shifted over there, closed the lid, reset the count and the pressure spot, engaged the lock, then stood waiting while Keyket finished pulling what he wanted from the second container.

Twenty minutes more and they were out of there, the warehouse sealed up again, no evidence anything had happened—except for some stuff gone missing off invoice and who could say where that went down. It hadn't surprised Worm that Grinder knew exactly what was in each of those boxes or that he wasn't simply cleaning them out. He'd worked for smart and he'd worked for dumb and from what he'd seen here, Grinder was on the high side of smart. Reminded him a lot of Mort. Which made him shiver when he thought of what would happen if he missed the snatch and blew his cover.

A few steps before they hit the main street, Keyket

gave his shoulder a friendly punch. "Never seen slicker, Worm. Grinder likes gits who know how to do the job. You better go shuck y' tools. I'll meet you at The Tank for the payout."

4

Worm followed Keyket into the small back office and stood by the door, his shoulders hunched, his eyes fixed on the legs of the blocky desk, his hands in the pockets of his jacket. Once they knew what he could do with locks, low-level managers like Tank got real nervous if they thought he was looking around too much. They never realized it wasn't what he saw that mattered so much, but whether he was carrying. And he was carrying; getting into Tank's office wasn't a chance he could pass by.

The sensacube in his pocket turned warm against his thumb, giving him a clear to start the tabs and tictacs sewn onto the jacket pulling in images and tracing energy flow.

Tank counted out the plaques into two piles, one larger than the other; his hands were quick and accurate, small hands for such a block of a man. Worm watched them and thought *gambler. Whatever he is now, he got his stake gambling.*

When the counting was finished and the plaques in canvas bags, Keyket stuffed his down the front of his shirt and went out, flashing a grin at Worm as he went.

When Worm came to get his bag, Tank cleared his throat. "Grinder was real happy with Keyket's report. He wants you over for dinner tomorrow, Worm. Which means you mind your manners and dress nice. He'll send a jit to pick you up at six hour sharp, outside Harron's Greenshop down to north end of Star Street, that's right next to the ring road. If he likes you, he'll probably give you a place. It's a good deal, and he won't be happy if you give him any shuffle about it. You know and I know, we don't want Grinder not happy."

Worm stood holding the sack. "Yah," he said after a moment. "Maybe it won't happen. Say it does, I'll be real enthused."

Tank blew out the breath he'd been holding and the hard line of his shoulders eased off. "Good. One last thing. If you stay the night, could be one of the women living in the house will come by. Grinder likes to keep them happy after he's moved on, so you don't need to worry about that. Just make sure she goes away feeling good. And keep your mouth shut after. You hear?"

"No lie?"

"No lie. He's a generous man to folk who don't cross him."

"Gotcha. Um, there a laundry around? Been washing my own, but. . . ." He shrugged.

"Transy Herm's over by The Rainy Season. Tell 'er how come, and she'll jump you up the line."

"Thanks."

When he got back to his room, Worm swept it for ears, but found none. Apparently Grinder wasn't that interested in him yet. He was exhausted and needed to sleep, but he stripped his jacket first, setting the tabs and tictacs in their slots in the decoder, plugging in the sensacube to download its more general data set.

5

Nervous and unhappy, Worm followed the humming serviteur into the dining room and nearly lost what calm he had left when he saw Lylunda Elang sitting next to the empty chair that was waiting for him.

He relaxed when she nodded absently at him, smiled, then went back to talking to the woman on her other side.

7

Hunting Cover

1

The Hegger Combine was a small dominion at the tip of the Ular Spur, four star systems with a fifth at the center, all of them within three days split travel from each other, the Combine itself on a major trade route. The inhabited worlds of these systems were prosperous, peaceful and controlled, with access to the surface severely restricted. An outsider had to have a sponsor and wear a locator tag at all times.

Shadith left her ship in the tie-down at the transfer station in orbit about the Hub World Ghysto; all commerce in the combine funneled through this place and the station was immense, almost as large—if not as massive—as the world it floated above. Having to be vetted like this was annoying and ate up time, but an untagged ship approaching any of the systems in the Combine would be blown to dust the minute it showed on a screen.

Digby's Shriek got her through Check-In without trouble; she rented a guide rod and slip plate and went skimming along the thruways, hunting for Adelaris Supply Systems.

2

The polished, pale young man gave her a good view of his perfect teeth as he rose from his desklet and smiled at her. "How may I help you, Desp'?"

Irritated by the eyes watching her, while the suspicion and control that was tangible enough to smell made her feel that her skin had shrunk until it didn't fit over her bones any more, Shadith decided she was tired of all this. She put on her most formal face and said with icy precision, "I need to speak to Adelaar aici Arash. Would you arrange the call, please?"

"May I ask why? I don't mean to be intrusive, but I'll have to give a reason to the Prossiggal."

"You may not mean to intrude, but you do. Tell your Prossiggal this: Shadith whom aici Arash met on Telffer and University wishes to speak to her concerning a matter which is to be kept private between them and which does not concern any others but the two of us. If that proves insufficient, then so be it."

"May I see your identification?"

"That is not necessary."

He let his smile fade. "If you were a friend, you would have the private number. I think I must insist."

"That I'm here without objection from the Combine is sufficient. Anything more is unseemly curiosity on your part. Make the call."

For a moment she thought he was going to summon security and have her removed; then he brought up the privacy shield, tapped on the com, and began talking. After the first few words, his neatly brushed eyebrows rose and a few faint wrinkles appeared in his marble brow.

Shadith waited, impatience like burrs in her blood.

A moment later he rose gracefully to his feet and stepped away from the desk. "Aici Arash wishes to speak to you, Desp' Shadith." He waited until she was seated, then stepped outside the door so it would be obvious he wasn't listening.

"So it is you. Well, what is it?"

"I need to talk to you. Face-to-face. You know where I'm working now?"

"Yes. It has to do with that?"

"Indirectly."

"Not Aslan?"

"Didn't your pretty assistant tell you there was no one else involved? Spla!"

Adelaar chuckled. "He is very decorative, isn't he. And intelligent in his limited way which is quite suitable for the job he's got." Her pale blue eye went distant.

Thinking it over, Shadith told herself. *Asking herself what price she can extract for her cooperation. She might owe me her life, but that's debased currency in these realms. I should have known that.*

"His name's Brad," Adelaar said. "Call him back and I'll have him set things up. You have your own ship?"

"Company ship, company registry."

"Give him the Shriek string, he'll need that for the tag. You'll have a three-day 'split from Ghysto. I'll be waiting for your call-down then."

3

When the shuttle from Droom's transfer station landed at the Visitor's Field, a girl was waiting for her in the small holding room, a lanky, odd-looking almost child.

"My name's Talit. The Patron sent me to give you the pass and bring you to Adelaris."

"Patron?"

Talit blushed. "It's what we call her, the other girls and me. Adelaar." She said the name in a rush as if it were too precious to be in her mouth at all. "If you'll hold out your arm, Desp' Shadith, I'll set the pass bracelet for you. Once that's done, you won't have to fool with those idiot clerks. Do you have luggage? I'll take care of that, too."

"There's nothing to take care of since I'm not going to be here long. You and the other girls?"

"There. Is that comfortable? Good. If you'll just follow me, Desp' Shadith. We can cut through here and reach the jit line without much walking." Talit opened a door half-concealed by an excessively clean plant that looked as if its leaves were washed every day.

They emerged from the building into a brilliant morning. Droom's sun was a greenish-yellow disk about two-thirds of the way to zenith. As Talit programmed the jit's destination module, Shadith looked around. The autumn day was brisk and cool, with the occasional brown leaf breaking loose and blowing free across aggressively neat yards and sidewalks. *Mop the leaves and sweep the grass! I'd go crazy fast if I had to live here.* She leaned back in the seat, brushing hair out of her face. *No sign of a Star Street. Well, there wouldn't be with the visitor restrictions in the Combine.* The road was a neat black line between the trees and the warehouse walls beyond them, with the jitrail gleaming down the center. There weren't many people around, a few in the distance walking away from the Landing Field's Admin Center and an old man with a leash draped over his arm, standing under a tree a short distance off while a small beast in a figure eight harness chased after leaves. Not a beast she'd seen before. It looked like a rat crossed with a monkey. *What people keep for pets, spla ah!*

She glanced a last time at the rat-monkey, smiled as it leaped at a tree and went scurrying up, while the bird it was after perched calmly on a denuded branch. "With a smile on its beak," she said aloud.

"Desp' Shadith?"

"Never mind. I'm just a little tired, that's all." She settled onto the back seat and watched with amusement as Talit got her legs tangled when she tried to get in. "How long will this take?"

Talit brushed limp brown hair out of her eyes, stabbed her thumb at the activator, and turned to face Shadow as the jit started smoothly off. "The Patron thought about sending a flier, but she said it's a nice morning and you'd enjoy the ride. Um, I'm getting things backward again, sorry. A little over twenty minutes. And you asked me about me and the others and I forgot to answer, sorry. Um. We're the Patron's apprentices. She does that, you know . . . of course, you didn't or you wouldn't ask. She has lines out all over the place. Foundling homes call her when they have a girl who's good at her maths and likes to make things but they can't find a place for. We're apprentices, like I said, then we take jobs in the company and the ones who're really really good, she sends to University for a while." She blinked as the bird Shadith had been watching gave a loud caw and went swooping past above the jit. "It's ever so much better with the Patron than the home. It wasn't a bad place, but you get lost in the crowd there unless you're really pretty or can do something special. The Patron makes us feel special. Because she chose us, you see." She gave her quick little smile, then turned away with practiced tact to give her passenger time to pull herself together before she had to face Adelaar.

Shadith was surprised at what Talit had told her, then ruefully ashamed of that surprise. It was a side of

Adelaar she didn't know existed, but it made sense when she thought about it. Adelaar might have pride in and a fierce love for her daughter, but Aslan had gone a different road and there was no chance she'd come home to take over the business that her mother had struggled so hard to build. These young apprentices were an interesting way Adelaar had found to look for someone to share her interests and have the drive to take over Adelaris when she was past it. And maybe she missed Aslan more than she wanted to admit. Loneliness. *I feel it sometimes, but there's nothing I can do about it. My people are dead. Even if I got pregnant, it'd be this body's child, not mine. No Weavers of Shayalin left anywhere in the universe.*

4

After Talit left her, Shadith looked about the room and found another surprise, not anything she'd expected from what she knew of Adelaar. It was not an office but a comfortable parlor; it might have been a place where people lived rather than worked. Padded chairs, a scatter of small elbow tables whose thick tops suggested that access ports might be concealed beneath the polished wood, a fireplace with a fire crackling merrily behind glass doors.

Shadith grimaced and settled herself in the chair Talit had waved at. She felt out of place, out of step. An office would have been more comfortable for her. She missed Autumn Rose. It would have been good to have that steely intellect to act as front and deflect attention from her.

She heard the click of a door and looked around.

Adelaar walked briskly into the room, her best business face on. She settled herself in another chair and tapped the top of a table which opened, displaying a terminal. She ran a sequence on the sensor squares, moved the table to one side, and nodded to Shadith. "Privacy shield up, recorder going. So what is this about?"

"To do a job for one of Digby's clients, I need to get into Marrat's Market. Digby has reasons for not wanting his connection with this client even hinted at. They know me there, they know I work for Digby, so slip and slide isn't going to work. You know Marrat's?"

"Yes."

Shadith waited a moment, but Adelaar said nothing more. "Right. Well, if I show up there without a reason, I get escorted to the tie-down, put in my ship, and told not to come back. Would you be willing to let me use Adelaris as cover?"

"You could have made a splitcom call. Why come here?"

"Comcalls are not always as private as one thinks. One of Digby's selling points is discretion."

"And if I asked you who these clients are?"

"Do you?"

"Yes."

"Turn the recorder off. Thank you. The Kliu Berej. A Taalav array has been removed from Pillory."

"Then we can expect Taalav crystals on the Gray Market soon. Or is it already?"

"Soon would be more accurate, I believe. In three or four years. Maybe. If the array survives and produces."

"Hm." Adelaar let her head fall against the chair's cushioned back and closed her eyes.

In the silence that followed, the fire crackled behind the glass doors and Shadith's breathing got louder and more uneven as she waited for the answer.

"Aslan says you're an extraordinary musician."

Adelaar turned her head, reached over to the table and
ran another pattern on the touch squares. "If I remember correctly, you like shara tea and lemon wafers?
Good. It seems odd you've left University to unravel
knots for Digby."

"I haven't the necessary passion to chase bookings
and bend my life to serve my art. Too much of a sol-
itary, I suspect. Perhaps in another fifty or sixty years
I'll change my mind. There's no hurry."

"I see why you and Aslan are friends. It's a way of
thinking I can't understand." Adelaar went silent again
as a serviteur hummed in to lay out the tea service and
the platter of wafers. When it was gone, she closed the
privacy shield and leaned forward to pour the tea. "I'll
do a deal, Shadow. In return for the use of Adelaris'
name, you work on a small problem for me. A bit of
serendipity here. Some connections of mine tell me
that my problem at the moment is actually in residence
at Marrat's."

"Mh?"

"I'd like discretion on this. Embarrassing, possibly
damaging to Adelaris' reputation. A scamjack managed to jump the line to Hegger Minitools and got
downside here on Droom. Among his other activities
he romanced one of my older apprentices, a girl named
Mirik. A young Fulladerin from Saber Minor." She
sighed. "They think because they've had a hard beginning they're street smart enough not to be fooled. It's
an illusion. He got away with a rather nice variation
for the programming of guard 'bots that my develop-
ment staff had not quite tamed enough to bring to market. The silly child ran with him. No doubt she's had
a rude awakening by now. I believe he left quite a
string of shattered hearts and careers behind him, male
and female both. A versatile man, as it were. I was

rather annoyed when I discovered all this. Hm. The sources that told me he's at Marrat's also mentioned that Mirik is still with him. The program variation is gone; I'm not worried about that, we've cut our losses. If I ever get my hands on him, he's going to be walking around minus some essential parts, but I'm not asking you to do anything about him either. Well, one thing, flake him if he's still there and collect as much information about him as you can without spooking him. If he's gone by the time you reach the Market, no problem. It's the girl I'm really interested in. I want to know if she was a dupe or in on the scam from the beginning."

"If she's a dupe and he's dropped her, what do you want me to do?"

"If she's clean, and unless I'm very much mistaken, she is, I want her back. Remind me before you leave to give you a credit flake in case you need to buy her out of something. She's a bright child with a remarkable questing mind, but little experience. Talk to her. Tell her she's got a place here if she comes and claims it. Tell her she's had a useful lesson, but she shouldn't let it ruin her life." Adelaar set her cup down, smiling at something she alone saw. "She'll find some other way to mess up, I know that. You've never seen such a klutz. She can trash a room just walking through it. Nearly burned the dorm down when she came up with an answer to a problem we'd been having on a program and let a tea kettle melt to slag. If she was fooled, she'll be miserable now. She gets that way. Could be close to suicide. Hm. Probably best if she doesn't come back here till things have quieted down a bit. The authorities might make difficulties for her and us. Tell her I'll finance a stay on University for a year, then she can come back clean. My word on it. She knows what that means."

"How much of this do I tell OverSec when they ask?"

"That I've sent you to search for the girl and provide return fare if she wants to come back. It's not the kind of thing Digby usually does, but since you're Aslan's friend, you can say you're just doing a favor for her mother."

"It's a deal, then." Shadith got to her feet. "If you'd call a flier, I'd like to get back to the Field as soon as possible. Thanks."

Adelaar stood, smiled. "And thanks to you, Shadow. Useful information to know that the price of Taalav crystals might slide in a few years. Should I wish you good hunting or not? I wonder. Wait here a moment till I grave that flake for you."

5

Travel times being what they were, when Shadith slid into the tie-down at Marrat's, it was almost a year standard since the last time she'd visited the Market, but the Directors hadn't forgotten her and were decidedly not happy to see her back there. About thirty seconds after the tug 'bots drifted the ship up to the hitch and locked it down, her shortrange com chimed, a Blurdslang face appeared and she was ordered to report to the OverSec complex immediately.

She sat in a small glassed-in alcove, the people passing by glancing incuriously at her, none of them coming in.

She sat.

And sat.

And waited.

This was deliberate. The Directors wouldn't want to get Digby annoyed at them, but they didn't like at all having one of his ops show up without his informing them that she was coming. And they were showing their displeasure.

She'd set herself a limit of three hours. If they didn't see her before then and let her soothe their little minds, she was leaving. Digby could stir his photons and see if he could identify the smuggler from the description she'd gotten from the Taalav. And then she'd have to decide once more how she wanted to play this.

The image of the Kliu Berej slaughtering the odd little creatures haunted her. Somehow she had to find the arrays and get them away, hide them in a place the Kliu couldn't reach. *Couldn't reach? Why didn't I think of it before? Vrithian. No, not Vrithian, the next world out. Storsten. It's a heavy world like Pillory. Vrithian's sister world. People have been looking for that system for centuries without getting a smell of it and Lee only found it because her Mum came and got her. Harskari . . . maybe she can help, she likes gardening . . . I need to talk to Lee . . . but I have to find the smuggler first. Have to get her to tell me where they are. . . .* She sighed. *Digby's going to have kittens . . . and I have to find something else to do with my life. . . .*

After about an hour and a half of the observers watching her doze, a juvenile Blurdslang drove his nutrient bowl into the room and clicked it in behind the desk. He activated the voice cube and fixed watery eyes on her.

"What is Digby's interest in the Market and why didn't he inform us of his intentions?"

"I'm on leave at the moment, that's why you weren't informed. I'm doing a favor for the mother of a friend. Adelaar aici Arash of Adelaris Security Systems."

"What favor?"

"I'm to find and interview a young woman who left her employ under clouded circumstances. If the interview is satisfactory, I am to arrange passage for her to University. It's a very simple business. A call to Adelaris will verify this."

"The young woman's name?"

"She may not be using it at the moment, but the name I was given is Mirik ac Vissyn. A young Fulladerin from Saber Minor." She slipped a cased flake from her pouch, set it on the desk. "Her bio data's here, if you'd like to take a copy."

After a moment's laborious cogitation he tapped off the voice cube and shrilled a spate of Blurdsla into the com, counting as usual on the fact that few people beyond his species could understand his speech. Shadith kept her face still. She couldn't get everything, some of the sounds were outside her hearing range, but she could pick up a lot of what was being said. It was hardly worth the effort because he was announcing they'd all wasted their time stewing in their dishes over nothing. And what was he supposed to do with the flake she was waving at him?

He listened, tapping irritably with the tips of the thready fingers at the end of a tentacle. When the burst of speech from the com was finished, he reactivated the voice cube. "You will remember that any action against a firm established in any Node of the Market will be dealt with severely. The list of Market Laws and the penalties for violations of them are waiting for you in the Mimarose Ottotel. Review them before you begin your search. You may leave now. Take your flake with you, we are not interested."

The Node diurn was nearing its end as Shadith left the OverSec complex, the bubble darkening, ripples of vermilion and saffron shimmering behind the flat roofs of the other buildings in the Security Complex. She was feeling quite pleased with herself and had to work to keep from grinning. "We are not interested," she murmured. "And if you believe that, see this phial I'm holding. Those few golden drops are the Vryhh formula for immortality. I swear it's true. Tsa!"

The street was empty except for a few peacer 'bots returning for an info dump and recharging. This wasn't a place where people strolled for pleasure. She marched to the chair pen and thumbed on a chainchair, climbed into it and let it click her toward the lock and the pneumo line that would get her into the Ottotel Node. A rain was scheduled in that Node. Nice. Clean the air and wash everything down. "Then I start hunting. Chatting up everyone I can get to talk to me."

6

Holoas swirled under the velvet black of the Node shell in its night phase, reflected in the wet pavements and the glass of the show windows. Lost in the mix of crew off the visiting ships, labor from the factories, off-duty guards, merchants, gamblers, thieves, smugglers, gun runners, druggies and druggers, Cousins and non-Cousins of every shape, color and attribute, some raucous, some musical, some silent, Shadith drifted along the Marrata Circle looking for the places she and her Hired Man had visited the one night she'd spent here last year. She'd thought about seeing whether he was still around, but decided against it. He was altogether too observant and no doubt had rather close ties to OverSec. If she were just playing, she wouldn't care, but working this double trace was complicated enough without that sort of close observation.

Music drifted into the street when doors swung open, sliding into her blood, changing the way she walked, the set of her head, the swing of her shoulders. She remembered the hushed elegance of the Hegger transfer station and laughed aloud, reveling in the difference.

She knew where she'd start her trace and how she was going to do it. *It was music. It was always music.* She laughed aloud. "The key to the universe," she sang. "Shadow's songs."

In the next three hours she went in and out of the smaller clubs, listening to the music, looking at the custom, sampling what was sold there, moving on again when the mix wasn't quite right, zigging from side to side around the Circle, sliding into all the dark holes where the crews blew their pay.

Shadith wriggled to a table the size of a washcloth, pushed up against the wall and continually threatened by the swing gate as the serving girls coming from a back room pushed past her, their trays loaded with everything from pelar pipes to jugs of obat raw enough that a sip would pickle the lining of the drinker's throat. Just the smell was enough to pucker her mouth.

The gloom was sporadically and inadequately lit by drifting spheres of psuedo-foxfire. Faces moved in and out of darkness as they were touched by the cold green light. Mostly they were the usual Cousinly variety, though a group of Lommertoerkans hunched over a table near the door, the deep creases in their faces puddling shadow as if they were filled with ink, and a few male Caan eyes flashed to silver then dark as the foxfire drifted near then away.

The stage was empty at the moment; the players finished a set as she came in and moved into the back where no doubt they were communing with their souls via whatever substance they found handy. They were the group she remembered.

It was toward the end of her Night Out when she

was feeling no pain and an urge to sing. Though she knew well enough what working musicians thought of pushy amateurs in the grip of wish fulfillment, she teased them into letting her join them, and the snatches of memory that were all she retained the next morning weren't that embarrassing—at least not the ones that dealt with her singing . . . though other images . . . the pile near night's end . . . sar!

The table beeped to remind her she hadn't ordered the rent drink yet. She ran through the menu, chose a white syntha wine that shouldn't be too poisonous and started to chuck a handful of Marratorium tokens in the slot.

"Uh! What . . ." She looked up into a man's grinning face. The swinging door had shoved him against her, but he hadn't resisted it all that much and he didn't move away when the server dashed past and let the door whoosh shut.

"Whyn't you let me buy that, chichi? Then you won't have to look anymore, will you?"

"Zaz off, grot. If I was looking and I'm not, it wouldn't be for you."

He ruffled her short curly mop with a big hand, leaned down till she was nearly choking from the haze of obat thick as smog around his mouth. "Your loss, hunbun," he said. "You sure?" His voice was amiable and lazy as the yawn of a well-fed tiger in a patch of summer sun.

"Yeah, genman, just want to hear the music."

He shrugged and wandered off.

She waved at the stink he left behind, shifted in her chair as sounds of movement on the stage trickled through the noise.

Flute in one hand, the other shading his eyes, a tall thin man with a bald head and skin that glistened like well-rubbed mahogany ambled along the edge of the stage peering into the crowd. *Chali,* she thought.

He came round to her side of the stage, grinned, dropped to a squat. " 'E Shadow. Bisa said she saw you come in."

"Yah, 's me. Since I was here a while, thought I'd come give you a listen."

"We using some of the stuff from last time." He grinned, broad square teeth flashing white against the dark brown of his lips. "Any more you want to gift us with?"

"Don't want much, do you?" She chuckled and got to her feet, wriggled past the table. A single step took her to the stage and she held up her hands. "Give me a lift."

She sang with them several times that night, Chali, Bisa, Herm, and The Max. Flute, viola, keyboard, and bass. At first her hands itched for her harp, then she noticed a change in her singing. She was beginning to develop echoes in the audience, almost weaving dreams again as she had when Kikun was there to give them form. It wasn't quite right, not yet, but it was coming and it was real, the ache in her head told her that.

She ended the night with just Chali playing and the song she'd written and sung on Ambela not so long ago. "I am fathoms deep," she sang, and felt those listening come into the circle of her arms, felt them seeing she didn't know what except it was a dark and melancholy vision as hers had been when she wrote the words.

> *I am fathoms deep*
> *In love with dark*
> *I fill my mouth with night*
> *And drink the absence*

Of the light
Dense and stark
I think
I will not endure
The pure white silence
Of the day
I will sleep the bright away
And rise
With the moon
To reprise
The melodies of night.

Stark black and white, her sisters danced for her, the veils they wore swirling about their angular forms. Their eyes were wide and dark with sorrow and fare-well, as if they knew they would not come again for her, no matter how strong her gift might grow. They would be wholly dead at last. Dead as Shayalin, burnt to a cinder eons ago, long before her second life in the Diadem and her third life in this body. Dead and gone.

When she finished, the room was silent for several minutes, then the hum of speech rose again and the rapid tinkle of the drink orders and the clunk of the Market tokens in the slots.

She watched the misty outlines of Naya, Zayalla, Annethi, Itsaya, Tallitt, and Sullan fade and vanish. Even with drugs and dreams she couldn't call them back; the knowledge chilled her to the marrow of her bones, never again, never never never again.

She let Chali and Bisa lead her away. In a little while she was going to tease from them all they knew about the Kliu while she asked them to help find Adelaar's protégée. In a little while. When she could get her head working again.

7

."Hoo, chals, I'm wiped." Shadith moved her shoulders, then patted a yawn; the room's single window was bright with the striated colors of the diurn dawn. "Been dogging on my job long enough."

Bisa grimaced, worked her mouth. "Something died on my tongue. Job, Shadow?"

"Looking for someone, what I should be doing. You all feel like having a peer at a phot?"

"Why?"

Shadith ignored the sudden wariness in Herm's voice. "I'm hunting for this girl. A rescue of sorts, no prosecution. She got conned by a scamjack and went off with him because she was too scared to stay behind. Poor kid. Her boss said she's near genius with tech stuff and a real klutz with everything else. Boss wants her back on the job. The jack's probably long gone, but the girl's supposed to be floating around the Market somewhere."

Bisa held out her hand and scowled when The Max caught her by the wrist. "The two of you can take a long walk out a short lock. Any dirtkickin' kid that hits the Market without a clue or connections is in bad trouble and you know it."

She took the flake viewer, clicked it on, and swore. "You didn't say how young she was, Shadow."

"She's around twenty standard. But a babe when it comes to knowing what's what. She came out of a foundling home and lived in a dorm when the client took her on as an apprentice."

Chali took the viewer from Bisa, glanced at the image and passed it to Herm. "Mind telling us who the client is?"

"I'll tell you this much. I've know her for a number of years now. She's the mother of a friend of mine, and we've done a bit of business together that worked out real well for me. She's prickly and hard-nosed and I don't much like her, but when she says she'll do something, she does it; she plays fair and doesn't hold grudges. If any of you happen to know the girl, talk to her first, see what she says." She yawned again. "Sar! I'm tired." She took the viewer from The Max. "Think about it. I'm hiving in Mimarose. If you decide to give me a call, as a favor, not before Node noon."

8

Shadith drifted out of sleep, shifting off her stomach onto her side. It didn't help. She didn't want to wake, but her bladder gave her no choice. Grumbling under her breath she rolled off the bed and stumbled to the fresher.

When she came back, she saw the message light blinking. She rubbed at her eyes, tried to wake herself enough to cope with whoever was calling. "Read message."

The words unreeled in a minatory tone as the Marratorium governors wanted to make sure she knew she couldn't receive pay for singing unless she had a cabaret license and was she planning to apply any time soon? She groaned. "Abort that. Any more messages?"

"One message received and read." The hum ended and the light clicked off.

"Ah spla. I was afraid of that. Ah well, I did my best. Now it's back to slogging along the hard way."

One by one she hit the smaller places along the Circle, showing the viewer, asking her questions. Have you seen this girl? She's a lamb ripe for shearing and I want to send her home. Do you know anyone who might know where she is?

She chatted with waiters and barmen, waitresses and barmaids, the occasional full-time drunk or dreamer, Cousin and non, even a meditating Sikkul Paem with ve's budlets sitting in pools of focvoda, doing ve's drinking for ve, passing the vibes along the rootlets that connected them to their parent. Sometimes she traded stories with all of them about what could happen to girls trying to get by without connections, sometimes she simply gossiped about this and that, her ears primed to pick up any information she could about female smugglers.

Footsore and hoarse from talking so much for such little result, awash from the drinks she'd had to buy, she reached the Tangul Café toward the end of the Node afternoon. The shell was beginning to darken and it was the slow time, too late for the working crowd and too early from the night owls. The place was almost empty.

She dropped into a chair at one of the tables near the bar, sighed with the pleasure of getting off her feet, then sat slumped with her head against the wall, her eyes closed. After a moment, she pried them open and inspected the menu written in liquid crystal above the bar mirror.

A jaje waitress came trotting over, her dusky fur absorbing light so efficiently she was little more than a blotch of darkness with a pair of shining gold eyes. "Hard day?" Her voice was as soft and muted as her fur.

"Oh, yes. I think a cup of tea's all I can manage." She glanced at the menu again. "Uplands Red."

"Ah. One of my own favorites. They do it right here, two pots and water on the edge of boiling."

"Well, would your bosses infarct if you sat a moment and had a cup yourself? I'll spring for it." She chuckled as the gold eyes narrowed and the small round ears flattened against the jaje's skull. "Only renting a moment of your time. You can always walk away."

"Why not." The jaje waved a three-fingered hand. "It's not as if we're rushed off our feet right now." A breathy sucking sound, jaje laughter. "If you come up with a tip, the time might be more fruitful." She went gliding off.

Shadith took a sip of the tea and smiled with pleasure. "You're right. Ah, that's good." She slipped the flake viewer from her belt pouch and set it on the table close to the edge where the tiny jaje could reach it. "I'm a bitty shovel in Digby's Excavations." She went through the patter she'd repeated so many times already. ". . . no friends, no connections, likely she's not enjoying herself much these days."

The jaje tapped on the viewer, examined the image with care, then shook her head. "Sorry. Haven't seen her. And she's unusual enough I'd probably have noticed. Too bad. Femmes on their own, even when they know what's what, they can get in a mess of trouble. At least we jajes have our bond. And the home tree. Sometimes, though . . . Z-juice . . . I hate that stuff. They got my bonds and me that way. We've a long line to swing before we get home again. You offering a reward?"

"I can go high as fifty gelders, higher I'd have to check with the client. I know what you mean. Had my own problems that way. I'm a lot older than I look, and a few years back I was so dewy I might have been just hatched. Ran into a guard on a transfer station who liked 'em young and scared. Tried to use Zombi on me. Ah spla!"

"What happened?"

"He ended in the garbage chute as molecular dust. Not my doing. Long story and complicated. Anyway, that's when I met Digby the first time."

The jaje shivered. "We had someone try it here a couple months ago. On this smuggler, at least that's what the talk was. I suppose she got off with something the Kliu wanted. That's who they said hired the ghoul. OverSec got real hot. The ghoul's brain-stripped now and doing a term under Contract. Cheered my bond and me up no end when we heard that."

"Wonder if she was someone I know. I've got several friends who fly the egg route. Caan?"

"Nah, that was her friend. Cousin. Lylunda—yeah, that's it. Lylunda Elang."

"Nah, her I don't know. Take another look at the viewer. If you see someone like that who does things like spill her drinks in her own lap, give me a call. I'm at the Mimarose."

"Poor tissa-la. Think you could make some dupes of this? My bonds are working several other Nodes. We could ask around."

"Not a bad idea. All right if I drop them by later tonight?"

"My shift is over an hour after Node midnight. That'd be the best time."

"I'll see you then." She finished the tea. "Nice break, but I'd better shift my feet some more."

9

The Privacy Cell in Digby's ship was a little bigger than a closet but not much, with the instrumentation completely insulated from outside contact. Shadith disliked the place intensely, but she had no illusions about OverSec's intrusion into the outer areas of the ship.

Luck had kissed her today and she wasn't about to waste time accepting its gift.

She keyed the scramble, beginning the recording with an explanation of the cover she'd arranged for the investigation. "I'm going to have to stay until I finish this, though it shouldn't take that much longer. In the meantime, I found a name for our smuggler and a reason for the Kliu's being locked out of the Market. Lylunda Elang. Smuggler, apparently rather well known, though I haven't come across her before. Find out all you can about her, especially about her homeworld. The Kliu tried to Zombi her and missed. I suspect she headed for the deepest cover she could find, probably that homeworld.

"After I locate Adelaar's apprentice, I'll be taking the girl to University. I'll check in with you there to see what you've come up with."

She ejected the flake, sealed it into a drone, and started the canister on its way to its target. "Over to you, Digby. Now I go back to talking my way round the Nodes, keeping the cover tight."

10

Shadith shuffled into her room at Mimarose, dropped into her chair, and tugged her boots off. She stretched out, wriggling her toes and groaning with the pleasure of letting her body relax. "Romance is dead," she said aloud and giggled. "Triddas never mention how boring this is and what your feet feel like at the end of the day."

She yawned, unclipped the notepad from her belt, and began scrolling through the list she'd bought from the Hub. There were two, no three small crewbangers that she hadn't hit yet, on the Circle only by courtesy. She tapped a fingernail on the pad's screen, frowning at the entries. Do them first, then try the Contractors?

Or leave them till the Labor Halls had refused to talk to her? They had that habit. She clicked over to the other list. Three Contract Labor Companies, each with its own niche. Factory and lab lineworkers. Techs. Unskilled for the low-end work where convict labor was cheaper than 'bots and easier to replace if it broke.

"If I were doing this by the numbers, I should have hit them first. Gahh." The almost year she'd spent under Contract was not one of her happier memories, and facing down junior execs determined not to talk was a job she'd rather postpone forever. "Time is, Shadow my girl. Tomorrow morning. Well, at least I can have myself a nice drench in the fresher and a good long sleep."

She pushed herself onto her feet and reached for the closure on her tunic.

The com bonged.

Working at the closure with one hand, she tapped on the speaker. The screen was blank. "Shadith here. Who's this?"

"Shadow, you know my voice." Bisa. As close to whispering as she could get. Not that OverSec would let that stop them if they wanted to know who she was. "Want to talk."

"Now?"

"Yes. Outside where I work."

Shadith rubbed at her eyes. "All right. Give me time to get there."

"Don't drag it. Twenty minutes and I'm gone."

The shell was night-black and mostly invisible behind the gathering clouds; rain was scheduled for the next hour so most of the Circle was empty, the usual strollers either back in their ottotels or in their hutches or inside the shops waiting for the next flux of customers. The holoas flickering across the facades had gone dark. The only lights left were the pole lamps marching along beside the chainchair line. Shadith stopped the chair short of the Tav, crossed to the sidewalk and started along it.

"Over here."

She followed the voice into a narrow alley, her *reach* identifying the woman and establishing that she was alone.

Bisa was standing in a shallow doorway. "Tell me the name of the client," she whispered. "I have to be sure."

"All right." Shadith leaned closer, murmured in the woman's ear, "Adelaris."

"That's the right one. Come on. She wants to see you." Bisa moved from the doorway and started off along the alley, heading away from the Circle, into grubby shell slums where the argrav diminished rapidly enough to make walking difficult. The Nodes were, after all, just large irregular chunks of rock, mauled a bit here and there, shaved and prettied up where the customers were. The back blocks that only workers saw were a lot less appealing and the farther away from the business center, the worse conditions got.

Mirik was waiting by a rookery with a grubby pothouse tucked into one corner; she led them inside, knocked on a hatch.

It opened to show the corroded face of an ancient bawd who tapped a bony finger on the ledge.

"Pay her," Mirik said. "Two minims."

Shadith dropped the token on the ledge, took the key the old woman pushed at her. "So?"

"We go upstairs now. We've just bought an hour in one of the kips."

"Just a moment. Don't say anything yet."

Mirik moved to the table beside the bed, reached inside her blouse, and pulled out a gadget that looked as if she'd crumpled together an assortment of miniature sensor boards and plugged in chips at random. She spread it on the table, touched it on.

Shadith felt the vibration at the edge of her senses that told her they were under a privacy cone. She raised her brows, decided Adelaar was probably right about wanting the girl back. "Why all the caution?" she said.

"You didn't read your rules, did you." Mirik sounded amused. "Conspiring to divert the services of a laborer under Contract is a large nono."

"I see. However, as long as compensation is paid. . . ."

"It's one of those things . . . um . . . Shadith, is it? Illegal till the offer is actually on the table."

"Adelaar was afraid you'd be depressed enough to contemplate suicide."

Mirik sighed. "I was close to that some four months ago when I woke up and found that miserable gila had hopped it and left me broke and alone. I felt such a damn fool. You won't believe this," she sighed, "but I didn't know what he was doing till I was with him on his ship and we were 'splitting for here. All he wanted was a bedwarmer and an ear for his brags. If I hadn't been so wiped from his thumping me about, I'd have walked out the lock. It was when the Governors sold me into Contract with Kapal Barush as Unskilled Labor that I got mad. That pulled me out of the glooms. Turn your head a moment. Ah. Yes. You're a friend of Aslan, aren't you. I had that mark of yours described to me. Does the Patron really want me back?"

"Yes. She thought a year on University would be a good idea, then you return to Adelaris and work off the debt. Another sort of Contract Labor, I suppose."

"At least it's my choice this time. All right. What do we do now?"

"How much do you owe?"

"Almost as much debt as that gila left me with. And Kapal Barush is pulling everything it can get to extend the Contract. They know about Adelaris and my training and they're putting on a lot of pressure to get me to violate copyright. In the meantime I do security maintenance and programming at Unskilled pay. What with Kapal's interest charges and the cost of my food and the air I breathe and the hole I sleep in, I manage to clear something like a minim every two weeks. Since they're guaranteed a twenty percent profit on the money they put out to pay my debts, I should be clear sometime around my hundred and fourth birthday. As of this morning, profit included, my contract's worth two thousand gelders. You'd better include around a hundred more to meet other claims they might dream up. Since I'm officially labeled Unskilled, there's one trick they can't pull. They can't up the prices for losing my services. It'd mean a hefty head tax and a fine for misrepresentation."

"Two thousand? That's all?"

"It's plenty when you're flat with no hope in sight."

"Ah, yes. Are there any buyouts you know about?"

"Around two weeks ago, there was this brain-wipe case. A broker handled it, took him outMarket."

"Know the broker's name? I was thinking it might be better to go that route rather than fooling around on my own."

"You're probably right. Actually, she handled both of the buyouts. I don't think she's really female, but she's certainly not male, so it's easiest to say she. Elegant creature. Not a Cousin, some species no one seems to know. Her name's Ruxalin and she has an office on the Barter Strip in the AgentNode. Um. I've got to get back. Mind waiting here till I'm well away?"

"No problem. Don't forget your privacy projector. I imagine there are some open slots you should refill."

Mirik grinned. "You're so right. I don't want more expense on my poor little head."

Shadith strolled beside Bisa, her mind busy with Mirik's bit of information about the brain-wipe felon as they moved through the rough narrow streets, walking carefully to avoid losing their footing.

"So it works out nicely." Bisa patted a yawn, threading her fingers through her hair. "Herm didn't want me to have anything to do with this. He likes your singing and your songs, but you scare him, Shadow. He has his little nest here, and he feels safe in it. You bring in echoes of the outside."

"You all right with it?"

"Chali can cool him down. Why *are* you doing this kind of work? With your gift...."

"Put it down to perversity, Bisa. Or just wanting some adventure while I'm still young. Digby offers that. I can write and sing anywhere, any time." Bisa's yawn triggered a yawn in her. "At this moment, though, what I want to do is get some sleep."

11

"My fee is five hundred minims an hour. All time spent dealing with Admin will be charged to you at actual rate which includes one full hour of waiting time. I eat anything over that."

"Acceptable."

At a short distance Ruxalin looked like a thin and rather beautiful woman, but up close the resemblance was gone. She was an ice goddess, eerie because she so closely resembled what she so clearly was not. Her skin was white and translucent as milkglass and delicately scaled, her hair spun glass, her nose a knife blade slightly turned up at the nostrils, her small mouth a pale bluish pink. And she was neuter. Completely and utterly neuter.

Shadith leaned forward and put the holder with Adelaar's credit chip on the desk. "I want to redeem a woman under Contract at Kapal Barush. I've been informed that the liability in question is approximately two thousand gelders. Anything greatly more than that will be Kapal trying it on. They'll be reluctant to part with her, but vulnerable because the woman is registered as Unskilled and they're paying her as such, but she's programming for them and supervising security. Um, once she's redeemed, I'll be responsible for any debts between the time of redemption and our departure."

"You seem to have covered the matter rather thoroughly. Do you have a phot of the woman?"

"Yes." Shadith set the flake viewer beside the credit chip. "Her name is Mirik ac Vissyn. As I said, Kapal Barush holds her Contract."

"The name of the individual or company providing the credit?"

"Adelaar aici Arash of Adelaris Security Systems. She requests confidentiality. It's none of Kapal's business who pays as long as they are paid."

"That's quite in order. Is there any prospective prosecution involved?"

"No."

"Have you examined the Contract and informed Admin of your intent?"

"No. Because of my connection with Digby of Excavations Ltd., OverSec was informed of my reason for being here at the Market. Otherwise, I've had no contact with them."

"Ah. Digby's interested in the woman?"

"No. Adelaar is the mother of a friend of mine. I'm

doing a favor on the side. Digby, of course, knows about this, but I'm on my own time at the moment."

"I see. Any other complications?"

"Beyond Kapal knowing they've got a good thing and wanting to keep it, I don't think so."

"I've dealt with Kapal before this. They know me and will give in with a minimum of foot dragging. May I check this?" She reached for the credit flake, but didn't touch it.

"Yes. As to dealing with Kapal, that's why I came to you."

Ruxalin dropped the flake into a verifier, made a soft popping sound as she scanned the readout. "Aici Arash seems to trust you quite a lot."

"We are well acquainted."

"I'll require a five hour nonrefundable retainer."

"Agreed. If you give me the flake and your cordak, I'll transfer the funds."

12

It took Ruxalin three hours to pry Mirik loose, another hour to clear with Admin while Shadith took a side jaunt to OverSec to inform them she was leaving, her favor completed.

Once the Contract was voiced, she took Mirik to the Tangul Café to introduce her to the jaje waitress, then to the Tav to meet Bisa, Chali and the others.

An hour later, Shadith eased away from the tie-up and headed for the Limit.

After she set the delouser to checking the ship, she swung around. "Quite a change, I imagine."

"Yes." Mirik's eyes went dark. "How I'm ever going to repay you . . . or the Patron. . . ."

Shadith glanced at the readouts, then smiled at

Mirik. "Me, it's easy. Just tell me everything you can scrape up about the brain-wiped man. Rumors, gossip. Everything. Plus anything about the Kliu Berej, even the smallest most insignificant details."

8

Lessons in Why I Left Home the First Time

1

A short scowling boy crouched before a screen and an extrawide sensor board, the exo straps gleaming dully in the greenish light. His hands were like his father's, broad in the palm with long fingers, but they were paler and softer, the nails ragged, bruise blotches stippling them, red and yellow or black and purple depending on the degree of healing. He was watching inventory flow, marking the items he meant to reroute without otherwise disturbing the file.

Lylunda pulled up a chair and watched quietly. At dinner last night Herred had had his company mask firmly in place, though he was still child enough to keep glancing at his father to make sure the game was going the right way. She didn't want that kind of cooperation; if he continued hostile, there were too many ways he could sabotage her. Which was why she'd told Grinder to keep out of this and let her deal with the boy in her own way.

As she watched the list scroll past, she was at first surprised by the amount and variety of goods that passed through the Star Street warehouses; it didn't take long, though, before she understood what was happening. And was angry with herself for not realizing long ago that the Behilarr had made Hutsarté a port of convenience for any shippers who had reasons to conceal the origins of their cargos. *Ba da, when I took up smuggling, looks like I was just going into the family business as it were. On the retail side. Puny operation compared to what Daddy Dear and his cohorts are running.* She took a wry satisfaction in knowing she was going to be used to siphon off some highborn Jaz's profit.

The boy was trying to ignore her. He liked this work. That was obvious. *Hm. Maybe that's his problem. He thinks I'm going to take it away from him. Grinder said he's fourteen. A hard age to be. He looks older. Grinder's Second. Herred. Bug. The Crip. The Gimp. The weird one who likes book stuff.* She could hear the taunts, like the ones thrown at her. Bastard. Mongrel. Whore's Git. High Nose. Because she was smart. Because she wouldn't put out like other girls her age. Except for Grinder, but then, he didn't bother asking. Because she was determined to get away from this swamp.

Zaintze said Bug's mum died before he was a year old, so he wouldn't remember her. This would probably be the first time he was valued for anything but being Grinder's son and that only because Grinder never let loose of anything he thought belonged to him. Except me and that was because he didn't have the power he does now. Warning, Luna. You don't watch it, he's going to start thinking you're his property again.

She waited until the final entries trailed off the screen. "Herred, did Grinder tell you why I'm here. Not here in this room, but here on Hutsarté?"

"No. Look, I got to pull and wipe before keph gets nervous." His high tenor was deliberately roughened;

he was trying for strength and maleness—or what he thought they were.

"No, you don't. What you did was passive and local. Keph won't feel it till you begin the pulls. Couple of things you need to know before we get started on this business. First, I'm not going to put up with any kakazhar from you. Either you listen and learn, or I get Grinder to pull your access because you just might be crazy enough to rojo the tap and kick the whole mess down round our ears. Shut your mouth. I don't want to hear from you yet. Second, if you've got the brains Jaink gave a cockroach, you'd see I'm back here because I need a place to cool off and once the flying weather's right again, I'll be gone so fast I'll leave scorch marks in the air. Unless you plan to be real stupid, your job is safe. Now you can talk."

"Why should I believe you? And don't call me Herred. My name's Bug."

"All right, Bug. I'm a smuggler and a jojing good one with a nice rep. Good enough to buy a ship and fly it on my own. Why in Jaink's Seven Hells would I want to hang round here? Think I'm after your father? Not hardly. I'm not going to say more about that because it's none of your business."

"Ba da, so what'd you do you had to run back to tit?" His voice was easier now; he'd let it go high, light, and what his peers would no doubt consider girlish. She didn't smile. Very carefully she didn't smile. This was his way of showing capitulation without actually admitting he'd accepted what she'd said.

"Some people want to know where my last cargo went and they're the types to ask the hard way. I'd rather not, thank you very much."

He brushed his hand across the board, tapped a sensor, and the chair hummed around. "Would you tell me about some of the things you've seen?"

"I don't think Grinder would like that." She grinned at him. "Sure, Bug."

"I can't leave here, can't take the pressure shifts. He doesn't want me to even think about it."

"Ba da, I know. And you'd better shut down the shield. It'll make him real nervous if he doesn't know what's happening."

"You didn't see me. You couldn't 've."

"You were really smooth, Bug, but we both know he's watching. And we both know you wouldn't talk like this if he could hear it. So put us back on show and let's get started going over Lerdo's lines."

2

When Lylunda left the warehouse's cellar, the sun was down and the sky a sullen black with clouds blocking light from the moon and stars, though there was no smell of rain in the air, as if those clouds were waiting for the month to turn before they let down the water they carried. She was tired, but pleased at the way things had worked out. Once his resistance was gone Bug had turned heartbreakingly eager for her approval and ravenous for the things she could teach him, as if he wanted to swallow them all in one day.

Krink walked beside her, escorting her to the apartment house on Saltoki Street, his presence setting Grinder's mark on her. She glanced at him and swallowed a smile. He hated this. He'd loathed her since the time he'd tried to corner her down by Milk Alley and she got him a good one in the family jewels. It was an accident, she was flailing all over the place trying to fight him off, but he always thought she'd done it deliberately. She knew better, but she was smart enough to stay out of his way until she got off Hutsarté. She wondered why it was Krink that Grinder had chosen for this escort; surely there were others. Hm. Things under the surface between those two men. And she was being shoved in the middle. She didn't like that. People in the middle got tromped by both sides.

When they turned the corner into Saltoki Street, Krink swore, grabbed her shoulder, and stopped her. "I don't like this."

The street was empty, none of the usual shoppers out; even Halfman Ike was gone from in front of Lester's cutlery. A short distance beyond Okin the Baker's shop a line of dark figures in robes that swept the ground walked in silence, unlit torches in their hands. Aptzers. Temple enforcers.

"I think you should go to Grinder's," he said and started to turn her around. "This isn't the first Sermoi they've held along here, they'll start emptying the houses soon for the Confessio, maybe this time, maybe next."

She pulled free. "I know the drill, Krink. It's not something you forget. I'll take my chances tonight."

"Grinder won't like it."

"He'll just have to live with it. I'm too tired to make nice. I want my bath and some sleep and I'm going to get them."

She heard chimes as she keyed open the door to her room. The first thing she saw when she stepped inside and turned on the lights was the comset installed by the window. She tugged the door shut and sighed. "So much for locks," she said. "Just as well I get this into my head right now. Where Grinder wants to go, he goes."

She crossed to the com, tapped it on. Acid in her voice, she said, "Greetings, oh, mighty Grinder-jun. And how may I serve you?"

Grinder scowled at her. "That mouth of yours will get you skinned one of these days, Luna."

"Could be."

The scowl lightened. "Just wanted to say you did good today. Bug's happier than I've seen him in a long time. Want you to come to dinner tomorrow night. Meet my other kids."

It was phrased as a request, but she knew her options well enough. There weren't any. "Thank you, Grinder. What time?"

"Krink will be over to pick you up round six. It'll still be light then, give you some time to walk round the garden."

"Um. Grinder, if it's all right with you, could you send someone else? No no, don't get yourself revved up, he did his job just fine, no problems. The thing is, I don't like being around him and he loathes me. You push him too hard, you might lose a handy tool."

The eyes that had gone flinty for a moment softened, and he smiled. "Always thinking. Maybe I want to push him."

"Uh-huh. Ba da, you'll do what you want, you sure haven't changed in that. I'm just asking find some other poor fool to do your levering, huh?"

"A' right, I'll do it this once. Dodo'll bring you. You'n Bug break off early, you hear? Get your hair done. Wear something nice."

After his image faded, she touched off the com and then dropped into the chair, shaking and nauseated, sweat popping out on her face, running down her back. She started to swear, then snapped her mouth shut. That was Grinder's com. Everything she said here, maybe even everything she did would be picked up and recorded. What she'd said to Bug applied to her, too. Grinder might pretend a sentimental attach-

ment to her and say all the right words, but he wasn't
about to trust her.

I'm a fool, she thought, *I shouldn't have come back.
I thought I knew how things worked here, but I'd for-
gotten a lot of it and I didn't know about Grinder.
Jaink!*

A loud cry from outside broke into her thoughts. She
tapped off the light, moved to the window, and looked
out. The hooded Aptzers were standing in a circle in
the center of the street. Their torches were lit now and
cast red shadows on the walls and the pale 'crete pavement.

One of the Aptzers lifted his voice in the Call; he
had a powerful tenor trained to cover distance. "O
Belovéd," he sang. "Surrender your wills to the tender-
ness of Jaink. Search your hearts and know that you
have sinned."

A second Aptzer took up the Call when the first was
done. "O Belovéd," he sang. "How easily you forget
that which Jaink requires of you. Search your hearts
and know that you have failed Him."

When the third sang the O Belovéd, Lylunda sighed
and moved away from the window. At least she could
manage a bath, though it seemed sleep was going to be
more elusive. They were going to keep that up till
dawn. The only good sign was that they hadn't brought
the drums, so the harrowing itself would happen another time, the scourging and purging, the bonfire of
vanities and the public confessions.

The Lekats of the Izar would come out, though there
were few who paid more than lip service to the
Behilarr god. They would play the Aptzers' games, in-
vent confessions, lay their clothes and ornaments on
the burning piles, let themselves be cuffed to the whipping posts, do anything they had to in order to survive.
They'd learned long ago the costs of rebellion. The

Behilarr controlled the water and the food; if they shut off the mains and closed the gates, the Izar died.

3

"Don't know if you remember me, Lylunda. Amalia Eskurat?"

"Forget the prettiest girl on Babalos Street?" Lylunda bowed, touching her fingers to lips and heart, her face carefully blank. *Jaink! She's younger than me, but she looks a hundred years old and all of them hard.*

"That's kind of you. Perhaps it was true, once. You look tired. Has Grinder been working you too hard?"

Lylunda grimaced. "How I look comes from O Belovéds chanted the whole night under my window. I maybe managed three hours' sleep. I'm giving serious consideration to moving into the keph vault's Overnighter."

Amalia nodded. "Not a bad idea. Come walk with me, I'll show you around."

She moved slowly along the flags of the walk in the arcade that ran round the outside of the court. "See the names on the doors? There's mine. Grinder's generous. When one of his women gets pregnant, he moves her in here. And the apartment is hers for the rest of her life. Some of the others have gotten married and brought their husbands here. He doesn't mind. You'll meet most of them at dinner. It's like in a palace, you see. Everyone comes to dinner when Grinder says he wants it formal."

When they reached the back of the garden, Amalia opened a door and gestured Lylunda through. She stepped into a smaller garden with graceful, dark-leaved minikuna trees, their long withes blowing like hair in the evening breeze. By each tree there was a small grassy mount with a flat stone on top. Each stone held a small urn. Amalia walked to one, stood looking at it. "My daughter," she said. "She killed herself when she was seven. I don't know why. She was always a sad child."

Lylunda shivered at the flatness of the woman's voice, a gray hopelessness she'd never felt, no matter how tight things got. "I'm sorry," she said.

"No matter. It's been five years now. Life keeps on in spite of everything. I come here so I can tuck her away for the night. Not really, of course, I know that, but. . . ." Her voice trailed off. "We'd better get back now. She's the only child here, you know. The rest were mothers. Once you give Grinder a child, you belong to him even after you're dead."

There was no change at all in her voice, the same soft sad murmur, but Lylunda knew she was being warned to walk very carefully or she'd find herself trapped the way all these women were. As she moved through the door, she set her hand on Amalia's shoulder and gave it a gentle squeeze to let the woman know she'd gotten the message.

4

The days that followed slid past with little to divide one from the next, even the Harrowing of the Izar. She missed most of the Harrowing, having moved into the Overnighter, a room opening off the kephalos' terminal chamber, no bigger than a closet with a basin and a toilet and a narrow, lumpy cot that made sleeping an endurance sport. Except for meals she spent her time with Bug and did her best to avoid Grinder and his men, though he insisted she dine at his house at least twice a week.

After three weeks, the Aptzers retired to the Temple,

satisfied with the havoc they'd wreaked on the guilty.
The Izar came to life slowly, warily, like a wounded
animal checking itself for more hurts. Lylunda moved
back to her room on Saltoki Street.

She was getting restless. No one had come after her,
not that she'd noticed. And Grinder would probably
have mentioned it if someone on Star Street started
making snuffling noises pointed in her direction.
Maybe the Kliu hadn't got onto her world of origin.
She didn't talk about it much in the Pits, only in a blue
mood when she was high on pelar. Jingko iKan knew
where to find her but he was no chatterer. It'd take
more than a dollop of Kliu gold or a threat or three to
pry his mouth open. Maybe she'd broken her back trail
effectively when she came here.

"You be coming to dinner tonight?"

"Don't think so, Bug, everything I own is starting to
smell, so I've got to do a wash and my hair's so gungy,
if I leave it much longer it's going to rot and fall off."

"Don't you like us?"

"It's not that. Truly, Bug. I just need some time to
catch up on all the stuff I couldn't do because of the
Harrowing." She made a face, looked around the long
narrow room, and sighed. "Button things up for me,
hm? I've got to get some air." She laughed at the face
he made, gently tapped his cheek as she turned to
leave.

There's another problem, she thought as she climbed
up the stairs to the double doors that locked the vault
away from the main part of the warehouse. She tapped
the code into the keyplate and waited for the door to
slide open. *I think he's getting the notion of pimping
for his father. A way to keep me here. Ba da, can't even
trust Bug.*

She glanced up at the landing in front of Grinder's

office. He was leaning on the stair rail, watching her. With the weight of his regard heavy on her shoulders she left the warehouse and walked briskly along the street, stepping over the drunks and ignoring the beggars. At least half of them were watchmen anyway, with Panicbuttons in their pockets to warn of security raids or challengers to Grinder's rule or even the chance stray from straighter regions of the Izar.

Grinder's notions—ba da, they scare me. So far I've managed not to see what he's getting at, and Jaink be blessed, he hasn't pushed me on it. But with Bug starting up ... I think it's about time I went somewhere else. Or I'll end up in an urn in that poor sad garden.

When she reached her home street, she stopped at Okin the Baker's shop for a fresh loaf of bread, traded sass with his oldest daughter, a fine freckled girl with a plain face but lively eyes and a livelier mouth, got a ready cooked bird, a cup of noodle soup, and a dollop of tuber salad from Sutega's Take Out next door, declined Halfman Ike's offer to sing her a song if she showed him her legs, and went laughing to her doorway, feeling better about things.

A man stepped from the street as Lylunda fitted a key into a lock. She swung round to face him when his shadow fell on the door, her hand going to the belt where the stunrod couched.

"Elang-mun Lylunda?" He wore a black leather vest with brass buttons and a round badge pinned high on his shoulder, the sigil of the courier service drawn with blackened silver wire set into the white ceramic surface.

"Courier? Whose?"

"The Anaitar of the Erzain. Hizurri-jaz Gautaxo." He bowed, touched his fingers to his brow and mouth. "And you are Elang-mun Lylunda?"

Her father. Not only her father, but the top cop of the Behilarr secret police. She'd known his name, but not what he did. He knows about you, Meerya said, the words almost lost in her struggle for breath. He's very important so he can't acknowledge you, but he asks about you all the time. It was him paid for your schooling. He did love me, you know. And he held you when you were a little thing. *But she didn't tell me who he was or what he did. Anaitar of the Erzain. Expeditor of the Question.*

Lylunda's face went tight; she took the key from the door, held it in her hand as she moved away. He stepped aside as she got close to him, followed her from the recessed doorway and into the street where his guards were waiting. A short distance off Halfman Ike had parked his wheeled box against a light pole and was juggling two of his knives. And she recognized one of the layabouts from near the warehouse. She turned to face the courier and the two guards who stood a short distance off; no one from the High City ventured into the Izar alone. "Yes. So?"

He bowed again, handed her a paper folded three times and sealed.

She broke the seal and read what was written.

One finds it necessary to summon you and speak with you. The Courier will bring you to the Erzainzala where speech is possible without ears to hear. There is no question of arrest or detention. You will be returned to your residence when the interview is complete.

She tore the note in half, tore it again and again until it was reduced to small fragments. "Hold out your hand. You'd best see he gets these back. I'm to come with you?"

"If you will, Elang-mun."

"I need to put my purchases away."

"We will wait, Elang-mun. Though it would be best not to linger."

"Yes. I can see that."

5

In the office wing of the Erzainzala, Lylunda sat with her head against the cushions of the comfortable chair, her eyes closed as she listed to the horrible bland noise no one with ears could call music. In this small waiting room there was nothing else to do. She tried not to think of the look on Grinder's face when she called him to let him know what was happening. He smoothed it out and said with a genial smile that he knew she wouldn't buy herself loose with his business and he wanted to hear what this was about as soon as she got back. Come over to the house, he said, and tell me exactly how it went.

She was sweating. She pushed back the hair that was sticking to her face. *If I go in Grinder's house, chances are I won't come out again. Joj' the house! If I go back through the Izar's gate, I won't see free air. . . .*

"Elang-mun?"

Who else, taik? She got to her feet, followed the young woman down a short corridor and into the side door of a large corner office.

The man had the broad body and big head of a high-bred Jaz, with dark hair still and the perfect silver streaks above his ears that marked his caste. She stared at him and knew her mother hadn't lied. This was her father; neither of them could mistake that. Her face was a female image of his.

He glanced at her, then looked at the pile of fac sheets on the desk in front of him. He took up the first, lifted his head again. "You are Lylunda Elang. Daughter of Meerya Elang."

"Yes."

"Read this. I acquired it. It was not sent to me."

She took the sheet, glanced down it. Her name. Her description. Description of her ship. A short summary of her activities for the past five years. Jaink be blessed, they'd missed a few things that would make her unwelcome in just about any stratified culture, let alone here. A request from the Kliu Berej to the Dukkerri of Hutsarté that she be sought for and, if found, turned over to the Kliu for unspecified crimes against the economy.

She returned the paper to the desk and waited.

"You're cautious," he said. "Good." He tapped a sensor, dropped the sheet into a sudden hole in the top of the desk, and watched it reduced to its constituent atoms. "To this point special notice has not been taken of that request. The minimum was done as a courtesy, government to government. Official records were searched without result and the Kliu so informed. If they are persistent and reach the right official, there might be difficulties. Should an order come from the Duk's desk, I could not ignore it." He hesitated. "I find you interesting," he said finally. "If the world and life were different, I'd like to spend a while talking with you. As it is. . . ." He tapped the sensor board. "Alert Eketari," he said, then turned back to Lylunda. "Your connection with Grinder Jiraba makes it imperative that you get away immediately. I will see to that."

"I expect you will. If you're finished with me?" She stood. "I'd like a Courier to escort me back to my apartment. I have things there that I'll need."

"We'll deal with that in a moment. Walk to the clan shield on the side wall, then back to your chair."

"Why?"

"Because I'll have you whipped if you don't. Walk."

He kept her walking about the room for several minutes. About midpoint in her peregrinations, while her back was turned to the door, a woman came in.

"You can sit now, Lylunda. Answer Eketari's questions."

"What is your name?" The woman's voice was soft, barely audible.

Lylunda looked at her father. His face was unreadable, not a muscle twitching. She drew in a breath, let it out as she turned to face the woman. "Lylunda Elang."

"Lylunda Elang. Say again."

"Lylunda Elang."

"Tell me what your friends call you."

"Luna."

"Greet me, Luna. As you would a friend."

"Kex zu, Eka. That what you want?"

"Say again."

"Kex zu, Eka."

"Kex zu, Luna."

The woman's voice was changing, becoming more and more like Lylunda's; it had happened so gradually, she hadn't thought about what it meant, but understanding came like a slap in the face. She swung round to confront her father. "She's supposed to take my place, isn't she. To fool Grinder into thinking I'm tucked in and waiting for him. Well?"

"It pleases me that you're intelligent, Lylunda, though you do talk too much. I brought you here because I wanted to see you, that's the truth. And because it became clear to me that you'll probably get ground up and thrown away if you stay here. And because I don't wish to face the choices you're forcing on me. Ekateri-mun, do you have sufficient material?"

"I think so, Anaitar-jaz."

"Excellent. Jaink bless you, daughter. May you fare well."

Lylunda saw the stunrod, started to protest. Before she got any words out, her father shot her.

9
Worm at Work

1

Worm leaned closer to the mirror, drew his fingers along his face; his skin was getting the orange peel texture it always did when the beard-inhibitor was nearing the weak end of its life span. *Sama sama, the cloud cover and makeup should do the trick. They say rainy season's about due. Wish it would rain, clear some of this crap out of the air.* He worked over his face until he had the look he wanted, an ivory white mask with a small curvy mouth painted pink, a pink flower stenciled onto his right cheek, another above his left eye. He eased the pewter wig onto his head and combed it out until it flowed in deep waves about his face and down his back.

He took the dark blue robe with the silver embroidery from its wall hook, slipped his arms into the sleeves, and stood for a moment simply enjoying the cool sensuous feel as the draft from the window blew the heavy silk against him. His father and his brothers didn't understand how it made him feel and he'd never dare tell them, but they were happy enough to use his talent for impersonation in their schemes.

He sighed, finished dressing, and went out.

* * *

The apartment's front door and the one that led into the weedy untended back yard were both plasteel with a thin veneer of local wood, the wood cracking and shrinking away from the hard gray core. Despite their appearance they were solid and sturdy, as were the frames into which they fitted. And the locks were better than the usual junk that builders put on rentals. They wouldn't keep Worm out for more than a minute or two, but once he'd worked them over, they'd do. The furniture sagged, the carpet was a dust trap and had long ago lost any pattern it might have started out with, the facilities in the fresher and the kitchen were hardly adequate, but there was a storage shed in the yard that he could rent along with the rooms; it was large enough to house the flikit and sturdy enough to discourage idle curiosity. And the back end of the yard was the Izar Wall, so he was close to where he needed to be. The place would do.

He counted out the first month's rent for the rooms and the shed, his hands in dainty white leather gloves that the landlord eyed with a covetous leer. Then he added two more plaques. "I am not to be disturbed," he murmured in the high, light voice he affected when in this role. "I desire peace and solitude for my meditations."

"Of course." The landlord's voice was so carefully free of innuendo that he might as well have shouted his thoughts.

"I will be bringing my possessions tomorrow in the evening. Late, I think."

"Would you be wanting a serviteur? I have a couple I rent now and then. Or I could point you to the 'bot shop down the street."

"There is no need. Possessions bind the soul, so I travel with few."

"Right, then. I'll leave you to it. The keypacs are on the table there. Anything you need, you know where I live, give a bang on my door."

"I thank you for your courtesy."

On the next night, Worm opened locks for Grinder, then hurried home, packed his surveillance equipment, and transferred it to the newly hired rooms. He rode a jit out to the landing field, tramped across the waste-land to the place where he'd left the flikit, brought it to the yard, and maneuvered it into the shed. After he set the new lock on the shed's door, he dragged himself over to his official residence and collapsed on the bed as the sun came up red and furious, half lost in barren clouds.

2

Worm sat naked in a chair he'd covered with a sheet because he didn't want to think of the diseases that might live in its cracks and crannies. The EYEscreen hummed subliminally on the table before him. The room was hot and steamy because he needed an open window, so he couldn't run the conditioner. He wiped his hand on a towel, slipped it into the control glove and began moving the EYE in small back-forth, up-down movements to bring back the skill that lay dormant in his nerve paths.

When he was ready, he sent the EYE zipping out the window, over the Izar Wall, then took it through the streets, gliding along in the shadow of the eaves where its faint shimmer was no longer visible. His father would skin him by inches if he let anything happen to that EYE. It was a bit of spoil from one of Mort's first jobs, and his father was sentimental about it. Besides, military EYEs with wide-spectrum viewers and built-in ice needlers whose poison was capable of dropping a Kirrgen giant were expensive and not all that available even at the darkest end of the Gray Market.

He spent almost an hour crossing and recrossing the Izar, making sure the preacher types had really cleared out. He was sick of listening to complaints about them. Got so it was all Keyket would talk about. Besides, having them about meant that the woman bedded down at the Warehouse and there was no possibility of getting at her while she stayed holed up like that.

He stopped the EYE under a window ledge of the building across from the Warehouse and waited for Lylunda Elang to emerge. The sun was oozing through banks of heat clouds, half of it already behind the horizon, and the light over the Izar was the bloody red of burner elements. The street was nearly empty; even the whores had gone inside to eat and talk and wait for dark when it would be cool enough to bring the customers back.

When Lylunda stepped into the street, Worm sent the EYE after her—and quickly discovered that he wasn't the only watcher. One of Krink's thugs, a local called Baliagerr, strolled along beside her, making no attempt to hide what he was doing although he kept far enough away so that she didn't see him.

When she stopped in the entry of a rooming house to key herself in, Worm debated sending the EYE in with her. By the time she got the door open, he'd decided that was a bad idea and set it hovering beside a dormer window on the house across the street. A short time later he saw her standing in a window, watching the sunset. Her room was third floor, corner.

"Right. Now let's have a look at the neighborhood." He sent the EYE exploring the area around the rooming house, paying close attention to possible places of concealment and the foot traffic, flaking the data transmitted so he could study it later. When his eyes blurred from fatigue and his glove hand started to shake, he pulled the EYE back to base and went home to see if Grinder's Exec had left him a call.

3

As rain roared down outside, Worm ambled through the basement of the Warehouse. It was the first night this week he hadn't had a job for Grinder and he was wondering if he should set a sono-pickup somewhere in here so he could keep better track of Lylunda as she went in and out of the keph vault. The more data he had about her movements, the easier it would be to plan the kind of snatch that would spring him clear with the woman without getting him killed.

He'd been watching her every night for a week now. So far she'd left the Warehouse at the same time, taken exactly the same route until she reached her home area; sometimes she bought supplies for the fresher or the kitchen, sometimes she stopped to talk to people along the street; mostly, though, she just went into her room and stayed there.

Whenever she left the Warehouse, she had a guard. There were four of them, rotating the assignment between them. Baliagerr, Arkel, Rodzin the Shrink, and Vlees. Grinder's men, all of them. *Could be she's hired her some protection after the miss at Marrat's. Could be Grinder's putting his mark on her. Maybe both. Grah! I hope not. That would mess things up so bad. . . .* It was maybe a good thing Xman wasn't here; he got impatient sometimes and rushed the job. *Like he rushed it at the Market. . . .*

Feeling disloyal, Worm stopped thinking that way.

He heard a scrape on the stairs, and looked up. "Atcha, Bug. What's doing?"

Bug negotiated the last stair before he looked up, his exo humming and clicking, his face intent as he watched where he planted his feet. "Hoy, Worm. Nothing on tonight?"

"What they say. Too much rain. You use a hand there?"

"Yah, if you'll just hold the door back till I'm through." He palmed the lock, then moved aside to let Worm pull the heavy plug door out of its hole. "You a lock man, do you know about kephs?"

"This'n that. Hadn't had formal schooling at it, but I 'prenticed to someone who knew 'm better'n most. How come?"

"You ever play Tac games?"

"Some. When I could get away to a Pit. My Fa, he put my brothers and me to working soon's we could walk almost."

"Gets boring, playing the keph all the time. If I don't dumb him down, he whacks me. If I do, what's the good of that? It's not like I was really beating him. Whyn't you come on down, we have a game or two? Daddo says things are going to be quiet a while now, so you got time."

"Bug, don't know if Grinder'd like that, me being new and an outsider and all."

"No big deal, man. We'd be using the dedicated terminals he got me, and keph keeps the record of what you do in that room so Daddo can see it's all right." He managed a shrug, expression wiped from his face. "If you don't wanna, though. . . ."

"Hey, I just don't wanna look up and see Krink and his crew coming round to stomp me." He pulled a clown face, then looked fearfully over his shoulder.

Bug giggled. "Come on. Daddo got me a new 'un. It

was in that box that you'n Keyket fiddled last night. So you and me, we can start off same level. Huh?"

"Why not."

Worm slouched in the chair as he watched the boy loading the game into the machine; he was nervous about the keph picking up on some of the dainties he had scattered about his person, but only a little because he could always explain them as being part of his tools he'd brought along in case a job turned up after all. He had no intention of trying to plant anything in here. That would be just plain stupid.

He was tired from working nights for Grinder and days on his own business, snatching at sleep when he could find an hour or two free, sleep that often wouldn't come because of the heat and the nearly intolerable humidity. Maybe with the rains it'd be better, but the season was too new for him to judge. This room was cool, the air clean with the comforting, familiar metallic smells that reminded him of his ship. For a moment he wanted desperately for the snatch to be done, wanted to be off this stinking, miserable mud heap and back in the clean clarity of the insplit. He winced away from the thought of his *Kinu Kanti* and the filth she'd be collecting in that canyon where he left her.

The terminal pinged and he sat up, gathering himself so he could get through the game without turning Bug off him. The boy had access to his father's plans and some of his thoughts and he'd be a good source if he were handled right.

4

"Lylunda."

Down on the floor of the Warehouse, Worm glanced

up from the game of hezur-hairi he was playing with three of Krink's men.

Grinder was leaning on the landing rail outside his office.

Worm saw Lylunda's shoulders tighten. She palmed the latch, locking the plug door, then she turned slowly, a smile pasted onto her face. "Yes, Grinder?"

"Labaki needs to see you about the Nameday feast. Come to dinner tonight, you can talk to her afterward."

"All right. I have to go home first, get cleaned up, and clear away some stuff that needs doing. Dinner around eight?"

He scowled at her, but it'd been his choice to make this public, and her response had been clever enough to maintain the distance between them. "Eight," he said and went back inside.

As Worm gathered in the hairu, he thought, *I was right. He's going to put the move on her any day now and she knows it. Doesn't like it much either. Any bets she isn't thinking of blowing off this whole business and hitting for the 'split? Which reminds me. Something I shouldda done a while ago. Got to get outta here.*

He shook the hairu, cast them into the kaxa, and swore as the numbers cleaned four of his five stakes off the board. "My luck's took a walk. Maq, any reason I got to hang round here letting you lot walk off with my coin?"

5

Cursing the horde of sticky, crawling insects and the corrosive sap of the vines that oozed out at the lightest touch, ate at his wholesuit and etched the clear plastic of the goggles, Worm wriggled through the fecund growth on the island and managed to crawl beneath the camoucloth without touching it.

The darkness meant he had to use the helmet light to find his way to the ship, which brought more hordes of fliers crashing into him. The wholesuit was sealed and he couldn't smell the stench he knew had to be out there, but the thought of it was enough to start his stomach churning.

He forced himself not to hurry, but it seemed forever before he found the markings on the maintenance hatch. He took the rod of memory plas from his pouch, twisted it, and waited until it finished extending to its full length and extruding rungs like thorns from the sides.

The hatchlock was simple, but once he had it solved, he didn't try opening the slide until he'd sprayed the area to clear it of spores and other contaminants and temp-bonded the sticktight to the hull. He spread a sheet of waldoplas over the clean spot, sealed it in place, then pushed the door back. Working through the plas, he broke the temp-bond, stripped the shrinkwrap off the sticktight, reached inside, and pressed the flat patch against the wall until he felt the brief heat as it glued itself in place and took on the coloring of its surroundings. It wouldn't activate its beacon until the ship had dropped into the insplit; until then it was just a bump on the wall and as near undetectable as anything he'd worked with—and it would go back to being a lump the moment the ship surfaced into real-space.

Getting out was faster than getting in.

An hour later the flikit was back in the shed, he'd shucked the wholesuit and run it through the sterilizer, and was in the fresher of the safehouse, playing the hand-held needle spray over his body, washing away even the memory of all that creeping, crawling life.

6

Bug glanced slyly at Worm, who was frowning over the situation his players were in and trying to decide how to extract them. "What you getting Daddo for his Nameday feast?"

Worm blinked. "Huh? I'm supposed to get him something?"

"You don't hafta, but he likes it if you do."

"Ha! Fa's like that, too, but he's never satisfied whatever you get. What would your Daddo think was the right kind of present?"

"Time's up. My turn. Doesn't have to be anything special, just show you took time to think about him. He likes knives. If you could find one that looked a little bit different. . . ."

Worm contemplated developments on the screen. "You are seriously evil, Bug. How am I going to get my men out of that bind? He going to be expecting everyone over to his house that day?"

"In and out. Some stay for dinner, some just come in and give the gift." Bug frowned at the screen. With Worm's hands hidden behind the workshield around the sensorboard, he couldn't watch the setup; he had to catch the small changes as they showed up on the mosaic so he could get ready to counter Worm's move.

7

Late at night in the safehouse, Worm bent over the board, trying out the steps of his plan, running it over and over so he could locate possible trip spots.

It was a simple plan. Whether it was raining or clear, Lylunda always went home the same time and the same way; her second turn took her through a short alley between two small manufactories, no windows, no foot traffic, lots of debris up against the walls. He could do the watcher there, roll the corpse into the debris, catch up with the woman, shoot a dose of Zombi into her, good stuff this time, walk her through the Wall and around to the safehouse, put her in the flikit, and take off for his ship.

He considered the four who guarded her. All other things equal, it'd be best to choose one of Baliagerr's shifts. He was big, but he was also lazy and rather stupid.

Worm tapped on the second screen and began replaying the flakes that had Baliagerr on them, watching how he moved, where his eyes went.

When he was satisfied that he'd worked things out as much as he could, he began thinking about the date; he erased the recording from the second screen, called up the duty roster and picked out the days between now and Grinder's Nameday when Baliagerr would be on duty. When to do it?

Not too close to the Nameday. According to Bug, Grinder was putting pressure on Lylunda to move into his house. Bug thought it was a great idea; he liked her and bragged to Worm about how he was getting that idea across to her. If it was going to happen, it'd be announced on the Nameday, that was as sure as anything Worm knew.

She was getting really fidgety. She didn't show it much, but he could tell.

The snatch probably should be a night in that last week, though. Bug said the Warehouse all but shut down then, meant fewer people hanging about. One of the Baliagerr dates was five days before the Feast. That felt about right. "I'd better fix a backup date, though. Vlees is on the day before. No. He's too spooky. He'd never let me get close enough to do him, not without more noise than's safe. Day before that, Rodzin. He's bored with this guard business, not paying much attention. Good enough. So nine days from now max, seven min. Then it's done and I'm out of here."

He leaned back, rubbed burning eyes. "Bokh! I'm tired. No call tomorrow night. That's good. Better go see Tank about the knife, he should know where there's something good. And let Grinder know I'm shopping, keep him happy."

8

Head thick with too much sleeping, Worm came yawning into The Tank. He collected beer and crackles at the bar and went to a table in a back corner with them, to sit in the shadows crunching and sipping and trying to wake up enough to keep up his front with Tank.

The sound of plucked strings drew him from his mind haze. He looked up. Dark and undefined because the lumins hadn't been turned on yet, a figure sat on the stage at the end of the bar, tuning a small harp. *That's something new. Wonder what happened to Musha and his lot?*

The lumins brightened slowly, catching glimmers from the sequins on the woman's dress. She stopped tuning and started playing a simple melody that grew more complicated under her fingers as her form grew more and more defined, warm brown skin and glittering white dress, opals in her ears, her nails painted to match.

"Time is a wheel," she sang, her voice a rich, fluid

contralto. He shivered with pleasure, pushed the glass aside and leaned forward, his eyes fixed on her.

> *Time is a wheel that steals our loves away*
> *Lost and gone in yesterday*
> *Time is the necromancer's terrain*
> *From the black plain of vanished years*
> *He summons the pale dancer*
> *She sways in swirls of moiré silk*
> *His tears are opals in her ears*
> *The pyrelights of dead suns burn*
> *In the hollows of her eyes*
> *Turn by turn*
> *He treads with her a languid pavan*
> *dead and gone, dead and gone.*
> *Time is a while a whorl a wheel*
> *It steals our loves away,*
> *Buries them in yesterday.*

As she sang, her words came alive for him; he was the dead dancer, called from his rest, star sprays shining in the empty eyes of his skull, his feet treading suns to oblivion. The image was so powerful that for a moment the room, the table, even his body vanished. Nothing existed except the dancer. . . .

When the song changed to a wordless croon weaving around the harp's mellow notes, he dropped into himself with a jolt and a shapeless grief from something without a name that had been lost.

She played with the melody a moment longer, then slid into a new tune, a rapid bubbly thing as if the harp were laughing.

"Howl, said the honeybear," she sang. "Nose in the honeyjar, tail in the air. . . ."

She leaned into the harp, rocking back and forth with the lilt of the song—and for the first time Worm saw the other side of her face, saw the drawing of a hawk etched in dark brown lines on the light brown skin. The description from the Kliu list flashed into his mind, the brand on her face and that gift for song. *Digby's agent. How long has she been here? Has she spotted the target and what's she doing to do about it? What am I going to do about her. . . ?*

When the set was finished and the singer had retreated to the back rooms, Worm gulped down the rest of his beer and sat a moment longer at the table. Between recognizing the agent and the effect her song had on him, he wasn't sure of anything any more—except that he'd better think real hard about moving up the snatch to this week and consign the old plan to The Harman's deepest Hell.

"New singer. Known about her, I'd a been back sooner. How long you had her?"

"Three days now. Off the worldship. She was traveling standby-and-work-it, got bumped. Heard it's Bug keeping you busy these days."

Worm shrugged. "Likes my name, what it is."

"Make sense. So what you want?"

"Bug was saying I need to get a Nameday present. I figure he's got the dump on that, but I don't wanna step on toes if you know what I mean."

"Hunh. You been this way before."

"Been and done and learned the hard way about overplaying it. Bug says a knife. I figure not fancy but nice. Who's got?"

"Go see Old Henry. He has a shop in the Izar down by the Gate. Anything else?"

"Yeah. The singer. She do more'n sing?"

Tank let out a roar of laughter, slapped his hand on the desk. "Gonna have to lay down razor wire about that stage if this keeps on." He coughed into his hand, gulped water from the jug on the shelf by his head. "No, she don't do. With the talent she's got she don't have to. Anything other than that?"

"Nah, guess that's it."

Worm left The Tank and walked back to his official residence, new plans whirling in his head.

10

A Day Late and a Synapse Short

1

Shadith strolled along Hutsarté's Star Street, past doss houses and taverns, beggars and street performers in a thousand shapes and colors with varying degrees of skill in whatever it was they did. The street was wide (one of the aspects of being on a newish colony world with plenty of room to spread), the center strip given to loaders trundling lumpishly along, heavy with cargo containers. The air was steamy, sweat beading on her arms and never drying, just getting stickier. And it stank.

She breathed in the sickly sweet aroma of rotting meat, rotting vegetation, the sour effluvia of inadequate plumbing, over it all the iodine bite of the wind from the sea, even though the water was several miles off and at least a mile lower in elevation.

Amazing, she thought. *Live for a few months in ships and transfer stations and you forget how saturated in bodily sensation a world can be. Hm, maybe a song in that. . . .*

Playing with rhymes and images, threading automatically through a crowd of hawkers, players, and crewfolk of the sort who milled about every Star Street she'd seen, she nearly crashed into a man who stepped from an alley in front of her.

"Hey, watch where you going."

"Sorry." She started to circle round him, but his hand clamped on her wrist and stopped her. "I wouldn't do that," she said mildly as she turned to face him.

He dropped her arm as if it were hot. "I know you," he said.

"What?"

"Shadow's your name, isn't it? I heard you sing. Nightfair. Bogmak. Maahhhh nanna! How you do that?"

She backed off a step. His words weren't slurred and he stood straight enough, but the liquid gleam of his greenish eyes most likely came out of a bottle and he carried the stink from the contents of that bottle in a fine mist around him. "The singing was me, the rest was someone else. We broke up a while back."

"Huhn. Too bad. Yah hai, come along and have a drink on me."

"Why not." Might as well use this one to start spreading her cover story. "Where? I just got here and don't know places yet. You know my name. What's yours?"

"Meddlyr Trych. Cargo master on the Free Trader *Timik*. Just got here, you said?"

"Off the worldship that left yesterday. I was riding standby and working my keep, singing this 'n that. They unstood me. Some Muck from the High City up there wanted space for his bodyservant."

"Still singing, then?"

"What I do."

He walked beside her without talking for several steps. She glanced at him again, but she was sure she didn't know him, he was just one of the crowd at the Nightfair and anyway that was over five years ago. He was an inch or two taller than she was, a compact man, not lean but no excess fat on him. His head was shaved and densely tattooed in patterns she recognized as luck signs, blue lines on the bright amber of his skin, the framework filled in with crimson, emerald, and gold. There were intricate fate knots between the middle two knuckles of his fingers and no doubt more needle paintings were covered by his shipsuit. His ears were pointed and flicked nervously as he walked and the pupils of his eyes were almond shaped rather than round. *Meddlyr Trych. A Cousin,* she thought. *Wonder what part of the Diaspora produced his branch?*

He pushed open a door and stood aside to let her precede him through it into the dimly lit room beyond, then escorted her to a table by the wall. "And what would you be having, Shadow? This trip I'm trying out a brandy they distill from some kind of local fruit, I don't know what it's called. It's smooth and tasty and warms you up lovely."

"Sounds good. I'll go for that."

He brought back two bell glasses with half an inch of a dark reddish-gold fluid puddled in the bottom.

She took a small sip, rolled it on her tongue, and smiled. "I like it."

"Me, too. So. You lookin' or movin' on?"

"Looking. Till I build up my stash a bit and can talk my way onto a ship heading the direction I want to go."

He tilted the glass, watched the brandy slide, then slip back, leaving a faint film on the curve of the bell. "I always wanted to tell you what it meant, that time you played your harp and wove dreams for me. Well, you and your partner. Didn't have time then, don't have words now. Except there was a hole in my heart, and after you sang it was gone."

"I'd say you weren't so bad with the words."

"Ah, you should hear my cousin. Now there's a man who can string word with word to make the stones themselves weep with the glory of it."

"Mayhap I'll come by his way some time if you don't mind telling me what world it is."

"Ah. Parcoshry is the name of that poor place and it is out beyond the Saber Worlds. A long and lonely way from here."

She lifted the glass. "To traveling, Meddlyr Trych. To finding what lies beyond the next star."

"To Home, Shadow Singer. Wherever that may be." Though she only sipped at the brandy, he drained his glass. His eyes went blank for a moment, then he was grinning at her. "Ol' Tank . . ." He stopped, stared past her as he ran his tongue around his teeth. "Ol' Tank," he went on, speaking with slow care. "He owns this place. The Tank, he calls it. He is not a man of words. He fired the last act. They were good, but two of them were Dusters and sometimes they just did not show. Even if you can't do the dreams any more, you sing good. I come here a lot. I could tell him you sing good. If you want."

"Why not. Got to work somewhere."

2

For the next two nights Shadith sang in The Tank for tips, then Tank added a base fee; he was pleased by the custom she attracted.

More cautiously than she had at Marrat's Market, she began building a web of acquaintances, the question she asked confined to the ins and outs of surviving here. Meddlyr Trych came round to listen to her for the first three days, bringing his mates with him, then they were gone, the *Timik* heading for its next landfall, but that chattering man had given her a solid background, so she marked down in her mind that she owed him a favor if ever she came across him again.

At the time Trych left, she'd absorbed a lot of information about the place, but had picked up no trace of Lylunda Elang. She wasn't too disturbed about that; all she'd learned in the millennia of her peculiar existence told her that this wasn't a place to ask blatant questions, perhaps not to ask questions at all. And how she'd get around that, she wasn't quite sure.

So much simpler just to march up to the Hall of Records or whatever they called the thing round here and start a name search working through the files. Or find some local sources and buy the information from them. Except Digby had ordered her to keep her head down and do this on the sly. That suited her just fine; she did not want to lead the Kliu to the arrays, no indeed. Still, it certainly made life harder.

3

Shadith patted a yawn, folded her arms on the counter at the cook shop, and gave the woman who ran it a sleepy smile. "Stiff enough to climb out of the cup," she said. "I will not not not drink any more rikoka brandy."

"Ha! That's what you said yesterday, Shadow."

"Curses on ol' Meddlyr's head, he chattered round to everyone and told them all that's what I liked so now that's all the clotheads buy for me." She took the cup and sipped cautiously at the scalding liquid.

"And it's such a horrible duty, eh? Sing me another, Shadow, maybe I'll believe it. And what'll you be having to sop up that kaff?"

"What else, Cara? Egg, easy, some of your tatta hash, and a nice bloody hunk of meat."

"What is it to be young." Cara chuckled and went to cook the breakfast.

Shadith chewed on her thumb and tried to work out a plan for what was left of the day. She'd managed to see most of Star Street, she'd been out to the Landing Field with Meddlyr Trych and used Digby's spyshot to flake the images of the ships parked there. Lylunda's was not among them. Nor was it anywhere in the tie-down up by the transfer station. If she was here, she must have cached the ship somewhere, presumably close enough for her to walk into Haundi Zurgile. *Hm. Might be worth looking at those islands north of here ... if I were stashing a ship, that's where I'd park it ... I pulled the boat trick on Ambela ... maybe I should start nostalgic reminiscences of dear old daddy and his fishboat ... all that metal should show up on Digby's patented prospector's detec ... if it does, I pretty well know she got here ... if it doesn't ... can't prove a negative ... maybe she parked the ship on the Wild Half and cut across the ocean in her lander.*

When she'd finished breakfast and complimented Cara on her way of searing cow, she strolled out and stood looking up at the clouds thickening overhead. The wind that plucked at her hair was heavy with the smell of brine.

"Lookin' for rain, Shadow?

She turned. "Oh, good morning, Getto. No, just smelling the sea on the wind. Anybody got boats around here?"

He tugged at the flesh loop that had been an earlobe before he had it stretched to hold his dari-mirror; the mirror pulsed there when he played his drums at his pitch on an alley corner near The Tank. "No fishing here. No reason to spend tokens on boats. The Bellies go where the tokens heap highest."

"Tsa! My da ran a fishboat, and when I light on a world with salt water I always go for a sail. And here I'm got some free time, and I was thinking I'd like to get out on the water a while."

"Kemros the Tinkerman, he rents out your open top flier, you could take one of those down low 'nough to skim the waves, suck some skempt, and dream a day sailer."

"Huh. That's a good idea. Thanks, Getto. Owe you one."

"Easy 'nough to get straight. Fetch you harp to m' pitch when you get back, and we play duo an hour come two."

"A' right. Why not."

She smiled with affection as she watched him ambling away, stopping every few steps to speak to a shopkeeper or a street player or just someone whiling away a moment or two staring at bugs on the pavement. Then she shook her head at her own obtuseness and went to find Kemros the Tinkerman.

Stupid not to grasp what an ocean full of poison water and poison fish would mean to the economy of a recently colonized world. And she knew about it, too; it was one of the warnings she had to thumbprint in the declaration of intent for temporary residence. *I UNDERSTAND THAT ALL WATERLIFE AND A HIGH PERCENTAGE OF THE VEGETATION ON Hutsarté IS POISONOUS TO AIR BREATHERS WITH HEMOBASED BLOOD AND THAT ANY ATTEMPT TO LIVE*

*OFF THE NATIVE PRODUCTS OF Hutsarté COULD
RESULT IN IN MY DEATH OR DISABILITY.* No fishing industry, the colonists concentrated into one city
and scattered ranches, not much heavy industry, the
other landmasses of the world left untouched so there
was no commuting to and from what they called the
Wild Half. Result, no boats. "I wonder what else I'm
missing. Focus, Shadow, focus."

"Talking to yourself, Singer?" Berm leaned from the
door of Meertl's Dosser, his voice purring, his eyebrows humping up and down as if they had a life of
their own. "You can come *talk* to me anytime."

"My daddy always said, you want to talk to somebody smart, talk to yourself. No thanks, Berm." She
moved hastily on before he worked that one out. The
Berms of the universe were one of the reasons she'd
passed on making music a career. She sighed. *So how
is that different from what I'm doing now? Hm. No
managers, I suppose. Hah, Shadow. How it's different
is you can get killed in this job. Killed on purpose, I
mean. Five hours left before I'm due at The Tank.
Should be plenty of time to get in a cruise and do my
set with Getto. Move those feet, Shadow. You've wasted
enough time setting up your cover.*

Ahead of her Teri the Switch came from Rat's Alley,
patted a yawn, and leaned against a wall waiting for
her next client. She'd gotten too old and too intermittently crazy for even the sleaziest Houses, but she was
cheerful despite what seemed a miserable life and on
those days when she was tracking, designed and sewed
costumes that were artforms in themselves, absurd and
enchanting. Tank paid her to make three changes for
Shadith; he got two of them and seemed to be content
with that. He was fond of her. He was not a sentimental man, so that surprised Shadith, but during the fittings she began to understand the woman's daft charm.

That there was no way anyone could really make life easier for her was a part of it. Frustrating, but a liberation in a shaming sort of way. It let you enjoy her nonsense and share in the impossible pleasure she got out of being alive without your being pushed to do anything for her.

"Teri, I'm going for a sea cruise. You want to come along?"

Teri smiled; she always smiled when people spoke to her, but her eyes were empty. It was one of her bad days.

"Ah well, see you around." Shadith hesitated a moment, made a note to tell Tank when she got back, and walked past the woman, more disturbed than before when Teri looked through her as if she didn't exist. When she reached the next alley, she turned and looked back, squinting against the dazzle as the sun moved suddenly from behind a cloud. A man was standing beside Teri, talking to her. Shadith sighed and moved on. She thought again about Tank, but what could he do? The question niggled at her until she reached Kemros' flier park and started negotiating for a half day's rent.

4

Shadith took the open flit low, swooping just above the wave peaks. The air was brisk and briny, the sea out beyond the clouds a brilliant turquoise, several degrees brighter than the sky. She played with the flit for a while, swinging it back and forth as if she were tacking against the wind, then went nosing along the offshore islands, racing in and out, between and around them as if she played a game with herself using them as markers. At the same time she kept an eye on one of Digby's specials, an asteroid miner's detec that he'd had titivated by someone until it could smell out a ship even at the bottom of an ocean of sludge. Or so he swore to her.

Whether that was true or not, the watchlight turned green when she swung around the fourth and largest of the islands. She sighed. No proof it was Lylunda Elang's ship, but she didn't really need proof. She went scooting out to sea after that, chasing cloud shadows, and spent the next hour whipping back and forth along the coast. At the end of that time she set the flit on hover, stretched out, and just enjoyed the feel of the wind and the smell of the ocean, layering impressions in her mind about the song she wanted to write.

5

Shadith nodded to Getto, played a phrase or two of the song to let him get a feel for it. "This one's for you, Gee, since you gave me the idea. It's a song I'm still working on, though I have enough for now."

The mirrors on Getto's drums shivered in the sunlight as he drew a whispering undersong from them, the mirror on his ear was a small sun itself.

"Briny winds," she sang.

> *"Briny winds blow clouds away.*
> *The sharded sea skips to their song.*
> *I slide from peak to peak on sapphire waves*
> *looking for answers in the sun.*
> *Nothing but shadows in the shine*
> *Sad shadows of friends that I left behind.*
> *Briny winds blow clouds away*
> *Spit fillips of foam into my face*
> *Gust through the ghosts within my mind*

Till even the dance of memory's gone.
Briny winds blow clouds away."

At the last word she segued into sweeping arpeggios meant to suggest sea winds, then took the sound back to let Getto reprise the verse with his drums. He could go wild on those drums, get your blood pounding till your feet moved on their own, but at times like these he had a precise yet lyrical touch that could make them sing until you could almost hear the words.

At the end of the set, when she brought the collecting bowl back to him, it was heavy with local credit tokens and coins from a dozen worlds. He wanted her to take half, but she wouldn't.

"I enjoyed myself out there and I'll probably go back," she said. "And I got a song, or at least the start of a song. Might not've thought of that myself. So I owe you." She stooped to slide her harp into its case, straightened when she'd snapped the clips.

She thought, *I can trust him not to talk about me. He hears things. What if I asked him about Lylunda Elang? He might even know.* She watched him taking apart the drums, folding them down and down so he could carry them back to his place, wherever that was. But she saw a distant sheen in his eyes that reminded her of Teri and she remembered how eagerly he tried to please the people he liked. If he didn't know, he'd ask around. And that might mean more trouble than she wanted to cope with.

"See you," she said, hefted the case, and slipped her arm through the strap.

That night, as she sang in The Tank wearing the silver fantasy Teri had crafted her, she looked out over the patrons and wondered if the Kliu's other agent was among them and if there was anyone at those tables who'd have access to the warrens on the far side of the Wall. It didn't seem likely. They were mostly traders and crew, transients who might pass through here several times a year for a while and then move on to another round.

"Oh, we shall go awandering along the secret ways," she sang and put a throb in her voice; the sense she had of this crowd was a lightly drunken sentimentality. Get them weeping in their beer and feeling vaguely heroic. "Ah, the lazy stars the crazy stars, they whisper in your bones," she sang and let her voice lose itself in the song of the strings. *I have to make a move,* she thought, *she's here. Not on Star Street, up the hill somewhere. In the Izar? Likely, Digby says that's where she came from. Heading for home with weasels on her tail. Home ground. How do I get over the Wall and make it look natural?*

"Rest a while, love a while, till the call's too strong," she sang. "Chase the singing stars and leave the ground behind." She played with the last word a while, letting it trail to a whisper, then finished the song and stilled the strings of the harp, bowed to the whistles and snapping fingers.

That was the last song of the set.

She bowed again, announced she'd be back in half an hour, then took herself and the harp off the small stage. Tank was waiting for her in the Green Room.

He was a short broad man with a brush of hair around a shiny bald dome and arms like tree trunks. His hands were so small they looked mismated to his body, as if he'd stolen them from another man. He brushed at his mouth. "Where'd you say you saw Teri?"

"She was working Rat's Alley. I thought about going

back, but she'd hooked a client and I didn't want to mess that up. Why?"

"Can't find her anywhere. Alive nor dead. You remember what the man looked like?"

"His back was to me and the sun popped out just then, couldn't see much through the dazzle. Cousin." She closed her eyes, tried to bring back that fleeting memory. "Was leaning against the wall, but he might've been maybe a head taller than her. Ummm. Not fat, not skinny. Wearing a one-piece something, gray and shiny. Might have been a shipsuit. Maybe a work overall. I've seen both along the Street. Maybe she's gone to ground somewhere. The time she was doing the fittings she told me she did that when things went whirly on her."

He brushed that aside with an impatient sweep of his arm. "I know her places. Anyone out front who might be that client?"

"Spla! Half of them at least. Or half the locals who do the muscle work out at the Field."

"You think it could have been a local?"

"Any reason why not?"

"The locals here don't much play outside their own pens. Hm. Could be one of them had a mind for cheap thrills. You get so used to them, you don't even see them, 'less you jump the Wall. . . ." He stared thoughtfully past her, his eyes narrowed, the creases deepening in his narrow brow.

"Tank, you know someone with connections over there?"

"Why?"

"Friend of mine. Well, friend of a friend who did me a favor a while back gave me a message to pass on if I saw the chance. A certain dancing Caan, should anyone want to know the wherefrom. The whereto is a woman of the Caan's profession by name Lylunda

Elang. Word was the Elang was hot and going home a while and home is here. I wouldn't want to shout the name around, could be touchy, but I figure you know how to talk soft when you need to."

"You want me to ask about this Elang?"

She felt him go cold on her. He recognized the name *Not so good, that. Someone else asking questions, maybe the Kliu agent? Or is it local trouble? Ease back, Shadow. Better make it clear you're not on the hunt.* "No. I don't think that would be a good idea. Don't ask, just put out a whisper about the message and where it's from. She wants to come she can, she doesn't, no harm done."

"So what's the message?" He was still tense, though he was relaxed and his eyes twinkled at her. *He does good face, our Tank.*

She clicked her tongue, shook her head at him. "Huh! you know better than that. I'll say this, it was an off chance my friend took when she knew I was heading this way. The sun won't nova if it doesn't get passed on, but it's something the woman ought to hear."

By the time she finished, the edge had gone off his alertness. "Good thing it was me you talked to, Shadow. I'll see what I can do, but don't say that name to anyone else."

She raised her brows. "Putting out that much heat, huh? Right. I keep my mouth shut. Owe you one, Tank." *That I do, more than you know.*

He hesitated a moment, but didn't say what was hanging on his tongue, just shrugged and left.

Hm. Wonder what that last was about. Hope it's not something that's going to jump up and bite me. She sighed and went on into the dressing room to splash some water on her face and sit with her feet up until it was time for the next set.

* * *

Tank was in the Green Room when she came back. "When you get changed," he said, "come over to the office." He left before she could ask him why.

He nodded at a chair, poured a sop of rikoka brandy into two bell glasses and brought one of them to her. The bottle was dark and squat, dust and cobwebs carefully preserved on its bulge to testify to the age and value of the liquid inside.

When he was behind his desk again, he lifted his glass. "Got Teri back," he said.

"She all right?"

"Alive. The cul that got her was a freak, cut her some and broke some bones. She won't remember once she's healed up, she never does."

"Least there's that. She was over the Wall?"

"Yeh." He scowled. "Don't know if I did you a favor or not, Shadow. Passed your whisper to my Touch over there. I don't like how nervous he was when he heard the woman's name." He took a mouthful of the brandy, worked his cheeks as if he sloshed it about in his mouth. Even after he swallowed, he said nothing, just sat looking down into the glass.

She waited, sipping at the brandy, saying nothing, letting him take his time.

"She's under heavy protection. Word's been out for a couple months. You talk about the woman, you end up poisoning fish. Same thing if you ask too many questions about her."

"Official protection?"

"Depends on what you call official."

"Mm hm. Gotcha."

"I gave the Touch the whole deal. Hope I got through that you're not nosing 'round, but you never can tell with those types. So slap a seal on your mouth and watch your back. Don't trust anyone. Not me. Not anyone." He got to his feet. "That's what I wanted to tell you and why I wanted it private."

He opened the door for her, waited as she hoisted the harp and slipped the strap over her shoulder. As soon as she was in the hall, he repeated, "Not me. Not anyone."

It was raining when she stepped into the street, a slow steady downfall that soaked her within a minute after she left the shelter of the doorway. "Ah spla! And me with no umbrella." She trudged along, thinking over what Tank had told her. *Heavy protection. Probably bought it when she came scuttling home like her tail was on fire, maybe with proceeds from a crystal she got for smuggling the array off Pillory. Be a hoot if I tolled her out when I was just trying to find out where she. . . .*

She woke, confused, her head throbbing. She was sitting in a chair, something pressed against her legs. She tried to move her arms and she couldn't. She was tied . . . strapped. When she looked down, she saw that the pressure on her legs was her harpcase. She stared at it, then lifted her head and looked around her.

She was in a sketch of a room, dark and shadowy. The door was steel with a small grill about eye level. The walls were packed dirt and irregular bits of sheet-rock interrupted by vertical two by fours, the floor was large square tiles the color of dried blood, the ceiling was fiberglass insulation faced with brown paper. Torn, filthy brown paper. A cellar of some kind? She swore under her breath. *Tank! You set me up, you zalup. I'd like to. . . .*

A clank from the door interrupted her thoughts. She considered pretending she was still unconscious, discarded that idea, straightened her shoulders, and lifted her head. *It'll probably be some kind of babble,* she told herself. *This is where you find out how good your timing is, Shadow, and get the ol' mind-move ready to jump.*

"A short life but a merry one," she said as the door swung open. And she laughed aloud at the figures who came through it—three men wearing heavy black robes and headsman's cowls that hid all but their eyes. "What are you? Black monks in some tridda farce?" One was tall and broad, menacing as a meat ax and about as subtle, one was tall and thin with a cold, snaky feel, the third was short and tubby. From him she sensed inquisitiveness of the peephole sort, the kind that made you feel dirty thinking about it.

The short one came toward her. When she saw the blowgun in his hand, she concentrated, used her small Talent to set a catchfield round her carotid. *Neck, I think. Yes, he'll go for the neck.*

As if he obeyed her thought, he shoved the business end of the blower under her jaw and tapped the sensor.

She slapped the field round the drug and caught most of it before it got loose, ran the encapsulated dollops of blood and babble through her system and peed it out on her underpants. Despite her efforts, she absorbed enough to turn her silly, though she was still in control of her mind. *Talent pays, pays, pays . . . no, I'm wrong, pees not pays.* Giggles bubbled in her throat but she kept them down. *Stupid zalups, pinch brain ground hobs, not enough sense in the three of you to keep an ant walking straight. Amateurs. Silly silly zots, I foolin' you to the max, no monitor, you uziks. Uzik ziks. Zikky ziklings. . . .* She caught what was happening and throttled that burbling fast. Get to feeling too superior and she'd start explaining in detail why they were so stupid.

The short man who'd blown the babble into her pulled a chair over and sat in it facing her, his hands on his knees. The other two were silent shadows behind him. "What's your name?"

"Shadow." A snort escaped from her, turned into a giggle.

"Your real name."

She considered that. *Real name? Whose real name?* "The body's real name?"

"Yes. The body's real name."

"Oh. Hawk, bird rider of the Centai zel. But I don't call the body that any more. That was before. Now it is Shadith. I am Shadith. Shadow. Shadowsong.":

"Who pays you?"

"Tank pays me. I sing in his place."

"Who do you work for?"

"I work for Tank."

"Who else do you work for?"

"I work for Shadith. Shadow. Shadowsong."

"Did someone send you to Hutsarté?"

"I sent me. I go nowhere at any one's order."

"Why did you ask about Lylunda Elang?"

"I have a message for her."

"Tell us the message."

"I don't want to. I'm not supposed to tell anyone but her."

"Tell us the message."

"Qatifa says there's a rumor round the Market that the Kliu have hired Excavations Ltd. to dig her out, and if it's true she should get as much cover as she can find."

"Who is Qatifa?"

"She's a Caan smuggler."

"Why should she bother?"

"You don't know?"

"Why should she bother?"

"Lylunda likes furries. She and Qatifa were belly friends for a while."

"Were you a belly friend to either?"

"No."

"Do you know Lylunda Elang at all?"

"No."

"Why carry a message, then?"

"Favor for favor. I pay my debts."

"Why did you wait till now to try finding Lylunda Elang?"

"I was busy and I kinda forgot till Tank talked about asking over the Wall when Teri turned up missing."

"Do you know what Lylunda Elang looks like?"

"Only what Qatifa said."

"Have you seen anyone like that in the past five days?"

"No."

"Have you seen anyone like that since you landed on Hutsarté?"

"No."

He got to his feet, crossed the short distance to the other two. When he spoke, he was muttering but loud enough that Shadith could catch what he was saying. "She'll be under for about five more minutes, then she'll start coming out of it. Anything more you need to know?"

The bigger man's voice was a low rumble and harder to make out. She thought she caught a question about a phot, but she wasn't sure until the short man came back holding a jewelcase in his hand.

He held the phot up so she could see the tridda image inside. A young woman with a pretty, round face, long black hair and white streaks like wings over her ears. Wide shoulders, wide hips, a narrow waist. Shadith almost burst out giggling. Even Digby hadn't come up with a phot and here her captors were showing her just what she needed to know.

"Have you seen this woman at any time?"

"No."

"Look closely at the phot. Look at her face. Look at her ears, at her left hand. See the crooked little finger. Think carefully. Have you seen anyone who looks like this woman?"

"No."

He lowered the phot. "I. . . ."

A hand closed on his shoulder. The big man bent, whispered in his ear. He nodded. "Shadow, if we let you go, what will you do?"

"Go back to The Tank, sing there till I can earn enough to buy a low passage on a worldship and go on till I feel like stopping."

The big man whispered again, longer this time.

Shadith decided it was time to start acting edgy. She tugged at the straps on her arms, put on a puzzled frown. "Wha . . . why . . ." She tugged harder, started moving her head about. "Where . . . what's happening?"

"Nothing you need worry about. We're not going to hurt you unless you make us."

Whimpering, panting, Shadith ignored him and started fighting the straps, throwing herself about, making the chair rock, putting on as reasonable a show as she could manage without falling over and cracking her head on the tiles.

The snake man moved for the first time. He came over to her, slapped her hard, then stood beside her with his hand closed on her shoulder, his fingers digging into her flesh. He still said nothing, but she decided that she could get his point and stop her struggles.

The big man moved to the door. "Gantz, clean her

up, flush her out, bring her upstairs. Krink, get over here. You stay outside the door, on watch. I've got a thought about using her and I don't want you messing it up. You hear me?"

"I hear."

Shadith's stomach knotted at the concentrated venom in those two words and found herself happy that Krink the snake was too afraid of Boss to go for him. She watched Gantz warily as the door shut.

He saw that. "Don't worry, woman. Grinder would have my guts for fishpoison if I laid a finger on you. You better remember that and do what he wants without smart talk or slacking. He isn't called Grinder for sweetness of temper and gentility of manner." He brought the blowgun from a pocket in his robe, worked over it for a few minutes. "You'll be feeling limp as overcooked noodles right now, what I'm going to give you will perk you right up, blow the fog out of your head."

"No. 'm all ri'. Don' do poppers."

"You don't really have a choice, love. Him, he wants you alert and ready to listen. And that's what he's going to get."

"Lylunda Elang belongs to me," Grinder said.

Shadith forced herself to sit still; though she'd done the catchment trick again with the popper, the residue had her so wired she felt as if her eyes were ready to explode out of her head and every sound was a scrape along her nerves.

"Maybe she doesn't know it yet, but she's mine."

She'd seen eyes like his before—after a moment it came to her where. Lute's eyes. Ginny Seyirshi's pet killer. That time she got snatched into one of the Deathmaker's scenarios. She swallowed several times and didn't have to pretend to be frightened.

"She's gone missing. Six days ago. Maybe on her own. Maybe Digby's agent got her. Yeh. I know about Digby. Who doesn't. Maybe the Kliu bought her father and got her that way. I can handle things this side of the Wall, you're going to sift Star Street for me."

Four days! Would you believe, the target disappears four miserable days after I get here. What stinking luck. She folded her hands in her lap and looked nervous. It wasn't hard. "Uh ... I don't mean to be ... um negative about this and I'll do my best, sure I will, but I'm just a singer."

He contemplated her a moment. "Don't play the ditzy fool with me. You're not good enough at it to be entertaining. Why you? I'll tell you straight, I can keep it quiet over here and out in backcountry, but Star Street's different. I don't want the word spreading I've been took over by a femme. Too many hopeful yappers biting at my heels. You've got a reason for asking, so I'm going to use it. Let me warn you, singer. I've got ears over there. You ran into one of 'em. If I hear you're talking too much, I'll send Krink over with his calf strap. He'll enjoy that. Yes, I see you know what I mean. Don't try conning your way onto a trader's ship. You'll be dead before you reach the ladder. You understand?"

"I'm going to have to ask questions."

"Word will be spread by morning. What you told us. That Lylunda's your friend and you've got a message for her. That it's good for you to be asking and better for them to give you the answers you want. I'm sure you can see the difference."

"Yes. Clever. I will be discreet and diligent. You've convinced me my health depends on that."

"Good."

"And my diligence starts now. I need to know the

circumstances of her disappearance. And I'd like a copy of that phot."

"Why? Not the phot, I'll see you get that. The other."

"As you said, I'm not stupid, merely reluctant. The fewer questions I have to ask, the less I give away. The more I know to start with, the fewer questions I have to ask."

"I see. Lylunda was working for me. You don't need to know about that, so don't ask. She left the job, went home to her rooming house. She was picked up there by one of Hizurri-jaz Gautaxo's couriers. He's the head of the Duk's Secret Police and he also happens to be Lylunda's father. She's the bastard he got when her mother was his hot little Izar piece, so there's no telling just what he wanted with her. She stayed there for a little over two hours. Courier brought her back through the Izar gate, walked her to the front door of her rooming house, left her while she was using her keys to open the vestibule door. She was seen by at least five different people who knew her well enough to be sure it was her. That was the last time anyone saw her."

"Late. After dark?"

"Yes and an overcast night. I thought about that. They recognized the clothes. More than that, they recognized the way she moved."

"Still . . . a good actress the right size and shape. . . ."

"Yes. I thought about that. I don't know."

"Did she have a credit chip? She hired you to watch her back, didn't she. To warn her if the Kliu got too close. Like me, I was supposed to warn her about Digby."

"Yes. Everything she brought with her was cleaned out of her room."

"What I've heard about the Behilarr jazzies, they've

all got fiefdoms out in the backcountry. Maybe he sent her out there."

"No. I've had that looked into."

"You told me you'd know if I tried to hop a ship. I expect you'd know it if she did."

"I would if she tried it after I found out she was gone. Before then, there's a seven-hour window when she might have made it."

"That's what you want me to check, isn't it."

"Part of it."

"Can you get me a printout of all shuttle and ship departures in those seven hours?"

"Yes."

"Hm. If you can get it, you might add to that a list of departures from the transfer station. I know enough about who's traveling around out there that it might tell me something it wouldn't tell you."

"I'll get it."

She sighed, rubbed at her eyes. "With all the stuff your bootlicker pumped into me, I'm about wiped. Can I go home now, get some sleep?"

"You understand what I want?"

"Yes, you made it quite clear."

"And I want results. Fast."

"Yes."

"Then you go like you came."

6

Shadith came out of stunner shock with a throbbing head and body that felt as if she'd been beaten with a rubber hose. The curtains to her single window had been drawn and the morning sun was streaming in. She looked down at herself and breathed a sigh of relief when she saw she was still wearing the damp dirty clothes from last night. She remembered her harp and sat up too fast, yelping with pain as her head threatened to explode, her stomach to erupt, and all she could see was a rainy silver aura with black spots in it that wobbled and darted like tadpoles.

When she pried her eyes open again, to her considerable relief, she saw the harpcase leaning against the wall beside the door.

She eased her legs over the edge of the bed and contemplated getting up. The thought of food revolted her, but she needed the energy. Lot of work to get through this day and the next.

7

Tank looked at Shadith, sighed, and shook his head. "I have to live here," he said. "I warned you, didn't I?"

"Yeah, that you did." She finished clearing off the table in the dressing room, snapped her bag shut. "You know what he's got me doing. I'll be too busy to sing as well as disinclined. See you." She swept past him, still angry at him. Reporting her activities she could accept as part of the game; setting her up for a snatch was something else.

When she unlocked the door to the room she'd rented and stepped inside, she caught a whiff of jorrat and went very still; a quick probe with her *reach*, though, told her the place was empty.

A cardboard folder lay in the middle of the rumpled bedspread.

No one here now, but there had been, someone with a jorrat pipe who'd left the stink of his habit behind. *Makes you feel really secure the way that lot waltzes in without breaking a sweat. And I suppose those are the printouts. Grinder works fast. Or he already had them.*

"And now I get to wear out my eyes on ship data. Tsah!"

She went out, leaned over the railing. "Orrialdy," she yelled. "You around?"

Her landlady came into the hall on the floor below, a big woman with an abundance of hair, wisps escaping the knot she kept it in to wave around her plush pink face. "Shadow, so?"

"Think you could bring me up a pot of your tea?"

"That I could. Right now?"

"If you will. Door'll be unlocked."

After Orrialdy left, Shadith filled her mug with hot tea and opened the folder. Her brows rose as she realized just how much data Grinder had included in the report. Not only the names and descriptions of the ships which left in that seven-hour window, but a history of their appearances here on Hutsarté going back at least ten years, along with short descriptions of owners and crew. There were only three of them, but still. . . .

She set that aside and took up the second set of printouts.

Shuttle flights. Five. Four were cargo lifts with stasis crates. Meat wagons. It might be possible to shove the woman in with the crates. Assuming Daddy was behind the disappearance . . . which seemed likely since he'd cared enough about Lylunda to see that she was educated and given a chance to get away from here . . . and considering he was head of government security, he could do things like that. But. It would also leave him open to blackmail or betrayal . . . hm. . . .

She looked down the lists of the crews. No disappearances or fatal accidents. And none of them had looked up Grinder with news for sale. Not a sure thing, but close enough to cross this one off.

One of the shuttles was a passenger lift. *Hm. Eleven riding it. Passengers and crew all male. Only place to stow her was the baggage compartment and . . . yes, crew still in business and no comment by Grinder. So, set this one aside, too. Which means the ships in the tie-downs at the Transfer Station are probably no-goes.*

She glanced over that list, found nothing that interested her, and set it aside.

Which left the three on-ground ships.

The K'Jatt, *a converted sting ship, owner Lomkael Jurd, dealing in hides and horn.* She looked at his history. He was in and out all the time, every few weeks. *Must stay in the Pseudo Cluster and do all his trading here. He hasn't got time to get anywhere else, not in that little ship.* She wrinkled her nose at the thought of what that hold must smell like, then noticed the last date. *He's back here now. Spla! Cross him off, thank whatever. I doubt Daddy would deal with someone in his face all the time.*

The second was a Jilitera trader. *The* Jherada, *owner listed as the Jilitera Trust. Hm.* She took a sip of the tea and grimaced because it was barely lukewarm. She poured more from the pot and went back to contemplating the readout. *Dealing in local plants . . . the poisonous ones, of course . . . here's a note—they'd asked about the fish, but no one was interested in supplying those . . . which reminds me . . . that ship . . . the Elang wouldn't have anything in there about where she dropped the array . . . smuggler . . . she'll be cautious about what's private and part of her assets . . . if Digby got his hands on that kephalos, though . . . he could go snooping through its innards . . . rumor is he can scrute the inscrutable and twist the tail on any enigma ever born . . . but do I want him to do that? He talks good flesh, but how much do I trust him on some-*

*thing like this? Answer to that is not at all ... but I
can use that ship to get out of here without Grinder
going nervous on me ... he gets nervous and I get
dead.*

*Set aside for now ... Jilitera, ship history ... set
down here seven years ago, then three years, then this
last one. I don't know much about them. Does anyone?
Jilitera. Homeworld unknown ... maybe they don't
have one ... ship born, ship bound ... langue unknown ... all contacts made with interlingue ... trade
in plants and plant derivatives ... whatever ... known
as poisoners ... trade a lot with University ... yes, I
remember that time when Aslan wanted to interview
some of them ... hmp! No outsiders on the ship ... no
crew even talking to outsiders.*

*Not likely Daddy chose that one for his little girl.
Hm. If the third ship blows out on me, maybe I'd better
reconsider those shuttles ... Ship, the* Vouist *... interesting ... there's a note—converted trooper, Rummul
Empire ... like Swarda's* Slancy Orza *... though I'd
wager she doesn't have anything like Orza's drives. ...*
She shook her head. "You'd think I'd keep my mind
on business. Stop rambling, Shadow."

*Rummul Empire trooper, owner Pitroc. Another note.
Cover name, real name Harmon. ...* "Sar! First
Sapato, now Harmon. Arms dealers I have known. Hm.
He dropped a cargo in one of the warehouses, it was
picked up three days later by a Chandava merchanter.
Definitely old home week. Note doesn't say what the
cargo was, but are we really baffled? And the answer
is no." *I think this is it, Shadow old girl. Arms dealers
have tight mouths and like to do favors for people in
power. Head of Security here? He has to know what's
shifting through those warehouses. And Harmon looks
such a twerp, Daddy would think his kid would be safe.*

And maybe he'd be right, I haven't a clue about Harmon's little pleasures.

She sat tapping the fingers of her right hand on the stack of papers, sipping at the tea, and staring at the three locks on her door—locks about as useful as a piece of string if the right people wanted to go through them.

After a minute of that, she got to her feet and started pacing about the room. Seemed likely the jorrat freak left more than the printouts. She could hunt for the pickups ... get the room sweep from the Trick Kit ... which she'd stashed up in the attic, gods be blessed, that would have blown her cover for sure ... hah! talk about blowing cover, kit aside, just doing a sweep and cleaning out the bugs. . . .

Figure out a way to use them? Everything I do everything I say here will be picked up by some watcher. . . . Clothes? No problem, she'd bought them for the role. The medkit? *Have to take that, too much of me in it.* The harp? *No way I'm leaving that behind. Have to figure something. Digby's toolkit. Have to collect that. Stinking Grinder ... but at least he's not official ... hm, Daddy dear the Muck Policeman, does he have his thumb planted on Tank, too? Gods! that would be a mess for sure, ol' Tank cringing to all comers. Ah spla, I've definitely got to get out of here. Use the bugs ... we'll have ourselves a little drama here. Act I scene 1: The spy is working hard but frustrated because she isn't getting anywhere. She stops her pacing, sits at the table. . . .*

Shadith pulled the chair out, settled herself, and once again began leafing through the printouts, frowning at them, looking up at intervals to scowl at the door. She used the time to think over her conclusions and ended more convinced than ever that Lylunda Elang had left Hutsarté on Harmon's ship.

Hope that's long enough to bore the hair off who-ever's watching. Act I scene 2: The spy vents her frus-tration on the folder, announces she's bored with this and is going to take a break. . . .

She slapped the folder shut, tossed it onto the bed. Rubbed her eyes. Tilted the pot over the mug for the last bitter drops of room-temperature tea. "Sar! Enough for today. Boooring. I think I'll rent me one of the Tinkerman's flits and go write me another song. Unless it's raining." She pushed away from the table and went to the window.

The clouds were high and scattered. It might rain af-ter dark, but probably not until then. *Time I had some luck.* "Harp, where's my harp. Ah there. My bag. Spla, my hands are mucky. Better wash first. Hm. Change my clothes, it's cooler out on the water. . . ."

Twenty minutes later she stuffed the folder into her ybag and reached for the door latch. *Act I scene 3: Exit one spy.*

8

"Eh, Shadow, you look like the world treating you good. Where you off to?"

"Eh, Getto, taking a flit out for a sail. Want to come?"

"Different strokes, Shadow. Me I get seasick if I even look at water. Gonna make another song?"

"Want to. Might. They come when they come, you know." She fluttered her fingers at him and went on her way.

Act II, scene 1: The spy walks down the street, greet-ing everyone she knows and spreading her story about, hoping she's soothing the jitters of the little worm who's tailing her.

She stopped in at Cara's cook shop. "Two of your

meat pies, hm, Cara my love. Wrap them up tight and throw in a couple of napkins, I'm going for a sail in a flit and the Tinkerman gets snarky about stains."

The older woman shook her head. "You've blown a circuit, Shadow. Anyone who'd go voluntarily out over that stinking soupmix. . . ." She clicked her tongue, then went to work wrapping up the pies.

9

"Act III scene 1," Shadith chanted to the wind as she took the flit in a sweeping curve across the water. "The spy has fooled them all and says an unfond farewell to Haundi Zurgile the chief city of the colony world Hutsarté. And Grinder Jiraba can go suck eggs."

As she took the flit low and finished the curve, she saw that she'd celebrated a bit too soon. There was a dark speck over near the horizon, almost out of sight. "Stinking Grinder, doesn't trust anyone. Let's see. Might as well open up my pies and have my meal while I'm thinking this over. Hm. Wonder if I can get him so bored watching me play around doing nothing, I can catch him on the hop when I take off." She chuckled. "Act III scene 2: The spy has her dinner and leads the tail round in circles."

When she finished eating, she sent the flit skimming across the whitetops, the lift effect churning the water into cream beneath her. It was dangerous and she was riding her luck hard, but it kept the watcher dithering in the distance, especially since she was careful to keep circling back toward the shore so he wouldn't have to worry that she was stupid enough to try escaping to the Wild Half. And while she played out that scene, she programmed a course into the autopilot, getting ready for the time when she had to ditch the flit.

After half an hour of skittering about like a waterbug
with the fidgets, she went up to a safer height, set the
auto-p on hover/drift, and let the wind blow her toward
the string of islands. She put her feet up, stretched out
and began to sing, fragments, phrases, repeating them
over and over with enough changes to suggest she was
trying to weave them into a song should the watcher
have a sound pickup aimed at her.

When she reached the first island, a rocky dot that
barely broke the surface, she sat up and began dancing
the flit around and between the islands. Half the time
the tail was out of sight completely. To her intense satisfaction he didn't seem to mind and didn't try to get
closer.

She flew faster, swinging up into sight, dipping low
again; she circled the big island, then took the flit
skimming low over the place where the metal mass had
registered on Digby's detec. Lylunda had set a camou
cloth over her ship and the vegetation had helped her
conceal it, a tangle of vines crawling across the porous
cloth, the broken trees and withered foliage swallowed
in the damp fecundity of these latitudes. Without the
evidence from a powerful detec no one would know
that anything nested there.

She turned the flit in a tight circle, brought it down
and set it on hover/pause, the programmed course to
kick in after seven minutes. She lowered the harp and
Digby's Trick Kit, then dropped overside herself. Using the cutting rod from the kit, she sliced through the
camou cloth and let herself down beside the shrouded
ship, wrapping herself in a mind spray of *don't-
touch-me* to keep the bugs off while she worked her
way along the ship's side until she reached the area below the lock.

She crouched beside the ship, sheltering under the
curve of the hull when she heard the ascending whine

as the flit revved up and took off. "Act III scene 3: The spy tries the old decoy trick. Gods, I hope this works. I need time to pry open this can."

10

"Act IV scene 1," Shadith chanted as the lock slid open. "Digby does it again. The spy enters the smuggler's ship. Huh! Enough of that, it's getting stupid now." She moved cautiously inside and started for the bridge. "I do hope you were counting on concealment and your folks' loathing for these waters . . . and planning for a hot jump if the Kliu were chasing you . . . after what happened at the Market, were I you, that's how I'd leave things . . . mmmm."

She settled herself in the pilot's chair and inspected the controls. "Well, you're old, but she keeps you up well. New kephalos, I see. Out of the Hegger Combine, looks like. Ah, yes. I know your kind. Let's see what the sequencer gives us." She whistled breathily through her teeth as she peeled the interface and clicked home the jacks. "You're a clever child, Lylunda, but rather conventional, I think. This shouldn't take long. Meantime, I'm going to have a look through your ship. Don't expect you'll be leaving notes to yourself in your writing desk like that idiot jock-pilot Autumn Rose told me about, but maybe there's something you forgot."

It was a compact little ship, swelling around the belly like a proper smuggler should, plenty of hold space with cells for handling tricky items and a mazy confusion of interior walls which was probably meant to conceal abditories used for really hot cargo. Nothing there that she could see, only the ghosts of old scents.

The single cabin was tidy and tucked up, clothing

stowed in a narrow closet and a few shallow drawers, the foldaway cot made up with clean sheets. The only extravagance was a flake player with hundreds of selections ready to go at a touch. When she glanced through the index, Shadith was astonished and flattered to find her own recording there, something she'd made as the final exam for one of her courses. It'd gone into University's library collection and had brought her a few small but much appreciated royalty payments. "Well, now, if I needed an incentive. . . ." She laughed. "Anyone with such excellent taste should never be thrown to the execrable Kliu." Still chuckling, she went back to the bridge to find that the sequencer had done its job, brought the controls alive, and gotten the kephalos ready for work.

She buttoned up the interface and settled into the pilot's chair. "Read new ID code." She watched the string flash across the screen. *Smooth. Coming through clear and intact.* "Read status of code." *Good.* Show me control configurations." *And here's where it starts to be work. I've got to know your jigs and jags before I dare take you 'splitting . . . which reminds me, I don't know your name yet. Well, that little frill comes later. Focus, Shadow, focus. You need to know this stuff. . . .*

11

The sea was buzzing with flits when she took Lylunda's *Dragoi* up through the camou cloth and went running for the line where the atmosphere officially ended, the point where dirt law supposedly ceased to rule. Of course, all that generally meant was that whoever was chasing you was free to nail you without going through the time-wasting formality of a trial.

Someone in the flits had acquired launchers and the missiles that fed them, but one of *Dragoi*'s neater tricks was an ability to shield herself while projecting an image off to one side, so the shooter blew a hole in the air but did the ship no damage at all, and by the time he discovered this, Shadith was long gone.

11

Bound on Bol Mutair

1

Lylunda blinked. The sudden brightness made her eyes water. She closed them again—and grew aware of the nearly intangible vibration humming through her bones. Cabin. Ship. In the insplit going who knew where. For a moment she didn't question this; then the oddity of it struck her and she jerked upright on the cot, swiveling around as she came up, her legs sliding over the edge.

She knew it was a mistake before her feet hit the floor. She lunged across the narrow cabin, slapped blindly at the sensor node, and got her head into the fresher just in time to heave up a bitter yellow liquid, which was all she had in her stomach.

After wiping her face with a damp towelette, she stumbled back to the cot and sat with her eyes closed, trying to think around the knives that ground into her temples.

She hadn't expected her father to use a stunner on her. She'd thought vaguely about confinement; maybe he'd send her off to one of his arranxes in the back country.

And it wasn't just a stun. I've been out too long.
Dear, dear Daddy. I wonder what he used on me?

She tried to convince herself that her father had
meant it when he said that he wanted to take care of
her, keep her safe, but she had a sick feeling that he
was just flushing a problem down the drain. That she
was a scandal he couldn't afford when the Ezkop
Garap was hunting sinners to fine and chastise and
even the Duk would have to face symbolic whip cuts
for the edification of the lesser Behilarr.

He was right about one thing, though. Him being
who he was, it wouldn't have been safe for her to go
back to the warren. *Grinder'd play with me a while,*
then dump me in the Jotun to poison the fish. I
shouldn't have gone back to Hutsarté. Home? What
was I thinking of? I could wait to get away the first
time, and I'm never going near the place again. . . .

Her eyes burned, wet oozed from under her eyelids.
She tried to swallow, but a lump closed up her throat.
"I won't," she said aloud. She didn't care who heard
her. "I won't. . . ." The word ended on a sob and she
was crying as she had not cried when her mother's
body trundled into the crematorium.

Before, there was the chance that her father would
be proud of her and claim her. Not much of a chance,
but not impossible.

Before, there was home as a refuge she could always
return to if things go too complicated in the larger
world she lived in now.

And before, there was always the dream of making
it so big she could go home in a sun-class yacht,
dressed in diamonds, with a train of servants so long
the line would wrap round the outside of the Izar Wall.
And the High would court her, even the Duk and the
Dukana. And she would snub them and hand out lar-

gess to folk like Halfman Ike and Melia the Standup
Whore.

A silly child's dreams, but she'd never quite let go
of them. She tasted the salt of her tears as they slid
past her smile into her mouth—and with that, the crying fit was over.

She coughed to clear her throat, wiped her eyes. "I
stink," she said to the ambient air.

"Then drop those rags you're wearing into the dis-
posal and take a bath. If you'll check the stowage,
you'll find we've put more suitable clothing in there
for you."

The voice came from the announcer grill, an incon-
spicuous circle of roughness above the door, a woman's voice, speaking interlingue with an odd swing to
the words Lylunda couldn't place.

"And when you're ready," the voice continued,
"come to the Bridge. The door's not locked. You're
free to move about as you want."

2

The ship was larger than hers and newer. *I forgot
about my ship,* she thought. *Looks like I will be going
back after all.* She smiled at a sudden picture in
her mind, swooping low over the Dukeri House and
the High City and giving the borts there the scare of
their stinking lives. *Grow up, woman,* she told herself, but she was still grinning as she stepped onto the
Bridge.

A man sat in the pilot's seat, not a woman. Age hung
like an aura about him and looked out of eyes like winter ice, though his ananiles were still holding, so there
was little gray in the thick braid that came over his
shoulder and was long enough to brush at his belt. The
lines in his face were shallow and fine, as if someone

had pasted a spider's web across it. Two young women sat in the other chairs, his daughters or granddaughters if appearance meant anything.

"So," she said. "I been sold to Contract?"

When he spoke his voice was rough, but not unpleasant, and there was that same swing to his interlingue that she'd heard in the woman's voice. "We would not consider such a thing, Lylunda Elang. It is a simpler task we have and a pleasurable pile of gelders from the doing. You will be tucked away safely in a calm and quiet place, and when I say tucked away it means that however cleverly you scheme, there you will be until the patron comes to take you home again. And fetch you home he will, he sends to you his sworn word on this." He put stress on the last words, but his eyes slipped away from hers.

"Kak!"

"Ah yes, you will be knowing him better than we. Our ship is yours to wander as you will, but lest you harbor wishful thoughts of taking it from us, you should know we are Jilitera. All things on board shut down after a time unless we whisper to them in the Secret Tongue which is more than words. Consider what it means to drift in darkness for eternity."

"I have heard that," she said. "Tell me the name of my prison."

"Bol Mutiar. Only the Jilitera trade there these days because it is death to outsiders who do not understand its ways. We will tell you how to go and we will put our Blessing on you. Unless you are irredeemably moronic, you will have a pleasant life ahead of you."

3

You will eat some tung akar every day, she read and
sighed as she looked at the knobby, dark yellow tuber
with its beard of fine white rootlets. "You look about
as appetizing as a dog turd. Maybe if I think it's like
taking vitamin supplements. . . ."

*You will bless and treat with courtesy the children of
tung akar.* "Sounds reasonable. Bless? Hope they give
me the local version of that. I've run into a few occasions when my idea of a friendly greeting nearly got
me handed my head."

*The blessing is Smarada Diam. Love and Peace. It
works best if you evoke some shadow of these things
within yourself. This is for formal occasions, when
meeting and greeting folk you have not met before. A
simple Diam is sufficient with those you have met more
than once. Do not concern yourself overmuch with pro-
nunciation; exactitude is not required.*

Lylunda settled back in her chair and watched the
figures moving through assorted greeting scenarios.
She didn't understand the words yet, hadn't gone under
the crown to get the Pandai poured into her head, but
it seemed a simple and mellifluous langue, one that
rolled easily off the tongue. She examined the figures
of the locals with considerably more interest than she
took in the greetings.

They were a smooth brown people, built low to
the ground, broad in shoulder and hip. "Eee! I'll fit
right in." She wriggled in the chair, sighed. "Except
for the hair. If that sample isn't skewed, it's mostly
light brown with a redhead in the mix now and
again."

The figures marched off and a new maxim slid onto
the screen. *Never take a plant or another living thing
for your food or for any other purpose without asking*

*its permission and thanking it afterward. Like the
greeting, this is a part of necessary courtesy. Ignoring
these strictures will not get you slapped, it will get you
dead.*

Lylunda made a face at the images that followed,
bloated, rot-blackened corpses. This was the third time
they'd run the lesson flake for her and those corpses
appeared after every four maxims, along with the stats
now scrolling down half the screen, telling her who the
dead had been and how they'd gotten that way. It was
meant to impress on the viewer how seriously she
should take those maxims, but even a litany of the hor-
ribly dead could get boring if you heard it too often.

When the lesson reached its end this time, the screen
went black and Beradea's voice broke into the silence.
"Come to the comroom, Lylunda 'njai. It's time you
learned the Pandai langue."

4

The Jilitera locked Lylunda in her cabin before they
left the insplit and left her there until the ship was in
a stable orbit.

The journey to Bol Mutiar had been shorter than
she'd expected; though she'd been unconscious for
part of it, it couldn't have been much more than eight
days 'splitting. Which meant they were still within the
Pseudo Cluster, just a hop from Hutsarté and perhaps even closer to the nameless heavy world where
she'd landed Prangarris and his stolen arrays. Which
was a rather unfunny joke on her when she thought
about it.

There was another word that haunted her. Why?

So many whys.

Why were the Jilitera treating her so well? Why
were they teaching her all this?

She knew free traders and how fiercely they protected their markets; she'd heard stories about the Jilitera, who were the most secretive of them all. What she was learning was inside information, something traders never sold or told. *Daddy dear,* she thought. *No doubt he paid them well, he's not stupid, but he has to have some hold on them, he has to know something so bad they'll do anything rather than let it come out. Jaink! It's only a guess, but what else explains this!*

"Lylunda 'njai, will you come to the Bridge, please. It is time that we blessed you."

The smoke that hung thick and greasy in the unmoving air caught her in the throat, and she coughed as she stepped through the door. There was a wide shallow brazier in the center of the floor, wood reduced to coals filling it, the red of the coals muted under gray ash. A layer of resin crystals was spread over them; these were subliming into the air, spreading a heavy sweet perfume. Beradea and Merekea knelt beside the brazier, stripped to the skin, their bodies covered with lines and whorls of thick paint, black and white mostly but with dots of crimson and amber.

Ordonai the Pilot/Owner stood on the far side of the brazier, stripped also, painted white from hairline to heels, with fingerdrawn designs laid on the white in a glistening wet black that kept its sheen after it dried. He beckoned her forward, then flicked his hand up, palm out, to stop her when she'd come far enough. "Eschewat ched doo ayal," he chanted. "Desu telab. Desu telab."

She stood erect and very still, fascinated because she knew she was hearing the secret tongue of the Jilitera, at least that part which she could perceive. And frightened because she shouldn't be seeing this or hearing that, not that she could understand a word of what was being said.

"Dabuxoo devoo," he chanted and held out a hand. Beredea put a shallow bowl in it, a bowl filled with a viscid golden fluid.

Lylunda's eyes blurred and she started getting dizzy. She concentrated on keeping her eyes open and her body still; disrupting this ceremony didn't seem like a very good idea.

"Degoo watuhbey." He held out his other hand.

Merekea dribbled a coarse meal into it until the curve of his palm was filled.

"Da oocid al di sec." He brought his hands around in front of them, held them into the incense rising from the brazier, then let the meal trickle into the fluid. "Lerxuadid." He mixed them together with his forefinger. "Ki ti ada."

Merekea and Beradea rose with a disturbing sinuous grace. For an instant Lylunda saw them as twin serpents, the paint marks converted to scales. They each took one of her arms and led her around the brazier until she was standing before Ordonai.

He chanted something else, but this time she couldn't separate the sounds from the pounding in her ears. At the same time he dipped his fingers into the bowl, scooping up a mixture of liquid and meal. Still chanting, he smeared the thick sticky mess across her brow, down her cheeks, then thrust his finger into her mouth and put another dollop on her tongue.

She concentrated grimly on keeping the contents of her stomach where they belonged.

The women's hands tightened on her arms and Ordonai slapped her lightly on the right ear, then the left, then shouted a great word at her.

It was as if he blew out the lights when his breath touched her face.

5

When she woke, she was stretched out on a patch of grass staring into a clear blue sky. "Huh?"

She got to her feet and touched her face. Someone had washed her clean; the honey mixture was gone. The memory of Ordonai's finger in her mouth hovered queasily for a moment, then she pushed it aside and looked around.

On her right the land sloped steeply down to a narrow white sand beach and beyond the beach blue sea glittered unhindered to the horizon. A short distance off to her left, she saw a wide path paved with white shells that glittered in the brilliant yellow sunlight.

She looked down. She was wearing a clean shipsuit and at her feet was a well-stuffed backpack. And a small square envelope was pinned to the pack.

When she opened it, she snorted. A message from her father.

> *Lylunda Elang,*
> *I won't ask for your forgiveness, only your understanding. I could not protect you here. I will have trouble in these next weeks protecting myself from those who would be delighted to use you to get at me. I have spent on you what I kept for my own safety. I have never forgotten your mother, nor how it felt when she put you in my arms. If Hutsarté were a different place or I were a different man . . . a zuz, there's no point in that. Whatever happens to me, I have made arrangements to free you from your exile if at the end of four years you still wish to leave. You will find all your gear in the pack, including your credit chip. Don't try bribing a free trader to take you offworld. The*

*only traders who land there are the Jilitera and
they would be more likely to kill you than offer
you any help. Be patient, daughter, and stay alive.*

She turned the letter over, but there was no signa-
ture, nothing to point to him, and the glyphs were carefully drawn, all character erased from them. "You're a
cautious man, Father," she said and began tearing the
paper into small pieces, listening to the ripping sounds
with a fierce satisfaction. When she was finished,
though, she remembered the strictures and stuffed the
pea-sized bits into a pocket of the backpack, then
checked the ground to make sure none of them had
blown away.

"No point in standing around here any longer." She
lifted the backpack, got her arms through the shoulder
straps, settled it in place, then crossed the strip of grass
and started walking along the path, the shells crunching under her boot soles.

6

"Lylunda Elang who was once a happily busy smuggler with her own ship, free to go wherever she took a
notion, and who is now a beachcomber exile on a
backwater world, sits in her hand-carved chair at her
hand-made table and prepares to eat her daily ration of
tung akar." Lylunda wrinkled her nose at the thin yellow slices of tuber laid out on the shell someone was
using as a plate. "Which, begging your pardon, O
mighty tung, tastes like mildewed cardboard."

The Pandai in the village had cleared out this house
for her and furnished it with bits and pieces from all
their houses. She didn't ask to whom it had belonged
before or what had happened to them, and the villagers
didn't say. The adults brought her fruits and berries

and fish they'd cooked for her, and the children took turns teaching her how to survive here and provide for herself. Friendly people, the Pandai.

She ate one of the slices, swallowed hastily, and dipped up water from the bowl in the center of the table to wash the taste from her mouth. "Seruchel says in a few days I'll like the taste. Don't know if I believe her. Don't know if I want to believe her. That's what someone told me about pelar and I suppose I was close to getting addicted to the stuff." She ate another slice and reached for the gourd dipper.

Water wasn't a problem here. There was an artesian spring on the side of the mountain that rose like an enlarged pimple in the center of this island. The Pandai had built a system of covered flumes that carried water to the cisterns in all the houses, the overflow dumping into a pond in the round open space at the center of the village—the Belau they called it, the Navel of the World—where the locals kept pet goldfish, five of them, each one longer than her forearm and supposedly as old as the island itself. She'd been introduced to them. Siochel, Blibur, Chadil, Iodes, and Nagarak. Rough translation: Precious, Goldie, Seaflower, Coin, and Halfmoon. With the Pandai watching, all smiles and expectation, she put her hand into the water and one by one they came, rubbing their mouth barbels against her palm, tickling her. Then they circled round her arm, brushing against it as if they were some form of aquatic cats.

Rather pleased with the memory, she washed down the third slice. "Ba da, if something lifted these Pandai from here and dumped them in the Izar, they'd get eaten alive."

When she was nearly finished with her breakfast, eating the bowl of berries, savoring their dark tart/sweet flavor, she heard the tink-tink as someone shook the shell string on the front door. "Who?" she called.

"Seruchel. You ready?"

"Diam, Seru. Come back to the kitchen. I'm just finishing up."

Seruchel was a light brown child with a dusting of darker brown dots across the top of her cheeks and a wide mouth that was always twitching into happy grins. When she came into the kitchen, she had a length of cloth draped across her arm, a green and brown batik print, a pattern of leaves and vines. "Diam, Luna. Mam said you shouldn't be wearing out your mekull clothes, and besides they look so uncomfortable and so hot. She said I should show you how to do the twist at the top and pin it tight. If you want. Fitting the mezu's easy, see?"

She dropped the cloth over the back of the chair and twirled in a quick circle to show Lylunda how the cloth was wound around her body, covering her from just under the armpits to her knees, the top tucked over and pinned in place with a pair of shiny, three-inch thorns.

"Omel oma, I'll try it. You wait here and I'll see how well I manage. And by the way, tell your Mam thanks, I appreciate this."

Though at first Lylunda felt as if the mezu would unwind and drop off every time she took a breath, she found it comfortable and cool. With a little care she could bend in it, kneel, get to her feet without offering more of herself to passing eyes than she'd feel comfortable showing.

"There, Luna. You see that greel hole there?"

"Which one? I see lots of holes."

"But they're all different. Can't you tell?" Seruchel took a step to one side, used her big toe to point out the hole she was talking about. "It's not round like most of the others, and the long side goes with the waterline not against it."

The eccentricity wasn't great, but obvious enough once it was pointed out and the long side was indeed parallel to the foam line of the outgoing tide. "I think I see. It's like that one about a step farther along, isn't it?"

"Uh-huh. That's another greel hole, all right. So watch me." Seruchel drove the point of her digging stick into the sand. "Smarada Diam, O greel, this is a lessoning; we'll not be taking you today." She gave the stick a twist, then shoved the end down with considerable force. The sand flew and a dark scuttly thing with far too many legs went hurrying off. "That's a greel. You usually have a scoop to catch him with and a basket to carry him, 'cause you don't want to touch him till he's boiled in kebui water; he's got this goo on him that'll take your skin off. But, mmmmmm, he's good when he's cooked right."

Shadith watched the scuttler vanish in a spray of sand and water; the last bit of it visible was a long narrow chela tamping the sand into the elongated breathing hole. She decided she'd rather not know what her food looked like when it was running about. Some of the things she'd eaten in cafés at Pit Stops. . . . She shuddered as she trudged after Seruchel.

Seruchel waded into the water beside a tumble of rocks, squatted, and felt about among the sea grass that grew like hair in sheltered areas like this. "Luna, come see."

"What is it, Seru?"

"A nice new clump of tiauch. The ones closest to shore are too young still for taking, but they don't have the sharp edges either." She parted the grass and used her body to create a patch of stillness so Lylunda could look through the water at some purse-shaped grayish lumps that seemed to grow from the stone. "When you gather tiauch, you push a flat lever against the muscle down at the base and work it under until the tiauch comes free, then you drop it in a jug of seawater to keep it fresh. The older ones taste the best and sometimes they have pearls in them. We use them to trade. One old tiauch I saw when I was a kid had five pearls. Of course it was black and ugly and almost dead." She waved the grass back around the tiauch bed, jumped to her feet, waited impatiently for Lylunda to stand, then went trotting on down the beach, pointing out things that a newcomer should know about.

"Oooh! You bringing luck, Luna." The girl ran a few steps, then squatted beside a patch of sand slightly darker than the rest. If you looked at it right, there was a faint iridescent shimmer to the grains. "Telilu, I'm sure of it. Luna, I don't want to lose the place, would you wait here and don't move, I've got to go get Mam."

Lylunda watched Seruchel go running off along the beach, then she frowned down at that irregular stain or whatever it was. "Why do you rev up so much excitement, hm?"

The patch remained enigmatic so she looked out across the ocean. This world was like something you'd see in a happy dream. A blue blue sapphire blue sky with a few shreds of cloud near the horizon. An intensely blue ocean shading to emerald as it neared the shore, small choppy waves with caps of white foam. Wind clean and crisp against her skin, filled with sea smells and just cool enough to feel pleasant as the morning heated up. A white sand beach curved away on both sides, interrupted by black outcrops of obsidian or red brown boulders. Clumps of tall trees with curved trunks flexed to the push of the wind, the

fronds that grew thickly at the apex of each curve rus-
tling loudly as if they spoke to each other.

"You are beautiful," she said and it seemed to her
the trees bowed to her and whispered their thanks.
"Yai! Whirly in the head already?"

She was getting very bored with the scene by the
time Seruchel came running back.

The girl stopped beside her, glanced down at the dis-
colored patch and let out her breath with a popping
sound. "Um . . . Luna, do you mind? Mam says just
smelling Telilu might be dangerous, seeing you're not
part of the Tung Bond yet, so she says you better go
back to the house." She looked unhappy. "And tonight,
you better not come into Chiouti with everyone, 'cause
tel-poisoning is something we can't fix and we don't
want you hurt."

"Tell your Mam, no problem." Lylunda tapped the
child on the cheek and left her standing by the patch,
still looking miserable.

On the way back to her house she saw Seruchel's
Mam Outocha, along with a number of the village
men, hurrying toward the beach. She waved at them,
called out the ritual *diam* and strolled on by, heading
for the house. That night she heard a rhythmic beating
and shouts that almost might have been song from the
village. *Some party. I wish . . . well, never mind, Luna.*
Don't go where you're not wanted.

When she went into Chiouti the next morning, there
was a faint bite to the air; it felt like sunburn when it
brushed against her skin and it made her stomach
cramp. People were usually out talking and doing the
day's chores by this time, but she saw only a few villagers about. A woman slouched in a doorway, head
down, hair falling across her face. Her mezu was
pulled about her, not twisted and pinned in place

and she looked like a bad end to a hard night. A naked man was curled up, snoring, in the shadowed alley between two houses. As she walked past him, nausea caught her in the throat and the cramps in her stomach turned to stabbing pains. She wheeled and ran from the village, kept running until she splashed into the ocean.

She swam a while, then waded back onshore, feeling considerably better and blessing the thoughtfulness of Seruchel's Mam.

7

By the end of her first month on Bol Mutiar, Lylunda knew how to choose her own tung akar—that when the tubers were too young they gave her the runs and a low fever, when they were too old the smell got so bad she couldn't put them in her mouth. You could tell the age by the leaves. Seruchel recited a rhyme for so she could remember what the shapes meant. *Long and narrow, stomach harrow, five holes, too old, three in sight, just right.*

She didn't have to look far to find the tung. As with every other house in the village, the western wall of her house, the one that was away from the shore, had no windows, just a thick covering of vines. Some with flowers, some with seed pods that exploded at a touch when they were ripe. The harvest area was a semicircular patch that grew at the base of the wall.

Her days were filled with little things. Digging shellfish for her meals, collecting fruits and berries from the Common Land. Walking around, exploring the island to see what was on the other side. And going with the children into the jungle that grew on the sides of the mountain and cutting vines for the retting pond or beating the rotted veins to separate out the fibers, rinsing the fibers and spreading them over the mats in the drying sheds on the shore side of the Belau. The Pandai demanded nothing from her, but they asked her if she'd help and it was something to do to fill the long hours of the day. Besides, she felt better when she was paying her way, not depending on the charity of others.

And they all knew why she was here, patting her on the shoulder, shaking their heads, telling her what a good father she'd got, wanting to make her safe. They were cheerful about it, too, expecting her to settle in like they had. *Some of us and all of our ancestors come from somewhere else, for all sorts of reasons. It's better here.* Each of the adults made a point of telling her that. *It takes a while to relax,* they told her, *but in a little you'll feel the tensions and the armor you wore from the old time peeling away. Like a snake sheds its skins and is beautiful in its bright new colors.*

They meant well, but she didn't want to shed her old habits. She wanted to get back to a place where she could practice them—especially her preferred sort of pleasures when it came to getting high or having sex. From everything she'd seen so far, she wasn't going to find many beautiful fur persons to belly dance with her. Celibacy and sobriety for four stinking years did not appeal.

There was another thing that did not appeal. The tung akar was starting to taste good to her. She found herself wanting it at other meals. Somehow everything tasted better after she'd crunched down a few slices of the tuber.

If she ate too much, if she became a part of the Tung Bond, would she be stuck here, for the rest of her life?

She had nightmares about roots coming up out of the

floor and wrapping round her, growing over her face and into the openings of her body.

8

"Grinder!" Lylunda brought the beating stick down hard on the soggy heap of rotted torech ignoring the spatters it sprayed over her. "Father!" Another blow, another spray of stinking green fluid from the vine pile. "Krink!" Another. She laughed and straightened. Using her body like that felt good, and shouting the names seemed to blow away some of the anger that simmered in the pit of her stomach.

Behind her she heard an odd creaking, then a crash. She swung around in time to see a spray of fronds quivering on the ground a short distance up the slope from the beating ground. She dropped the stick on the vines and made her way through snaky twists of vines and small brushy trees to the fronds, followed the trunk along to the men who were glugging down gourdfuls of biang beer to celebrate the success of their efforts. There was a two-handed saw on the ground by their feet and a pair of axes, the first metal tools she'd seen since the Jilitera had landed her here.

"Meki, Gebar, what's this, huh?"

"Wood for fires, Luna. In a couple months it's going to be rainy season, so we need to get green wood dried by then. Gets colder'n you think it would some of those nights and if we want hot meals, we get the wood for cooking now. Even if you think you've seen rain, you don't know what *real* rain is."

"Ah." She frowned at the fat bottom of the tree, an idea churning at the back of her head. "You think you could cut me a round off that, say about as long as my forearm?"

"Sure. Why not, we're going to be cutting it up anyway."

When she finished beating out and washing the torech fibers, she carried them into Chiouti, spread them out on the drying mats, then went back for her chunk of wood. It was light wood, with a papery texture. As she rolled it down the mountain and around to her house, she told herself it was still green and would harden up as it dried.

She set the chunk of tree on her kitchen table and gazed at it while she ate the supper one of the women had made for her.

There was no music on this world.

At least, not on this island. She'd seen birdlike things flying about, but she'd never heard them make a sound. When Seruchel taught her the leaf rhyme, she didn't sing it, didn't even chant it. Nobody whistled here, none of the Pandai sang while they worked. They were cheerful, friendly people, they worked, though not hard, enough to keep themselves in comfort, they carved every surface they could set a knife to, they made bright colored dyes for the cloth they wove. But she'd never seen them dance and she'd never heard them sing.

The food was dust on her tongue and the craving for tung akar was like a fire in her, but she fought it off and continued to stare at the trunk. "Smarada diam, log. You'll be a drum some day. When I'm finished with you. And someday I'll dance to your sound."

For the next month she labored over the piece of stump, hollowing it out chip by chip. She had to be very careful because the grain was so straight, the texture so soft she could break the round she was trying to create with the slightest extra pressure or a careless cut with the knife. A chisel or a gouge would have been better, but the knife was the only tool she owned; her father had carefully removed her weapons before he returned her belongings. Perhaps he was afraid she'd commit suicide with them, but knew she'd need the knife. Or maybe it was the Jilitera who'd purged her pack. It didn't really matter.

As the hole through the middle grew larger and larger, she had to work to restrain her impatience. She wanted to dance. She needed to dance even more than she was coming to need the tung akar. Since she was born, she'd been immersed in music of one sort or another. Her mother was a singer and had clapped hands for her when she was a baby and sung songs for her to dance to when she was older. On her ship she had a library of recordings she played constantly so she lived in sound like a fish in water, only marginally aware of it most of the time, yet needing it for her soul's health.

Seruchel climbed onto the black lava outcropping where Lylunda was sitting and crouched beside her, watching her hands as she chipped away at the interior of the log section. "Diam, Luna. What you making?"

"Diam, Seru. I'm hoping it'll be a drum." Lylunda brushed chips of wood from her mezu, watched them splash into the sea water lapping gently at the base of the rock.

"Oh. I know drums. We don't make them, but the Berotong Pandai have some."

"Berotong Pandai?"

"Mm-hm. Canoe people. They come by two, three times a year." Seruchel wrinkled her nose. "Weird folk, they make me feel itchy when I think about them. They're Pandai like us, but they're unh! different."

"How different?" She turned the log a few degrees

and began working on a new section, tucking away the shudder in Seruchel's voice to think about later.

"Omel oma," Seruchel tapped a short stubby finger against her knee as if she were counting the ways of weird. "They live on those berontas all the time, they're biiiig, like they're two sometimes three boats with a floor built across them and house on that floor. They brag they go all the way round the world each trip. I've never seen the same ones twice, so maybe that's true. We trade stuff with them. Like for axes and knives and needles and stuff like that. They get them from the starmen, they say, and maybe that's true also because Pandai don't work metal."

"And they have drums?"

"They beat on them to let us know they're coming so we can bring out our trade."

"Do they *chorous?*"

"What's *chorous?*"

Lylunda stilled her hands and stared at the girl, startled. The language didn't have a word for dance. She'd used the interlingue without thinking about it. She must have been doing that all along when she thought about the drum and dancing. "Moving to *mousika* ... ah! You don't have a word for that either. I'll show you."

Lylunda carried the knife and the log to the end of the outcropping, set them down out of the reach of the wind, and jumped to the sand. "Stay up there and watch, Seru. And listen."

She moved a few steps until she was standing on sand that was damp enough not to drag at her feet. For a moment she stood with eyes closed, clapping her hands to catch the rhythm she wanted, then she began one of the stamping swaying dances she'd learned from the Tiker worlds, a child's version of the voor tikeri. She wasn't a good whistler, but she did manage to improvise a few trills to the clicking of her thumbs and fingers.

When her mouth went dry, she stopped and walked back to the lava outcrop. "That's *chorous* and a bad attempt at *mousika*, Ser. . . ." She broke off. The girl's eyes were glazed and she was staring out across the water; it was obvious—and disturbing—that she hadn't seen or heard any of Lylunda's performance. "Never mind," she said. "Best, I suppose, that we just forget it. Come on, teach me how to find more tiauch, I've got a want in my mouth for tiauch stew."

When Lylunda had the inside and outside of the wooden ring rubbed smooth, she passed her hands over it, smiling with pleasure in her work. Then she set it aside and went looking for waxberries and chedik vines. The Pandai used the berries to make candles for their scraped shell lamps and, mixed with chemidik, they made good polish for furniture and the inside walls of their houses since that mix kept insects away from the wood. Chemidik came from sap milked from chedik vines and cooked over a slow fire for several days.

Lylunda was getting more than a little tired of things like that. Every time you wanted something, it took days, maybe even months and lots of planning. If you wanted a new mezu, you had to go cut enough pieces of torech vine to fill up the retting pond and wait till the fibers rotted clear of the rest, then you had to beat the fibers, get them spun into thread, then the length of cloth woven on a loom, then you had to dye the cloth, either a solid color or spend yet more time with the tedious process of batiking to get a pattern dyed into the cloth; to set the colors so they wouldn't wash out or fade, you had to steep the cloth in mix of cold water and oma which you made by macerating a fungus that grew from the roots of lalou trees. Everything was like that. The Pandai shared the jobs, but they were always working with an eye on the months ahead, getting things ready so they would be there when they were needed to get other things ready. It wasn't hard work or even unpleasant, it was just so damn constant.

When she first walked up that white sand path that ran along the beach, she thought with despair: How am I ever going to get through the days? What will I do?

She shook her head. "Idiot that's what I was." The more she had to do for herself, the more she wanted additional hours in the day to give her time to get it done.

Lylunda stroked her fingertips down the smooth wood; after the waxing, it had a lovely golden brown glow. "I need something for a drum head. Which could be a problem. They don't do leather, and the cloth they weave is too coarse, too soft, no snap to it. Maybe I should wait until the Barotongs come drifting by." She shivered. "And maybe not. If I cut up the gearsac . . . it's got some bounce anyway . . . borrow a needle from Outocha and hem it so the cord doesn't pull through . . . I'm not going anywhere . . . I wish I knew what I was doing. . . ."

The drum looked good when she was finished, with its matte black heads, its greenish cord, and the golden wood. She reached toward it, drew her hand back. Not yet. It has to be special. *Moonlight. Yes. I'll take it to the beach. I'll play my drum in the moonlight.*

The sky was clear of clouds, filled with the brilliant glitter of the closely packed stars of Pseudo Cluster, enough light to turn the beach into an abstract painting in black and white. The two moons were already high, the outer one a hairline crescent, the nearer, several hours behind it, in its gibbous phase.

She stood, her feet cold on the damp sand, but not so cold as she was inside as she realized just how long she'd spent working on the drum. Days had sneaked away on her ... weeks ... no, more. At least a month and a half. What else had she lost?

She climbed onto the lava outcrop and walked slowly to the pillow humps at its tip, working her tongue in her mouth, seeking to taste how much tung akar she'd eaten without being aware of what she was doing. She couldn't, of course, and it was a silly thing to try, but she had to do something to push back the billows of panic that kept trying to drown her.

She settled herself on the cold stone with the drum between her knees, closed her eyes, and tried to call up music she knew, let it flow through her body. It was hard. As if she were being pushed away. . . .

When she could finally feel a simple beat, she set her fingers on the drum head and began to tap it out.

The sound was thin, dull. There was no resonance. It wasn't music. It wasn't even noise. She could barely hear the sound above the siss siss of the waves.

Maybe it's me, she thought. *I don't know how to make it talk to me.* She closed her eyes and struggled to remember what she'd seen drummers do, but the memories were faint as faded watercolors and they kept slipping away for her.

"Aahhhhh!" she screamed and flung the drum away from her, then sat with her head resting on her crossed arms, her body heaving as she sobbed out her frustration, fear and grief.

9

Lylunda lifted her head as the shell string by the front door clattered and clanked; she sighed and snuggled into her covers, closed her eyes and tried to drift back into the dream she'd been having. It wasn't a pleasant dream, but it was better than being awake.

A hand closed on her shoulder, someone shook her.

She pried her eyes open. Seruchel bending over her, the smiles fled from her mouth. "Luna, Luna, get up. Please."

"Di'm, Seru," she mumbled. "Go 'way."

Seruchel shook her some more, but Lylunda closed her eyes tightly and ignored the child until Seru gave up and left. Then her mind started going round and round about her father, his promise to come get her, how much she didn't believe that, the addiction to the tung akar, her horrified suspicion that if she completed the Tung Bond and he did come, she couldn't leave without the tung killing her. She tried not to think of that, but the notion sat like a dark fungus in her mind.

"Jojing doors without locks. Everybody and his dog can walk in." Muttering obscenities under her breath, she crawled out of bed and stumbled into the kitchen, vomited into the sink, an acrid yellow fluid that she washed away before it made her sick again. She splashed water onto her face, stood leaning against the counter, her body shaking, her knees threatening to fold under her. "What's happening to me? I'm acting like I was three years old and sulking because Ma took my candy away. I'm not like this."

"No, you're not. Diam, Luna."

Lylunda eased herself around, scowled at Outocha. "Seru ran to get you, didn't she. So I don't want to be here."

"We know. Sometimes, Luna, when you fight what is, you only hurt yourself. If you could just accept us, you'd have a good life here."

"Turn Pandai?" Lylunda pushed away from the sink, made it to the table and lowered herself into one of the chairs. "Sit if you will, Outocha."

"Thank you." The Pandai woman arranged herself in the chair across the table from Lylunda, reached out and touched her wrist lightly, then drew her hand back. "Yes. As our elders did. Is our life so bad, Luna?"

"It's a good life for those who like it, but for me, it'd be like cutting off an arm and a leg. I'd have to be someone else, not me. And I'd lose my *mousika*." She watched Outocha's eyes go blank. "You don't have a word for it. You can't even think about it. I want my life back, Outocha."

"You won't have any kind of life if you keep on the way you've been." The older woman reached out again, wrapped her hands around Lylunda's wrists, her thumbs pressed on the big veins; there was electricity in her touch, then a sense of drawing out, as if she pulled strength from Lylunda to augment her own. She closed her eyes, the vertical line deepening between her sun-bleached brows; when her voice came, it had a distant, hollow sound. "It is difficult . . . sometimes . . . to remember . . . my mother told me of . . . of a way to slow the closing of the bond." She got the last words out in a rush, squeezed her eyes more tightly shut. "A tea . . . yes, an infusion of . . . ahhhh . . . of cherar leaves."

There was a long pause. When Outocha spoke again, Lylunda had to strain to hear the faint whisper. "It is dangerous; if you get the wrong leaves, gather them at the wrong time, try to store them, cherar will kill you. You must pick the pale green leaves without the red veins, they're the youngest and the only ones it's safe to use. And you have to gather them when it's light enough to see but before the sun has cleared the world's edge. No more than twelve leaves. You must take a bowl with you and a pestle and mash the leaves into a paste as soon as you've gathered the twelve. You bring the paste home, soak it in cold water, not hot water, never hot water. When the water turns a dark blue-green, you strain it through cloth into a bottle with a wax stopper. You drink two fingers of the liquid a day until it is gone. Then you gather more." her eyes went blank again, her hands left Lylunda's wrists to rest on the table, wholly relaxed with the fingers lightly curled.

Lylunda leaned forward tensely. "Will you show me where to find cherar and what it looks like?"

"What?" Life came back to Outocha's face. She frowned. "Why?"

For an instant Lylunda was as astonished as she'd been when Seruchel wasn't allowed to be aware of music. This was the aspect of the Tung Bond that terrified her most; whatever acted to diminish that bond was counted as enemy and as much as possible not permitted to happen. The kindness of the Pandai woman could for a moment override this, but not for long. *And that's the joy of the telilu,* she thought suddenly. *It lets them remember what the Bond has forced them to forget. No wonder I thought I heard something like singing. Oy, Jaink help me, I have to get away from this world. Somehow....* Aloud, she said, "It's part of my lessoning, isn't it. To learn all the plants of the island, I mean. The bad as well as the good."

"Are you feeling well enough to walk a while?"

"Slow and easy, if you don't mind, but it'll be good for me to get out. You're right, I can't sleep my days away without getting really sick." *Hope,* she thought.

*Better than a hit of pelar. If only she shows me the
right plant. With the Bond pulling her about, who
knows ... when she took my hand she could override
that ... maybe that'll work, she points out the plant, I
take her hand and ask if she's sure ... jojing tung....*

10

Lylunda tilted the cup, then straightened it and
watched the murky liquid oil back down the sides.
Even after the straining it looked like cheap ink that
was beginning to separate its solids from the liquid
base. "Two fingers a day? I don't know...."

Closing her eyes, she downed the mess, then groped
for the water gourd so she could wash the taste from
her mouth. Taste? As if something had solidified the
stench off a slaughterhouse on a hot, steamy summer
day.

Her stomach cramped. She staggered to the table,
caught hold of the edge, and crabbed around it until
she reached one of the chairs. She lowered herself onto
the sea, then she hunched over, hugging herself, rocking from buttock to buttock.

The cramps only lasted a few minutes, then the
churning in her stomach and the pressure against her
sphincters gave her just enough warning to let her
reach the fresher and get herself seated before everything let go.

She spent the afternoon swimming in the sunwarmed
seawater of the small inlet north of Chiouti. The sea
cradled her and fed energy into her. When she reluctantly dragged herself from the water, wrapped a spare
mezu around her shoulders and started walking back to
her house, she felt more like herself than she had in
weeks.

She walked through the village, greeting folk involved in the continual work of supplying themselves with the necessities of life. They smiled and nodded and answered her greetings, but it seemed to her that once again they were on the far side of a glass pane and not quite real as ancient museum dioramas were never quite real no matter how much art was expended in their making. In an odd sort of way it was comforting, a sign that her morning's ordeal was not worthless.

When she showed up later in the afternoon to do her share of the work in the combing and spinning sheds, the women there seemed to have trouble remembering that she was among them though there was the usual laughter and jokes as they passed the hanks of dried fiber about, or wound the spun thread onto cones for the looms. They weren't trying to be unfriendly, but the startled looks when they noticed her and their shaky smiles made her uneasy. She left the sheds after half an hour and went to sit on the lava pile staring out across the blinding blue of the sea.

She tossed a fragment of black rock into the water hissing about the foot of the pile. "I went too far," she said. "Purged too much. I have to find a balance, something that will let me *be* here, but keep my roots shallow enough so I can tear loose without bleeding to death."

After a while she heard a clunking sound, got to her feet, and looked down. The drum she'd spent so much futile effort on was bobbing in the water and bumping against the rocks, driftwood of a different sort. She lay on her stomach, caught hold of the cord that laced the heads on, and pulled it up. The chemidik wax on the wood had kept water out and the working of the sun and the sea had tightened the heads. Water had gotten inside, but only a little, just enough to slosh about when she shook it.

She settled back on the rock and tapped the head. The sound had changed. Or was it that she'd changed? It still wasn't loud or like any drum she remembered, but it sang to her. She closed her eyes and called up the music she and Qatifa had danced to, it seemed a century ago. Tump tump ti tump ti tah tump ti tump. . . .

She played till her fingers were raw and the day darkened toward sunset and the evening breeze came cold off the sea.

In the days that followed she experimented with the cherar infusion and the slices of tung akar, at first alternating them, eating the tung one day, drinking the infusion the next day, then changing the number of the slices and the amount of the liquid until she finally found a balance where the Pandai were easy around her, but she could still hear the music in the drum.

The rains came and brought wild storms with them, but the bulk of the mountain protected Chiouti from the worst of the winds, and the only problem the Pandai had was bringing in enough food to supplement the dried fish that everyone but Lylunda kept in storage jars. They passed her around like a party favor; each night an invitation to share the evening meal came from another family, a call to join in the gossip and play games with the children while the adults were absorbed in one of the intricate games they were addicted to, small distorted figures pushed about on a painted board at the whims of thin, intricately carved sticks cast from a tall cup. Klekool, they called it.

Seruchel had tried to teach her the game, but Lylunda found it impossible; she told herself it was probably something you had to be in the Bond to understand.

The craving for the tung akar came back and she couldn't get up the mountain to fetch more cherar leaves—rain, rain, more rain, mud slides, trees, and thornvines blowing dangerously about, broken fronds, limbs, wheeling on winds that came howling round the mountain. She berated herself for not thinking of something so simple as uprooting one of the plants and transplanting it into a pot of some kind, one she could keep inside the house, but food was around every day and she hadn't given a thought to what day after day of slashing rain might mean. *When I can get up there,* she thought, *the moment I can get up there, I'm bringing a plant down. Maybe it'll die on me, maybe I can't keep it growing enough to make the new leaves I need, but I have to try.*

She fought to limit what she grubbed from the tuber patch, but in the intervals when the rain lessened to a heavy mist, the smell of the tung blossoms crawled through the windows and tickled at her and she'd find herself out there, mattock in hand, digging tubers.

The drum sat in a corner of the kitchen collecting cobwebs and dust.

In the second month of the rains, she played her first game of klekool and almost understood the nuances of the moves. She was the bangg at the end, bangg being a bright colored fish of extraordinary stupidity and ugliness. The only reason the species survived is that no one—beast, fish, bird or Pandai—who ate one bangg ever ate a second. The taste of bangg was awful beyond the capacity of human description. The family teased her and laughed at her, and she plodded home through the rain feeling vaguely pleased with herself.

* * *

By the end of that month the heaviest of the down-pour was finished. There was still a thundershower almost every day sometimes between noon and mid-afternoon, but it was possible to go up the mountain again to gather fresh food and cut trees for fuel, bringing the chunks to the drying sheds where the fibers had been before.

Lylunda went to gather waxberries for candles; she had only one left of those she'd made and she needed to begin the long process of giving back all the care that had been taken of her during the rains. As she gathered the berries, she saw a patch of cherar nestling deep beneath the brambles. She felt a sudden strong revulsion, as if she'd seen a viper; in spite of that, she stared and stared at the dark succulent leaves with the brilliant red veins. She wanted to vomit, she was terrified, but she remembered why she knew the cherar and she understood that all she'd gained before the rains she'd lost. She'd have to start all over again, finding a new balance, fighting nausea and the runs again, fighting the pull of the tung akar.

The next morning she overslept, woke with the sun streaming through the cracks in the shutter onto her face. She fought the craving, ate a single slice of tung akar and took the basket of berries into the village so she could use the single big boiling pot the village had to boil them and skim the wax, then pour it into molds with the wicks she'd gotten for her help with the fibers. Working was hard and hot, she had to stir the berries constantly so they wouldn't stick to the bottom and burn, but the work helped her forget the clamoring of her body as it demanded more tung akar.

The big green berries had a sharp, pleasant scent, and the wax she skimmed was a pale green with a muted version of that scent. Burning the candles perfumed the house, and they also kept away the small bloodsucking insects that were hatching now from every pool where rainwater was sheltered enough to turn stagnant.

By the end of the day she had two dozen candles. She left six for the use of the kettle, ladled the basket full of the pulp and took it uphill to spread it on her tung patch; it was useful mulch, gave nutrients to the soil, and it kept saw flies away from the vines.

All that night she sat at her kitchen table, beating on it with a pair of spoons. She got no feeling from that sound, there was no rhythm beating in her blood, but it kept her awake. When dawn came, she took the bowl and pestle, left the house, and went up the mountainside.

When she pushed the waxberry vines aside, she could only find seven cherar leaves without the red veins. She plucked them carefully, mashed them, then carried them back down the mountain, walking slowly, warily. The tung was everywhere, it knew what she was doing, vines reached out to trip her, a flitterbat dived at her, nearly knocked the bowl from her hand, a frond from one of the trees cracked loose and almost crashed down on top of her. But she threaded her way through these attacks, or what she thought of as attacks, her mind and body in a dark knot of suspicion and rage.

Though the infusion was weaker, the racking her body went through this time was considerably worse.

The next morning when she woke, the food basket was empty and no one rattled the shell chain by the door. She was cut off again, isolated. When she went out to get fresh tung for her breakfast dose, the smell of the flowers nauseated her so much she could barely endure the time it took to dig up a small tuber. The smell and taste of the tuber when she got it washed off and sliced was so bad, she had to chop it into small bits with her knife because she couldn't force herself to chew it. She got it down and spent the next ten minutes hunched over in the chair trying not to vomit.

When her stomach settled a little, she managed to swallow a few berries left over from yesterday's breakfast; then she took the drum and went down to the beach to sit on the lava and talk out her problem, herself talking to herself because until she was stabilized again, no one from the village would *see* her and they wouldn't understand anyway what she was fussing about.

She settled with the drum and began tapping out a rhythm, relaxing into a full-body smile as she felt the beat and responded to it. A tune came to her and she whistled a snatch of it and it was like cool water across her ears and along her nerves. Ignoring the short burst of rain that beat on her back and head, she drummed until her hands grew tired, then leaned on the drum and stared out across the water.

"The rains come twice a year they say. And even if I believed that lying letter, even if he does send for me, it'll be four years. Four years! I can't go through this again and again and again, each time worse than the last. Four years? No way. I don't know. Maybe I should just give up. No! It'd be like killing myself. Maybe I should do that and cut out the middle man. Dead is dead. No problems left. No. I won't give up, I'm not going to let him win. Or let the stinking Kliu off me, because that's what it'd be, them pulling my strings. I've got to get away from this world somehow. Only one way to do that. Find a free trader and use his splitcom and call someone. Qatifa maybe. All right. That's it. Now the only problem is how."

She brooded over that for several hours, then trudged up the beach and over to her house. She left the drum there, went to gather food for her supper and breakfast. She'd be on her own for the next several days, until she'd gotten the mix right and the Pandai would notice her again.

10

Lylunda drew the pole knife across the torech vine, stepped back to let the sticky white sap drip from the cut, then finished slicing through the vine and used the hook set into the back of the blade to pull the vine away from the tree trunk, twisting it to break loose the tendrils that had knotted themselves into the fibrous bark. She grimaced as the black flies that she'd dislodged with the vine swarmed about her face and shoulders. She'd rubbed herself with juice from waxberry leaves, but the effect was starting to wear off and the flies were landing and biting.

The vine rustled away as Seruchel and Beroos tugged it free of the tangle. The two girls would strip off the tendrils and the leaves and wind the length into a coil for Emiud to pick up when he came by and carry over to the retting ponds.

Before she started work on the next section of vine, Lylunda crossed to the water jug and poured herself a cup of water, then stood sipping at it and watching as the girls worked with their tiny crescent-shaped knives, nip nip scrape, tug another section in front of them. She pushed the hair back from her face. "The Berotong Pandai, Seru. Should we expect them soon?"

"Mm hm. They usually come around when the time of the big storms is past. You've got those pearls you found, you should be thinking about trading for a pot. Me ..." She giggled and poked her elbow into Beroos' arm. "I'm going for stuff I need for my gonna-be family, you know, needles and a knife and maybe some beads just for me. Mam says it's time to start thinking about gonna bes. She says probably next year I'm a woman and the year after that, maybe there's a chebech feast and I go move in with. . . ." She giggled again, blushed a little. "What you thinking about trading for, Berry?"

"I think those red dyes like Aleko got last year. I like red and it's so hard to get a good bright color."

"Red. Chebech color." Seruchel dropped her knives and clapped her hands. "Who you gonna go with, Berry? Tommas? I saw you'n him the other night."

"Silly Serry, 'tisn't just for chebech mezus; your own Mam puts red in her batiks. Anyway nothing's settled yet."

Lylunda looked at the smiling pink face of the girl, shook her head, and took up the pole knife again. She couldn't be more than fourteen. *Not that I've anything to brag about where I come from. What do you call a teenage femme in the Izar? Mother. That's what. Which brings up another thought. I've got my implants, but who knows what the tung is doing to those? Anyone around here want to wager that the tung akar doesn't like antifertility drugs?*

She separated out a second vine of the proper diameter, cut one end free as high as she could reach, and hooked the vine away from the tree. Pulling with the hook and prying with the blade, she unraveled it as far as she could from the rope of smaller vines that looped from tree to tree, then cut that section loose.

When she finished, she looked back. Seruchel and Beroos were working over the vines again, the knives flying as they cleaned the stem, but they'd looped it around so their heads were close together and they were whispering and giggling together. A pang of longing and loneliness surprised her. She wanted that intimacy again. But not here. Never here. Back to dangerous hauls and high times in the Pits, belly dancing

with Qatifa or another of the partners she'd found in
the past five years. She wanted that so terribly that for
a moment her eyes blurred. Then she shook off the
malaise and went back to work cutting the vines and
trying to plan her escape from all this.

*The Berotong ... the canoe Pandai ... they traded
with the Jilitera ... maybe with other ships ...
Ordonai said only Jilitera came here, but maybe that
was hope more than truth ... maybe ... this place is
spooky enough to scare off some of the free traders I
know ... but not all of them ... if there's a reason to
be here, there'll be others ... maybe the Canoe Pandai
don't tell the Jilitera everything ... maybe? Odds are
good on that if they're anything like the Chioutis ... if
I can convince them to take me along ... how? I have
to talk with Outocha ... she's the only one who's tried
to help ... maybe. ...* She sighed and moved on to the
next rope of vines.

She worked at cutting vines until her arms were
trembling and her joints started aching. This was something else that worried her. With the tung and the
cherar warring inside her, she had no stamina at all.
*When I get away ... when when when ... let it be
when not if ... when I get back where I belong, I'll
spend some of the crystal money on a work-over at the
nearest meatfarm. Jaink! I won't go like my mother. I
won't!*

She was sitting on the lava outcropping singing a
sad song to the whispery tump ta of the drum when she
heard what at first sounded like an echo—but an echo
louder than the source. She sat up and listened, her
hands on the drumhead.

TOOM TOOM TOOM came across the water, blown
on the brisk wind that swept the whitecaps off the
waves. She set her drum aside and jumped to her feet,

stood staring in the direction of the sound, holding her breath in shock and desire as a horn of some kind wove a simple tune about the drumbeats.

A raft came gliding around the end of the island. No, not a raft, a trimaran with three crescent-shaped bows rising dark and elegant from the water, a fenced floor built across the middle of the three hulls, a large triangular sail on a central mast and a smaller jib cleated to a stay from the tip of the central bow to the top of that mast. A Pandai in a red mezu stood on the floor in front of one of the structures built on it, beating on a broad drum half as tall as he was. Beside him a smaller figure wrapped in bright gold stood blowing into a huge shell.

As the beronta came closer, the size became more evident. It was huge. No wonder Seruchel said the Berotong Pandai spent most of their lives on their canoe. Their beronta.

She stood shading her eyes and watched it come sliding along the coast, moving at a speed that surprised her. When it was even with the outcropping, it was close enough for her to see children hanging perilously over the railing round the deck, waving at her. She waved back, then snatched up her drum and went running for her house.

By the time she reached the village, half a dozen small boats were tied up at the jetty, and the open space was swarming with Berotongs and Choutis. Standing in a ring of laughing preening girls, a teen boy blushed and smiled and was gradually recovering his poise enough to laugh and answer the girl's teases with quips of his own that made them giggle and wiggle into the closest thing Lylunda had seen to a dance since she'd been here. She smiled and eased through the crowd until she was standing next to Outocha. "Who's the boy?"

"He's from Emtoched, that's an island about two days west of here. All the girls on Emtoched are either too young or related to him, so he's traveling with the Berotong till he can find a girl he likes and a village to settle into."

"And we have several extra girls here. Do girls travel, too?"

"Sometimes. If she's eighteen or more and no one's come by that she likes."

"I see. So they do take outsiders on those berontas?"

Outocha didn't look at her, but as usual she cut through obliquity with the razor of her mind. "That might be a good idea, Luna. Perhaps the Berotong life would suit you better than ours. You are welcome here, but we do want you to be happy."

Lylunda wandered about, listening to the gossip from the other islands, watching the rituals of trade, watching the boy maneuver around local boys his age, another sort of courting ritual. It couldn't be easy, making himself welcome in a new place—even with the Bond to help.

She walked out to the end of the jetty and stood looking at the beronta, wondering what it'd be like to live so cramped together for so long.

"Her name's *Remeydang*."

Soaring House, she thought. *Nice. And a bit disconcerting.* She turned her head, smiled at the Berotong boy. "Pretty name," she said. "How far do you go?"

"Round the world and round again." He had sun spots like Seruchel, looked a little like her when he grinned. "Me, I've only been halfway so far." His hand was closed in a loose fist and he was shaking it gently, two shells or stones or something similar clicking together inside the fist, making a small music. "Name's Tudil."

"Mine's Luna, Tudil. Smarada diam."

"Diam," the boy said, then looked startled when he saw her catch and echo the beat, snapping her fingers and swaying her body; after a moment's thought, his face lit up. "You're the star woman."

"Yes." *The Bond,* she thought and groaned silently. "I miss *mousika.*"

"Huh?"

"That."

"Oh. Chelideyr."

"I don't know that word."

"Well, you wouldn't. The land Pandai don't have it. It's only us Berotongs who can know what it is and that's because it's part of the sea dance."

"I tried making a drum. It's not very good."

"Would you like to see ours?"

"Oh, yes. I'd love that. Would your folks mind?"

"Why should they? It's not like you're going to steal the beronta." He grinned again, slipped his clickers into a pouch on his belt, then swung over the side of the jetty into one of the boats tied there. "So come on down."

"Mengar, toss the ladder. I've brought a visitor."

One of the oldest Pandai that Lylunda had seen peered over the rail at them, his mouth stretched in a broad grin showing mostly toothless gums. "Star mama, hah? Treat her gentle, boy."

Lylunda blinked, startled.

Tudil chuckled. "Omel oma, Luna, don't be worried by him. Ol' Mengar sniffs all the news in the world from the air that runs past that nose of his." He caught the rope ladder as it unrolled down the side of the outer hull. "Can you climb if I hold this steady?"

"I can climb better if I do the following," she said.

He giggled, shook his head. "Omel oma, watch close, then." He went up the ladder as if he had fingers instead of toes, shook his narrow behind at her, then was over the rail with an easy kick of his feet.

She followed more cautiously, but found it no more difficult than working an umbilical in an unlicensed fueling station. She got over the rail with a bit more decorum than the boy, then let the two Pandai show her about the ship, smiling at their pride, but understanding it thoroughly, a small ache around her heart because her own ship was so far out of her reach.

Tudil led her to the Great Drum, but he didn't touch it, so she didn't either. He slid out some pegs and opened the top of a chest, took out two much smaller drums, closed the top again, and pegged it tight. "We practice on these," he said.

"May I?"

"You are my guest."

She turned the drum in her hands, tested the weight of it, drew her fingers across the single head. Parchment. Someone on Bol Mutiar knew about skins and how to treat them. The wood was dark and tight grained, hard enough to carve thin. She sat on the chest, held the drum on her knees, and tapped the head. The sound was sharp and pure. It was joy. She closed her eyes and touched it some more, testing the different areas of the head, using all the hand gestures she could remember. Then she made a song for herself and Tudil with her hands and this giving drum.

After a minute, though, she sighed and stilled the sound. "Better than food," she said. "But I don't know how to play it, not really."

Tudil was crouched by her feet, looking up at her. "But it's there. It's in you. You should come with us, not stay with them on land. You don't belong there."

"I don't belong here at all," she said and sighed as she bent to give him back the drum. "My father forgot I'm not a child any more. But that's the way he is. He thinks he knows better than most people how to run their lives and he has the power, so he does it."

Tudil nodded gravely. "I've seen that," he said. "The Bond rejects folk like that. After a while, anyway. And then they die."

"Either you're in the Bond or you die? Is that the way it is? What about the traders?"

"They respect the Bond, they don't hurt any Pandai and they leave in a few days." His teeth closed on his lip and his eyes glazed. After a minute he said, "You're fighting the Bond. Trying to be with it but not of it. You want to be like them. The traders. Come and go."

"Yes. Traders. Do you know if there are different kinds of traders or only those who call themselves Jilitera?"

Tudil looked down. He scratched uneasily at a sliver that was separating from the wood of the deck. "Maybe you should talk to Menget about that, he's the Drummer. I could ask, if you want." He sighed. "You think you can't play, but I watched you, you know things about the drum I hadn't even thought of. I wish you'd want to be of us."

"I can't, Tudil. I think the land Pandai's life is good, and yours is even better, but not for me. It's just the way things are. I'd like it if you talked to the Drummer about what I asked." She got to her feet. "Thank you for showing me your home. I think we'd best be going back now."

11

The Drummer came to Lylunda's house that evening; he was a big burly man; he wore his coarse brown hair in a thick braid that reached past his waist. A large enameled copper amulet covered most of his bare chest and his dark red mezu was narrower than most, wrapped about his hips, the set-fold held in place by a long steel pin with an enameled copper head and a copper point guard. When she greeted him, he touched his forehead, then the amulet. "Smarada diam, Luna."

"The kitchen is the kindest place to sit. There's fruit if you wish and an infusion of iya leaves."

He sat at the kitchen table and smiled as she brought out a plate heaped with dark purple-red berries and slices of golden imekur fruit. She filled two mugs with the iya, then settled herself across from him. "What I have is yours," she said. "May it be acceptable."

"It is so." He helped himself to the fruit and took the first bite as was custom, then spooned down the rest with a gusto that matched his size.

When he was finished, he patted his lips with the napkin she'd laid beside the plate and smiled at her. "You have had a difficult time, Luna."

"Yes."

"And coming here was neither your choice nor your intent."

"Yes."

"What do you know of the Berotong Pandai?"

"What the Chioutis have told me, what Tudil said, what I saw when I visited your beronta. What I heard when the beronta came around the end of the island. That you will take young people from where they are excess to where they are needed. No more."

"Then you know everything and nothing." He

pushed his mug across the table, waited till she refilled it. "We are of the Bond, but we live within it in another way than the Land Pandai do. We eat the tung akar when we are on the land, but when we are on the sea, we do not touch it. You might find that more to your heart's liking, Luna. Tudil tells me you have a gift for the chelideyr but no teaching."

"Tudil is young. I have a deep need for chelideyr, but no gift. It's just that I've listened more widely than he has and known more drummers. I was remembering, not creating. I do know the difference."

"Ah. I see." He lifted the mug and drank, his eyes fixed on the window open above the sink. She could see he was thinking something out and she understood what it was when he spoke again. "The Jilitera have been forbidden to take you away or let you call for help," he said, "so you want to know if there are other traders who come here."

"You have it."

"You've been here almost half a year. Do you understand that even with the cherar you drink and the purging you've forced on yourself, it is not likely you can live away from the tung akar?"

"I don't know that, though I'm afraid that's how it'd go." She sighed. "I have resources if I can reach my friends. With enough coin you can buy almost anything." She held up her hand to stop his objection. "Out where I come from, I mean."

"Why would you want to go back to that?"

"Because it is *my* life. Not something imposed on me. It's something I've reached out and taken for myself. Do you understand?"

"Yes. It is my duty and my pleasure to take you with us on the beronta *Remeydang* to the place where we meet the trader Tangavik. You will need patience, Starborn; it will be another half year before we reach the landing place. He comes every third year, slipping down under the Jilitera's noses, and this year is one of those. I read that as an omen and a command."

Three days later Lylunda hugged Seruchel, touched cheeks with Outocha, then climbed into the small boat and let Tudil row her out to the beronta *Remeydang*.

Three hours later, she stood at the back rail, out of the way of those working the ship, and watched the island Chiouti slip slowly over the horizon.

12

Worm Wriggles Faster

1

"The Harman be blessed, at least it's stopped raining."
Worm patted at is head with the towel he'd set beside
the EYEscreen; even with the sun close to setting, the
air inside the room was so steamy he was worried for
his equipment. He'd moved the table close to the window so he could shut it once the EYE was outside, and
the conditioner unit was struggling to wring out some
of the heat and damp, but sweat kept rolling from his
hair into his eyes, making them burn and blurring his
vision.

He was following the target home a last time, making sure the afternoon deluge hadn't changed her habits
or the habits of her watchers. If this was what the rainy
season meant here, it wasn't such a bad thing he had to
move up the snatch. He felt mold growing in every
crevice of his body. "And last week I was wishing it
would rain. Zull!"

Lylunda walked briskly, circling the puddles. "Wise
woman," he muttered. "Who knows what grunge is in
that slop."

It was Arkel on guard duty—big man, rather stupid.

Worm had cleaned him more than once at hezur-hairi; he kept coming back, his faith in his luck untouched by experience. Arkel slouched along half asleep, splashing into puddles and out again, going through the motions. Too bad it wasn't him tomorrow. Rodzin was the sharpest of the four; he was bored by the guard duty and slack at the job, but if he sniffed trouble, he could turn mean real fast. Worm swore. Anything to make his life harder.

When Lylunda reached her home street, she stopped at Okin the Baker's shop, came out with a loaf of bread in her net bag, looking over her shoulder, grinning and trading sass with someone inside. At Sutega's Take Out next door, she added a cooked bird and two closed containers to the bread, joked with Halfman Ike, and turned into her doorway still laughing.

"You're in a good mood," Worm said. "I wonder if I should worry about that."

A stocky man in a black leather vest with brass buttons stepped into the alcove behind her as she fitted the a key into the topmost lock. The two guards with him stood back, wary and taut-bodied, stunners in their hands. "Enemy territory," Worm said. "Behilarr from up the hill. Bad news?" He flew the EYE closer, clicked on the speaker so he could hear this real-time.

"Elang-mun Lylunda?"

"Courier? Whose?"

Worm scowled at the screen. *Courier? What's that about?*

"The Anaitar of the Erzain. Hizurri-jaz Gautaxo. And you are Elang-mun Lylunda?"

"Yes. So?"

He handed her a bit of paper with a slash of wax on it. She broke the wax and read the note, then she tore

the paper in half, tore it again and again. "Hold out
your hand. You'd best see he gets these back. I'm to
come with you?"

"If you will, Elang-mun."

Puzzled by her reaction and alarmed by this irrup-
tion of enigma into his plans, Worm sent the EYE after
the two of them, following them up through the Low
City and into the level of the great Houses until they
went into a huge pile of stone up by the Temple. He
didn't know what for sure what that place was, but it
had a familiar smell. Cop shop. No way he could take
the EYE inside there.

"Zoll! I bet it's those joddadin Kliu. They messing
me up again." He scratched at his nose with his free
hand, shook his head. "And maybe not. Looked like
she knew what this is about and I don't think she'd
be so calm if it was Kliu. Is it worth hanging around
to see if she comes out again?" He established the
EYE on a ledge of the Temple, focused it on the front
of the cop shop, and set the alarm to tell him when the
woman came out. "Arraaa, I'll be glad when this is
over." He shed the control glove, got to his feet with a
groan, and went to work, packing the belt sac for the
job.

"Sleep gas six caps, timers for caps, nose plugs two
pair, Zombi cartridge, injection gun. . . ."

The soft beeping brought him hurrying back to the
table. He slid his hand into the glove, activated it, then
checked the screen.

Four figures had emerged from the gate and were
walking down the street, the courier first, the woman
in the middle, the guards coming along behind.

Worm took the EYE closer, managed to get a look at

the woman's face. Not Lylunda, but a woman wearing her clothes and fixed up to look like her; she even moved like Lylunda.

He flew the EYE above the cop shop, high enough so he could see all four sides of the massive pile and the streets around it.

During the hours that followed, individuals came and went, mostly men but also a few women. None of them were Lylunda in any sort of disguise. There were no boxes or chests taken in or out. Nothing like that came from any of the other houses nearby.

By morning he was too tired to go on with the vigil and didn't see any point in keeping the EYE hovering up there. Either she was still inside, or whoever had her brought there had gotten her out the back before the decoy left. Besides, it was starting to rain, light rain, not a storm, just a steady downfall—a monotonous drip drip drip that made him want to scream.

He brought the EYE in, closed the window, set the scrubber on high to pull the damp from the air and began to pace back and forth across the room, fighting to stay awake and keep his mind working. He had pepperpops if he needed them, but he didn't trust the fake clarity of mind they gave him. Xman swore by them, but if you didn't keep a firm hold on him, Xman would always be rushing the trap and tripping over his own feet.

"First thing. I need some sleep. That's all right. Fits the pattern I've set up. Hit the warehouse the usual time. Hope Bug's around. Yes, he's the best source. If he knows the woman's gone missing, he'll be wanting to talk about it. See if I can bust loose round midnight, get across to Kanti and put in a call to the Kliu. They won't bother talking to me if they've got her, so if I get bounced, I better call Fa, 'cause I dunno what else I can do." His stomach knotted at just the thought of telling his father he'd missed again. He swallowed nervously and went on pacing.

"If it's not them, then all I can think to do is watch Digby's agent. She's here in deep cover, so I'm fairly sure it can't be her working with the locals, but looks like she's a smart 'un or she wouldn't be here at all." He went over to the table, looked down at the dull ovoid of the deactivated EYE. "Hm. Think I'd better retire you. Shouldn't be too hard to find out where she's staying . . . peep that place, set for passive collect, transmit on code . . . and her dressing room . . . no, maybe just an ear there, she wouldn't be up to funny stuff at Tank's, but she might say something useful. . . ."

He collected the recordings from his web of bugs that he hadn't yet watched, clicked the flakes into the viewer and began playing them. As he listened, he began the activation and reconfiguration of the new peeps and ears which he planned to plant as soon as he got back from calling the Kliu.

2

When Worm recognized the pattern of splotches on the ugly face, he almost vomited with relief.

The Kliu didn't wait for him to speak. "You have her?"

"I'm working on it. Why I called, sources tell me the Kliu have asked the local cop shop to pick up the woman. You're making it harder when you stir up the locals like that."

"Cop shop?"

"You know what I mean. How come?"

"What we do is none of your business, srin. What's taking you so long to get about yours?"

"You want the Behilarr screwing a joddida humungous fine outta you by way of Helvtia for interfering with a local on her own world? What I'm saying is, back off."

"And what I'm saying to you, srin, is your brother Mort butchered two Kliu guards a week ago and we'd be stretching him over the nearest mrav-hole if he weren't in escrow to that miserable family of yours. Don't push too hard or wait too long, srin. Or what you'll get back will be well-polished bones."

The screen blanked.

Worm slumped in the chair, closed his eyes, and just breathed for a while. The good news was that they didn't have her. He would have cursed Mort's stupidity, but one doesn't curse one's brother, so he shoved that thought away. He was so tired, and it was clean and cool here on Kanti's Bridge. He didn't want to leave; he wanted to crawl in his bunk and sleep for a week.

After a few moments, though, he got to his feet and went down to the flikit's berth. There were Mort and Xman and Fa to take care of; he had no choice but to go back across the stinking ocean and climb into his stinking life on Zurg's Star Street and see if Digby's agent had come up with some new angle.

3

Flake 10. Audio. EAR in Tank's Office.
Tank here. Get me on to Grinder.
Grinder here. What's this about?

The new singer, she's asking questions about the Elang.

Kliu Spy?

Don't think so. She's the real thing when it comes to music and she's got the kind of background it wouldn't be easy to set up. Says she's got a message she needs to pass on private-like; says it's a favor, so no big deal if it doesn't happen. What you want me to tell her?

[extended period of silence]

When's she leave your place?

Hour past midnight. She's got two more sets to go.

Call her to your office before she leaves and tell her you've put word to your Touch over here, but she's not to talk to anyone else about the Elang. Send her off sweet. Got it?

Got it.

> Flake 11. Band 6 Aud/Vid.
> Peep in Singer's LQ.

[Door opens. Krink walks in. Two men follow, carrying the body of the Singer. A third carries her harp in its case. They dump her on the bed, set the harp beside the door; then while Krink watches, the three men proceed to search the room, checking out everything the woman owns. There isn't much to check, just some clothes and a few flakes that are professional recordings. The entire time they are there, not a word is spoken.]

> Flake 11. Band 13 Aud/Vid.
> Peep in the Singer's LQ

[The singer comes in, stops, sniffs, looks around. Her head stops moving when she sees folder that the men in band 7 had left there. She goes back out the door.]

"Orrialdy, you around?"

"Shadow, so?" [the voice is faint as if from a distance]

"Think you could bring me up a pot of your tea?"

"That I could. Right now?" [still distant]

"If you will. Door'll be unlocked."

[Some minutes later a big plushy woman brings in a tray with a pot, a mug and a plate of wafers. The singer is seated at the room's sole table. She closes the folder as the woman approaches, takes the tray.]

"Thanks, Orrialdy."

"Well don't you work too hard, not good for your eyes, dear."

[As soon as the woman leaves, the singer fills the mug, opens the folder again, and begins studying the papers inside. The peep is at the wrong angle to get a good look at the pages, but they seem to be lists of something. She studies them intently. Time passes. The only sound is the click of the mug against the table when she sets it down, the rustle of paper—until something catches her attention.]

"Sar! First Sapato, now Harmon. Arms dealers I have known. Hm. He dropped a cargo in one of the warehouses, it was picked up three days later by a Chandava merchanter. Definitely old home week. Note doesn't say what the cargo was, but are we really baffled? And the answer is no."

Worm stretched, rubbed his eyes, and considered what he'd seen. "Harmon. What'd I hear about Harmon . . . gotcha! Arms dealer. Blew his last two sales and is running on debt. Lifting gray freight to keep eating. Looks like Grinder thinks Lylunda was took offworld and has set the spy to figuring out how and who. If she was somewhere in backcountry, he'd have her by now. The Kliu are clueless." He grinned. "Bad Worm."

The lift to his spirits was brief, though, and he went back to brooding. "Those lists. Ship landings. If Harmon's as bad off as they say, he'd sell his grandmother and keep his mouth shut about it." He glanced at the screen.

The Singer was lifting the harpcase. She slipped the strap over her shoulder and went out. "The table's clean. The papers are gone. What's she up to now? If she's on the move. . . ." He scowled at the screens set up on the table. Most of his gear was packed in the lockboxes of the flikit; he wanted to be ready to jump when the spy did and figured he wouldn't have much time for packing. "I can always set up again . . . leave the EARS and the peeps . . . you're working Xman time, Worm. So do what he'd do and jump."

He broke down the screens and the flaker, packed them in their case and stowed the case in the flikit. He locked the door and the shed and scurried for Star Street. And almost ran into the spy as he came charging from a sidestreet onto the walkway.

He slowed to an amble, stopped to look into one of the windows of Kautkas' Anything Shop when the spy paused to talk to Getto. He didn't have to strain his ears to hear what she said. *Announcing it to the world,* he thought. *She's definitely got plans.*

". . . even look at water. Gonna make another song?"

"Want to. Might. They come when they come, you know." She fluttered her fingers at him and went on her way.

Hiring a flit? Going out over water? Zoll! She's got it. Found something in those papers. Harmon. That's it. She's figured out he's the one took Lylunda. Bet any-

thing on that. And she's heading for her ship, going after him. . . .

He snapped his fingers as if he'd forgot something and went hurrying back the way he'd come.

4

As Worm swung the flikit south, skimming just above the long surges of the ocean waves to avoid being spotted from Haundi Zurgile and chased by the local authorities, he saw a dark seed flying low over the water near the northern horizon. "Must be the spy's flier." He clicked on the screen and focused the pick-ups north—and blinked at the gyrations of that flier; it was swooping in long arcs, racing low enough to cream the water, lifting and darting about like a waterbug having fits.

"What's all that? Has she lost it?"

The flier turned suddenly and swooped north, vanishing over the horizon. Worm took a chance and sent the flikit higher. He saw the flier swoop toward the first of the island chain, a hump of rock with a tree and some seagrass, dart round it, dive toward the next island. He saw something else, too—another flier hovering over toward the land. "Gotcha. Grinder or the local lice. She knows the watcher is there and she's holding cover until she can get loose enough to run for the Wild Half."

He dropped the flikit again and squeezed all the speed out of it that he could manage when he was flying this low. Too bad he couldn't go up-and-over, but the locals got mean with any unauthorized flights they happened to spot. He understood that. It was a matter of cash; they wanted their passage fees and their storage fees and their taxes.

He'd gotten most of what he needed from the

woman, a new target. He was going after Harmon, going to get there first and shoot the clot full of babble, pry out of him where he left the woman and go pick her up. No more fussing about, catering to locals. He didn't have time for that. He wasn't happy about having to admit to his father that someone had scooped the smuggler out from under him again, but he needed his father's sources. Fa would know where Harmon was headed next. He kept up on that kind of thing. Funny how he could, since he was stuck in that Sustainer back on Teripang. The drain of keeping him alive was why Worm and Mort and Xman had to do so much work. More coin. All the time more coin, so Fa could pamper his sources. Sasa, this time for once, that pampering might pay off.

When he'd nearly reached the shore of the Wild Half, he heard the scream of a full-power lift and saw the flare of a ship's drivers burn an arc toward the Break-Point.

"Zoll! She wasn't heading here, the bint went and nicked the Elang's ship." He grinned. "I like her. She's got class. She really must have come here on a worldship as part of her cover. Din't have her own, knew one was handy, so she went out and got it." Neat solution to the problem of getting away from Grinder without handing him her head.

The locals started firing at her. He saw the dot seem to jump sideways, the missiles swerved and missed. Then she was gone.

He tapped the controls, had the flikit berth open and waiting as soon as he reached the canyon. He left the servos to locking the flikit down and raced toward the Bridge. If he could just get into the air fast enough and into the insplit behind her, he could track her. That way he wouldn't have to bother Fa; he could put off the skin peel he was bound to get when he had to tell him what happened.

"Spy, sweet spy, I owe you a favor. Now let's see if I can get off this mudball without a sting up my tail."

13

More Detours

1

Shadith slid the *Dragoi* into the berth next to Digby's
ship in the University tie-down, took the shuttle to the
surface and a hopper to the main campus at Citystate
Rhapsody, an immense complex on the coast of the
largest of the three continents. As one who owned Voting Stock, she had a studio apartment in one of the
Megarons. She'd kept it even though it was likely
she'd not spend much time there, because it meant
she'd always have a place to go no matter what happened to the job with Digby.

It felt good to be back, clicking along in a
chainchair, basking in the sunlight of a late spring day
and watching the crowds of students and Scholars
moving through the streets. She didn't see any faces
she knew, but she'd been on Digby's payroll nearly
three years now and gone most of that time; the popu-
lations in all the Citystates of University were fluid as
mud geysers, shifting and changing with the phases of
the moon as it were—the same types, though, over and
over, Cousins and non, curiously alike in their common
purpose. It was a good place to be, for a while, at least.

* * *

Feeling weightless and free, very much like she felt when she left Pillory and crawled out of the exoskeleton, she touched on the light in her apartment, tossed her bag into a chair, and combed her hands through her hair. "Aaaahhhhhhh. . . ." The sound was concentrated pleasure and ended on a brief happy laugh.

She clicked on the viewer, ran through the menu, chose a chamber group she knew, then rambled around the apartment moving to the music, touching her books, the small carvings she'd picked up here and there (cat, she thought, renewing my scent marks), pulling off her clothes and kicking them into a pile, going into the kitchen where she snatched packs of tea from the stasis box and started water boiling on the stove.

She took a long shower, washed her hair, pulled on a robe, settled in a chair with her feet up and the teapot beside her; at first she watched a news summary, then she tuned in a drama by one of the writers she'd worked with when she was taking a course in musical theater.

Vul ri Pustan-ili was a Sparglan from a world he called Makusij, which he said was so far out of touch it was a good thing the local life spans were numbered in centuries rather than decades. He was fascinated by the ephemeral qualities of Cousin views on life and love and was immersing himself in them in order to understand the joy and tragedy of such a swiftly passing awareness. From what she could see, he was persevering in this, his peculiar humor and odd angle of approach still part of his charms as a writer.

Twenty minutes into the play, though, she fell asleep.

2

She woke nine hours later with a stiff neck and the message chiming gently in her ears.

Vul's squeaky voice: *Shadow! Caught your name as a watcher. You back for just a visit, or are you staying a while? I've got this new project, want you to look at it, see what you think, I need music, a single instrument I think, subtlety over noise, I really do want to talk even if you can't stay. Come see me, hm?*

Digby: *Why are you on University, Shadow? I'd like a report, if you don't mind. Have you found the smuggler? Try to keep traveling times as short as possible, this is a race we're in, remember?*

Aslan's contralto (Shadith blinked with surprise; she'd thought Aslan was still on Béluchad): *Shadow, Vul told me you're back. If you have the time, it's Mirik's birthday, near as she can figure it, so we're having a party in The Eager Seagull, the usual lot, you know. Love to have you come if you can. Tonight, supposed to start around seven, but you know how these things go.*

Shadith checked the timer. Tonight was indeed this coming night. She smiled. "Digby, you can go on hold. I've just finished a month of agonizing boredom and I want to play. Hm. On second thought, I'd probably better give him a call. Grmp. He's going to want more than I want to tell. Do we mention Lylunda's ship? For sure, we do not. Would that keep him off it? I doubt it. Too many records, all of them transparent to him. Which means, when I leave, I take *Dragoi* in tow.

Gods! What happens when your life gets so convoluted
you forget which is back and which is front. Well, we
do the best we can with what we've got. I hate this,
I'm taking his money, supposed to be doing the job he
hired me for. Makes me feel lower than ... hm ... I
should make sure he gets his full fee. I owe him that
even if I've already quit. Looks like the only person I
can work for is me. Have to figure out something ...
but not now. Time for that later."

3

Away from his main nest Digby was a ghost of himself, a painted translucent specter, hip-hitched on the
corner of a desk in the satellite office he kept here on
University, scowling at her as he listened to the carefully edited account of her activities on Hutsarté.

She ended her tale with the delivery of the readouts.
"I brought them with me," she said. "I'll scan them for
you and give you my reasoning after that. Then we'll
see if we agree, hm?" This was the tricky point. If she
could get him interested in the data, perhaps she could
slide over how she got from Hutsarté to University.
She took the pages from the folder, smoothed them
out, then fed them one by one into the slot on the scan-
ner.

After a moment's pose as the contemplative thinker,
the ghost lifted his head, raised a brow. "Not much difficulty there. So, tell me."

"Harmon," she said. "With the Jilitera a distant second. The other ship, the shuttles, the transfer station,
all of them out of it." She explained, waited.

"I find no flaws in your reasoning. Why University?"

"The Regents try to keep track of arms dealers and
people like that. I was going to give them what I know

about Harmon's activities and run that name through to see if they have a new loc on him. And I thought I'd pull what they have on the Jilitera. Might be unlikely, but they were there." She shrugged. "You said use your ingenuity and your resources. Just doing the job, Digby."

The ghost contemplated her, a skeptical look on his sketch of a face. "Your discretion thus far has been admirable, so I won't pry into the gaps in that report. At the moment at least. I'll expect your final report to be considerably more detailed." He seemed to relax, then grinned at her. "The Kliu are agitated and are trying to wring what information they can out of me. I suspect they lost track completely of the Elang when she vanished from Haundi Zurgile. They've certainly lost their smug. You've won some time, Shadow, but probably not a lot. I'll give my resources a shake and see what falls out. Let me know what University comes up with, hm?"

"Will do. Um . . . just in case, if you've got lines to the Jilitera, it might be a good thing to get them ready to pull. Never hurts to have a backup no matter how convincing the logic."

4

Pleasantly tired, Shadith eased her way through the crowd to the bar in the corner of the room. The party had migrated to Aslan's apartment after dinner at The Eager Seagull and was still going strong though the noise level had begun to abate a bit. She searched through the empty bottles, boxes, and more esoteric containers, found a bottle with an inch of Carta Blue in it and refilled her glass.

"Any of the gartienta left?" Aslan caught her by the shoulder, leaned rather heavily against her, breathing a sweetish fog of alcohol past her ear. "Whoo! I'm going to hate myself tomorrow, but it feels good now."

"What's it look like?"

"Dumpy black jug thing. Smells like apricots."

"This?"

"Mm hm."

Shadith shook it gently. "Something left. Hold your glass out."

They moved around the edge of the room, found a futon rolled up and pushed against the wall, and eased themselves down on it. "I was wondering. . . ." Shadith said after a moment.

"Why I'm not still on Béluchad? Funding dried up. Yaraka thought we were teaching the locals a bit too much instead of studying how to manage them."

"You don't sound unhappy about being kicked offworld."

Aslan grinned. "I'm not. Left a lot of local students behind and University sprung for a couple splitcoms; the Meruu of Medon Vale are enthusiastic scholars and they like the idea of setting down their history. The Yaraka are going to find that the Keteng and the Fior are rather more than a match for them, I think. Do I ask about you? Got a letter full of restrained enthusiasm from Mum. Well, you know her."

"I'm in the middle of something. Can't talk about it now." The milling groups of talkers split a moment and she saw Mirik melting against Sarmaylen, his battered fingers moving absently along the elegant bones of her shoulder, a sculptor's appreciation in the delicate touch. "Mirik and Sarmaylen. She understand what she's getting into?"

"Does anybody ever?" Alsan sipped at the gartienta. After a minute, she sighed. "He doesn't mean to act like a merd, you know. He just gets so interested in what he's working on he forgets you're there, and you can get pissed at him and leave and he doesn't even notice for months maybe. And there's always another sighing femme waiting in the wings. She'll enjoy these first weeks, Shadow. He can play symphonies on a woman's body." She smiled fondly at memories that Shadith couldn't see, but she certainly could feel them through the reactions of Alsan's body.

Aslan got to her feet and ambled off, heading toward a tall, lean man with a gleaming bald head and a gray-streaked brown beard that reached halfway down his chest. Shadith watched her smooth her fingers along the line of his jaw, saw him smile down at her.

Abruptly she didn't feel like partying any longer; she looked down at her glass, sighed, and set it by the end of the futon roll where it wasn't likely someone would kick it over, got unsteadily to her feet, and edged along the wall till she reached the door.

The air outside was crisp and cold. She took a deep breath and the wine hit her, turning her knees to rubber and churning in her stomach. She dropped onto the edge of a granite planter, lowered her head to her knees, and fought the urge to upchuck everything she'd eaten. *What a stupid thing ... less sense than Mirik showed when she loped off with that scamjack ... gods, I'm horny and hopeless ... I want ... I want more than I've got ... why can't I just pick something and stick with it ... sleepy ... I'd better get home before I end spending the night on the steps here ... call a jit ... I'm in no shape to chain it or to walk. ...*

Cautiously she sat up. She was still a bit dizzy and wine tears blurred her eyes, but at least she could navigate now without embarrassing herself. She hunted till she found the jit pole, then thumbed back the slide and touched the sensor. She leaned on the pole and waited for her transport to arrive, weeping with loneliness and too much wine.

* * *

The messager woke her again.

Notice from University to come pick up her print-outs, message from Digby informing her that Harmon was on his way to Sauva Kutets, a world in the Sakuta System, one of several newly settled planets in a miniature cluster close to the Saber Arm. "Mouse, it's called," he said. "Because of its size and a tail of dust curling off one side."

Sauva Kutets was a colony in the throes of a savage revolt against the mother world, a planet called Agregossa in a system way out at the tip of the Saber Arm.

> *... because the Agregossans haven't fought a war in a long time, depending upon coercion and indoctrination to keep the peace rather than crude and visible force, they're not very adept at it though they have been learning rapidly. The most recent reports have the Agregossans making an attempt at an embargo of the system, most inept and futile unless you're unlucky enough to surface in front of their outer patrols. Most of the hostile attention is focused on Sauva's surface, so keep away from there if you can. Otherwise you shouldn't have much trouble getting in and out again. Oblique attacks and ingenuity, Shadow. Shouldn't be hard for you to manage.*

5

When Shadith reached the breakout point at the Sakuta System, the alarm signaled *ships too close*. She hovered at breakout until the clear-light blinked green at her, then emerged to find she'd just missed a line of three sting ships prowling inside the Limit—Agregossa guards on what was essentially an attempt at embargo on the cheap.

If Agregossa sowed breakout beepers in a globe inside the Limit and kept a dozen interceptors ready to move when one of the alarms was triggered, they might be able to slow the smuggling to a trickle.

Even pulling the patrol back until it didn't activate a clutter warning on the incoming ships might work. A nose to tail procession hard up against the Limit—like the one she'd just avoided—looked more like punishment detail than guard duty.

Passive receptors as wide and sensitive as she could crank them to prevent other, possibly fatal surprises, worrying about having to drag Lylunda's ship along beside her, she slipped into the shadow of a gas giant, then went scooting toward the asteroid belt, the sublight shield drawn tight about the twinned ships, though the hot tail on the *Backhoe* was impossible to camouflage completely; all the field-sculptors could do was extend the emanation block backward in a slightly flared tube to narrow the chances of detection.

After a few hours of heavy sweating, she edged the linked ships into the Belt, crept along it according to the plan she'd worked out on her way here. When she reached the point closest to Sauva Kutets, she settled into the shadow of a large rock, locked onto it with fore and aft lines, then reconfigured the shield, turning the ships into a craggy node of the asteroid, both to the eye and to most detec systems. The locals were most likely to choose a meeting place that gave them the least possible exposure to Agregossan patrols.

"Spla! I need a bath. That was a bit more sweatmaking than I expected. First, though, I see if I figured right about how to locate our happy arms dealer."

According to her data file, Sauva was the larger

twin, the one with the most people. There was no mining or heavy industry because the world was expected to produce food for the homeworld and nothing was allowed to distract from that task. Sauva was divided into huge salashi owned by the Families that ran Agregossa and by their friends; the salasheri rented the land they worked from those Families and paid taxes to the colonial government. They also had to buy hardware and machinery from the owners at what they knew were inflated prices. In spite of this triple drain, the salasheri prospered—to no small degree by growing speciality crops of various kinds and smuggling the harvest offworld.

The rebellion came with the last increases in the rent and in the tax laid on the salasheri by the homeworld, which convinced them that the absentee owners would squeeze them dry in their greed and ignorance. They sent a delegation across to Kutets to protest. The members of that delegation were arrested, convicted on the spot of insurrection and signed into Contract Labor; their families were thrown off the land they thought of as their own. Outsiders were brought in to work it. It didn't take much deliberation for the rest to figure out where that road led.

Most of Kutets' population belonged to one of three groups—the Agregossa colonial government with its mix of politicians, police, land agents, and bureaucrats; security forces; the Contract Labor used in the mines and factories. No rebellion there according to the report.

"Dumb system all around. Almost guaranteed to generate dissatisfaction on Sauva. I expect Agregossa figured it had the high ground here and the Sauvese would follow orders, like it or lump it. Hm. High ground in this case depends on who's got the most bang in hand. Hence Harmon. Gods be blessed, I don't have to plunge into that mess, just locate old Harmon and squeeze out of him where he dumped Lylunda Elang."

Her chosen rock was on the inner side of the Belt and in good viewing range. Sauva Kutets was between her and the sun, the dark side toward her with similar crescents of daylit world on the trailing edge. No city lights shone in the larger of those velvet black ovoids, but here and there she saw the flashes from explosions and in several places wide swathes of fire. All so very pretty from way out here even with amplification, and nicely silent, no screams from the burned and dying. She shivered and blanked the screen, though she left the pickups working and transferring data to memory cells.

"From the lack of fooforrah, I got here first," she said. "Well, I *was* closer, if I did start later. Digby said Harmon left The Accord with a nicely vicious assortment of their products three days before I 'splitted from University. Interesting that he could get that kind of information. Spooky. Digby as a virus in the com system. I'm starting to wonder more than a little where he's aiming. More stuff to think about later.

"So where's Harmon? At a guess his ship's not all that much faster than this one. If he came directly from The Accord . . . and I'd say that's likely with the load he has . . . and if he had no more problems than I did getting here, then he may have arrived around six hours ago. So it's just possible he could have dumped his cargo and got away before I stuck my nose through. Not likely, though; he'd have to spend some time making contact with his buyers. It'd go faster if he grounded the ship on planet, but setting down in the middle of a war is a gamble. Me, I'd do the trade up here. Let the buyers dance with the Agregossan patrols. Get your pay and get out. So if you're around here like you should be, you little weasel, you're doing just what I'm doing, playing least in sight and waiting for the Sauvese to signal their arrival."

She tapped the screen on again, pulled most of the receptors away from Sauva Kutets and set them mapping the local asteroid configurations. She get more precise data once Digby's pooter moles were deployed, giving her a delicate web out there collecting data about everything that happened in this area of the Belt.

She smiled as she watched the moles creep away from the ship. When she was testing out the abilities packed into Digby's fleet, she asked the tech why they were called that. He told her to watch the screen. She did and saw this nebulous little object doing a quick odd jig across the space between the ship and the rock that was its target. You see? he said. Like it's farting its way across. Slow enough to get you chewing on your elbows, but they don't trigger alarms and when they've got their paint on they don't show up on most search screens, so they're useful little buggers. And you can pickaback them if you have to show some speed, let the carriers draw the fire after the moles have dropped.

Twenty minutes later when she was scrolling through the data from the mole web, examining hundreds of medium- to large-sized rocks floating in the middle of nothing, the alarm beeped at her and threw the readout off the screen. She found herself looking at an insystem ship that seemed to be coming straight for her. When it passed one of the larger asteroids, though, she saw the nose begin to turn away; the battered craft was creeping along very slowly, almost as if it were tiptoeing across a creaky floor. It nestled up against that rock with a delicacy of increment that suggested the pilot was probably a smuggler or perhaps an asteroid miner recruited to the cause. *Hm. Close enough to be handy, far enough to be safe.*

As she watched it power down and set its mooring lines, Shadith played with the controls, pinning the location and maneuvering the pooter moles into a mosaic for a beacon watch. No need to go looking for Harmon; there was the bait to draw him here. "There's an ego booster—setting my piece on the board just right."

Bmmmp cwmmp, the beacon watch told her, then went silent. Bwmmmb. Very short-range signal—faint and so low it was a basso mutter rather than the usual beep.

"Lovely. Now we wait for him to come to the call. And sit here sweating till I know if I was careless and he spotted me or if he was focused insystem and not worrying about the Belt. University says he's missed the last two drops he set up, barely got away with his life and no cash. Reduced to ferrying cargo to pay expenses and burning the papers on his ship for this load. Only way to get them back is make good on the sale. He'll come. Oh, yes. Sweet if he can. Nasty if he has to."

She waited.
The beacon did its pattern every twenty minutes.
And she waited.
Nothing else to do. Her gear was in the lock, ready to go, the plan was made during the trip here, tweaked a little to suit local conditions, no need to go over that again.
Two hours. Three. Four.
Bmmmp cwmmp. Bwmmmb.
Thwop thweep. Thwop thweep thweep.
She shook herself out of her half doze, began watching the screen intently. At first she saw nothing; then

she noticed that the glimmer of the Belt dust was occluded by a roughly spherical object moving counter to the general direction of rotation. "Hello, Harmon."

6

As Shadith eased from the sled and used a sticktight to moor it to the side of Harmon's ship, she caught flickers of light from the cargo transfer that was moving at frantic speed on the other side of the bulge. As she crossed to the ship, she'd seen Harmon's 'bots handling much of the work, with the men from the insystem ship adding their muscle to the process, stowing the sealed bundles in their own hold with the care of men who knew they had little leeway with much of the stuff they were hauling.

She slid the probe over the latch of the maintenance lock, raised her brows as the reading remained null. No juice through the latch. *Burning paper, all right. Nothing drawing except what is absolutely necessary. Nice of you to make things easy for me, li'l Harmon.*

Before she did anything to the latch, she pulled herself against the side of the ship and *reached* inside, searching for life fires.

Three men. One nearby, probably in the hold overseeing the 'bot loading. Stranger. The second was Harmon, faint, much farther away. On the Bridge. With the third. Another stranger, probably the paymaster waiting till the transfer was complete before handing over the cash. *Hm. Don't underestimate the little man, Shadow. He hasn't survived this long by being stupid. . . .*

She focused her *reach* on Harmon so she could act the moment she felt him go tense, inserted the mutator key at the end of suit glove's fifth finger into the slot and started the attack on the latch.

Five minutes later she was inside and climbing cautiously along the catwalk in the space between the walls, working toward the Bridge, using her *reach* to give her an estimate of how close she was getting. Twice she came on interior maintenance locks, but they were too far from her goal; she noted the locations and the areas they gave access to and kept moving. The third lock was on the Bridge level; she used her suit arm to wipe dust from the small bronze plate, read *dichio komugan. Aux Com. Good. Running on the cheap, he's probably closed this one down. So, li'l key, do your tiny thing and get me in there clean.*

She emerged from the lock into the secondary com room, found the screens and sensor boards sheathed in a skin of crashwebbing and a layer of fine gray dust on every surface, dust that came floating up as her steps disturbed it. The wrist readouts on her gauntlets told her that the air in the room was stale, barely breathable, impregnated with slough from every surface in the place. She grimaced and moved to the door. Again there was no power through the latch. He was conserving to the point of absurdity. Or necessity. She was beginning to feel sorry for the man, though she loathed arms dealers. This was death by inches and the thought revolted her.

Harmon was still tense; this close she could read an overlay of forced cheerfulness that confused but didn't worry her. She slid the door open and moved through as quickly as she could, clicking her tongue against her teeth at the in-gust of air as the pressure on two sides sought to equalize. Nothing she could do about that but hope Harmon was too busy with his conversation to notice the blink of a telltale.

She checked her own telltale. Air. Thin, but breathable. She unzipped the gauntlets, clipped them to her

belt, removed the stunner from its pouch, and ran on
her toes past a dark access that from the smell of stale
food led to the galley, then past two closed cabin entries; she stopped just outside the door to the Bridge,
dropped to her knees and crept close enough to look in.

Harmon sat with his chair turned slightly away from
the controls, though he glanced at the readouts now
and then. He was smiling at a burly man who stood beside the Co chair, a locked case at his feet. ". . . come
up with the cash, I know where I can get some out-of-
date cpe at a big discount."

"Out of date?" The burly man's hands closed into
fists—briefly—until he forced them open. Anger and
the effort he was making to hold it in grated in his
voice.

"Oh, it's still plenty potent. Tricky to handle, I'll
grant you that, but also going at one-tenth the price."
Harmon leaned forward, fixed his eyes on the other
man's face and spoke with an apparent candor, beneath
which Shadith could hear his desperation. "Look, I live
by my reputation. I sell you worthless, word goes out,
nobody buys from me. You've got techs who know
how to handle it, see what they say, they'll tell you it's
a good deal. Scrape up the coin and give me a call."

"I . . ." He broke off at a ting from his wristcom.
"Blue leader here."

"Stowed and sewed up. Let's get."

Shadith eased back, got to her feet, and ran back the
way she'd come until she reached the galley accessway
and plunged into the darkness, where she pressed herself against the wall and waited. She was a bit surprised that Harmon was leaving his Bridge; then it
occurred to her that the man in the hold wasn't crew
but one of the locals and Harmon was operating the
ship solo.

The two men were still talking deal as they marched

along the corridor. She heard a soft hiss and smiled to herself. Face. That's what that sound meant. He fed enough juice to run a lift tube. Keeping up the prosperous image in front of his customers.

She left the accessway, moved into the Bridge, and waited for him to come back.

3

Eyes mean as snake's if still a touch blurry from the stunner, Harmon twisted his wrists against the comealong tapes. "You're dead. I'll find you. . . ."

"That's a stupid thing to say." The distorter in the suit hood deepened and roughed her voice. "Gives me a good reason not to want you healthy or whole."

"If you're after the money, why didn't you just take it and go? You want my ship?"

"Only one thing I want and that's the girl."

"Huh?" His face went totally blank for an instant. "What girl?"

She ground her teeth together; his body shouted to her what she didn't want to hear. He didn't know what she was talking about—which meant she'd spent months of travel and a year's worth of computer time on University for nothing. Less than nothing. Clinging to a last sliver of hope, she said, "Three months ago you landed a cargo on a world called Hutsarté. The Chief of Security put a young woman in your custody and told you to take her somewhere. I want to know where."

"You've got mold in your head. Yeah, I dropped off cargo all right and picked up some, too, but no femme. Don't like femmes on my ship. Bad luck." He blinked at her a moment. "What femme's this and how come you want to know?"

"The Kliu bounty, fool. Ten thousand gelders alive,

zip dead." She didn't try to disguise her disgust with
the situation and could hear it even in the gravelly
tones of the distorter. All she could do now was get out
of there as clean as she could. "Reason I'm telling you
is you'd pick it up anyway the first Pit you tie-down
at." She swore as she glanced at a readout she kept
concealed in the palm of her gauntlet so he wouldn't
see it was an ordinary air sniffer. "Li'l Henry here says
you truthspeaking so hail and farewell, I'm off."

"Ee! Don't leave me tied like this."

"Time keyed, Harmon. So contemplate your sins and
cultivate the virtue of patience and in around twenty
minutes the ties fall off." She backed from the Bridge,
and went running for the maintenance hatch and the sled.

4

Drone: Shadith to Excavations Ltd/Digby
. . . no question he was telling the truth. Spla! he
was perfect for the part, everything I would have
postulated were I creating him. Well, enough self-
justification. I thought the Jilitera the next most
likely, but I've gone off pride in my logic right at
the moment. Also pride in what you delight in
calling my ingenuity. So. I've reread the data collected so far and twisted it every way I can think
of. Grinder Jiraba was convinced the woman was
taken offworld and I see no reason to dispute that.
He wasn't a man to make that kind of mistake or
one to bring in strangers to do something he could
handle himself. So, the Jilitera are it. If you've got
a way to pry information out of them, now's the
time to use it. If not, locate the Jherada for me and
I'll see what babble can do.

Drone: Digby to Shadith aboard *Backhoe One*. Install enclosed Shriek ID on ship. Take name Drina acMorah, use enclosed materials for the role. Meet one Jaskara at the Crowndome, The Tricky Deacon Pit. Ninth hour of the Pit diurn. Week's window, so don't linger on the way. Ask him no questions other than the location of Lylunda Elang. If he says he doesn't know, believe him. Tell him nothing about yourself.

Shadith finished the terse message, raised her brows. "Curiosity up. Slap curiosity down. For the moment. Anyone want to wager Jaskarah is as phony as Drina acMorah? No? Wise. Deacon, hm? More travel. I'm getting really tired of all this crawling about in the 'split. After I quit, maybe I should drop over to Vrithian and vegetate in Harskari's garden." She sighed. "I'd like that, I think, mucking about with plants and trading lies with Willow and ol' Beetle Bodri and watching Sunchild airdance. For a while, anyway."

5

A blue-black woman with eyes that glowed like yellow fire above a discreet breathing mask strolled across the lobby of the Crowndome. She wore a skintight sheath of garnet avrishum, a silver turban that completely covered her hair, and silver, elbow-length gloves. Shadith blinked as she glimpsed herself in one of the mirrored walls; she still hadn't got used to the guise Digby'd thought up for her.

A little man with a yellowish, wrinkled pseudoskin mask left the shadows where he'd been standing and met her near one of the carved pillars of colored marble that were scattered about and connected to a complex play of arches as if they were really loadbearing instead of freeform art pieces. "Drina acMorah?"

"Jaskarah?"

"Yes. I have a shielded conference room reserved. If you'll come?"

"Lead the way."

Jaskarah tapped the seal on the door, walked to the table, and sat down. "You have a question for me?"

She frowned at him a moment, wondering if he already know what she wanted, knowing at the same time she had no leeway to ask him about that. "Do you know where Lylunda Elang was taken?"

He blinked at her and she could feel his surprise. *Hunh! That answers that and makes me wonder why he doesn't know.* "I don't know the name," he said.

"Hm. Perhaps if I put it this way. A young woman was taken aboard a particular ship on Hutsarté by instructions from an official there. She was transferred to another place. I wish to know that place."

"Ah. That's different. Bol Mutiar in the Callidar Pseudo Cluster. An island called Chiouti. Is there anything further?"

"Can you give me more information about this Chiouti?"

"No."

"Then I thank you for your help and would you prefer to leave first, or shall I?"

He stood, bowed, walked to the door, unsealed it, and left. It resealed behind him, a red light blinking on the monitor.

She waited till the red blink turned green, walked away from the room, her *reach* sweeping out to make sure the little man wasn't hanging about, meaning to follow her until she removed the trappings of Drina acMorah. Remembering the implicit warning in Dig-

by's message, she expected to find him out there, and
he was, lingering in the shadow by one of the columns,
his curiosity about her overlaid with a sense of need
that disturbed her—more things she had to figure out
about Digby. It wouldn't surprise her much to learn
that the faux-Jaskarah didn't know who it was pulling
the strings that got him here.

*Not that I know either. Who can say what Digby did
to get this.*

Deacon's rules were a lot looser than Marrat's. There
were no respectable folk here, no Gray Market with
citizen types coming to buy. Murder was frowned on,
though duels were common enough and killing in self-
defense with even the faintest of justification rated a
minor fine. Theft and the false report of theft were cap-
ital offenses, with trial by verification and the sentence
carried out approximately twenty seconds after the verifier extruded its report. It was not a place for the gentle and the unaware. Which meant if she trapped and
zapped the little man, no one would bother noticing.
He had to know that, too, so it was going to be tricky.
And, she reminded herself, *I've got watch out or he
does the same to me. Don't get too sassy, Shadow. You
aren't the champeen wizard of the universe. Just think
what Lee or Harskari would do to you if the need
arose. Or even Autumn Rose, if she took a notion.*

She clicked her tongue, shook her head. *I'm getting
so used to deviousness, I forget the short way. All you
have to do is get back to the ship intact, Shadow. The
way Digby set things up, skinface can follow you till
his feet rot and bribe the Deacon's Guards for the
ship's Shriek and he won't know more than he does
now. Keep it quick and easy and let's get out of here.*

Ten gelders bought her a 'bot escort out to the tie-
down, the credit chip in Drina acMorah's name paid
her mooring fee, and a few minutes later she was

'splitting for the Callidara. It meant another month of travel, but maybe this was the last of the zigs she'd have to zag.

6

Shadith dropped the *Backhoe* into orbit around Bol Mutiar and breathed a sigh of relief as she finally cut the umbilical to the *Dragoi*. She could leave the ship parked here, hand it over to Lylunda when she got the woman offworld.

She inspected the globe turning beneath her. There was very little about the world in the memory files on the ship and she didn't want to alert Digby just yet.

An island named Chiouti.

She watched the parade of islands sliding past below her and swore with considerable fervor. No cities, just villages, one or two to an island depending on its size. No landmasses more than fifty miles on the longest axis. Almost all of the islands in a wide band about the equator, the rest of the world wind-churned ocean. She had no local maps, not a clue which of those humps of dirt might be called Chiouti by the people who lived there. "Looks like I unship the lander and do the lucky dip and hope I don't have to spend the next ten years at it."

She put the small lander down on one of the larger islands, choosing as landing site a barren spit where the weight and heat of the lander would do least damage. When you're visiting someone else's home to ask a favor, you don't break the furniture or kick the cat. She crawled out, circled the lander, and was pleased to see she'd made a neat set-down. Then she started walking south along the beach toward the small village nestling at the back of a halfmoon bay, trying to ignore an uneasiness that tickled at her like flies walking down her back.

She had a feeling of something watching her, measuring her—not hostile yet, but a sense of lurking danger. She tried a sweep with her *reach,* but there was nothing alive nearby except a few bugs in the sparse grass and shellfish under the sand.

The first people who came running to meet her were children, brown, happy, unafraid, throwing words at her she couldn't understand as yet, though the pain in her head meant the translator was working hard to remedy that.

"A droo eoeo a mei."

"A mei erra blyek."

"A mehil erra tiang."

"Diak a woman?"

"In bail like that mno er el?

"I think yes, I think she has tuttas. And look at the way she meraii." It was the oldest of the girls; she giggled and went strutting ahead of them, shaking her small behind. After a few steps she grinned over her shoulder. "Men don't walk like that."

"You might be surprised, young woman," Shadith said. The words came slowly, but they came. The accent wasn't quite right, but she could see from the startled look on the girl's face that she understood the words well enough.

"Then you are a man?"

"No. You had that right."

"You come to trade?"

"I came to find an island. Chiouti. Have you ever heard of a place with that name?

"Chiouti? I don't think so. Too bad you missed the Berotongs when they came by last month on their beronta. They sail all round the world and know just about every place."

Shadith stopped walking. When the girl turned and came back to her, she bowed, straightened. "Blessings on you, young woman. You have saved me much trouble and travel. I will do as you say and seek out a beronta of the Berotong Pandai."

"But you must come and eat with us. We'll have games and stories and a fine feast to celebrate your being here."

"I thank you for the thought, but my need is urgent. Greet your elders for me and say that I wish they would celebrate the joy that your words have brought me." She bowed again, swung round, and ran for the lander.

"And I wasn't exaggerating," she told herself as she took the lander up to the edge of the atmosphere. She put the craft on autopilot and began a search of the ocean round the islands, looking for a beronta. "Which shouldn't be so hard to spot. Big melanggas. Melanggas? Translator still on the job. Spla! Forcegrowing new dendrons is not a fun experience. Wonder what happens when I run out of room inside this skull. Does it explode on me? I can see it now. One langue too many and kaboom, the lady's head's a tomb. That what they mean when they say go out with a bang not a whimper? Tsah! I could work up a good whimper right about now. Ah! there we are. One beronta riding the waves."

She increased magnification, frowned at the image on the small screen. "Kids! Hm. Looks like whole families travel on those things. Interesting as that is, it's got nothing to do with my problem. How do I talk to them? Should I wait till they make their next landfall? Probably best I do. This is not the most maneuverable of platforms. Right. We get a measure of average speed, see which island is the likely target.

Then we drop down and say hello. I really don't like that place and I'd rather not spend more time there than I have to."

.

7

Shadith bowed. "Drummer Orros. And you may call me Shadow."

"Yes, I do know Chiouti. Is it the island you wish to find, Shadow, or the woman who was on it."

Shadith blinked, startled by having her question answered before she voiced it. "Thank you. It is the woman. I've come to find her. I need to talk to her."

"Do you mean her harm? She is of the Bond."

"No harm. I've a question to ask and an offer to make."

"She can't leave. Do you understand that? If you take her now, she'll die and so will you."

"You're sure?"

"You come too late, Star rider."

"Perhaps so, perhaps not. I don't understand this Bond of yours, but there are things you don't understand about me. In any case, I do need to talk to her."

"She drums on a beronta these days. They make landfall next at an island called Keredel. It is on the far side of the world, six months sail from here."

"How can I recognize Keredel?"

The Drummer snapped his fingers and a young boy ran to him with a stick, some stones, leaves, and bits of grass. He dropped to his knees on the damp sand, smoothed out a patch and, using the stick, began to carve. He labored over it for nearly half an hour, cutting bits of grass and leaves and fitting them into the sand, using the stones as rock outcroppings and to form a curving tail of small, rocky islets. When he was finished, he dusted off his knees, rubbed his palms against his mezu. "That is Keredel."

"You leave me in your debt, Drummer Orros." She examined the small exquisite miniature, amazing in its detail, and knew she'd have no trouble locating that particular island.

"No. The woman is unhappy here and more so every day. It . . ." He paused, hunting for words. "It disturbs the Bond. The debt will be ours if you can find a way to make her content or to help her leave alive."

Shadith bowed again, then went back to the lander. She had a lot to think about, but more to do before she could find the time she needed for that thinking.

14

Bargains

Lylunda took the small practice drum, left the bustling trade fair in the village belau, and went to sit on the bench, her bare feet in the foam from the retreating tide. She'd gathered cherar on the first island that the *Remeydang* stopped at after leaving Chiouti, but she could not make herself drink the infusion. Her throat closed up, her insides cramped, her hands shook so badly she dropped the glass. In the end she poured it out and fought the pull of the tung akar by drumming herself into exhaustion—but when morning came, she ate slices of the tuber with the rest of the Pandai. That night she curled in a knot and grieved for everything she'd lost. The Pandai understood her struggle and left her alone with it.

They knew, everyone knew everything, around the world and back all Pandai knew what one Pandai knew as if they ate the information with the crisp yellow rounds of tung akar. No privacy of thought and feeling on Bol Mutiar. Each time she saw evidence of this, her body screamed with rage and terror, though she swallowed the words she wanted to shout at them. Rape of the soul. Taking what she didn't want to give. Taking the last thing that was hers alone.

When she was out on the ocean, the pressure was gone, as if the brisk winds that sent the beronta scudding along blew the addiction from her head; she was happy there and it was enough respite to help her keep going. But there was always the next island, the next meal, all around her the smell of the tung and the awareness of its presence that went beyond the senses.

She touched the drum head, listened to it speak. She'd not eaten the tung yet, so she could still feel the song in her bones; it helped her push away the clamor to eat and be One in Bond with the others. Bond, the tapping of her fingers sang to her, bond, bond bondaaaage. Though the Pandai were freer within their limits than anyone she'd known, happier . . . real joy in them . . . in the games and the making of things . . . laughter and no fear . . . yet, what they gave up for this. . . .

She felt something tweak at her. A coldness, almost anger, in the aura of the tung. She got to her feet, stood holding the drum in front of her like a shield as she watched a dark figure coming toward her. A woman. In a shipsuit. A trader? The Berotongs had never spoken of femme traders.

As the woman came closer, Lylunda watched the vigorous alertness in her body, the fierce energy of her walk; her eyes blurred with weak tears. She'd walked like that once. She'd danced that way.

The woman stopped in front of her; she was tall and slender with a tangle of gold-tipped brown curls and eyes like bitter chocolate. "Lylunda Elang?"

Lylunda sighed. Whatever the woman wanted, she had no will left to fight her. "Yes." She felt the coldness grow, felt the peril in it. She didn't care, she was just too tired to be afraid anymore.

The woman shivered. "I'm not here to hurt you in any way. Do you believe that?"

"Does it matter?"

"You tell me."

"All right. I believe you." She felt the coldness draw back; perhaps it did matter. She had no reason to wish harm on this woman.

"Thanks. I'm tired of this sand. Any place where we can sit and talk?"

"If you want to talk, talk here."

The woman raised her brows, startled at the violence in Lylunda's voice, but she wasn't about to apologize. If she went away from the water, the tung's call would grow too strong for her and she wouldn't be able to think.

"All right. My name is Shadith. I work for Excavations Ltd., and the Kliu hired us to find you and either get the location of the Taalav array or hand you over to them so they could extract it. I don't intend to do that, by the way. Hand you over, I mean."

"Oh." Lylunda sighed. "You came too late. If you take me away from here, I won't live long enough to reach the Limit."

"So I was told. Also that I'd be dead right beside you. Why?"

"To stay alive on this world for any length of time, you have to eat the tung akar. Once you've eaten enough of it, you can't live without it. It's more complicated than that in ways I wouldn't understand unless I gave up and became part of the Tung Bond."

"I've an ottodoc on board my ship. That wouldn't flush it out of your system?"

"The Jilitera warned me about that. It won't work. I think the tung has become part of my cell structure and the ottodoc can't get all of it without killing me. It's aware, the tung I mean. I can feel it."

"Yes. So can I. Your father chose well. You're certainly safe here. If the Kliu come after you, the tung kills them."

"You know about my father?"

"When I was on Hutsarté looking for you, I tangled with someone called Grinder Jiraba. He figured out what must have happened."

"I see. I see something else, too. No ethical problems telling the Kliu where to find me. I'm safe, you're away clean, not even any bad dreams."

"Maybe no ethical problems, but an interesting practical one. We don't get paid if we just give them your location. They want actual possession or a firm location for the array."

Lylunda turned away, eased herself onto the sand, and sat staring out at the sea, her hands flattened against the sides of the drum so their shaking wouldn't betray the surge of hope that was like fire racing through her body. She heard Shadith drop beside her, but she didn't turn to face the woman, this too-clever hunter who'd sniffed out her hiding place.

When she had control of her voice, she said, "I'm not going to tell you."

"Unless . . ."

"You are quick. Ba da, considering that you found me, I shouldn't be surprised. I'll sell Prangarris and the Taalav for a way off this world. That's the only coin that will buy me; there's nothing else you've got that I want."

"I know a healer; I think she can keep you alive. I'd best go have a talk with her. Travel times being what they are, could be around several months before I'm back, so hold tight, hm? And hold onto this." A beeper landed in her lap. A warm hand closed on her shoulder in a quick squeeze, then she heard the sounds of running feet thudding on the sand.

Lylunda kept staring at the sea, trying to calm the turmoil inside her and at the same time wondering how she was going to survive the next few months.

15

Worm Trails

1

The pulse from the beacon cut off as the Spy emerged from the 'split.

When Worm reached the Limit and surfaced, he listened to the Shriek of the transfer station, swore when he heard the University ID. "Why here? I don't understand. Harmon wouldn't come near this place."

Instead of continuing on to the tie-down, he slipped sideways and took the *Kanti* into a polar orbit about one of the outer planets.

His respite was gone, run down the drain. He sat for some time scowling at the com screen. "I should have called Fa. It was the right thing to do. I wasted a month's travel time because I lost my nerve." He rubbed at his eyes. "Maybe I'm wrong. Maybe she's figured out something else. Maybe . . ." He sighed and punched in his father's call sign, then waited for the connect.

When the screen lit, it was a girl's face he saw instead of his father's. Trish. "Where's Fa, Coz?"

"Having a flush-out. Kliu called, said about Mort hanging on a thread. He took it bad. You got good news? Don't know how he'd take more bad."

"No good, no bad, just got more traveling to do. Need Fa's sources."

"You know he don't let no one tap the source node. You gonna have to wait till he can talk, least twelve hours. That too long?"

"Maybe so, maybe no, but I damnsure can't move without I've got some place to go to."

"Ta, then. Talk to you when."

Worm went limp as the stiffening he'd summoned drained out of him. It was all to do again, nerving himself to face his father's anger and maybe give him another seizure when he had to confess what happened. He got wearily to his feet and went to scrub the galley once again. At least when you cleaned something, you could see what you'd accomplished.

2

"... just a couple a days 'fore I was at go on the snatch, some local piv'r hauls her in to cop shop and she don't come out, what comes out is some femme fixed up in her clothes. I get on com to the Kliu and complain they interfering with the op, that I hear they trying it on with the locals to pick the smuggler up and ship her over to Pillory so they can get out of contract they got with us. I din't ask if they got her, I just said they were messing me up. And what ol' Kliu he says makes me some sure they han't got her. Grinder's kid, he said it was her Fa who got her, he's some mucko in the cop shop. The kid thinks mucko got biters up his ezel when Kliu ticket come by him and he whiffed her off somewhere he don't have to look for her in. Anyway, I see this femme who's Digby's agent fijjing around trying to finger the smuggler, so I put the ear on her and I pick up she's got her hands on ship lists and she figures the mucko passed his daughter off to

Harmon, you know him, scurf who sold Snake that stale cpe, so he could dump her in some Never Find. So I figure I get to Harmon first, shoot him to ears with babble, go where he dropped her. Isn't likely she'll have the same kind of protection she bought on Hutsarté. So I need to know where Harmon's going and how long it's gonna take to get there."

When the spate of words was finished, words he hoped didn't sound too much like whiner's excuses—Fa hated whining—Worm sat stiffly upright, hands curled tight about the arms of the chair, waiting for the blast he knew was coming.

It didn't come. His father's mouth shaped itself into an unconvincing smile and when he spoke, it was in a tone of mild disappointment. No thundering scarification, no skin-peeling scarcasm. "Sasa, I had hoped for better news. You done good, Worm. You done right. Give me a minute, I'll call up what you want and pulse it through. A father's Blessings on you, boy."

The screen blanked and a moment later, the keph tinged to let him know the data blip had arrived.

Worm stirred. He felt sick.

His father was frightened. He'd never seen his father frightened of anything.

"I'm the last of his sons maybe and he's licking up to me so I won't go off and leave him. Cousins aren't the same. He shouldn't do that, makes me feel ... he shouldn't do that."

The ship was still well-enough supplied for a couple more months of 'splitting, but the comp on Harmon had him heading for a warzone in the Sakuta System, so Worm had another bite at Kliu credit and topped off at the University Transfer Station. Still uncertain about his father, replaying the call, worrying over every word, watching his father's every expression, trying to convince himself it wasn't fear he was seeing but only the result of the purge Fa had just been through, he headed for the Limit and the two-week journey to the Mouse Cluster.

The beacon started pulsing again four hours after his journey had begun and the pulse stayed with him, the locator showing it behind and off to one side.

So that was why University. Someone there had told the Spy where to find Harmon and she was going for him.

3

Worm set the keph to fiddling the exit point until he was above the ecliptic and, he hoped, away from any patrols. He surfaced to realspace and sent *Kanti* slipping toward the asteroid belt where he could bide unseen and do a manual reactivation of the beacon to trace the Spy and slip up on her when she whipped her net over Harmon.

He watched her come sneaking along and cheered silently as she settled in the shadow of a rock only a few shiplengths from his hidey hole—though he was startled to see two ships, not one, Lylunda's little darter tucked up against the flank of a bigger one. Just as well the Spy was into umbilicals, meant he could track her some more if this didn't work out. He wriggled in his seat. On the good side, taking Lylunda's ship along should mean she was expecting to run across the smuggler sometime soon; on the bad side, this could get real tight real fast. *Watch how she works,* he thought. *Gotta know what I'm going against.*

He settled in to brood over what the Spy was planning and to wait for events to unfold.

When he saw the Spy's sled come slipping through the shield round the ships, Worm left the chair and hurried to get himself dressed to follow her.

By the time he was out the lock and riding a hand impellor toward Harmon's ship, she was already at the maintenance inlet and working on the latch. That was a datapoint of sorts; she knew what he knew—that it was the least regarded area on any ship, forgotten or ignored until it was needed. He blinked as he realized suddenly that he was as bad as everyone else at protecting *Kanti*'s flank. He'd never thought about being boarded, so he'd never done anything about alarming or trapping that hatch. He made a note to do it during the next trip to wherever.

When he reached Harmon's ship, the Spy had been inside for several minutes. He was happy about that; he didn't want to be treading too close upon her heels.

He followed the slight sounds she made and the marks in the grime on the walkway, hesitated outside the hatch to the aux com. If she was inside, she'd pick up what was happening and be waiting for him. He edged back until he reached the first of the locks he'd passed up, cycled through, and found himself in crew quarters, a sixer once but little more than a stinking hole these days, with the remnants of a crate in one corner, a busted dolly beside it, stains and scratches on the floor. He eased the door open and stood listening by the crack.

Voices came up from the hold, briefly, as if a hatch had opened. He couldn't hear what they were saying, but there was a certain urgency about it that told him the buyers had finished loading and wanted to get away from here like ten minutes ago.

He slid out and began making his way to Bridge level.

5

"What femme's this and how come you want to know?"

"The Kliu bounty, fool. Ten thousand gelders alive, zip dead. . . ."

Worm knelt in the shadows of the corridor outside the lighted arch that led onto the Bridge. Though he could hear well enough, he couldn't see either Harmon or the Spy. *Kliu bounty? Truth isn't in the femme. At least I don't . . . no . . . not the Kliu . . . not when they're using me to get out of paying Digby, trying to get out of paying me even with Mort and Xman. Too mean to put down good coin for what they could get free.* Another datapoint. She was good at laying down false tracks, voice distorter, too. Hm. Didn't want Harmon to know she was female. Interesting. Meant she was squeamish. Planning to leave him alive or she wouldn't bother. He blinked as he heard her buying the truth of Harmon's denial. Why? It didn't make sense.

"Ee! Don't leave me tied like this."

"Time keyed, Harmon. So contemplate your sins and. . . ."

Worm got to his feet and hurried as silently as he could to the galley accessway, ducking into it as he heard the sound of running feet.

Harmon was tugging at the ties and cursing with a deplorable lack of imagination as Worm walked in. He stopped, scowled at Worm. "What you doing here?"

"Got the same question you been hearing. Where's the woman?"

"I told him and I'll tell you. I don't know shays about no femme."

"That's what you said, yeh. Maybe she believed you. Me, I don't. So we're gonna find out the hard way."

"She?"

"Uh-huh. Delicate little femme, barely old enough to vote like they say. Whipped you good." Worm stepped close, pushed the shotgun against Harmon's neck, and triggered it.

When the babble had him, Worm leaned close, spoke slowly and carefully. "A woman was brought aboard your ship."

"No woman. No."

"You were told to take her somewhere."

"No told. Told nothing."

"Where did you take her."

"No woman. Nowhere."

"Where did you go when you left Hutsarté?"

"The Accord."

"Why?"

"The pay for cargo transfer on Hutsarté. With what I got laid aside, it was enough to buy loan and stock. Make contract with Yobany Fitz. Get back in business."

"Zoll! She was right. And she'll be hitting her other leads now. I'd better . . ." He shoved the shotgun into his belt sac, scowled at Harmon. "You know me and you're worse'n Mort for holding a grudge till it squalls. Sorry 'bout this, Harm, but I gotta protect myself. I'm all Fa's got till I can ransom Mort and Xman." He took hold of Harmon's hair and used his cutter to slice neatly through the dealer's throat. Then he collected the satchel of coin that the Spy hadn't bothered to take and went running for the nearest lock.

6

The soft squeal of the locator was the only thing that kept him sane in the next month he spent following the Spy.

First there was The Tricky Deacon Pit which he didn't understand at all until after she took off from there. *Information, that's what it was, she was looking for something and she found out where it was.*

Hope rising, he followed the beacon's intermittent squeal until she surfaced at an out of the way world in the Callidara Pseudo Cluster. Bol Mutiar his Chart told him and the keph said, "Restricted world. Rated purple 9 on the danger scale. Further information interdicted."

Which raised his brows up to his hairline. He hid in the shadow of a moon and watched the paired ships come round beneath him.

The smuggler's ship jerked, then began to move away. "Tractor shove. And the umbilical's cut. Zoll's Teeth. That has to mean that the smuggler's here. I've got to get down there, no more waiting. I've got to drop a loop on both of them before the Spy cuts out on me again."

He chewed on his lip as he watched a lander emerge from the side of the Spy's ship, wondering if he should drop a sticktight inside before he went. Maybe she wasn't like him, maybe she had the maintenance hatch trapped. She thought of things. But if she got away from him this time . . . no, if she got away this time, it was over. She'd head straight back for Digby, Digby would call the Kliu and collect his fee, and Mort would be dead two heartbeats afterward.

As soon as the shields flared as the lander hit atmosphere, Worm went arcing away. He hit atmosphere twenty minutes later, landed *Kanti* on a barren islet just big enough to hold her, bonded the EYE to its zipper sled and sent it racing toward the place where the lander touched down.

As he watched her walk toward the children playing on the beach, he thought about activating one of the EYE's darts and killing her then, but she hadn't found the smuggler yet and a world is a big place to search and she was a better searcher than he was and she knew things he didn't.

He watched her face change as she seemed to absorb the langue the children were speaking, though he couldn't make any sense of it. In less than a heartbeat she was talking back to them and being understood. "Talent. Word is Digby likes Talent, buys it wherever he can. I bet she can truthtell, too, and that's why she believed ol' Harmon without worrying about babbling him. No wonder it's her Digby sent. Spins lies quicker'n a Menaviddan spins web and looks through your lies like you're made out of glass."

When she went back to the lander alone, he started the EYE home and chewed on his lip until Kanti's screen showed her taking the lander up and hovering in the clouds. "She's looking for something. Those kids told her something. Not enough, I think, but something."

7

Through the EYE which was hovering in the fronds of a tree, he watched the local messing with some sand while the Spy crouched beside him. After a while he understood what the man was doing. He was making an island. A particular island. Once again Worm thought about darting the woman, but he still wasn't sure. It was better to wait until he was actually looking at Lylunda. He couldn't understand what they were saying, so that island map could mean anything, and he'd already made too many wrong choices.

The Spy bowed and walked back to the lander. The local looked at the map, his face troubled, then he smeared it out with his foot and went the other way along the beach.

Uneasy, Worm called the EYE back, hoping he had time to reclaim it.

As he watched the lander shoot for the horizon, Worm swore and pushed the flikit after it. The flikit was a lot slower than a lander, so he didn't dare go back to his ship or wait for the EYE to come home or even stop to scoop it up as he passed over it. In the time any of that would take, she could drop the loop on Lylunda and be on her way off planet.

There was enough fuel left in the zipper sled to take it around the world and back, so he set the call and concentrated in getting the most speed he could out of the flikit while keeping a wary eye on the screen, watching for any sign of the lander.

The chase seemed to go on forever across the mostly empty sea, though he overtook and left behind several large sailboats. Since the Spy had ignored them, he did also. He passed over several islands, most of them with locals doing this and that on the beaches and in the villages, ignored these.

Then he saw an island he recognized. The one the local had sculpted—and a good job it was, too. He'd got the coast just right, that spine of mountains like bony teeth, the thick jungle round the base of those teeth, the wide apron of pale yellow sand.

And belly down on that sand, the lander.

And a short distance off, two women talking.

He clicked the mufflers on, dipped to tree level, using the fronds as a sketch of a screen, cranked up the visuals, and focused on the women. Lylunda all right, looking angry, upset, sitting with a drum held between her hands, staring out at the sea as the Spy talked to her. He ground his teeth. If only he hadn't deployed the EYE the last time, if he'd just kept it with him, he could listen to what they were saying. He could kill the Spy, stun Lylunda, and get off this stinking mudball. On the other hand, they could be talking local jabber. Be just his luck. . . .

Cutter in one hand, Worm began easing closer, keeping as low as possible, the fronds of the treetops brushing against the side of the flikit as he crept past them. He had to be careful; he didn't want the Spy sheltering herself behind Lylunda. The closer he could get before she noticed him, the less chance she'd have to think up something nasty.

The Spy turned and began trotting toward the lander. She was inside before Worm had time to react; she fired up the lifters and took off.

She was leaving. She had the woman and she let her go and now she was gone. All he could think of was that Lylunda had given her the information the Kliu wanted, so the Spy didn't have to take the trouble to carry her off.

Sick with anger, Worm brought the flikit down on the sand, piled out of it, and ran to Lylunda. He jerked her to her feet, started shaking her. "What did you tell her? What? Tell me what you told her." He coughed, saw flecks of red splatter her face, but that didn't matter. He shook her some more, not giving her a chance to answer him, shouting the same questions over and and over.

She broke his hold with an ease that surprised him. He hadn't expected her to be that strong.

"Worm. Sit down. Just sit down." Her voice was

soothing and it only increased his rage. He reached for her again, but she stepped between his arms, slapped her open hands against his shoulders and a moment later he was flat on his back staring up at the sky, wondering what had happened.

She knelt beside him, a sadness in her eyes that he hadn't expected. "That you're here tells me why you're here," she said.

It took him a while to sort out the sense of that. She waited for him to understand, then she went on, "If you keep being angry at me and trying to hurt me, I can't help you."

"What?" His throat was raw and trying to talk made his head dizzy. "Help me?"

"Didn't your keph warn you?" She helped him sit up. He couldn't believe how weak he was, how suddenly that weakness had flooded through him. "This is a deadly world if you don't know how to cope with it."

"Help me on my feet. I have to get back to my ship. There's an ottodoc in it. . . ."

"That won't work, you know. You should let me take you into the village."

"No! The flikit. I got to get back to my ship."

"All right. If that's what you want. Take my hand." She pulled him up, set his arm about her shoulders and helped him stagger over to the flikit.

When they reached it, he grabbed onto her wrist and with remnants of his strength, fueled by desperation, he tried to pull her into the flikit.

She wrenched her arm free, slapped at his hand when he reached for her again. "If you managed to get me in there, we'd both be dead before we left the ground."

"What? What are you talking about?" He barely got the words out before a fit off coughing seized him and nearly turned him inside out. "What . . . what what's happening . . . ?"

"Be quiet. It's the only chance. Be qui. . . ."

The darkness closed round him, cutting off her words.

8

He woke inside a room somewhere, stretched out on a hard, lumpy bed. His face was a sticky mess and there was a foul taste in his mouth. Lylunda was sitting in a chair beside him, a bowl in her hands.

"You'll live," she said, "but I don't know if I've done you any favor feeding you the tung akar. Did you need money that much, Worm? That you'd come here to earn it?"

"Not money," he said. Speaking hurt his throat, but he wanted her to understand. "I need you to trade for my brothers. That's the price the Kliu put on your head. Mort and Xman. They've got them. They're going to hang Mort if I don't bring you back. Or bring back what you know. You told the Spy, why can't you tell me?"

"The Spy, that's what you call her? I made a bargain with her, but I haven't told her anything. Not yet."

A blissful ease spread through him. There was time. There was still time. All he had to do was get his strength back. He closed his eyes and let sleep take him.

16

Family—Where You Go When There's No Help For It

1

Message drone: to Wolff/Aleytys Greybond
from ship *Backhoe*/Shadith
(written message, not recorded)

Lee, I need your help. It's touchy since Digby is moving to compete with Hunters and I'm on a job for him, but you're the only one I think can do what has to be done. I don't want to make a comcall, hence this letter. I'm heading for Wolff on the off chance that you're home and that you can help. I'm in the Callidara, so it'll be a while. I know this is vague, but I'm just letting you know I'm coming with a problem we've got to talk about.

Shadith reread what she'd written, wrinkling her nose. *You're really getting paranoid, Shadow. Just because this is Digby's ship, it doesn't have to mean he's watching everything you do. Uh-huh. Maybe no, maybe so. I like that playful little git, but. . . . Hm, think about it, Shadow. What are you really seeing there? Is the Digby you know just a face he puts on to charm you?*

She shook her head, dropped the cargo shell into the drone insert, keyed in the destination, and sent the drone on its way to Wolff. It would get there in a few days, rather than the weeks it would take her to make the journey. Drones didn't 'split like ships, it was some other, quicker way they took, but no one knew exactly how they worked, even on the Hegger world where they were invented and manufactured.

> Message drone: to ship *Backhoe*/Shadith
> from Wolff/Aleytys Greybond
> (written message, not recorded)

My my, aren't we being cautious. This is the second time you've written instead of sending a voice flake. What's up, Shadow? As to me, I haven't had a Hunt for two years now and there's no prospect of action anywhere in sight. We'll deal with conflicts of interest if and when their ugly heads pop up. I'll be delighted to see you. How long has it been? Three years? Four? You won't recognize Lilai, she's such a big girl now. I'll take your cue, Shadow, and won't bother with questions about this mysterious business until I can ask them to your face. But don't you dawdle, you hear? You've got my curiosity steaming.

2

Shadith set the flit down in the paved patio on the south side of Aleytys' house. She left her gearsac in it and moved along the path that led round to the front door. Flowers bloomed everywhere in the frantic exuberance of the brief summer of these latitudes and the vines were overgrowing the windows again. Aside from the chirping of the hoard of meuttertiks moving in and out of their mud nests plastered on the wall up by the roof and the whisper of a half-hearted breeze through the conifers, a deep and peaceful silence spread like a quilted comforter over the place.

She palmed the door's latch sensor, raised her brows when it didn't open, just triggered a recording. "Shadow, come round to the stables. Lilai's having a riding lesson."

Aleytys was leaning on the fence, watching her daughter's lesson. Lilai was a red-haired eight-year-old, a thin and wiry girl with eyes too big for her face. She was perched on the back of a black gelding moving at a walk, her face intent as she listened to the old man who stood in the center of the ring.

"Lee."

Aleytys turned her head, smiled at Shadith and waved her over. "You made good time," she said, keeping her voice low so she wouldn't distract horse and rider. "Look at that little flea. Like she was born in the saddle. I was remembering my first ride. I can't believe how ignorant I was. Good thing I had the mind touch or that poor beast would have shucked me in three steps and gone home to his herd."

. . . watch your shoulders. That's better. Soften the wrists . . . (Chuff chuff from the gelding, dull clop of his hooves, tink-clink of the bridle)

"One way or another we've had our fling with horses, Lee. Me, I remember the ride across half of Ibex. Lilai is looking good. How long has she been having lessons?"

. . . canter, right lead . . .

"Two years now. She's been crazy about horses since she started walking. I'd look up from something I was try- ing to get done and there she'd be, heading for the pasture or plowing through snow to the barn. So I found Maestre Vassil, hired him to teach her, and gave her a new god." Aleytys chuckled, then shook her head. "I don't know what I'm going to do when she gets a few years older."

Shadith smiled at the poorly concealed pride in Aleytys' voice. "Considering who her mother is. . . ."

. . . head up . . . not so much leg . . . better . . . yes, yes . . . keep your mind on what you're doing . . . better . . . keep going. . . .

Aleytys sighed. "I keep hoping Grey's part in her is strong enough to give her a little common sense."

Walk . . . wrong lead . . . that's better . . . shoul- ders. . . .

"Is he out on a Hunt?"

"He's more or less given up on Hunting. Canyli Heldeen is thinking seriously of retiring as Head and Grey wants the job. I complicate his maneuvers." She moved her shoulders. "So I stay as far away from the Council and politics as I can manage, which means he's gone a lot."

"Lee, if my being here makes problems. . . ."

"I don't think so. And even if it did, I wouldn't care, Shadow. You and Swarda and Harskari are my family, and I'm not going to let that bunch of pinch noses erase you from my life."

. . . once more . . . yes yes . . . watch your wrists . . . good.

That's enough for today. Take him in.

There was a whispered violence in Aleytys' words and Shadith sensed a darkness in her that she hadn't seen before. Was there trouble between her and Grey? Or maybe a crisis in the uncertain peace between her and the other Wolfflans?

Mouth twisted into a wry half-smile, Aleytys patted her arm. "Not to worry, Shadow."

Shadith snorted. "Put two empaths together and conversation can get more complicated that a Menaviddan web maze."

Aleytys' smile broadened. "We might as well go in. Lilai's going to be busy a while polishing tack and cleaning out stalls." She shook her head, "Don't have to get after her to do it. She loves it. Loves everything that smells of horse."

3

The screens were engaged and the windows open, the evening breeze blowing along the living room. Lilai was in her room working with the Tutor Circuit. Shadith and Aleytys sat drinking tea and watching the setting sun color the shrunken snow pack on the mountain peaks.

Aleytys set down her cup with a sharp click. "All right, Shadow, stop wallowing in guilt and tell me what this is about."

"Have you ever heard of a world called Bol Mutiar?"

"No. That's in the Callidara? I've never been there."

"It gets a bit iffy here. If you were anyone else, I don't think ... well, you're not, so here it is." She sketched her line of investigation and what she'd discovered, the mistakes she'd made, the talk she had with the Drummer, the final conversation with Lylunda.

"She's desperate." Shadith ran the heels of her hands

back and forth along the leather chair arms, needing a way to vent the pressure that had built up in her. "I got to know her rather well while I was tracking her, Lee. She was smart, tenacious, independent. It hurt seeing what'd happened to her. As if the Lylunda she'd been was being eaten away and someone else was being poured into empty places." She slapped her hands on the leather. "She's watching it happen, Lee, fighting it and losing and losing and losing. Gods! Whatever else happens, I want to break her free of that world."

"And you want me to purge her of that tung akar and whatever else that's got its claws in her."

"That's it, Lee." Shadith passed her hand over her hair, then looked at the palm. "I suspect there's something in the air. A virus maybe, an organism of some kind. And the tung akar keeps it benign as long as there's some kind of balance. The longer you stay, the more delicate the balance. And sometimes the organism hits a reproductive high that's triggered by who knows what, and it consumes the person. A collective intelligence? There was something there, I could feel it pressing at me, not liking me much. I was very glad to get away. And I spent a good while in the ottodoc, trying to make sure I wasn't bringing any of it with me. It reads me as clean, but with the story the Drummer told me. . . ." She shrugged, grimaced.

"How do you feel?"

"Ready to wallow in the glooms, otherwise healthy enough."

"Hm. I'm not picking up anything peculiar, but in a moment I want you to let me check you over. What's the other thing that's worrying you?" Aleytys clicked her tongue when Shadith raised her brows. "A rather obvious deduction, Shadow. You didn't need to tell me all that just to persuade me to help get the woman off Bol Mutiar."

"It's the Taalav array. My job is to find out where they are and give the location to Digby to pass on, but if I do, they'll be destroyed. I can't let that happen, Lee."

"Hm. It's possible they've already died, you know. Intelligent or not, transferring a complex species to a new environment is apt to be chancy. You have to think about that."

"I hope not. It'd make things a lot easier for me, but I really don't want them to be dead. I've quit this job, Lee; I just haven't told Digby yet."

"Talking with him wouldn't work? Maybe you could come to an arrangement."

"Would you really expect Digby to kiss his fee good-bye just because one of his shovels has a qualm or two?"

"Shovel? Hmp. I'd get bored with that the second time I heard it." Aleytys inspected her cup, refilled it from the samovar. "Right. I know that. Must have been sheltered here too long, growing illusions like weeds. The sooner we see about Lylunda, the better, so we'll take my ship. You can leave the company ship in the tie-down upstairs. Harskari called last week; she and Loguisse have been ambling about . . ." she chuckled, "looking for trouble, if you ask me. She's coming by here next week. If you don't mind, once we've left, I'll call her back and tell her to meet us at Bol Mutiar." She got to her feet. "I'd better go tell Lilai she can't come with me this time. I don't want her anywhere near that virus or whatever it is." She smiled, shook her head. "I won't get an argument this time. Mothers are way down on the list of important beings. Vassil has the place of honor."

She left, trailing an aura of jealousy and pain. And amusement turned on herself. And interest.

Shadith stretched out in her chair, put her feet up on

the hassock. *Harskari. That's good. She'll know if Storsten would work for the Taalav. I still have to talk to them first, find out what they want.*

Storsten, the next world out from Vrithian—a heavyworld, in the same range as Pillory; its largest life forms were wormlike grazers with chitinous armor to protect them from smaller and faster predators like dog-sized scorpions. Since Vrithian had never been located by outsiders in all the centuries of Vryhh existence, the Taalav would be safe there. She was pleased with herself for coming up with that idea.

Hm. It'd be a hoot if the Kliu swooped down on the smuggler's planet with death and destruction in mind and ran into a pair of Vryhh ships standing guard. She giggled at the thought of the Kliu pulling up in consternation when Harskari snapped a beam across their bow and told them to get out or get ashed. A tridda comic, that. Of course, it wouldn't happen. Too boring for Harskari. She dipped a finger in her cup. The tea was cold. She looked at the samovar, sighed, and set the cup down; she didn't really want more tea.

Outside, the sun had vanished, taking most of the color with it except for a last fugitive gleam lighting the needle peaks. For a moment she envied Aleytys this house, but only for a moment. Lee had paid a price for it and was still paying. *I'm not willing to do that, not yet anyway. I wish I knew what was wrong here. I wish I knew if I should do something about Digby. I wish I could do something about the Taalav, get all of them someplace where they'd be safe. . . .*

"Shadow, I called Grey, he'll be home in a bit. Um, I'd like to talk to him here. Neutral territory as it were. Would you mind . . . ?"

"No problem. If you're doing the transport, I should probably get back to the ship, make sure I've got everything I need."

"He'll want to say hello. You don't have to leave yet."

"All right." *I doubt that, Lee, I truly do. Last time I was here you'd need a q-scan to measure the amount of welcome he was putting out.* She knew Aleytys could read her skepticism. She was sorry for that, but there was nothing she could do about it.

"Let me take a look at you now, hm? See what you brought away from your visit to that world. If anything. Stretch out on the couch. You know the routine."

As Lee's fingers moved lightly over her, Shadith was aware of heat and an uneasiness so faint she could barely feel it—an uneasiness that was not part of her but something else. There was a sudden flare of intense pain which vanished almost as soon as it began, then only the familiar lassitude from the deep relaxation Lee's touch induced.

When she was finished, Aleytys got to her feet, worked her shoulders. "You had some visitors in a few cells. Cysted and dormant. Didn't like it when I poked at them, but you're clean now."

"Akh, horrid thought." Shadith sat up. "Two years since your last Hunt?"

"Canyli took Grey on as her Second around then. Funny how it happens." A quick unhappy twist of her mouth, then Aleytys walked to the window and stood looking out at the developing stars. "Suddenly there were no suitable assignments. Don't make a fuss, he says. I've seen what's been available, he says. You wouldn't want any of them, he says. Maybe so. Two years. It's nothing, a snap of the fingers. We've had problems before, but we've worked them out. Now . . . he looks at me now, he looks in the mirror . . . and he sees an aging man, while I don't change . . . when he can't handle it any longer, he stays in town or at his own place. I've tried, Shadow. He won't talk to me or

let me ... I can't ... I don't want to let this fall
apart ... I think something broke in him that time on
Avosing ... you were there ... sometimes I hate you
for that, Shadow ... that you were there and I wasn't
... I think more than anything that's why I had Lilai.
And of course there is Lilai. And I remember what it
felt like when I knew my own mother had run away
and left me. And you were there, Shadow, still in the
Diadem, that time on Cazarit, you remember, when I
begged Stavver to let me talk to Sharl. My son. You remember. Sharl wouldn't talk to me; my son wouldn't
even let me look at him. I can't let that happen with
Lilai. Happily ever after the old stories say. Well, when
it's really *ever* after, happily goes out the door."

Shadith hadn't turned the lights on after the sunset
watch, so Aleytys was a shadow against the faint
flicker of the bug screen. She lifted an arm and Shadith
thought she rubbed at her eyes, but she couldn't be
sure.

"Grey's coming. He'll be landing in a few minutes.
Shadow, would you do me a favor and clear away the
tea things? I've got to wash my face and get myself set
for this."

When Grey walked into the room, Shadith was
shocked. Sometime in the years since she'd last seen
him, he'd turned into a pinched old man—not old in
the body exactly, his hair was still mostly dark, his
muscles were firm, his hands steady; when he walked,
there was no shortening of his stride. The sense of age
lay in the stiffness with which he held himself, the expression on his face and the fragility she felt inside
him. The joy's gone out of him, she thought. "'Lo,
Grey," she said and managed a smile to go with the
greeting.

"Shadith." He was polite, controlled. "You're looking well."

"And it's good to see you, Grey. Lee tells me you're possibly in line for the job as Head. Best of luck."

"Will you be staying long? There's a shooting party next week; we could arrange an invitation."

"Thanks, but this is just a drop-by. I'll be leaving tomorrow. And I'd best go get ready to do that." She smiled and went out, knowing he was looking after her with barely repressed anger.

4

As Shadith was doing a last runthrough of her kephalos files, checking to see if there was anything else she should download to transfer over to Aleytys' *Tigatri,* the announcer tinged to let her know she had an incoming call.

Aleytys' face had a brittle quietness. "Shadow, I'm coming up to *Tigatri* in an hour. Would you be ready to transfer by then?"

"Fine. I've about got things wrapped up here. Let me know when you're in and I'll sled across."

"Will do."

Shadith scowled at the screen, shook her head. "I say good-bye to my sisters' ghosts and now Lee's life is starting to break up. I never thought how much it meant, knowing she was here, a place I could always come back to. All erased. Or will be in a few years. Not a place I want to visit after this. No Digby. No job. No idea what I want to do. Funny how it's all happening at the same time. The Flux is fluxing royally."

She sighed, got wearily to her feet, and went to start packing the bubblesled for the transfer to the other ship.

5

Tigatri's prime mobile waited at the lock to greet her. "Welcome aboard, Shadow. Your quarters are ready for you. Is there anything you need immediately?"

"'Llo, Abra. No, all that gear can be stowed." She took the flake case from her belt sac. "If these could be read into the kephalos, I'd appreciate it."

"Of course. Simply stowed, or do you wish *Tigatri* to comment?"

"Comments would be more than welcome, along with any data you have on Bol Mutiar. And she might check the flakes for sneaky hitchhikers. Hm. And my other gear, too. For the same thing."

"Understood."

She stepped onto the skimmer flat beside the mobile and hummed through melting mutating interior space until walls stabilized about her and she was standing in a pleasant, ordinary room, much like her apartment on University.

"Your gear has been put away. Doll will be your serviteur. If any questions occur, she will have the answers for you. You are free of all areas of the ship except for the Archira's quarters." Abra bowed with liquid grace and was gone.

The last time she'd seen *Tigatri*'s prime mobile, he'd looked rather like Grey. That was gone. Now he might have been a twin to Swarda if he'd had anything resembling flesh.

That startled her, and when she thought about it a little, depressed her, because it told her more than she wanted to know about the way things were going between Aleytys and Grey. *Tigatri* was sensitive to Aleytys' moods because her kephalos was configured to be in part a duplicate of Lee's mind/brain and it was that which took care of Abra's appearance. It wasn't a good sign to see Aleytys wiping Grey away so completely and retreating, symbolically at least, to the days before she settled on Wolff, when she still had that drive to find her mother and a place where she could fit in.

"Doll, what's the estimated travel time to Bol Mutiar?"

"Four days, nine hours." Doll was a small, delicate mobile with huge eyes and daintily pointed ears. She was a remnant from the time when Aleytys' old enemy Kell had owned this ship, an image dredged up from who knew what corner of that Vryhh's twisted psyche. Her only changes were interior; she no longer cringed when you spoke to her but grinned like a happy child. How much of that was illusion born of programming, how much a result of the AI Doll shared with the ship, was something Shadith didn't know and didn't worry about.

"Tell me what *Tigatri* knows about the tung organism on Bol Mutiar."

"The organism is indeed a collective awareness, its intelligence unmeasurable but probably not much above the higher animals. It is rather more complex than you assumed; that which exists within the tung akar produces toxins which slow the rate of reproduction to tolerable levels within the bodies of the hosts as long as the host is in contact with the totality. Remove the host from such contact and the organism will reproduce in such numbers that it will eat the body. One must spend more than a day or two on the surface for the organism to invade all the cells of the body, which is why the Archira only discovered the fragments cysted and dormant in you, Shadow. There is a single exception to that. If a host is attacked or seriously threatened by a nonhost, the collective awareness reacts to protect the host by a massive invasion of the attacker's body. This counterstroke is usually fatal."

"Would it count an attempt to remove a host from the surface as a threat?"

"Yes."

"How quickly would it strike?"

"The moment it felt the loss. As a speculation, this might occur at some arbitrary location within the atmosphere, perhaps that point where the density of the ambient organisms approaches nil."

"Vindictive little merds. Kill the hosts to get the attacker."

"As I said, it is not a particularly intelligent organism."

"Hm. Might be possible to construct a warning device with a bit of Lylunda's blood in it. When the organism begins its explosive growth pattern . . ."

"Yes. That would be possible. I would suggest a more sensitive warning device already exists in your empathic response. It seems quite likely that you will sense its agitation before the multiplication actually begins."

"Maybe so, but it never hurts to have a backup, so if you'd construct such a device and have it ready for charging with the blood. . . ."

"I'll do that."

"And work on a plan that will let us take Lylunda offworld without getting ourselves killed in the process. I'm thinking this is going to be very complicated."

"Yes, I will do that."

Shadith sighed. "And I hope you'll come up with something better than the mishmash I've been churning out. Take me to the garden, I've got a song starting in my head and it wants to come out."

6

Aleytys drifted into the garden space, lowered herself onto a boulder, and sat with her feet in the running stream.

Shadith looked at the words she'd just written, sighed and slashed a line through them, the black ink from the stylo canceling out another failed attempt. She set the pad down, let the stylo click home in its magnetic holder. "Lee."

"Sorry if I'm interrupting."

"Wasn't getting anywhere anyway. Figured out how we're going to do this?"

"*Tigatri*'s been reconfiguring a lander. She's set up a cleanroom where the air can be changed every few minutes, dumped outside the ship, with fields around it to block anything getting back in. We go down, you identify Lylunda for me, we get her into that room and head for changeover fast as we can punch it. Abra blows all air in the lander except for what's in the room with us. With the air exchange going, I clean out Lylunda, probably you, too, this time, myself as needed. We should be flushed sufficiently clear by the time we reach *Tigatri*. To be sure of this, Abra will scan Lylunda on the way up, get some subcellular mugshots of the organism and *Tigatri* will run a full scan on the lander, do another clean on it before she lets us onboard. Then we do a quick jump to one of the outer planets in the system, link with Harskari and Loguisse and head for the destination Lylunda gives us. Might be a good idea not to let her know about Harskari and your plans for the arrays. What she doesn't know, she can't babble."

"Hm." Shadith felt uneasy. Silence shouted questions she didn't want to ask, but every subject she thought about bringing up seemed worse than silence.

"Did you ask Harskari about Storsten as a new home for the arrays?"

"Not yet. Let's leave that until we've pulled Lylunda out."

"All right."

"You're sure about quitting Digby?"

"I'm sure. I managed to keep faith with myself and him last time, but it was a shaky peace I made. And this one? This is really a simple job. He said that and it's true. In a little while I'll have the answer he needs to collect his fee. I need to be able to do that, Lee." She sighed. "But the Taalav aren't beasts. They're people. They make songs. And I like them. I suppose that shouldn't make a difference, but it does."

"Would you do as much for them if they were little horrors?"

"I like to think I would, but who knows." Shadith rolled onto her back, laced her fingers over her ribs and stared up at the blue shimmer meant to represent sky. "With you and Harskari helping me, there's half a chance I can pull this one out. The next, though. . . . " She sighed. "It's better if there is no next. Hmp, University is all right for a while, but too confining over time. Music's necessary but not enough. And in a year or two, I'm going to need a way to make enough money to keep my ship going. My agent on Helvetia is doing fairly well with the coin I left with him, but I can't live on the income for long. Swarda's found his niche and he's happy with it. Why can't I?"

"Is that a real question?"

"I suppose not." She turned her head. "Lee, what are you going to do?"

"Nothing until Lilai leaves for University. Another nine years. Maybe ten. Depends on how she matures after she passes puberty. Grey will be living in his house, she'll move between the two of us."

"Has she inherited the Vryhh long life?"

"Harskari's been after me to have cell studies made. I've put it off. I don't really want to know. Easier on all three of us if I don't. He asks me that, you know. Every year or so. She's his daughter, too, I want him to love her, not resent her. And I won't lie to him. So, no tests until Lilai herself does the asking."

"What about Talents?"

"Early days for that. Took me a while to grow into mine, you know. Right now, all she wants is horses. Hm. I just had a disturbing thought. What if Lylunda Elang decides she doesn't need to keep her bargain?"

"Hah! That's a cheerful one. I don't like using it because it's so apt to do more damage than you expect, but I'll pump her full of babble and pry the answer out of her."

"I was wondering. . . ."

"Whether all this fussing about morality means I'll dither about, resplitting split hairs?"

"Something like that."

"No. That comes under not-nice but not-fatal and it'll get the job done."

"Hmmmm. . . ." Aleytys moved her feet in the little stream, lifting them at intervals so drops of water cascaded musically from her heels into the rush of the current. The minutes slid past in a deepening silence.

On the other bank of the stream Shadith lay watching the blue of the pseudo sky and the small creatures flying about in it. Two of them looked like tiny green and gold dragons and were swooping in interlocked figure eights. Others were small bright birds, silver and blue and crimson and a dark metallic green, with trailing silky tail feathers and elaborate crests. There were soft brown moths that sang more sweetly than any bird. Around her in the grass and the ferns that grew under the trees she heard small rustles, sometimes saw red-brown squirrels run up a crackled trunk.

The whisper of the stream and the tink tink tink of the drips falling from Aleytys' feet crept into Shadith's bones and soothed away the worry and uncertainty.

After a while she slept.

17

Waiting

—1

Lylunda looked up as one of the village girls came into the house. "He's worn out. He should sleep for a good while now. What's your name?"

"Delala, Drummer." She came across the room, her bare feet silent on the mat. "He looks like just a boy."

"Don't let that fool you, Delala. He's clever and rather dangerous." Lylunda stood. "Get him into the Bond as soon as you can."

"Oh, we'll do that in any case."

"Omel oma, I leave him in your care. There's tung stew simmering on the stove. Soon as he stirs, get some more of it down him. I'll look in again before the beronta leaves."

Lylunda left the guest house and walked down to the beach where the flikit sat like a metallic cricket, already starting to corrode. Tudil was waiting for her, standing beside a small sailing canoe pulled up on the sand.

She waved to him. "See you at the edge of the Deep," she called.

He laughed. "Edge of the Deep." He pulled the canoe out into the water, swung himself inside with the liquid ease that still amazed her. After he got the sail up, he went running straight out to sea, the canoe bobbing up and down like a rubber toy as it lifted and fell with the waves.

Lylunda waited until all she could see was the tip of the mast, then she climbed into the flikit. "You or me, Worm," she said as she took it up. "With this out of the way," she patted the arm of the pilot's chair, "by the time you can get back to your ship, you won't want to. And I'll be gone. One way or another, I'll be gone."

She caught up with the canoe, slowed down and drifted along ahead of it until Tudil dropped sail, tossed a sea anchor overside, and turned into the wind. Blessing Worm's habit of keeping his tools meticulously maintained, she clipped the lift harness around her, took the flikit spiraling up until she thought she was high enough. She disabled the altitude interlock, started the flikit racing down a long slant toward the surface of the water, a slant pointed away from Tudil and the canoe. A moment later, she ejected and went tumbling away from the machine.

The lift harness was set to Worm's weight. He was thin and short, without a lot of muscle mass, so her heavier body plunged swiftly enough to put a lump in her throat, but it let her reach the water before the flikit did. The flotation bubbles deployed and she began kicking toward the canoe.

The flikit hit as Tudil reached for her. He got her inside, made her crouch beside the mast. "Hang onto that, we gonna be jumping." He got the sail up, cut the drag, and ran farther out to sea, letting the swell from the crash lift the canoe and thrust it onward.

* * *

The sun set before they got back to shore.

As she stumbled from the canoe, Lylunda could hear the beronta drums sounding in the village; they drew her, but she was really too tired to answer the throb in her blood. She touched Tudil's arm. "Tell Menget I'll be sleeping in the guest house tonight. We still leaving tomorrow?"

"Yes. After the morning market."

"Omel oma, come get me when it's time, hm?"

2

Lylunda sat with Worm while Delala was fixing breakfast for them. His face was knotted with the intensity of his sleep and he looked absurdly like a baby. She'd have felt worse for him if he and his brother hadn't used Zombi on her. Xman. Hah! Exi Exinta. What an idiot ploy that was. She couldn't see much resemblance; Worm and the Xman must have had different mothers. The other brother was a convict on Pillory. "Not a political." She shivered. If you weren't a political, governments sent you to Pillory because they didn't do death and cringed at the thought that you'd ever get loose. "I think it's probably just as well for the universe if your Mort stays right where he is."

He stirred a little at the sound of her voice. His mouth worked; he closed one hand into a fist, pressed it against his lips, and settled back to sleeping.

She leaned over him, pinched his earlobe.

He woke reluctantly, scowling at her.

"You don't talk Pandai," she said. "And I'm leaving. So I want to be sure you know what you're into here. Make up your mind to it, if you live and I think you probably will, you'll never leave Bol Mutiar again. There's something in the air, a virus or something like

that. The Pandai call it the Tung Bond, for what that's
worth. Make it mad and it'll eat you alive from the inside out. You should know, because it started to do just
that yesterday when you grabbed me. Remember how
it felt, Worm, and walk carefully around these folk.
Even an ottodoc's no good, so don't count on that. The
Pandai on this island will take care of you. It's called
Keredel, by the way, and the Pandai here call themselves Kerdela. I've explained about your brothers and
why you were trying to attack me. They're good people and are really sorry about what's going to happen
to you, though they can't do anything about it. The
flikit is at the bottom of the ocean. I did that, so don't
blame the locals. The girl who will be bringing your
breakfast is called Delala. Remember the Bond and
treat her nice. Good-bye, Worm."

He shoved himself up and tried to grab her, but he
was too weak and fainted instead.

Tudil came while she was still in the kitchen, drinking the last of the tea. "Luna, Menget says you should
come now; there's a storm blowing up and we need to
get clear of land before it hits."

3

When Worm woke a second time, a pretty, smiling
girl was bending over him, washing his face with a
cool cloth. She fetched a cup of water, lifted his head
and helped him drink.

"Delala?" he said.

She giggled. "Ngar ngi," she said. "Delala. Kau tkoy
ak?" She touched his brow, repeated, "Kau tkoy ak?"

"Worm," he said, guessing at her meaning, though it
seemed obvious enough.

"Warrum," she said and giggled again. "Ak moi er a tiktut." She patted his knee. "Nga mengii."

He watched her trot from the room, listened to the soft pat of her bare feet as she went somewhere to do something. His whole body hurt and he was so weak he couldn't stand. It was enough to make anyone sink, especially when he'd done it to himself, coming here like this without even wondering why the Spy took off without Lylunda when all she had to do was put out her hand and take her.

Mort and Xman. He'd killed them. No way to get around that. His father was going to get hoiked out of his place because who could defend the Stead now? Cousins was all and cousins don't have the same blood bonds. Cousins betrayed you all the time. His eyes burned with tears that wouldn't stop coming. He was shamed, but he couldn't stop that crying.

Delala came in, clicked her tongue, and began talking at him. He didn't understand a word of it, and that just made the misery worse. She helped him sit up and empty his bladder into a pitcher of some kind.

It was odd, when he was wrung dry below, he stopped leaking from his eyes. She washed his penis and his hands, eased him back onto the bed, pulled the sheet over him, and trotted out again carrying the pitcher with her.

When she returned, she lifted his head and made him drink something hot and stinking. He almost threw it up again, but by the time she'd got the mugful of slop down him, the woe had retreated somewhere over the horizon. It was still there, but he was too numb to feel it.

After she went out for the third time, he lay staring at the ceiling trying not to think. Then he sighed. "I'm sorry, Fa. I'm sorry, Mort. I'm sorry, Xman. You'll have to get on however you can." Another sigh. He

let heavy eyelids droop shut and in a moment was
asleep.

4

Early in the morning, a little over a month after leaving Keredel, Lylunda looked up from the mezu she
was washing and saw a strange lander go whispering
by overhead, its shadow slipping like a bird across
the beronta, a bird with stubby wings and a flared
tail.

"The woman has come for you." Menget's voice.
She hadn't heard the Drummer approach, but he was
very light on his feet for such a big man.

Lylunda was annoyed, though she tried not to show
it. Here was another case of the Bond stripping her privacy from her; what one Pandai knew, they all knew,
as if the Bond thought something and those thoughts
were echoed in all Pandai minds. "I didn't expect her
so soon. You sure?"

"Yes. We'll be making landfall in three hours if the
wind stays steady. The island Oreallin. The woman
will be waiting for you there." He set his hand lightly
on her head. She could feel the warmth of it through
her hair. "Omel oma, I don't know what to think about
this. You aren't happy with us and you make the Bond
itch with your fighting against it. Yet you are enough
of the Bond that I'm afraid. . . ."

"She knows about that. She said she might have a
way."

"If you can go, we'll miss you, Luna. You've taught
us as much as you've learned and we're grateful for
that. Don't forget us. Or your drumming. Though I'll
ask you to leave the drum behind. It is of the Bond."
He tapped her head lightly and went away.

Lylunda bent over the scrub board, rubbing the mezu

up and down, up and down it, working absently, her eyes fixed on the water beyond the rail. Around her she could hear babies crying, women and girls gossiping as they repaired sails and prepared food for the one large meal spread out at mid-afternoon, men gossiping as they mended nets and worked at the constant maintenance it took to keep the beronta in good order, boys chasing each other across the deck and through the rigging—the thousand sounds large and small that she'd got used to in the months she'd spent on the *Remeydang*.

Already she felt separated from them. And impatient to be gone. The things she'd found pleasant a day before were suddenly so restrictive that she was choking on them. As she wrung out the mezu and got to her feet to hang it on the line stretched from the cabin overhang to the rail, she murmured to herself, "Naked I came from my mother's womb, naked I go forth from this second womb. And the only thing I'll miss is my drum."

5

The beeper in her hand, Lylunda walked along the beach.

Shadith was waiting beside the lander, but she wasn't alone. A red-haired woman a handspan taller stood beside her. Lylunda wondered about this woman, but tried not to let hope get too strong a hold. If this fell through, the loss of that hope would kill her.

As she got closer, she could feel the tung stirring in her. The Bond didn't like that redhead and the closer she got, the more it started fighting her. She took two more steps, then stopped, about two body lengths from the lander, unable to walk closer, the tung cramping her muscles and threatening nausea.

Shadith spoke. "Are you willing to come with us, Lylunda Elang?"

Lylunda understood the formality in the words, an offered contract. When she tried to speak, though, her throat knotted and she couldn't make a sound. She managed a nod before her whole body froze on her.

"I take that as agreement. My companion is Aleytys, the Hunter from Wolff. If you're heard of her, you know that she's a healer. If anyone can keep you alive, she will."

Aleytys the Half-Vryhh, Lylunda thought. *Maybe I will make it. . . .* She started shaking, her eyes watered until she couldn't see much but blurs, her stomach jerked, and hot vomit filled her mouth.

A moment later she felt hands on her. Someone stripped the mezu away, someone grabbed her arms and pulled her toward the lander. As she stumbled and nearly fell, someone swore, then hands were lifting her, carrying her.

Words came through the roar in her ears. "Abra, go!"

Broad straps are drawn tight over her body. Metallic clunks as they are locked down. Something hard and heavy on her mouth, collecting her spew and suctioning it away.

Words. "Hang on a moment, Shadow, soon as I've finished here. . . .

Hands on her.

Pain. Worse than the last time she'd drunk the cherar infusion. Knives scraping along her bones. Muscles cramping, trying to throw her into convulsions. Straps holding her, bruising her.

Coughing. Vomit hot in her mouth, sucked away. Again. Emptying herself into the sucking machine.

Wind. Hurricane. Driving across her, snatching her breath from her nostrils. No wind. Again the wind. No wind. Again. . . .

The tung desperate in her, clawing at her as it is driven forth. She hangs on, feeling the tung torn out of her.

Between one breath and the next, there was no more pain.

Aleytys' hands were warm on her, feeding her strength, pouring life into her body.

She was strong again, as full of energy as a berry with juice.

She opened her eyes, looked up into that blue-green gaze. "Thanks."

Aleytys smiled wearily. "It's not done yet, not quite. Rest a while. I'll be back to you in a minute."

Lylunda turned her head to watch and was appalled at what she saw.

Shadith lay on a cot like hers, strapped down. An ugly gray and ocher fungus grew in patches on her face and body, some of it even on her eyes, blood trickled from her nose and mouth with each labored breath. She was shuddering and moaning . . . and the moment Aleytys set her hands on her, she screamed. With her mouth and her whole body, she screamed, spewing blood and bits of rotten flesh over the healer's face.

The hurricane roared again. Air exchange, expelling the organism as Aleytys killed it and drove it from the body.

It was like watching a replay of what had happened to her, only seeing it from the outside, this time.

Lylunda coughed. And was afraid. The infection was in her again, growing in her. Exploding through her. It wasn't fair. She was clean a moment ago. It wasn't faiiir.

An eternity later, well-being returned to her, Lylunda watched Aleytys lean into the harness that she wore to keep her in place during the rush of the air exchange; her face had a faint webbing of fatigue lines that made her look for a moment as if she were a thousand years old, her body was slumped in utter exhaustion. Without opening her eyes, she said, "Sterilize, Abra. It's time."

A mellow baritone voice answered, "Heard and done, Archira."

The pumps hummed again and in seconds the room was filled with a gas that stank and stung like pepper essence. Lylunda's eyes teared and her body felt as if she were being whipped with nettles.

The baritone voice sounded again. "Take several deep breaths, Lylunda Elang. It will be painful, but it is necessary."

She grimaced, but followed instructions.

"Thank you, Lylunda Elang."

The pumps hummed again and the gas was drawn out. She sucked in cool clean air and thought that no pleasure would ever be as great.

Aleytys unsnapped the harness and moved alongside Shadith, undoing the latches that held the straps in place. When she'd finished and was turning to do the same with Lylunda's straps, Shadith sat up, stretched, and groaned. "Merd, Lee, that's nasty stuff, that organism whatsit. Whew! I definitely don't want to go through that again."

"Agreed. The Jilitera can have that world without any complaint from me." Aleytys straightened after she'd dealt with the last catch. "Abra, if you've finished sterilizing the rest of the lander, send Doll with the clothing I set aside for us."

"We're ready to berth, Archira. The outside clean was finished a moment ago."

"Good. The clothes, please."

The robe Aleytys handed Lylunda was a silky material that seemed to caress her skin as she drew it on, a dark blue that changed tones with liquid grace as it moved with her. She stroked the sleeve, sighed. Avrishum. Expensive enough to pay rent on a tie-down slot for several months. The robe Shadith was tying on was a dark crimson and Aleytys' was a dark green. *And I'm about to visit a Vryhh ship. Walking into one legend with another strolling before me, wearing the finest avrishum. Daddy dear would die to be here.* She grinned as she followed the two women from the cleanroom.

This time there was no lock to tumble through, only a melting wall that put them onto a skimmer flat that might have been stationary while the ship dissolved and reformed about them or might have carried them through a liquefying chaos until they were in another place.

What solidified around them was a room that looked like images she'd seen in triddas about forgotten times, paneled with rich carved wood and shelves with books on them, large leather chairs scattered about, elbow tables by each one; there were other, larger tables, a soft dark green rug on the floor, a fireplace with a screen in front of it, wood burning on firedogs, the sound perfect, snapping and crackling as sparks flew, the steady hiss of the fire. On shipboard it was so out of place it shouted luxury even more than the avrishum.

Aleytys and Shadith turned to her then. Shadith was the one who spoke. "You're free now, Lylunda Elang. We've paid your price. Where did you take the Taalav array?"

18
Solutions

1

In the screen Aleytys had called into existence, blanking out one wall of the library, the world at destination code 87950 KLD MLYD 3 was a cold, stony planet roughly equivalent to Pillory in size and surface gravity, but colder and harsher. The sun had a greenish cast and was smaller and paler than Pillory's crimson star.

Shadith raised her brows as she examined the star chart displayed at one side of the screen. The xenobi's choice was only two systems over from Hutsarté.

Lylunda sighed. "I thought that was deliciously ironic the first few days after I got back home. If they only knew, I thought. Not so funny now."

With a flick of her hand Aleytys banished the screen. "Shadow, why don't you get Lylunda settled in. *Tigatri*'s Belle is waiting in your quarters, Lylunda; she's been assigned to you as serviteur and will show you how to move about the ship. The public areas have been programmed to accept you." The room rippled around Aleytys; an instant later she was gone.

Lylunda brushed her hand across her eyes. "That is . . . weird!"

"Come on, our slide flat is disguised as that throw-rug over there. It's Lee's ship, so she doesn't need one, but Tigatri doesn't sublimn to us like she does to her, so we ride the slides. Actually, it's rather fun. Like a magic carpet in its sly way."

Shadith watched Lylunda's eyes widen as she looked around the cabin and widen again as the mobile Belle rippled into existence beside the communications complex set into a desk of dark rich wood.

Belle was another of the elfin serviteurs. Her face was triangular, her smile three-cornered, freckles were dotted across her nose and the tops of rosy cheeks. Like the rest of *Tigatri*'s mobiles, her substance was more energy than matter; despite that she was a warm, friendly presence. Her voice was a deep contralto, absurdly big for one so tiny. "Anything you want, Lylunda Elang, if I can get it for you, I will."

Lylunda glanced at Shadith, caught her nod, said, "Well, first thing, call me Luna."

"Of course, Luna. Whatever you wish."

"Do you have anything like a shipsuit available?" She smoothed her hand along her sleeve. "This is lovely, but I don't feel comfortable lounging around in something worth a couple months of ship fuel."

"We can do that, Luna." Belle's green eyes glazed for an instant, then brightened again. "It will be here in a few moments."

Shadith leaned against the wall, thumbs hooked over the belt to her robe. "You needn't worry about cost, Luna. Lee has connections and gets the stuff straight from the loom."

"Even so, Shadow, I'd rather play in cutoffs or something like that. Um, Belle. Do you have a drum around? Or could you make one to my specifications?"

"One could be made simply enough. Metal or wood?"

"Wood, if possible."

"Would you indicate dimensions and shape? If you could give us a plan. . . ." Belle waved a hand at the communications complex. "There's a light stylo you could use."

Shadith watched as Lylunda sketched the drum, the program turning the crude drawing into a professional plot; Lylunda made a few final adjustments, then turned to the mobile. "Belle, how long?"

"We can have it for you by tomorrow, mid diurne. Enough to let you try it and see if it needs adjustment."

Belle flickered out. When she returned an instant later with three shipsuits draped over her arm, Shadith stepped onto the slideboard. "Luna, you'll want food, a bath, and some time to recover. When you're ready, have Belle bring you to the garden. You'll like that, I promise you."

"Do all Vryyh ships have places like this?" Lylunda settled herself on Aleytys' boulder and gazed at the stream flowing past her feet, disbelief written in every line of her face.

"Lee tells me each ship is different. I've only seen this one so I wouldn't know. It's not quite as odd as you think because the garden looks bigger than it is. If you wandered around off the paths, you'd hit walls rather quickly, but what's the point of that? Might as well enjoy the illusion. You willing to talk about the Taalav?"

Lylunda shrugged. "Why not, seeing I've sold them out already."

"What's his name, your friend the xenobi, and how did he get them on your ship?"

"Prangarris. No friend of mine. I did the job for three Taalav crystals, not for any fondness I had for him. I'd done transport for him before. Pharmaceuticals. He pays prompt and doesn't argue. Not a nice man. For all that he was a political and not on Pillory for mass murder or the like, he was a first-order zorrit and probably ought to be squashed. As to how he got the two arrays on board, I was too busy watching screen and holding camou fields in place to pay attention to anything but the time it took."

"Who chose that planet?"

"He did. And got out a list of things he wanted me to provide. Food supplements for the Taalav, a year's food supply for him, a split com, a flikit adapted to heavy world flying, a spare exo and a survival pod with an argrav field powered by rechargeable light cells. The pod was the hardest to get hold of. I picked it up through Marrat's. Took a hefty prepayment before the broker would even look at my offer. What gripes me most about this is seeing the Kliu win."

"Way it goes, Luna. If you want them off your back, this is what'll do it. Hm. Something to cheer you. When I decided to skip from Hutsarté without Grinder noticing, I hot-wired your ship and took off in it. Lee's got it in tow now, topped up with fuel and completely resupplied. So you can go your way anytime you feel like it."

"You mean I just say Ta, folks, it's been fun—and that's it?"

"Mm hm. Though you might want to hang about till Digby's made his report and the Kliu are satisfied. Lee's offered her house as sanctuary if you feel like accepting her invitation."

"Huh! Think I'd refuse?" Lylunda grinned. "It'll feature in my Pit conversation for a decade at least."

"Did you know you had one of my recordings on your ship?"

"Yours?"

"Harp music and some songs I wrote."

"Shadowsongs?"

"Mm hm."

"Why you doing this sort of work, then?"

"Everybody asks me that, Luna. Just restless, that's all."

"I know the feeling. I was about to go crazy back there. Lovely place, nice people. Peaceful. Plenty of food. Work enough to keep you from rotting away, but no heavy labor. I mean, it's the kind of place folks dream of. And I'd go through that mess getting clear a dozen times a day, if that's what it took to get away."

Shadith blinked. "Paradise is none . . . hm . . . gives me an idea. . . . "

2

Harskari sipped at the tea, the firelight painting her face red and black; it was the only light source in the library at the moment. "Shadow, transferring the Taalav to Storsten sounds like one of your better ideas. I've checked the specs on Pillory and it's fair match—except for light quality. Might have to do something about that, a filter, shadow panels . . . hm . . . well, that can wait till later. We'll definitely have to fetch plant samples from Pillory, along with water, soil, the rest, so we can set up a duplicate ecosystem. The Taalav will need that for health and happiness in a new place."

Shadith rubbed at her nose. "That might be a problem. You know what Pillory is."

"Hah! Shadow, you mean to say you think a pedestrian little smuggler like Lylunda Elang could play the fox better than me?"

"Well, I didn't want to presume." Shadith opened her eyes wide and looked as demure as she could.

"Idiot." Harskari shook her head, smiling. "Loguisse and I talked this over. Since we don't want people connecting the Vrya with this, we thought we'd lay an ambush for the xenobi, keep him in stasis while we dealt with the Taalav, turn him loose elsewhere with a few crystals in his pocket to encourage silence. You've taken care of your smuggler friend; she doesn't know about my *Tiauchi* and needn't find out. Hm. Once Abra has worked a thorough clean of the site, making sure we've left no traces of our presence, you can report that you found where Prangarris was camped but that there was no sign of him or any living Taalav hanging about. The Kliu can look for themselves, collect the crystals we'll leave lying about, and go home satisfied."

"As long as I can avoid a verifier. Which shouldn't arise if they see the site with their own blinky eyes and get their grippers on those crystals." She looked down at her hands. "Since you'll be going there anyway, any chance you could get the rest of the Taalav off Pillory? The adult I talked to was sad and hopeful at the same time when he sang about the arrays being free with a whole world to themselves."

"If the arrays have managed to thrive away from Pillory, I don't see why not, but it does rather depend on what we find when we get to Lylunda's world and how well they adjust to Storsten. Not much point in a freedom that's a quick road to extinction."

3

The parlor in Lylunda's quarters had been reconfigured to make the whole wall above the comstation into a screen that picked up visuals from the Bridge and displayed them in a smaller, rather more congested form. Lylunda was stretched out on the long chair, her ankles crossed, her hands laced together behind her head. Shadith sat cross-legged on the floor beside her.

"The diamond-shaped continent just coming into view," Lylunda said. "The one that crosses the equator. I set him down by that freshwater lake near the northern tip of the diamond. Western edge of the water."

For a moment longer the nameless world at 87950 KLD MLYD 3 turned massively in the screen, the land areas a paisley pattern of dull browns and ochers with the occasional splash of dark purple. Then the screen was resorbed into *Tigatri*'s substance.

Aleytys' voice came through the grill. "Thank you, Lylunda. That will be sufficient, I believe. Shadow, will you come to the Bridge, please?"

4

The mobile Abra stood at the left edge of the screen that took up the whole front wall of the Bridge, his golden non-skin shimmering palely in its light.

Aleytys sat in a massive swivel chair, her hair a brilliant splotch of color against the black molding that supported her head. "Abra, expand the image of the western shore of that lake. Scan for mobile life, set up a cell for each instance, whether it's bipedal, Taalav, or other."

She's looking a lot better, Shadith thought. *Not so tired and drawn. Working over Luna was good for her. Wolff and Grey are abrading her soul, I think. If she feels she has to stay for Lilai, she better make sure Grey finds Hunts for her. And I can't say anything. Nothing worse than friends getting on your back about things you can't change. Spla!*

The screen divided into small cells like spreading soap bubbles, and images began to appear in them—a few adult Taalav and some juvenile forms moving rather feebly about, some worms and armored beetles. The main screen showed the survival pod, a flikit sitting beside it. And a large object made from interlaced crystal threads.

Aleytys flicked a finger at it. "Abra, can *Tigatri* see into that?"

Another cell opened. In it, the cocoon's layers peeled back, the image shivering and hesitating as the resonances of the crystal threads interfered with the probe. Finally, a body appeared, the face clear enough to be recognizable.

"Send that to Lylunda, Abra. Just the one cell. Got it? Good. Luna, do you recognize the man?"

"Prangarris." The voice that came through the grill had a dry edge to it. It was obvious Lylunda didn't appreciate her isolation from what was happening. "That's him, all right. He dead?"

Abra spoke. "Sensors indicate he has been dead for more than a year, Luna. There is evidence of several aneurysms in the brain that seem to have burst about the same time. He died within minutes of the event. The body has been preserved by the cold and the spun crystal."

"So much for Prangarris and his plans."

Shadith clicked her tongue. "What a dreary place. Looks like the Taalav are as dead as he is. The Kliu won't be getting much for their coin. Luna, did Prangarris ever say why he chose it?"

There was a moment's hesitation, then Lylunda's voice sounded again. "Mostly because no one in his right mind would try to settle it. At least, that's what he said. And he laughed when I agreed with him."

5

Shadith rubbed at her nose. "Lee, could we do a circuit with *Tigatri* scanning surface for more signs of Taalav? I'd like to be sure we've found them all."

"Abra, if you will. . . ."

It was a desolate world, large land masses separated by narrow, sinuous oceans that were ocher and crimson vegetable stews; there were several volcanoes in the process of erupting, spewing huge clouds of matter into the atmosphere, further cutting down the amount of sunlight reaching the surface. The seas were the world's repositories of strong color; on the land only a few colored lichens and mosses broke the dull monotone of mud, stone and coarse sand.

When they were stationary once again above the pod site, Shadith grimaced. "Maybe the Taalav like it. When I go down there, I'll ask them."

6

Shadith eased herself into the frame that was supposed to help the exoskeleton support her body so she could cope with the complicated language of the Taalav, with her breathing and the precise control of her voice. Because too many stilters might frighten the arrays into hiding and keep them from answering the song query, Aleytys was waiting a short distance off in the lander.

When Shadith was settled, she looked round. Neither array was anywhere in sight, not even infants and juveniles, but according to *Tigatri* and her own sense, they were within reach of her voice. She sucked in a lungful of the cold, thick air, ran through a series of vocalizations to help set her up for what she thought could become a long and difficult bargaining session.

===

Greet you **of the new land**	From tied-to-old-land
I, Singer	No-harm **offered wanted**
Who stand **on your land**	Their song I offer.

===

She cleared her throat, drank from the stem of the waterbottle.

Silence all round. She swept the area with her *outreach*. The Taalav stayed hidden and she could feel a feeble startlement mixed with anger and distrust.

She sang again:

===

Tied-to-old-land	**If ours thrive**
I, named Shadow	I **hear and repeat** for you
Sing **for the old-land this song**	Let them be.

===

Warning	**Truth and trust**
I, named Shadow	offer with open hands
Sing **to you-of-the-new-land**	Death comes.

===

The Two-Mouthed thieves	**swarm, disturbed nest**
I, **named Shadow sing warning**	run here, run there
Burn, fire and more fire	search out the-new-land

===

She continued singing for around ten minutes, amplifying the warning, saying she had not come to take them against their will, though she would mourn their deaths if such were their choice.

She dropped into silence and waited.

And waited.

She could feel two adult Taalav circling warily about her, edging in closer. . . .

When one of them finally appeared, moving into view around a pile of lichened rock, she was appalled. It looked sick and mean, the once bright cherry hood mottled with black and khaki, the large eyes of the headbeast filmy and oozing mucus. Around it was a dull aura of anger/resentment/hate that was thick enough to stain the air.

===

Why	**Why**	**Why**	Why
Shadow Singer	**trust not/trust you who speak**		
We the betrayed	**land-tied, taken, stolen by you/**		
	kind		
Listen should	**who die** (this/place) **starve** (this/		
we	place)		

===

(Woven around this, asides that commented on her likeness to Prangarris, the deep distrust of the singer, her smell, the inadequacy of her true-speech, and other things that once again were too subtle for the translator in her head to catch)

It was a passionate outcry, all the more so because the Taalav's voice was weak from hunger and worn to a thread from coping with the bitterness of this world, breaking and wavering on some of the more difficult harmonies.

In the exchange that followed, Shadith discovered

just how brutal life had been for the arrays that Prangarris had brought here. The sun was the wrong color, the Taalav sang to her, there were things in the water that did grief to the littles so they grew weak and died, the food plants that Prangarris had brought withered and died and the food the arrays found here was not complete. Prangarris fed them liquid supplements which helped them live, but something went wrong inside him and he was gone. They couldn't get into his place and reach the supplements, so they starved. Slowly. The food they could find kept them just enough alive to feel the agony of that slow dissolution. This was a bad place, so many things were wrong here. We die, the Taalav sang to her, we rot here and die.

Shadith sang to the Taalav: I will call to you a healer. This person will give you strength and health again, adults and littles alike. This person need only touch you to heal. Will you trust enough to allow this?

The Taalav brooded in silence for several minutes, its eyes dropping shut, its body sagging in the cradle of its legs. Finally it sang: For the good of the newplace-people, this person before you-stilter/singer will allow the touch.

When Aleytys left the flier and came toward Shadith, the Taalav stirred, gave out a flare of desperate hope. Its eyes were fixed on the healer's bright red hair. Shadith thought about the cherry hood of healthy Taalav adults and understood. The Gestalt must be thinking, ah! an adult at last.

Will you permit? Aleytys sang.

Shadith kept her face carefully blank. Lee couldn't carry a tune if you gave her a universal gripper. Her voice wasn't unpleasant but she had no grasp of the relationship of the tones and her approximations were enough off to make any singer wince.

She watched Aleytys set hands on the head and body of the Taalav, close her eyes, and begin work. For a while nothing seemed to be happening; then a healthy crimson crept back into the hood and the head's eyes brightened. When Aleytys stepped away, the Taalav's lively cheerfulness was back. The difference in its emanations was astonishing. And when it sang its gratitude, the harsh dissonances had vanished from the speech.

The other adults and the littles of the arrays came from hiding, scuttling and wriggling and slithering. Shadith watched Aleytys take up the tiny head forms and body forms, hold them in her hands until the distressing feebleness was gone, then set them down to run and play about the feet of the adults. It was as if they were reborn and reinfused with the stock of happiness that this world had sucked out of them. With a whine of servos, Lee knelt and began passing her hands across the wormforms that were also part of the Gestalt.

While she worked, the sun moved past zenith and a cold wind rose off the lake, bringing with it the rancid, sickening smell of rotten vegetation.

Even with the exo and the frame supporting her, exhaustion dragged at Shadith and she didn't want to think about how Aleytys felt; she told herself it was like the struggle to keep Lylunda alive, it reminded Lee of her strength where forces on Wolff conspired to remind her of her weaknesses.

Shadith sang a soft query to call the first Taalav from its contemplation of the healing. You have strength now, she sang to it, and you've seen our good will. If you stay here, the Curl Ears will surely find you and kill you. Do you want to go back where you came from? I will take you there if you ask it. Or there is another world that you can visit that might prove better for you than this. Will you risk that?

We went with One-bump 'Garrs, the Taalav sang, we had no choice, it took us, gathered us as we gather fruits from the grony bushes, yet we went with a certain willingness for we wished a new place, a free place that would be ours alone. We understood that the Curl Ears looked on us as beasts and harvested our histories because they were pleasant to look upon and their songs were prized. We thought One-bump 'Garrs was weak and alone and we could escape its hand easily enough when there was room to run. We did not understand that places could be more deadly than Kadbeasts. This person looks on your good will and accepts that. This person feels whole for the first time in many days. Yet this person has learned fear of new things and it is hard to contemplate the choice you-stilter/singer offer. Must this person choose?

I-Stilter/singer don't understand. How possible that you-of-the-new-land could be returned and not-returned at the same time?

This person would look upon the new world, yet if the new land is bad also, this person would go back to the tie-land.

I see, Shadith sang. Yes, that is sensible. The sun's color will be wrong on this new world also, but it will be warmer and, I think, more hospitable. She glanced at Aleytys, sang: The healer is nearly finished with its work. Will you call your folk of-the-new-land together and come with us?

7

The hold in Harskari's *Tiauchi* had been set to a proper gravity and the light provided was a close approximation of that on Pillory. The arrays left the flier with twitters of excitement and pleasure; they'd expected to have to suffer the same primitive conditions they had endured in Lylunda's *Dragoi*.

Shadith introduced them to the mobile Grace who had taken on the semblance of an adult Taalav and acquired the Taalav langue from *Tiauchi*'s kephalos through *Tigatri*'s tie to Aleytys.

===

This place **fit/not-fit**   **desired be your comfort**

   You of-the-new-land   **sing to Grace**   food and more

Dark and light is timed for you   what can be done will

===

The Taalav who'd spoken first to Shadith stood beside her; it sang an acknowledgment then went silent as it looked around the hold.

The baby body forms were chasing each other over the spongy flooring, in and out of the pseudo plant forms, whistling shrilly through their long dangly noses and having a grand time. The baby heads were crawling more slowly, nudging against each other and piling into sloppy heaps for the comfort of feeling others around them. And the other, more ambiguous juvenile parts of the Gestalt were wriggling and squirming around, wrapping themselves around head forms and licking at them, getting their taste re-registered, coiling round each other, looking more or less like knots of earthworms chased out of their holes by a morning rain. The other adult gestalts were moving about, exploring the place, singing their complex songs as they commented on what they saw.

The huge dark eyes of the Taalav turned on Shadith

for a moment. She sensed wondering/tentativeness/interest/tension and understood the mix as the Taalav moved over to the mobile Grace and sang a request for open water and food.

Shadith waited until Grace sang her answer, then she stepped onto the slide flat and was transported to the living areas.

8

"Loguisse."

The Vryhh had the fragile look Shadith remembered from the first time she'd met her, delicate bones with barely enough flesh to put padding between them and the skin, but she'd lost her aura of ancient desiccation; her dark blue eyes sparked with life and there was color in her pale face. "A fascinating species, Shadow," she said after giving Shadith a brief nod to acknowledge the greeting. She was examining a small Taalav crystal mounted in a dagnoster envelope, plotting the intricacies in the weaving of the extruded threads. "You say these are histories?"

"So the Taalav say. Some of the crystals anyway. Some are story books. And some are just for the pleasure they give. Harskari hasn't come across yet?"

"Not yet. She's doing some last minute planning with Lee. Should be finished soon, we'd agreed to be gone in another hour or so. Themis tells me the Taalav are settling in quite nicely. I can see why you like them so much. Charming creatures and very intelligent. If they prosper on Storsten and agree to it, I mean to bring more of them there; for a viable colony they need a larger breeding base. Hm. The crystals being sometimes histories, I wonder what effect a transfer of them between the two groups would have. It would be interesting to see how their society changes and develops. Both on Storsten and on Pillory." She smiled vaguely at Shadith, then went back to her examination of the crystal.

Shadith turned to *Tiauchi*'s Master Mobile. "Themis, arrange my transfer to *Tigatri*, please."

9

"What are you going to say to Digby when you tell him you've quit?" Aleytys was sitting on the boulder again, swinging her feet in the garden's stream, kicking up sprays of water and watching the drops fall back.

Shadith shifted position; a root from the tree she was leaning against was poking too assertively into her back. "I don't know. Wouldn't be polite or politic to tell him it was because I just didn't trust him anymore. Though that'd be the truth. The more I learn about him, the more spooked I get. How far does his reach go? That's a lot of power he has. What happens when that face he clings to turns into a mask with nothing behind it? How does he know who he is then? What does he want? What will he do to get it? What happens when he does get it? Does he turn into something like Kell? All malice with no internal limits?"

"Heavy list of questions." Aleytys pulled her legs up, folded them into a lotus knot. "Thinking of getting answers to them?"

"No. Not unless I have to. If he leaves me alone, I'll return the favor."

"Mm. You told Lylunda the Taalav were dead. Tell him the same thing, but that you were really unhappy about the thought of the Kliu slaughtering them. So you've decided to find another way of making a living. And then go play around Vrithian for a while till the whole thing cools down. What are you going to do about his ship?"

"Take it to University in tow to mine, do my talking from there. He can send someone to pick it up. I'm not going back to Spotchalls, that's for sure. Lee, what am I going to do?"

"What do you want to do?"

"You're no help."

Aleytys grinned sleepily at her. "Well, what kind of help were you when you were infesting my head?"

"Ah, so it's revenge you want." Shadith wrinkled her nose. "Having opted for mortality, I suppose I want that choice to mean something. I want people to be glad I walked through their lives. Like the Fior and Ketang of Béluchad. That was, well, satisfying, though I suppose it's Aslan who made the big difference. But I helped."

"See. You do know what you want."

"But that kind of thing doesn't put fuel in my ship or food in my belly. That's why I signed up with Digby in the first place. I do the jobs while he takes care of logistics. Seemed like it'd be the perfect blend. Tsah!"

"While you're on University, why not talk to Aslan? She might have some ideas."

"I don't think so, Lee. She's a friend and I like her, but she's very much into the University ethos. I'm not, and I don't want to be."

"Picky. Hm. A while back you said you were getting royalties off your lightsailors. I've started hearing about them, I do still get some of the gossip on Wolff, and word is they're hot. You might be making more than you think. And if you could come up with something else Adelaar could handle for you. . . ."

"I suppose I'd better check with Ti Vnok and see what's happening. I don't really count on them much, Lee. Fads explode and wither so fast sometimes, you blink and they're gone. Or the Gray Market rips off the design and undercuts your prices." She twisted her face into a clown's sad grimace. "And don't tell me I've gone all negative. It's just ... I don't have anything to aim at, Lee."

"I know, Shadow. You've got to close out this bit first before you can look ahead. I'd tell you to stop fussing, but I expect that's useless." With a quick twist of her body Aleytys was on her feet. "You need your harp. I'll have Doll bring it out to you. And you can pay your way with a concert tonight. Lylunda and I—and *Tigatri,* of course—we'll be your guests.

19

Report and Farewell

1

Shadith stood irresolute for several minutes outside Digby's branch office in Citystate Rhapsody, dredging through memory for any loophole she might have missed in the story she'd cobbled to cover the abstraction of the Taalav. She passed her hand over her hair, patted the soft springy curls into place. She needed a trim, but she wasn't going to bother with that now. Once her report was finished, she was booked on a flier heading for the Landing Field and on a shuttle to take her to the University Transfer Station and her own ship. Digby's *Backhoe* was parked up there too, but she wasn't going near that ship again. Then she'd make the jigs and jogs on the long and complicated flight to Vrithian. She was tired and unhappy. Some time spent in a place where she didn't have to worry about anything would be a blessing.

This street wasn't far from Star Street and was busy this late summer morning. She was rather like a boulder diverting the flow momentarily of the traders, crew, and others moving past her in a steady stream. When she started to get annoyed stares, she sucked in a breath and plunged inside.

2

The Greeter 'bot having been programmed to admit her whenever she called, Shadith walked through into the inner office without having to wait. The office manager looked up. "Yes?"

"I need a Clear room and a connect to Digby. Tell him I've got the location and I'm ready to report."

"We've just swept Two. Touch the announcer and I'll let you through."

"Thanks." Shadith left and walked down a short hall, tapped the announcer outside door number two and waited for the massive plug to slide to one side. The Clear rooms were baffled and insulated, as free as possible from any sort of insinuation from outside.

She seated herself by the desk, moving her shoulders uneasily as the door slid shut and sealed itself. This was a bit too much like a cell to please her. If Digby got irritated enough at her quitting, it might run from security to prison between one breath and the next. She told herself that was crazy, he'd never shown any inclination to over-control his agents, but the unease wouldn't go away. She leaned back, closed her eyes. While she was waiting for the connection to go through, weariness swept over her and she drifted into a doze.

She woke with a start as a soft chime announced Digby's arrival. When she opened her eyes he was sitting in a simulated armchair behind the desk, still in his professorial guise. He leaned forward, a lock of shining gray hair falling across his brow, a grave and disapproving set to his face. "Why University, Shadith? I expected you to report to Spotchalls."

"I had reasons for making the full report here, Digby. I'll explain them later. First, the location. In the Universal Catalog, the sun is listed as 87950 KLD

MLYD. One of the stars in the Callidara Pseudo Cluster. The world in question is third from the sun. The xenobi's name was Prangarris, a Herthite. He's dead, by the way. The Taalav wrapped him in a crystal cocoon, then proceeded to follow him into death, leaving very few traces behind. A few crystals and some decayed organic matter with enough definition left to identify it as Taalav."

"The transplant didn't take?"

"From what I saw, definitely not."

"The smuggler?"

"You told me we weren't required to produce her. I see no reason to turn her over to the Kliu; they'll have what they want. At the moment she's on Wolff, visiting Aleytys until it's safe to get on with her life." She leaned forward, set a flake on the desk. "The complete report, everything I've done, everything I've learned about Hutsarté, my expenses—it's all there."

"So you've pulled it off again. Congratulations, Shadow. Good job." He leaned back, the chair creaking realistically as he shifted his non-weight. "I have a feeling you're not happy about this."

"I'm not." She went through the speech she'd worked out with Aleytys, finished, "When I saw they were dead, the problem went away. But when you lean on luck, it melts under you and you fall on your face. Who knows what I'll come up against next time. So. No next time. Why I'm here on University. No point in going all the way to Spotchalls just to say I quit."

She pushed the chair back and got to her feet. "It's been interesting, Digby. But it was a mistake from the beginning."

He said nothing, didn't try to stop her, simply watched as she left the room.

3

She was yawning as she palmed the lock on her apartment; all the strain of the job, all the suspicion and the chewing over and over of what might happen, how she could counter it, all that had caught up with her and weariness was like a blanket smothering her. What she wanted more than anything was to stretch out on her bed and sleep for a week.

Instead, she put on water to boil for tea, logged a call through one of the Rhapsody skipcoms and had a shower while she waited for it to go through.

Aleytys raised a brow. In the screen her face was slightly distorted and her skin had acquired a greenish tone, but her voice came through clearly enough. "I see you survived."

"I took your advice and was tactful." Shadith patted a yawn. "Spla, I'm tired. All tensed up and ready to act, then the whole thing just dribbled away. Whatever. Tell Lylunda she should probably hang about for the rest of the month, but after that the heat should be off her." She yawned again. "You talked to Harskari yet?"

"About an hour ago, matter of fact. She says the injection is taking just fine and the new plants she picked up are thriving. She'll be going back for more in a few months, give the source time to settle down. Have you decided what you're going to do?"

"Probably I'll go see if Swarda's home. I need to talk to him. Then I'll probably go have a look at Harskari's garden."

Aleytys' mouth twitched; it wasn't a smile. "I might join you for a few months. I'm tired of the sniping round here. Nice that your severance was a friendly one. And go get yourself some sleep, Shadow. You can start your new life tomorrow."

4

Shadith came to awareness abruptly.

She was seated in front of a sensor board. In a familiar pilot's chair. She was on the *Backhoe*. Her body leaned forward, her hands lifted, began moving over the board, entering a destination code. She watched the code print out on the main screen, committed it to memory automatically, then realized with dull horror that she couldn't turn her head, that no part of her body answered her will.

This was confusing.

She'd meant to leave the *Backhoe* in the University tie-down. If Digby wanted it back, he could send someone to fetch it.

She should have been frightened and angry.

She couldn't feel anything.

It was as if she were back in the Diadem, looking through the body's eyes, but with no connection to the other senses or to the body's emotions.

Her mind barely worked. A word or an image rose to awareness, then faded. A long time later a new thing welled up to take its place.

day 1

Digby . . .

day 2

Digby's techs . . .[[image of Tron Ga working over her body with humming, blinking readouts, fitting the exo to her, adjusting the probe blockers]] day 3

... know me. Template ...

day 4

[Nothing. Blackout.]

day 6

...tailored ...
... Zombi ...
... no.

day 7

Mind ...
... mindlock ...
... no.

day 8

[Nothing. Blackout.]

day 9

...both ...
Clearroom ...
... yes.

[[image of self waking, seeing Digby seated behind the desk]]

And so it went, word by word, dredged up from the
edges of her mind, putting the picture together. There
was time, plenty of time, nothing to do while the *Back-*

hoe 'splitted toward its enigmatic destination and her body moved to someone else's programming, feeding itself and keeping itself clean—nothing to do but struggle to think, to understand what had happened to her.

day 15

At measured intervals her awareness left her for about a day. It wasn't sleep, it was as if someone had touched a button and turned her off. The timer on the sensor panel told her how long she was gone, but she had no internal sense of time passing and that bothered her a lot—all the more because she could do nothing about it.

Interval by interval she pieced together what this was about.

day 19

Through his techs and their reports, Digby knew her body and her consciousness—at least as much of them as could be measured from the outside. And he could do anything he wanted to her because he had a fine and frisky scapegoat to blame it on. The Kliu.

He wanted everything she knew. Her history. Aleytys. Vrithian. The Diadem. Everything. He'd been after her from the beginning to tell him things, pressing as hard as he could without driving her away. He'd accepted her evasions because he had no choice about that. When she quit, though . . . that ultimate evasion was something he must have decided he couldn't allow. And with the Kliu hanging about, he didn't even have to kill her when he was finished; all he had to do was brainwipe her and turn her loose. He could even get her back to University and let her be found wandering mindless, traces of drugs in her that might be linked to the Kliu. He didn't like them; it would appeal to his peculiar humor to get them barred from University as they'd gotten themselves barred from Marrat's Market.

Information. Miser of knowledge, sitting in his electronic parlor turning over the golden rounds of his secrets.

As the days passed, her thinking became measurably quicker, the alternate pathways strengthening and growing more complex with exercise.

day 25

Huh! Omphalos had some use after all.

The work she'd done to slide around their mindwipe had set up so many subroutes and branches that even the most effective lock couldn't cut all of them out of service.

Digby's techs are the best around, but they've got the limitations that come from knowing too much. Blessings be for that. Let's see what else they missed. . . .

She couldn't feel anything, couldn't smell or taste the food she consumed, couldn't turn her head, couldn't even twitch an eyeball. She tried. Over and over she tried to wriggle around the bounds of the lock and tease out a way of getting her body back. Over and over she rammed against a wall there was no penetrating.

Hm. If I can't go around, maybe I can pull my memories and shove them in a cyst like I did for the thing with Omphalos. Then he can probe all he wants and get nada for his pains.

But nada was what she got when she tried it. It was as if memory were marked Read Only. She could see

but not touch. She crashed into the wall until her mind
ached with the effort.

And in the trying she called up memories she didn't
want to view again, images that oozed through the
mindlock and flared into brief existence in front of her
eyes.

IMAGE flares of light, red and blinding white, long
       torturing squeal of landers as they came rush-
       ing through the night and dropped the
       catchnet on the Weaver's house, her mother's
       house. Dark figures pouring from the landers,
       it seemed as though there were thousands of
       them though later she knew it was only a
       dozen men. They came through the catchnet
       as if it didn't exist, the web that paralyzed
       whatever it touched, they killed her mother
       and the breeding male who lived there, they
       took her sisters, her six shining sisters who
       danced dreams for the Shallana, they took
       her, too, but only because she was young
       enough there'd be a market for her.

IMAGE She bent over the narrow casket she dug from
       a wall in an ancient ruin, ran her three-
       fingered hands over the panels, brushing the
       dust away so she could see the patterns some
       long-dead artist had carved into the stone,
       white jade it was, the walls thin as fine porce-
       lain. Amazing that it was intact so long after
       it was made. Her touch triggered it somehow
       and the lid rose upward. Inside she saw a pile
       of ash and something else, a necklet she
       thought at first, a delicate gold chain, com-
       plex and supple, draping heavily over her
       hand when she lifted it, fine wires spun into

the petals of stylized blooms with jeweled
hearts, jewels that sang single pure notes as
she turned her hand and inspected them. She
spread out the circle and fitted the Diadem
onto her head.

IMAGE Darkness. Nothing. Struggle to be, to see, to
do anything she could to break the intolerable
tedium of existence inside the treasure tower
of the RMoahl. Day upon day of wrestling
with her limitations as she learned to ride
the Curator's mind so she could get beyond
the boundaries of her patterned life. Then the
gem that held her soul sounded its note as a
hand snatched it from the case. Darkness
again as the Diadem slid into a loot sack and
the thief Stavvar began retracing his steps.

day 31

When she emerged from the memory dreams and the
futile campaign to free herself from the lock, she began
watching as much of her body as she could see in the
glimpses that chance allowed her. Knowledge was
about the only lever she had access to.

The pattern of the body's actions around the black-
outs told her what was happening there. Every four
days, when the body moved into the cabin and
stretched itself out on the cot, she'd catch a glimpse
from the corner of her eye of something descending,
little more than a sense of movement and a glint of
metal. A moment later she'd be gone—not into sleep
but into the blackout. It was easy to tell which was
which. Sleep came gradually, settling like a blanket
over her. The blackout would cut a thought in half.

And when she woke, her mind had slowed again.

She had to exercise it as she would stiff muscles to get
the flow moving steadily once more.

*Drugs. He's got me set up so he can reinforce the
lock and replay the program. He doesn't want to take
a chance on them wearing off before I get to where I'm
going.*

day 32

[Nothing. Blackout.]

day 33

*He couldn't have installed the drugs and the delivery
system in* Backhoe *any time after he assigned her to
me. He had to have set this up before then. What did
he say? Ah. 'There's a pattern that ... shall we say,
limits your usefulness.' And this. 'It just means I have
to be careful.' This is how he's being careful. He fixed
it so he could control me if he had to. I wonder if he
has this kind of thing installed for all his agents?*

day 35

Memories. They were some use after all, not just an
additional torment, replaying for her what she'd been.

In the distraction of her struggle, she'd forgotten she
was a mindrider. The images that appeared and reap-
peared in her efforts reminded her of this.

The only minds available on this ship were a few
spiders, some anonymous insets, and a roach or two;
manipulating them gave her a small triumph and drove
back the grays that had been closing in on her as she
exhausted every possibility she'd thought of to escape
this trap.

At first she could only feel them, but the more she

searched them out and the more she settled into one after the other, sending her tiny mounts scurrying here
and there, the more access she had to that part of her
mind. She was pleased with herself and delighted at
this new joke on the certainties of superior techs.

day 41

When much of the stiffness from the blackout had
worn off, she *reached* for one of the spider minds,
looked through the compound eyes at the bug it was
sucking dry. And sighed. So what if she could play
with bugs? Where did that get her? Her melancholy
lightened briefly as she visioned roaches dancing over
the sensor board, but that was not practical. . . .

A flood of sudden thoughts overloaded the still la-
boring pathways of her awareness and for a moment all
she knew was chaos.

When she could think again, she picked out the idea
that sparked the deluge, shaped it into a small neat
statement and contemplated it. *If my mindride talent
escaped the lock, maybe other talents are also available to me.*

The translator was useless, but her ability to mind-
move small objects close to her (close being within
reach of her arms) seemed to offer interesting possibilities. Digby didn't know about that one. At least, she
didn't think he knew. So maybe he hadn't programmed
the *Backhoe*'s kephalos to counter it.

*First I see if I can move something, then I figure out
how to use it.*

day 43

When the square lit, Shadith saw it from the corner of her eye and in her relief felt her focus diffusing. In the screen in front of her, the first number of Wolff's destination code was a bright amber glyph.

Mind on your business, Shadow.

Amazing how hard it was to deal with tension when she couldn't vent it through the body. She regained control and began entering the other elements of the new destination code, working by hope and estimation; there were several of the sensor squares that she couldn't see because her head was turned the wrong way. As she went on, though, the figures before her were the right ones and her confidence grew.

She finished and would have held her breath if she'd had any control over that.

The numbers vanished, were replaced by COURSE CHANGE DENIED.

Wolff's out. I could try University. Hm. I don't think so. Spotchalls. That's the best chance. . . .

She visualized the sensor board, worked out the moves and entered Spotchall's code.

Once again the numbers vanished. Once again she saw COURSE CHANGE DENIED.

One more. Hm. Why not Pillory? He wouldn't expect me to go there.

She finished, screamed, a silent scream of frustration and anger. COURSE CHANGE DENIED.

Because she was so fatigued by this time that she could barely string two thoughts together, she rested for a few hours after the last DENIAL, letting her favorite songs flow through her mind, the imagined sound and the play of the words distracting her from the fear that threatened to swamp the tiny area that she'd managed to pull away from the mindlock.

* * *

Her body was planted in the pilot's chair and she couldn't move it; all she did was sit for hours and hours until she could feel muscle tone oozing away. That made her angrier than anything else. It was just so stupid. Digby could at least have programmed her body to exercise itself on this trip. It was going to last two months; by the time she got to where she was going, she'd have bedsores on her behind.

She'd recognized parts of the code, so she knew the place the ship was traveling toward and the time it would take to get there. Swardheld had a commission out that way while she was playing songmistress for Aslan on Béluchad. He came to see her when he dropped his cargo at the Cliostara citystate on University. He was vocally annoyed with Proctor Haldron for sending him out there with only the sketchiest of warnings.

"So offhand, you'd think he was saying it's an old gouty hound but you'd better be careful of its temper. Hah! Some temper; a pair of Dragonships chased us halfway back to the Arm. He didn't mention that was disputed territory. He'd have had to give me danger pay if that'd come up, the miserable skint." He wrote out the string for her. "There it is, Shadow. If your titchy boss wants to send you out that way, decline with thanks and be firm about it. Taking chances may add spice to life, but out there, trouble's not chance but certainty."

Dragonships. Big and black. At once sinuous and angular. Named by a free trader with more imagination than sense—an eternally optimistic little Cousin pooting about the edge of Civilization in an ancient singleship held together by spit and prayer.

No one knew what the entities in those ships looked like, but there was no question of their belligerence;

they chased away or blew to ash anyone who crossed
into what they considered their space.

Her destination was definitely in Swarda's disputed
territory. She thought about calling up what the
kephalos knew about the place, but decided that wasn't
such a great idea. At least, not until she'd found some
way to get word out ... get the word out, now there
was an idea. ...

day 46

As the words flowed across the screen, the body's
eyes followed them. *Out of habit*, Shadith thought.
*Complicates things, but at least if I get it wrong, I'll
know it. And if I get it right.*

LEE, DIGBY HAS DONE HIS THING. HE HAS
GOT ME IN A MINDLOCK AND PRO-
GRAMMED TO KEEP MYSELF ALIVE TILL I
GET TO ONE OF HIS HIDEAWAYS. 570554
RZT MMXS 2 IS THE DESTINATION CODE.
THE WHOLE TRIP IS AROUND 60 DAYS
AND 45 OF THEM HAVE GONE PAST, SO
THERE IS NOT MUCH TIME LEFT. AFTER
FAR TOO MANY FAILURES, I HAVE
WORKED A FEW SYNAPSES FREE. USING
THEM, I HAVE ACTIVATED A DRONE AND
AM MANAGING TO GET THIS WRITTEN
WITH SOME TICKLES FROM THE OLD
MINDMOVE. I EXPECT HE IS GOING TO
SQUEEZE MY MIND DRY OF MEMORY,
THEN WIPE IT AND DUMP ME SOME-
WHERE. I WOULD REALLY RATHER NOT
GO THROUGH THAT. I HAVE TRIED TO
CHANGE COURSE, BUT THE KEPHALOS
WILL NOT PERMIT IT. I HAVE TRIED TO

WIGGLE LOOSE FROM THE LOCK AND
FAILED. LEE, I HAVE TO CALL FOR HELP
AGAIN. YOU KNOW HOW MUCH I LIKE
THAT, BUT I REALLY DO NEED YOU.
                SHADITH

She rested for the remainder of the day, playing her
songs over and over in the small area of brain available
to her, letting the poisons of fatigue wash away.

day 47

Shadith reread the note, then pecked away at the
sensor board, transferring the message onto a flake and
routing it into a drone.

After a pause during which she recollected her
strength, she called for a status report.

MESSAGE TRANSFERRED 0 ERRORS
DRONE CHARGED AND IN TUBE
DETINATION: WOLFF 402504 QMT BBEF 3
ACTION DESIRED?

She would have closed her eyes, but she couldn't.
She might have held her breath, her hands might have
been shaking. This didn't happen. She gathered her
forces, sent the release signal. The words on the screen
vanished and two more appeared.

DRONE RELEASED.

day 57

The musical bong that announced emergence from
the insplit came as she was surfacing from a blackout.
She lay on the cot and squeezed enough slow

thoughts out of her stiffened brain to wonder if the program was going to keep her there until the ship touched down. Usually the body rose immediately, tended itself, ate, then moved to the pilot's chair where it sat staring at a mostly empty screen.

She lay and fretted.

This was one more chain Digby was wrapping around her.

Time passed.

The body rose. Went to the fresher, took care of its wastes, washed itself. It came out, changed to clean clothing, then it stretched out on the cot once again, lay with its hands crossed on its breasts, eyes fixed on the dull metal of the ceiling.

Helpless prisoner in her own head, Shadith would have wept in frustration if she could.

Some hours later, the vibrations in the walls changed. The sound changed.

And yet later the sounds, the vibrations stilled. The ship was on the ground.

20

Turned Loose

1

A timid scratching on the door.

Lylunda looked up from the remote and saw Lilai hesitating in the opening. "Come on in." She blanked the screen and smiled at the girl. "I wasn't doing anything important, just looking over my finances."

"Oh. Maybe I should come back. Mum gets scratchity when she's working numbers."

"All depends on what the numbers say. Besides, till I get back on the job, I can't really do any planning. Guessing without hard data is good for passing time and not much more."

Lilai sidled in and perched on the edge of a chair. "That's sorta what I came to tell you. When you'll get back, I mean. Mum said I could. Mum said Shadow called and said she'd made the report to Digby and as soon as the Kliu check it out, you can go whenever you want." She sighed, then stared down at her hands, the fingers of one scratching the palm of the other. "I'll miss you," she whispered, so softly Lylunda had almost to guess at the words.

For the first time Lylunda realized how lonely the child was and saw some value in the messy, often dan-

gerous life she'd led while she was growing up. Lonely
wasn't something you suffered in the streets of the
Izar. This place was lovely, there was every comfort
here you could possibly want—everything except other
people. She was bored after a month of it. Lilai had
been here all her young life. "You have Vassil and the
horses," she said.

"But I can't talk to him about anything but horses.
And Mum, well, she's my mother. And she's. . . ." Lilai
sighed again. "You know. She loves me and I love her
and we do lots of stuff and she's a great Mom. But it's
not like just . . . I dunno."

Aleytys had been friendly, but she wasn't the type to
sit around chatting with strangers and besides, she was
distracted; it hadn't been to hard to pick up the growing strain between her and the kid's father. And on top
of all that, it was rather hard to get chummy with a legend in the flesh. *Lilai must feel that too. I wonder if
she wishes sometimes that she had an ordinary mother.
Too smart for her own good. Eight years old going on
fifty. Sort of like Bug. Everything hurts when you're
like that. Jaink's nethermost hell, what do I say? I
don't know anything about kids. And I swear I'm never
going to have any.* "You're lucky to have a mom, Lil.
Remember, I told you how mine died when I was fifteen?"

"But you got to go learn to be a pilot and you have
your own ship and you can go wherever you want
now."

"So what do you think you want to do?"

"Mum says she'll get me a place on University. I
think I'm going to study animals. Well, I already am.
Swarda and Shadow bring me books and things when
they come to visit and Aunt Harskari always has something new in her ship garden and she tells me about
how it lives and stuff. Shadow has friends who hunt

for animals. I thought may I could go work for them after I finish school."

"Sounds good to me."

"And Mum says when I make twelve we'll do my first run in the Wildlands and I'll see the silvercoats live not just on flakes and we'll gather the first stones for my cairn. And when I'm eighteen, I'll go by myself and put a stone on the cairn. And they can't call me brat any more or say I'm hanging on Mum's belt to pull myself along."

Lylunda repressed a shiver. Her childhood kept looking better the more she heard about Wolff. This child was anticipating with pleasure being dumped in the coldest, most barren part of this unfriendly world with just what she could carry on her back and no weapons but a knife and a bow. She was supposed to survive out there for at least a week—and not just survive, but cover Jaink knew how many kilometers, make her mark on some pile of rocks and come back out by foot power and gritted teeth.

"Luna, there's a tutorial on a little while about the Wildlands. You want to come watch it with me?"

"Sure. Why not. While the show's running, you can tell me all about the silvercoats."

Grey and Aleytys spent the next day in a bitter quarrel, arguing in undertones, no shouting, all control. They filled the house with a tension that twanged at Lylunda's nerves and had Lilai shivering like a frightened deer.

Fiddling with the remote screen, trying to pretend she was working, Lylunda stayed in her room until the little ghost that wore Lilai's shape wandered past the door for the tenth time. With an impatient siss, she wiped the figures from the screen, shut down the remote and marched into the hall. "Come on."

She didn't wait to see if the child was following her, just strode along the hall to the drop tube.

The barn was warm, smelled of horse and hay. Lylunda threw a blanket over a bale to keep the stubs away from her flesh, then settled herself on it and waited for Lilai to slip in. She wrinkled her nose, remembering her first day here when the girl grinned at her and told her they had to be friends, their names were almost twins, then hauled her off to see her horses. *Looks like a parent doesn't have to be a stone bort like my own daddy dear to mess up a kid's life. At least he's out of my life for good. Poor little Lilai has got another ten years of this. At least. Well, it's not my business. I'm outta here soon as it's safe.*

Lilai came hesitantly through the partly open door. She stopped just inside and stood slouched, staring at the planks of the floor with the wisps of grass hay strewn across the wood. Her mouth trembled.

"It's tough, kid. I know. Come over here and sit down. You don't have to say anything."

Lilai nestled close to her. She was cold and shaking, but she didn't cry, even when Lylunda slipped an arm about her shoulders and held her close.

"One thing you learn after a while, Lil, these things pass. You live through them and life gets better."

Lilai sucked in a long ragged breath, but she didn't say anything, perhaps out of loyalty to her feuding parents. Lylunda hugged her; she, too, stayed silent, mostly because she didn't know what more to say.

A horse in one of the stalls that ran along the side of the barn whickered and shifted his feet, his shod hooves muffled by the straw bedding. Another snorted and thumped against the barrier between the stalls. Two barn cats hissed and yowled in a brief fight, then there were scratching noises as one of them fled. Up near the rafters there was some soft peeping from owlets in their nests. Outside, the little brown meuttertiks broke into scolding chirps; something must have been threatening their nests.

Lilai's shaking slowly went away. She leaned her head against Lylunda's shoulder for a moment, drew a sigh up from the soles of her feet. A moment later she wriggled free and got to her feet.

At the doorway she turned and gave Lylunda a wavery smile, then she was gone.

Lylunda scrubbed a hand across her eyes. "Jaink! I hate this. I want to get away from here. Now."

Grey took Lilai with him when he left.

Lylunda did her best to keep out of the way, but she did stand at her window as the child walked to the flier with her father. Lilai waved to her mother, climbed inside. Aleytys was watching from her garden, half hidden by a flowering sehnsur, the wind blowing delicate lavender petals from its lacy blooms onto her head and shoulders.

She stood there until the flier vanished into the thready clouds; then she walked with quick energetic steps toward the barn, brushing away the petals as she went. Shortly afterward she rode away from the house on one of the blacks, keeping the horse to a controlled trot, not pushing it, but her eyes were fixed on the horizon, as if being in motion were something she had to do, as if that jagged line between sky and earth were someplace she had to be.

Lylunda stepped away from the window. "This whole visit has been a letdown. You expect legends to have perfect lives, not this kind of kak." She sighed. "I think I'll give Digby a call. With any luck I can be on my way and out of her hair."

2

Lylunda smiled as she patted the arm of her pilot's chair. It was good to be back in her own ship; she could feel the tension draining out of her. She woke the kephalos and initiated the call to Digby, then sat back and waited for it to go through.

Digby was a silver-haired docent, handsome and stately, with what Lylunda took to be a smug gleam in his bright blue eyes. "What can I do for you, Lylunda Elang?"

"I was wondering if the Kliu had finished inspecting the site and were satisfied with what they saw."

"That's proprietary information, you understand. However, I'm willing to let it out. For a price, of course. Nothing extravagant, just a brief report on your views."

"My views about what?"

"About the events between the time you left Bol Mutiar and arrived at Wolff."

"Shadith will have given you that already."

"And do you never cross-check your information?"

"Hm. I see no problem with that; the whole thing was a disaster." She went through the meager calendar of events after the healing, adding no commentary, keeping strictly to what happened and what she was told.

"You're sure the dead man was the xenobi Prangarris?"

"I didn't go downside, but that wouldn't have helped anyway, he was inside that crystal weave. I watched *Tigatri*'s keph peel through the crystal until you could see the man inside. It was Prangarris, no doubt about that. And there were shells of dead Taalav all around the site." She tapped impatiently on the chair arm. "So, have the Kliu been there? Are they satisfied?"

"My fee was released from escrow two hours ago. They are satisfied. I would advise staying away from that sector of Cousin space; they won't be looking for you, but if you fell into their hands, your life would be short and messy. Mmh. Should you take a notion to look for steady work one day, come see me." The screen blanked as he cut the connection.

Lylunda wrinkled her nose. "Not likely, my friend." She stretched, groaned with pleasure at the feeling of chains dropping off her body. "We say good-bye and thanks much, O Aleytys of Wolff, then I go find a Pit and throw myself a party. Oooo eee, it's been a while."

21

Endgame

1

Once the ship was down, Digby wasted no time. He had the body on its feet and moving before the engines cooled; it was out of the ship and installed in a bubble car so fast Shadith only caught a few glimpses of the lichens and rubble that seemed to make up most of the local landscape.

After the flat metallic atmosphere of the ship, the air was cool and crisp with a sharp, fungal tang to it. She was irritated at being dumped back into the sterile blandness of machined air and made a note to do her version of the Vryhh ship gardens once she got back to her own transport. Having plants about would make more work and introduce more contaminations into her ship, but the feel of the atmosphere would certainly be worth it.

The car zipped from the recamouflaged pad and plunged straight at a granite cliff rising a hundred meters straight up.

Idiot poseur. Playing infantile games of scare the prisoner. Tchah!

She ignored the rock and mused over what she'd have to do to her ship to get it ready for use. It had

been sitting at Wolff since she signed on with Digby
and would have developed the quirks and crotchets all
moth-balled ships picked up. At least those with complex kephaloi. She hadn't run across any major problems 'splitting from Wolff to University, even though
she was towing the *Backhoe* and putting more strain on
the ship, but sometimes it took a while for the quirks
to start showing.

The membrane that sealed out the local atmosphere
and mocked the mottled gray of the granite twanged as
the car passed through it.

The weight of the mountain pressed down on her as
the flimsy car scooted deeper and deeper into it. And
even more oppressive was her growing fear that she
wasn't going to get out of this with mind intact. If
Digby wouldn't let her speak before he tried the probe
. . . all she could do was try to short it out. Which
would work once. . . .

A second membrane squeaked. The bubble car
stopped and stood shuddering on its supports as jets
of fluid hammered at it from above, below and both
sides.

After the wash was done, Shadith heard a series
of clunks and clanks; then the car began gliding forward, drawn along by some exterior method of pro-
pulsion.

During the next fifteen or so minutes the car was
scrubbed thoroughly, the air in it expelled and replaced
repeatedly until she was as battered as the small vehicle, the body she couldn't feel coughing with irritation
from the sterilizers carried by that air.

The car passed through a third membrane and
stopped. The gullwing doors swung up and the body
moved stiffly out. It walked to a massive plug in the
wall, waited for it to slide open, then stepped into a

rock lined with shining white tiles where it was inundated once again with antiseptic fluids. If she could have, Shadith would have sighed with frustration and impatience.

Hair kinked into curls so tight and close to her head they hurt, throat raw and temper on the point of exploding, she moved with the body into a white room beyond the lock; it marched to a chair facing a wall, plopped itself down, and folded its hands in its lap.

The wall irised open.

Behind thick glass she saw a nude male body wrapped in a cocoon of wires and tubes, a Sustain unit almost as complex as those she'd seen on Ibex when Aleytys was hunting the last clues that would put her in touch with her mother. In a sort of irony she was in no mood to appreciate, it also looked rather like the crystal mass the Taalav had woven around Prangarris. *Digby,* she thought, *the original, the one and only. Wonder how old he is? From how he looks, he was here before this world formed. Gods, unless I talk really fast, for sure I'm not getting out of here knowing that.*

Digby's simulacrum formed, translucent so she could see the outline of the body through it. "You're aware," he said. "You aren't supposed to be aware."

He gestured and her face came back to her control, her throat, her voice.

"I'm a lot of things I'm not supposed to be," she said. Her voice was hoarse, her lips trembled, and it was difficult to speak, but the relief in that much relaxation of the lock was enormous. She tried not to let it affect her; she had to remain focused—and avoid the temptation to talk too much.

"How?"

"Practice."

"That's not responsive."

"It isn't, is it."

He gestured again, and the chair she sat in began to shift around her.

"No!" She spat the word at him, rushed the rest of it while she still had the ability to speak. "Before you touch me, check *Backhoe*'s kephalos." The chair froze in midshift and she went on more slowly. "I saw the destination code and I programmed it into a drone's message flake. Along with my speculations as to what this was about. Aleytys should have it by now and be on her way here."

The simulacrum looked away for a moment. When it turned back, she faced its fury with her first degree of hope.

"How?"

She'd gone over this moment again and again on the way here and had changed her mind as many times as she thought she'd finally made it up. On top of that, the Sustained body on the far side of the glass was a factor she had to fit into her reasoning and she didn't have much time. *Go with instinct,* she thought. *Trade him secret for secret. That might be sufficient to tilt the balance. . . .*

"I was hatched twenty millennia ago, Digby. You may be old, but you're a child compared to me. For a long time you've wanted to know who I was, what I was. So listen. I was a Weaver of Shayalin, born to a family who danced dreams for the Shallana and any who came to listen. You wouldn't know of Shayalin. It was ash before your species left the ocean that spawned them. That's what I was until I died. Then I was a pattern of forces caught in the RMoahl Diadem and I watched the years pass through other eyes than my own. It was useful training. The techs who craft mindlocks have limited imaginations; they don't dream of someone like me. When the Diadem came to Aleytys, after a while I traded eternity for mortal flesh. This flesh. We are sisters of the soul, Digby. We are more than sisters. I would die for her and she for me. More important to you, she'll come for me and she won't be alone. The Vrya will come because I know how to reach Vrithian and that's not a secret they'll trust you with. And there are the other souls I shared space with in the Diadem. Like Aleytys they are bound to me in ways you'd never understand. If they find a shell, not their sister soul, you're dead. The Vrya and my soul's kin, they'll destroy this place and purge you from every inch of the systems you control until you simply do not exist any more."

"And why should I believe any of that preposterous story?"

"Wait a few days. Vryhh ships are fast; it won't take long for Lee to get here. Two weeks at most. The others might need more time, but they'll come, too."

"My defenses are considerable. What if I simply deny you're here and let them do their worst?"

"That's your decision. By that time you'll have done your probing and your wipe, so I'll be dead even if this body lives and I won't care what happens to you."

"Seyirshi was right, you're a mutagen, transforming everything you touch. I should have taken his warning and kept clear of you."

"I survive," she said. "One way or another. A bargain, Digby. You leave me and mine alone, I'll go my way and not interfere with you."

"I want to talk to Aleytys. Give me her call-sign."

"If you're thinking of infesting *Tigatri*'s kephalos, I warn you she's self aware and apt to react murderously to intruders." She saw the smug glint in the simulacrum's eyes and sighed. "Send me out to *Backhoe* and I'll make the contact for you. I don't want to be under all this rock when you make an idiot of yourself and get your plug pulled. You've got control of *Backhoe*'s kephalos, so I won't be going anywhere."

The white non-corpse in the Sustain lay stony and immobile and for several minutes the gaze its spokesimage turned on her was as unyielding.

The body was still held in Digby's grip, so Shadith could do nothing but sit and wait. She'd considered using the *mindmove* to attack the Sustain since Digby had unwittingly brought her close enough, but that might mean all systems would go out and the thought of being sealed into this hole in the ground nearly sent her reasoning paths into overload. She put that aside to save for a last and desperate stunt, taken in the hope that Aleytys would arrive before air and food were gone.

The body coughed, coughed again as the remnants of the disinfectant gas irritated its lungs.

The noise woke the simulacrum from its stasis. "The ship's com has been tied to the skipcom here. You can watch, but you won't be permitted to speak once the connection is made." A gesture and the last of the mindlock dissolved. "The car will take you back. This is not to be considered an agreement, you understand, but I am contemplating your offer."

2

Aleytys' blue-green eyes burned through the screen. "I don't know if I want to listen to you, kak. Who threatens Shadow, threatens me. You'd better believe that."

"I seem to have made an error in judgment." Digby's voice dripped penitence; he'd chosen a sad puppy look and was doing his best to project rueful contrition. "Is there some way we can resolve this difficulty without mutual destruction?"

"For one thing, you can stop trying to worm through *Tigatri*'s defenses. If you get her annoyed enough, she'll seize your trace and do to you what you're trying to do to her."

"Ah. I must apologize to Shadith. I thought she was exaggerating for effect."

"Hm. I think more than apologies are called for."

In the *Backhoe,* watching this exchange on the forescreen, Shadith smiled. *Squeeze the bort good, Lee, squeeze him till he squeals.*
She blinked as the screen suddenly added a third cell as Harskari appeared and joined the conversation.

"Yes. Considerably more. Shadow is my sister, my daughter, Digby. Lee is not alone in this. Look to your health, you thing of painted light. We'll pull your house down and melt your flakes to slag." She was smiling as she spoke and her voice was soft, her dignity pulled like a robe about her.

Shadith was bouncing in her chair and grinning widely enough to threaten her ears. "Go get 'im, Mama Harskari." She drew a deep breath, chortled as she watched Digby's face go stiff and his eyes empty as he contemplated the nearly identical faces of the two women. The load was off her shoulders now, she could sit back and watch her soul-kin operate. For a little while she could revel in being a child again.

Digby seemed to sigh. "It was an extravagant tale . . . that your daughter, you say? Mm . . . that Shadith spun for me, but it seems she underspoke the truth. What do you require?"

"She is indeed the daughter of my heart and of our long companioning. In addition to her immediate return to us, WE," Harskari laid stress on that word, "require indemnity deposited on Helvetia equal to one year's gross income of Excavations Ltd; Aleytys will give you the details in a moment. As to what Shadith requires, you'll have to ask her."

3

The screen blanked and Shadith found herself in darkness; around her the faint, subliminal soughing of the ship's life support was hushed. Digby's voice was silky in her ears. "I can do more than stop the fans. I can evacuate the air from the ship and you'll die gasping."

A moment later the lights were back and a faint current of air tickled at the tiny hairs that curled about her face.

"That's to remind you what happens if you drive me too far," he said.

Shadith laughed and enjoyed the look on his face when he heard the freedom of the sound. "I've died twice already, why should I fear a third death?"

"Then why bother with your friends out there?"

"If I had to go, I wanted company. You're wasting time, you know. My offer is still open. Leave me and mine alone and we'll leave you your secrets and your life."

"So I have to run every job past you to make sure I'm not violating your precious ambiance?"

"Leave legalisms to lawyers, Digby. You're trotting
out problems that don't exist. Go about your ordinary
business and there won't be a pattern. If by chance you
and I meet as adversaries, we can work out an accom-
modation or declare all-out war and see who emerges
at the end. If you go after us again, you'll make a pattern and we'll know it. You haven't any notion of the
capacity of a Vryhh-designed kephalos; I suggest you
don't try to test it. If you do, we'll come after you, the
ones you know and the ones you don't."

"I could still fight this out. My Sanctuary is land-
based and the atmosphere will limit the weapons your
friends can bring to bear on me. Plus the fact that
you're sitting here, more vulnerable to them than I
am."

"Don't count on that, Digby. There's a lot you can't
know about Aleytys. Or Vryhh tech."

"Threats about what I don't know get thin very fast.
I do not like the thought that I exist on your sufferance,
Shadith. In fact it's so unappealing, that I find myself
just about ready to call you back in here and take my
chances with your champions."

"You can try." Shadith sighed. "I'm not going to argue with you, Digby, or let you distract me. Agree or
fight. Make up your mind."

There was a long silence.

Shadith stretched out her legs, shut her eyes, and
waited with what patience she could scrape together.

4

An hour later, the screen lit, split into cells with
Digby's Simulacrum in one, Harskari and Aleytys in
the other two.

The simulacrum put on a wry ruefulness and spoke,

"Let it be, then. A year's gross profit into a specified account on Helvetia. And I give my word that I will not search out you or yours with hostile intent. Is that sufficient, Shadith?"

"It is sufficient."

Epilogue
—Tieing the Knots

WORM

Delala giggled as Worm swung his gathering scoop at the scuttling greel, missed, and swore as it dug itself back into the sand. She took her digging stick, popped another greel from his hole, and cooed as Worm got this one and dumped it into the basket.

Later, as he followed her along the path to the village, he heard a long, low whine and raised his eyes to see the bright seed of a lifting ship arcing across the sky. He watched it a moment, groping for a memory that wouldn't come.

Delala looked over her shoulder. "Ke mo?"

"I'm coming, I'm coming, I don't want to spill this." He forgot about the ship and walked beside her, his mouth getting itself ready for the feast that night, his naming feast and his formal welcome into the Tung Bond.

LYLUNDA

The perpetual party in the Loft of the Buzzard's Roost had come alive again two days after Lylunda reached Sundari Pit.

She wandered in, glanced around, took a glass of white wine from a serviteur's tray, and went to lean against the wall, sipping at the wine while she watched Virgin and Hopeless dance a strutting pavanne to a tune provided by Henry the tentacled centaur as he used his physical advantages to play a harp-guitar.

"No pelar?"

Lylunda looked round, grinned at Qatifa. "You might say I've gone off the whole drug scene. Right now anyway. Didn't expect to see you here, Qat."

"You clear of that mess at Marrat's?"

"Uh-huh. Why?"

"I've got this deal . . . a good one, it'll set your belly grumbling when you hear it. But it needs two to make it work. You interested?"

"Sure. Been out of it too long, *Dragoi*'s all shaped up to run."

"I've got a room over Junker's Bar, say you meet me there tomorrow, Pit noon?"

"I'll be there."

Qatifa's nose quivered with Caan laughter, her eyes were narrowed to golden slits. " 'Less you want to come home with me?"

"After the job's finished, Qat. I just got out of one mess, I don't want to make another."

"Po po, you were more fun when you were on the pelar. See you tomorrow." Qatifa twitched a mobile ear, wriggled her nose again, and ambled off.

Lylunda emptied her glass, set it on a window ledge, and began her own circuit of the room. She was back in her chosen world, the scattered anarchy of the Pit Stop circuit; she had prospects for a job that was certainly dangerous and probably interesting. At the moment, life was very good.

SHADITH

Supported by one of Harskari's exos, Shadith sat on a tussock of rotten stone held together by the complex root system of the grasses that grew over it. She watched the Taalav moving with noisy cheerfulness about their adopted home, rambling in and out of the reddish shadow cast by the translucent shades Loguisse had set up for them, tending the shoots of the polychrome reeds that were already breaking the surface of the water in the small lake at the heart of this equatorial island. The other plants Harskari had snatched off Pillory seemed to be rooting themselves and growing with a similar enthusiasm.

A horde of infant body beasts were running about, getting underfoot, hooting with tiny but exuberant joy, and infant head beasts lay in slowly heaving piles, contributing their modulated hums to the noise. Most of the worm forms of the Gestalt had settled themselves in the mud at the edge of the lake, but here and there she could see a bright pink fingeroid popping out of the water to snap at the bugs skating on the surface.

Harskari and Loguisse were some distance off, supervising a clutch of 'bot gardeners as they set more plants in place.

The sun Avenar was warm on her back and the air heady in her nostrils. The gravity pulled at her and she was growing tired, but she was happy as she looked at the Taalav arrays working so diligently at settling into their new home.

It's an object lesson, she thought. *One phase of my life has closed and I don't know where I'll go from here, but at least I can rejoice that nothing is finished and everything is new again.*

SEAN RUSSELL

☐ **THE INITIATE BROTHER (Book 1)** UE2466—$5.99
In this powerful novel rich with the magic and majesty of the ancient
Orient, one of the most influential lords of the Great Houses is marked
for destruction by the new Emperor and must use every weapon at
his command to survive—including a young Botahist monk gifted with
powers not seen in the world for nearly a thousand years.

☐ **GATHERER OF CLOUDS (Book 2)** UE2536—$5.99
The army of the Golden Khan is poised at the border, and Lord Shonto
is caught between it and his own hostile Emperor's Imperial Army. Yet
even as this trap closes, Brother Shuyun faces another crisis. For in
the same scroll that warned of the invasion was a sacred Udumbara
blossom—a sign his order has awaited for a millennium. . . .

MOONTIDE AND MAGIC RISE

☐ **WORLD WITHOUT END (Book 1)** UE2624—$5.99
It is the dawn of a new era; an age of reason, science and exploration,
and Tristam Flattery is one of its most promising young naturalists.
But when Tristam is summoned to the royal court of Farrland to try to
revitalize a failing species of plant which seems to have almost magical
medicinal powers, he gets caught up in the grip of a destiny which will
lead him to the ends of the known world—a voyage of discovery that
has more to do with magic than with science . . .

Tanya Huff

☐ **FIFTH QUARTER** UE2651—$4.99
Bannon and Vree, brother and sister assassins trapped in a single body, are confronted by a master of a magic beyond their comprehension and offered a terrible choice—to continue their dual existence forever, or to betray the Empire they'd served all their lives.

☐ **SING THE FOUR QUARTERS** UE2628—$4.99
For Princess Annice the call of magic was too strong to be denied, even if it meant renouncing her royal blood and becoming a fugitive in her own land.

VICTORY NELSON, INVESTIGATOR:
Otherworldly Crimes A Specialty

☐ **BLOOD PRICE: Book 1**	UE2471—$4.99
☐ **BLOOD TRAIL: Book 2**	UE2502—$4.50
☐ **BLOOD LINES: Book 3**	UE2530—$4.99
☐ **BLOOD PACT: Book 4**	UE2582—$4.99

THE NOVELS OF CRYSTAL

☐ **CHILD OF THE GROVE: Book 1**	UE2432—$4.50
☐ **THE LAST WIZARD: Book 2**	UE2331—$4.50

OTHER NOVELS

☐ **GATE OF DARKNESS, CIRCLE OF LIGHT**	UE2386—$4.50
☐ **THE FIRE'S STONE**	UE2445—$3.95

Mickey Zucker Reichert

THE RENSHAI CHRONICLES
- [ ] **BEYOND RAGNAROK**   UE2658—$21.95

THE RENSHAI TRILOGY
- [ ] **THE LAST OF THE RENSHAI: Book 1**   UE2503—$5.99
- [ ] **THE WESTERN WIZARD: Book 2**   UE2520—$5.99
- [ ] **CHILD OF THUNDER: Book 3**   UE2549—$5.99

THE BIFROST GUARDIANS
- [ ] **GODSLAYER: Book 1**   UE2372—$4.99
- [ ] **SHADOW CLIMBER: Book 2**   UE2284—$3.99
- [ ] **DRAGONRANK MASTER: Book 3**   UE2366—$4.50
- [ ] **SHADOW'S REALM: Book 4**   UE2419—$4.50
- [ ] **BY CHAOS CURSED: Book 5**   UE2474—$4.50

OTHER NOVELS
- [ ] **THE UNKNOWN SOLDIER**   UE2600—$4.99
- [ ] **THE LEGEND OF NIGHTFALL**   UE2587—$5.99

Melanie Rawn

EXILES

☐ **THE RUINS OF AMBRAI: Book 1**   UE2668—$5.99
☐ **THE RUINS OF AMBRAI: Book 1** (hardcover)   UE2619—$20.95

Three Mageborn sisters bound together by ties of their ancient Blood Line are forced to take their stands on opposing sides of a conflict between two powerful schools of magic. Together, the sisters will fight their own private war, and the victors will determine whether or not the Wild Magic and the Wraithen-beasts are once again loosed to wreak havoc upon their world.

THE DRAGON PRINCE NOVELS

☐ **DRAGON PRINCE : Book 1**   UE2450—$6.99
☐ **THE STAR SCROLL: Book 2**   UE2349—$6.99
☐ **SUNRUNNER'S FIRE: Book 3**   UE2403—$5.99

THE DRAGON STAR NOVELS

☐ **STRONGHOLD: Book 1**   UE2482—$5.99
☐ **STRONGHOLD: Book 1** (hardcover)   UE2440—$21.95
☐ **THE DRAGON TOKEN: Book 2**   UE2542—$5.99
☐ **SKYBOWL: Book 3**   UE2595—$5.99
☐ **SKYBOWL: Book 3** (hardcover)   UE2541—$22.00